Cat on a Hyacinth Hunt

By Carole Nelson Douglas from Tom Doherty Associates

MYSTERY

MIDNIGHT LOUIE MYSTERIES
Catnap
Pussyfoot
Cat on a Blue Monday
Cat in a Crimson Haze
Cat in a Diamond Dazzle
Cat with an Emerald Eye
Cat in a Flamingo Fedora
Cat in a Golden Garland
Cat on a Hyacinth Hunt

IRENE ADLER ADVENTURES
Good Night, Mr. Holmes
Good Morning, Irene
Irene at Large
Irene's Last Waltz

Marilyn: Shades of Blonde (editor of anthology)

HISTORICAL ROMANCE
*Amberleigh**
*Lady Rogue**
Fair Wind, Fiery Star

SCIENCE FICTION
*Probe**
*Counterprobe**

FANTASY

TALISWOMAN
Cup of Clay
Seed Upon the Wind

SWORD AND CIRCLET
Keepers of Edanvant
Heir of Rengarth
Seven of Swords

*also mystery

Cat on a Hyacinth Hunt

A MIDNIGHT LOUIE MYSTERY

Carole Nelson Douglas

A Tom Doherty Associates Book

New York

CAT ON A HYACINTH HUNT

A Forge Book
Published by Tom Doherty Associates, Inc.
175 Fifth Avenue
New York, NY 10010

Forge® is a registered trademark of Tom Doherty Associates, Inc.

Library of Congress Cataloging-in-Publication Data

Douglas, Carole Nelson.
    Cat on a hyacinth hunt : a Midnight Louie mystery / Carole Nelson
Douglas.—1st ed.
        p.   cm.
    "A Tom Doherty Associates book."
    ISBN 0-312-86634-8
    I. Title.
PS3554.O8237C285   1998
813'.54—dc21   98-14537
                                                    CIP

First Edition: July 1998

Printed in the United States of America

0 9 8 7 6 5 4 3 2 1

For the real and original Midnight Louie,
nine lives were not enough.

Contents

8 • Contents

Cat on a Hyacinth Hunt

Home for the Holly Daze

I know one thing about the forthcoming New Year's weekend. At least I am going to hit ye olde home town before they dim the Christmas glitz and glitter along the Las Vegas Strip. Not that you can tell much difference between the normal wattage and the extra icing the city establishments put up for the holidays. The usual blinding is the usual blinding on any occasion and in any season.

I am not sure jolly old Saint Nick could navigate his sleigh through this glitter-strewn sand-dome without embedding Rudolph's red-light nose into the tip of the Luxor pyramid or entangling the reindeer in the mane surrounding Leo's three-story head at the MGM Grand or, perhaps most amusing to imagine after my sojourn in the Big Apple, crashing King-Kong-level into the tip of New York-New York's downsized version of the Empire State Building.

The flight from La Guardia airport in New York to McCarran airport in Las Vegas is a three-hoursome jaunt with the clock springing back an hour to match each hour in flight. So I while away what passes for six hours hanging in the sky and controlling my bladder while hunched underneath a seat within a carry-case zipped tighter than a drug lord's lips. Jonah and his adventure with Moby Leviathan had nothing on me.

Like Jonah, I cannot say much for the view from within the belly of the beast.

But once we land and I am pulled out, slung over, bumped past and trekked through the airport, I am soon listening once again to the Lullaby of Broadway as it is played in this little town in the West: in the metallic hip-hop fascinatin' rhythm of the slot machines.

Once on the ground, I doze my way home. Luckily, my kind long ago learned the secret to travel without tears. We simply assume the fetal position and retreat into an appalled ball. Some favor the piteous wail rigorously applied at forty-second intervals as an appropriate response to uninvited transportation. I go for the silent treatment. Let them wonder what you are really thinking! It is too easy for humans to ultimately ignore even the most piercing howls. They have astounding powers of concentration when the situation requires—as the infant Homo sapiens has proven in experiment after experiment.

So why strain my throat merely to insure that the humans around me share my anxiety and discomfort? A vocalized grievance, no matter how just, ultimately becomes an annoyance. An unspoken rebuff is also inevitably magnified in the mind of its recipient until it reaches the proportions of a globe-trotting guilt trip.

"Oh, poor Louie!" I hear Miss Temple Barr croon under her breath above me, as I bobble against her body to the beat of her mush-soled New York City tennis shoes. You would think we were Fred and Ginger, could either one of us tap dance. "You are being so good. We will be home soon, I promise, and then everything will be back to normal."

I am not so sanguine. For one thing, in Las Vegas "normal" is never the norm.

For another, the Santa slayer on Madison Avenue may be

identified and facing an interminable wrestling match with the long arm of the law in a Manhattan courtroom, but I suspect that other, less violent crimes were committed during our New York visit, and those too will have more personal consequences, although perhaps not legal ones.

For one thing, while I enjoyed my unauthorized trek to Midtown and the Divine/Sublime Girls' digs at the Algonquin Hotel, it was not lost on me in all the excitement that Miss Temple Barr was also Absent Without Leave to the tune of one entire night away from the sheltering roof of Miss Kit Carlson's impressive Greenwich Village condominium.

(Although it is quite expected that I have in the past, and may in the future, spend the night away from our shared accommodations, Miss Temple is not allowed that privilege, which is a male prerogative common to every species.)

But back to my abandonment in Miss Kit Carlson's fancy digs. I admit that I was busy catching up on some well-deserved rest during the "missing time" on Miss Temple's part, after the double strain of auditioning for television and detecting a murder and a murderer, but I do not believe that abduction by aliens would explain her strange behavior after the absence in question.

Throughout our last day in New York, she was nervous and distracted to the point of conducting an extremely banal telephone conversation with someone I cannot identify but I suspect was of the male persuasion. She and the delightfully nicknamed Miss Kit spent the rest of the visit with their heads together. Even during the farewell party that evening, which Miss Temple's thoughtful maternal aunt put on for her benefit, I caught my winsome roommate brooding while standing alone in the spectacularly pointed prow of Miss Kit's flatiron-shaped apartment, gazing upon the dark bulk of Manhattan lit up like a cruise ship on speed.

I rubbed against her wine velvet sleeve until it was nearly black with my stray hairs, and produced my most gently inquisitive murmurs, but she barely noticed me.

These humans are so delicate of feeling and difficult to read at times. Inscrutable would be the word, I suppose, rather like the statues of Bastet, the goddess of all things fine and feline.

Well, I am quite up to solving yet another problem in the always-puzzling realm of human behavior. Miss Temple need not worry! I will bend all my gumshoe skills to getting to the bottom of her bad mood as soon as we get home.

Chapter 1

Murder on the Home Front

Temple's recent holiday trip to New York City had convinced her of one thing: she would make a lousy undercover operative. (Although her five-alarm-fire-red hair should have tipped her off to that likelihood long before now.)

Today, on her return home, she was discovering how hard it was to scurry anonymously through the vast, gleaming Las Vegas airport while toting a twenty-pound black cat in a purple knapsack affixed like a baby-carrier to her décolletage.

Temple had no décolletage worth noticing at the moment (or any other moment, in her modest opinion), just Midnight Louie hanging limp as a sack of couch potatoes front and center. If anybody tried to shoot her, she'd be more protected by feline flab and fur than by Kevlar body armor.

Of course, no one (that she knew of) wanted to shoot her at the moment, but someone might be hoping to spot her. She didn't want to see anything but the Whittlesea Blue cab that would whisk her home to the Circle Ritz.

No surprises, she thought, dragging her rolling luggage behind her through the hectic between-holiday crowds that besiege the Slot-machine City over Christmas and New Year's.

No Electra Lark checking the plane schedule Temple had left with her, then deciding to drop by McCarran Airport and pick up her returning tenant on some good-Samaritan whim.

No Matt Devine playing Boy Scout gallant. No Matt getting Temple's car keys and arrival time from Electra. No aqua Storm idling eagerly at the ground transportation curb to waft Temple home in its aging but game style.

And no, please God, no Max Kinsella appearing from behind a mirrored pillar to load Temple and belongings into his oh-so-discreet inherited ebony Taurus. No Max to transport the whole kit and caboodle back to the scene of the crime, the Circle Ritz, where they might encounter Electra Lark or, worse, Matt Devine and have to explain things. Or *not* explain things. Which was even more incriminating.

"Don't nobody even remember me for at least twenty-four hours," Temple whispered fervently to herself.

She was running on an emotional jet-lag high that the three-hour turn-back in time wouldn't help. She needed to get her feet on the ground, Louie off her back (or front, rather), her mind in the proper time zone and her emotions on some course resembling an even keel before she wanted to see a soul, or a soul to see her.

"Temple Barr!"

"Oh, no!" She stopped and turned, stricken.

Oh. Only Crawford Buchanan, the slime reporter. To think that she would ever be *relieved* to see *him*. His brown distressed-leather jacket had to have escaped a J. Peterman catalog, along with an ivory silk aviator scarf that dangled almost to his knees and would look infinitely better on either gentleman of her acquaintance that she was so intent on avoiding at the moment.

"Well. If it isn't the Munchkin Hunchfront of Notre Dame," Crawford went on, as he was always going on, his conceited drawl emphasizing his one good attribute, a deep, thrilling, radio-mike voice. "Does that cat ring bells in his spare time? He certainly does nothing for your figure."

"Louie and I are both too travel-worn for chitchat. What are you doing here? You don't look like you're heading in or out. No baggage."

"Elementary deduction, my dear Watsonette. I'm here to pick up my squeeze. Her and her kid visited family for the holidays."

"I loathe the expression 'squeeze.' "

"Too bad. It's here to stay, T.B. Just like me." He leered.

Crawford Buchanan was the only man outside of a silent movie melodrama who still knew how to leer.

Temple turned and resumed her race for the airport exit. "Tell it to the marines. I have a feeling they could fix that."

A Whittlesea Blue cab was waiting. Several were. Temple took the first one and collapsed into the backseat. The ride from McCarran airport was almost laughable. Seen from the runways, Las Vegas Strip landmark hotel-casinos made a crazy-quilt skyline: the Luxor's pointed pyramid jousted with the fools-cap Disney-blue towers of the Camelot, which tilted at the new New York-New York's boxy art deco skyscrapers, which contrasted with the Mirage's tidal-wave wall of gilded glass.

Entering Las Vegas was like driving into a town of half-scale architects' models, a *Twilight Zone* set that even Rod Serling could never have imagined in quite this unlikely juxtaposition.

Temple and Louie were deposited before the Circle Ritz's round fifties silhouette in no time flat, for an absurdly low fare.

She had asked the cab driver to drop them at the wedding chapel in front. Not that she was expecting imminent nuptials, but this way she could sneak in the attached apartment building's side entrance, avoiding the back entry via the parking lot and the pool, where she was likely to confront the Ritz's usual suspects.

In the deserted marble-lined lobby she pushed the elevator button, glad to have only one elevator to deal with and only four floors of building ahead of her, after her sojourn in high-rise New York-New York, the Original.

The elevator doors opened, revealing . . . nobody. Temple darted in like a daylight robber, cussing when her wheeled baggage rollers caught in the brass-edged gap between lobby and car. She wrestled her key out from her tote bag during the one-floor journey and clenched it between her teeth for safekeeping while both hands were busy dragging baggage.

The thick hall carpeting nearly derailed her bags, but she finally turned down the cul-de-sac leading to her front door.

There she leaned the bags against the wall, reclaimed the moist key and unlocked her door. Solid mahogany heft drew it open of its own accord. Sighing at this small boon, she stepped over the threshold.

She broke through an invisible skin of her own absence, encountering the undisturbed peace of rooms abandoned for a while. Everything in its place, including silence, and a blessed familiarity. The effacing hum of the refrigerator. The place even looked neater than she had remembered leaving it, but that was just the Alzheimer's effect of being away kicking in.

She unhooked Louie's CatAboard Seat, letting him and it ease to the floor.

He was out and sniffing around like a bloodhound, then edging out of sight. She heard a muted thump atop the kitchen counter as she wrestled the luggage inside.

A sense of déjà vu subdued her like an opiate as she warily moved through each room, hunting nameless snares and traps. She entered her own bedroom like a thief, expecting another's spoor. Nothing but her own imagination and some hallucinogenic fragrance. Being away always brought her back a temporary foreigner attuned to smells and sights residence had made undetectable.

Too weary to unpack, she tilted her luggage against a bedroom wall before returning to the main room to lock the front door. Then she rooted through the cupboards for something succulent to spoon over the eternal mound of dry Free-to-be-Feline pellets occupying Louie's dish like one of those lifelike ceramic desserts restaurants parade before jaded diners' palates nowadays.

The cat thumped down from somewhere in the living room and came running for smoked oysters in shrimp sauce. Temple collected and folded his—her—carry-pouch and tucked it away in the tiny guest closet. She returned to the kitchen, wondering what she should do. Eat. Rest. Or sit down and stare at the walls.

Someone knocked at her door.

Temple's jump made Louie look up resentfully from his eating. The knock had not only startled Temple but it had interrupted the total concentration Midnight Louie required for dining.

Heart pounding for no good reason, Temple went to open her door without peeking through the tiny peephole. She had to face the music some time, no matter who was playing what instrument.

"Electra!"

"I heard your cab arrive and thought you might want your mail." Her landlady hefted a cardboard box overflowing with rolled-up newspapers, mail-order catalogs, bills, solicitations and Christmas cards.

"Thanks. I think. Did you have a nice holiday?"

"Great. A couple of the kids got to town, only one with grandchildren. And you?"

"Interesting."

"Oh?" Electra, clad in a seasonal muumuu whose pattern somehow blended orchids and evergreens, paused after depositing the box of mail on Temple's coffee table, awaiting a report.

"Sit down," Temple said, capitulating. Of all the people she might have encountered immediately on returning home, Electra was the least harrowing. "Want something to drink?"

"Nope. Eggnogged, wined and Mimosa-ed my way through too many meals out while the kids were in town. I'll just get a load off my feet—and it's more load than before you left—then settle next to my pal Louie. Oof! He's got oyster breath."

Electra's weight not only dimpled the love-seat cushion, but caused Louie to roll right into her evergreen orchid patch. Too rotund himself to fight gravity, they stayed hip to hip and floral print to fur. Louie even began to purr.

"Aw, he missed me. My little big boy. Well? Did you two win the commercial contract?"

"Don't know. We didn't exactly endear ourselves to the advertising agency. I managed to implicate a murderer among them."

Electra clapped her hands until the copper, silver and brass bangles on each wrist jangled. "Some people would be so greedy for their own advancement that they'd rather conceal than reveal such a thing. I'm sure your integrity made a big impression on them."

"Integrity is not the desirable commodity it used to be. And concealing things isn't as easy as it sounds," Temple answered grimly.

"Is there something I should know?"

Temple paused, rubbing her . . . temple. "No, but there's something I should know. Is Matt back yet?"

"Last evening, just in time to rush to his job at ConTact. But he seemed in a peach of a mood. Must have had a good Christmas visit home in Chicago. Poor guy. He was moping around after you left for New York."

"Not merely over my departure!"

"Well—," Electra, a card-carrying justice of the peace, seemed to toy with a temptation to fan the flames of like into the ashes of true romance. "No. He seemed to have a lot on his mind. But you were definitely in there."

"I think I know why." Temple grinned. "Have you been inside his place recently?"

"Me? No. I do not snoop when tenants are off the premises. Although, now that you mention it, I heard a lot of strange thumps from his apartment. Almost sounded like a body being dragged around."

Temple nodded sagely. "A dead weight indeed. I persuaded him to invest in a flashy vintage sofa before I left. It must have found its way home."

"Flashy? Matt? That doesn't sound right. He's such a dear boy and I love him to death. . . . really, I mean that, though not literally, given your track record with corpses—but sometimes he seems rather näive and a little staid."

"No law against that," Temple said rather briskly. "Sometimes I feel rather näive myself."

"And you all of what—? Thirty?"

"Don't mock me, Electra. Between my recent immersion in murder, among other things, I'm aging rapidly."

"You do look a little peaked."

"Electra, nobody's called me 'peaked' since I was in high school and my mother was on my case."

"Thank you," she said complacently, patting Louie. The cat stretched as long as a yardstick and kneaded his claws against a particularly lurid orchid on Electra's knee.

"Ouch!" she complained. "Cut that out! His claws are sharper than needle-nosed pliers."

"He hasn't been able to run around nights and use them. He was strictly a lap cat in New York City."

"Lap of luxury," Electra said fondly, scratching Louie's chin while he stretched his head back and slitted his eyes. "It's really nice that you found each other," she added.

"Huh?" Temple was having a panic attack, wondering if Electra were as psychic as she claimed her cat Karma was.

But she hadn't detected memories of Max floating among Temple's conflicting thoughts; she was speaking of the current resident male, Midnight Louie.

"He's a great companion," she went on.

"I don't know. He runs around a lot nights and comes in at ungodly hours expecting to be petted and pampered, and usually fed."

"It's a good thing you're solo these days—and nights—though."

"What do you mean?"

"Louie doesn't strike me as the type to share."

"Louie doesn't own me. I didn't promise to forsake all others when he tripped into my life at the convention center. Actually, he tripped me quite literally."

"Such a rapscallion." Electra tickled Louie's considerable tummy while he rolled under the attention. "Call me a hopeless romantic, but I can't resist these devil-may-care boys in black."

Temple refrained from adding, "Me too."

After Electra had left, Temple sat on the couch idly sorting her mail into intimidating stacks without reading it. Usually she loved diving into a motherlode of hoarded vacation mail, especially when it included notes from distant friends.

"I must be tired," she told Louie, who certainly had the part down pat himself.

The big tomcat sprawled upon his back as languid as Adam on the Sistine Chapel ceiling. Temple doubted that even God's lightning bolt could move him. His lazily curled limbs pointed to Temple's intriguingly vaulted white ceiling on which the Las Vegas sunlight played chiaroscuro peekaboo with indoor shadows. One of his back feet was particularly elevated; when he assumed this lounging lion position, Temple always felt she should extend immediate permission for him to leave the classroom to go to the little boys room.

Louie yawned, a major production that revealed a pallid rose blooming on his otherwise black palate.

"It's called a 'letdown,' " Temple told him, dramatically driving her Mexican onyx dagger through another envelope and creating a jagged edge. "Like when actors finish the run of a play, or a PR woman is done with a big publicity campaign or a cat no longer is the toast of Madison Avenue."

Louie blinked. Feline body language always struck Temple as inherently foreign, like a Parisian shrug or an eloquently obscene Italian hand gesture. When a cat blinks, one senses one is being paid a profoundly flattering attention as has not been offered the human kind since Eden. Like Italian sign language, the feline dialect had its ruder side as well, but today Louie was luxuriating. Temple flattered herself further that he not only was attentive to her every thought and mood, but that he was glad to be home.

She sat back and closed her eyes, like Louie.

Letdown. Like when a woman has resumed a romantic liaison without knowing *why*, or *when* again or *where* again or *wherefore art thou, Romeo?* Max had called her three times at Kit's after leaving New York so suddenly, so literally anticlimactically. So Maximumly.

As usual, he couldn't discuss over the telephone any particulars for his midnight call back to Las Vegas, and in Kit's airy but intimate rooms, Temple couldn't murmur anything but inanities against the background noise of her aunt's pointed attempts to pretend she was too busy elsewhere in the apartment to hear Temple's half of the conversation.

Temple couldn't forget waking up in the hotel whose name she hadn't bothered to remember that post-Christmas morning, its barely glimpsed geometry assembling around her like a dreamscape in reverse, with nothing left of Max but a note and a rapidly dissipating afterglow.

The magician exits, stage left, leaving the audience begging for more, with the lady sawed in half and hanging by a hair.

Wasn't that just the way he had exited eight months before, without explanation, leaving her stranded to defend him? Leaving her to fend off thugs who came looking for him and left her bruised and battered? Leaving her to steadfastly stonewall a Las Vegas homicide cop about any facts relating to the Mystifying Max and all his works?

Temple smiled to recall C. R. Molina's frustration; a petite, feminine woman often dismissed as "cute," Temple had proven a hard case to crack, even for a nearly six-foot-tall lieutenant who was something of a power-suited amazon herself.

Temple's smile faded. Max's abrupt departure hadn't left her simply facing the legal music. It had also left her unsure and lonely, free to meet Matt Devine, new neighbor, new personal project. Temple always wondered what had attracted her to Matt while she was still freshly smarting from Max's defection. Sure, Matt was the handsomest man she'd ever known. And, more rarely, the nicest. Too bad he was also an ex–Roman Catholic priest whose sexual experience came from the confessional. Or was that fact "too good"? Had she been so quickly attracted precisely because Matt was a freshman at the usual single, thirty-something sexual gavotte? Had he merely been a convenient safety zone to idle in while she waited for her true love to ride back for her?

Because she'd always known Max would return. A powerful instant rapport had knocked them both off their feet, professionally and personally: she the repertory theater publicist, he the touring magician. She had deserted Minneapolis stability for the sands of Las Vegas and a freelance career without a qualm, although her family had plenty and let her hear every one.

Now she should be ecstatic. Max was back and better than ever, though the explanation for his absence involved murky international politics a law-abiding publicist couldn't know too much about. And Matt? She had helped him track down personal demons from his Chicago childhood, playing pal, big sister and the sort of sweet-sixteen girlfriend who would coax him a few baby-steps over the sexual threshold and no further until he was ready. Which he might never be.

So here she sat, lost in her own love story, worried because Max's mysterious past made him a more dangerous partner than she could have imagined, and because Matt's present progress had come perilously close to depending solely on her.

She loved Max, but feared that she might not be able to live with what he really was. She cared for Matt, but she worried that he had come close to loving her, and her heart had chosen sides long before she had met him.

Temple muttered an Anglo-Saxon epithet she rarely used on grounds that it lacked finesse and tossed the letter opener atop a leaning tower of Christmas catalogs. And then the phone rang, startling her as if she had been shot.

Letdown. The morning after. Sometimes it made one a trifle edgy. Not Midnight Louie. He yawned again.

She didn't have the energy to stand at the kitchen wall phone, so she went to bedroom-office for the portable. Public relations people lived and died by the phone; they were multipurpose tools: personal accessories and lifelines and the puppetmaster's strings, the pianist's hidden harp that could play soft and persuasive or stormy and driving.

A phone was your best friend.

But she hesitated before answering this call. She wasn't ready to reenter reality. Especially the reality of an impulsively resumed love affair.

It wasn't Max, as she had half-hoped and half-feared. It was Matt, as she had half-feared and half-hoped.

"Welcome back," he said, sounding too close for comfort.

"Thanks. I'm still on jet lag."

"I know, though Chicago is only two hours off-time compared

to New York's three. Listen, Temple, I've got to work the next few nights straight to make up for my time off. Can we make a date for New Year's Eve? I've got it off."

Temple blinked; only she knew her gesture was devoid of feline profundity.

"There's so much to tell you," he went on. "You wouldn't believe what happened."

"What about Effinger?"

"Oh, Molina had to let him go, but that isn't important."

Effinger wasn't important? Had Temple's plane landed in the true *Twilight Zone*? Effinger wasn't important, and Matt wanted—nay, expected—a "date." This was more than she could take standing up. She sat down at her desk.

"You sound exhausted," Matt said.

"I haven't said enough for you to tell *how* I sound."

"That's what I mean. Usually you're bubbling over with info-bits on this and that, and you must have a lot to tell me too. I'll let you go. But, what? Nine Monday night? I thought we'd try to see the New Year in, if you can stay awake that late, so crack out your Louie shoes and something jazzy. We'll have to take your car, of course."

"Of course." Matt taking her car for granted? Taking her for granted? "You don't really have to take me out someplace ritzy—"

"Celebrations don't need justifications, like red sofas don't, right?"

He couldn't see her wan smile, but he must have sensed it.

"Temple." When she couldn't muster more than an inarticulate hmmm in a questioning upglide, he plunged on. "I really can't wait to see you. I hope you had the Merry Christmas you deserve. 'Bye."

Temple cradled the droning phone on her shoulder long enough for the operator's tart, schoolmarmish voice to come on and shrill that her call was disconnected.

Temple punched the unit off, then on again and pounded in a flurry of eleven numbers. Three rings later, she was back in New York City, in a manner of speaking.

"Kit, Matt just called."

"Did you say Matt or Max?"

"And you think *you're* confused."

"Just tell me, blond or black?"

"Blond. I don't know what I'm going to do."

"What *did* you do?"

"He wants to take me out for New Year's Eve. For a celebration. An upscale celebration, apparently. And I said yes."

"Modest Matt is taking you out on the town? Wow. I'd say send him here, but I don't believe in Santa Claus anymore. So you said yes. What a wimp."

"I owe him an explanation."

"But not a romantic rendezvous."

"This isn't necessarily a romantic evening. But he did call it a 'date.' He's never used that word before."

"Right. You're wondering what Max will say about this."

"I'm not wondering what he'll say at all. I know. What I'm wondering is how I'm gonna keep them in separate corners. There hasn't been a word from Max since I got back."

"For what . . . three hours? Temple, give me a break. Maybe he left a message on your answering machine. Did you check it?"

"No. That's a good idea. He probably invited me out for New Year's Eve," she added dourly. "Kit, what am I going to do?"

"What you always do: the best you can. Max has to understand that his eight-month absence didn't mean your life was in deep freeze, even if your relationship was. He has to respect your other obligations."

" 'Obligation' doesn't quite describe Matt Devine."

"Relax, honey. Emotional involvements aren't like European principalities; they don't occupy neat borders within your heart. Life is messy. There's nothing to do but wade in and clean it up the best you can."

"Right. I'll check my messages."

"Was your flight okay?"

"Fine. Louie didn't even yowl. I think he's as worn out as I am."

"From what you told me of the auditions, Louie has his own romantic dilemmas to exhaust him."

"What do you mean?"

"Gold and silver, the lovely leading ladies, Solange and Yvette. Jeez, what names! I sound like I'm discussing a Françoise Sagan novel."

" 'Bonjour, Tristesse,' " Temple quoted an appropriate title. Hello, sadness.

"I didn't know your generation knew Sagan. Espresso and angst, youth and despair. Check your messages, hon. I'm sure Max has left one, and it'll be good for him to face some competition for a change. Builds character."

Temple thanked her aunt and disconnected, switching on the answering machine, whose small red flashing light had been blinking on the edge of her consciousness since she entered the office.

She pulled over a minisized legal notepad and dug out a pen from beneath her stratified papers while the tape rewound. And rewound and rewound. On her left hand, the glorious, still-alien ring Max had given her flashed its ambiguous message of fourteen-carat gold and fire opal. It didn't look like an engagement ring; it didn't feel like a bribe or a sop, but it did weigh as heavy as a commitment.

Finally, the voices began parading as Temple scribbled phone numbers and notes.

The first message was a computer-generated solicitation. Nothing from her family, but Temple and Kit had called her mother's house from New York and had found the clan gathered the day after Christmas. Funny how your parents' house was always your mother's house after you left.

"It's Van von Rhine at the Phoenix. Happy Christmas, Temple," the machine replayed. "I'm so sorry to call you during the holidays, but we've—you've—received the most wonderful surprise Christmas present for the renovation project! You must come over to see after Christmas. Call me as soon as you can."

Temple felt a restorative prick of curiosity. Van von Rhine was the most tactful, if businesslike, of hoteliers. She rarely spoke in such imperatives or with such enthusiasm.

There was a reminder from her dentist's office. Why had she scheduled an appointment right after Christmas? Hadn't she known she would be too emotionally challenged to dive into mundane matters like flossing, plaque and mouthwashes?

She jotted down other numbers, other messages of routine importance. Not a word from Max.

Boy, the big rush in the Big City and the big silence on home turf. Guess she'd been smart to book something else for New Year's, right, Louie?

By now Temple was passing the cat still airing his undercoat on the loveseat, and heading for the bedroom. When in doubt, take a clue from a southern belle and take a nap. The necessary grocery store trip could wait until, if not tomorrow, late this afternoon.

Like all temporarily abandoned places, the bedroom was waiting with bated breath for Temple to reclaim it with the unmistakable clutter of her presence.

Temple hated bending over to unlace her homely travel tennies, but she finally struggled out of these engulfing marshmallows of the footwear world. Her black plane getup didn't show Louie's cat hairs, but had attracted more than its share of itinerant white lint, so she peeled off the top and leggings as she hopped and stripped on the way to the bathroom.

She let the black knit clothes puddle on the white-tiled floor, inhaling a scent of soap she'd been too familiar with to notice before. Nice.

Temple only wore perfume for dressy occasions; strong scents turned elevators into torture chambers, and in her profession it was bad business to risk alienating people who might be allergic to Emeraude or Poison.

But she relished the subtler scents of soap and shampoo, and had forgotten that until she had left her bathroom long enough to sense it with refreshed eyes and nose.

She loved its wall-to-wall shiny fifties tiles, its small but elegant quality, the deep, deep porcelain tub. But she was too tired—suffered too much ennui, the heck with sadness, Françoise!—to brood in the bathtub. A fast, hot shower, and then to bed.

She opened the frosted glass door, with its silver stripes at top and bottom that were so very fifties . . . and gasped as a wall of silk flowers drenched her bare body like a melting rainbow. The faint, pleasant scent enveloped her, and the jump-start shock it had given her heart soon softened into an edgy, expectant throb.

She wouldn't have been surprised to find the magician himself standing behind the cascade of his upscale paper flowers, but Max was never predictable.

Temple sighed, inhaling more of the fugitive scent, wondering what would contain so extravagant a shower of flowers.

One thing was decided. She took a bath after all.

Chapter 2

Bagged

Only one bag of groceries.

It sat sedately in the Storm's passenger seat, all but buckled in. Usually Temple loaded the trunk with enough bags to hold each other upright, so she could take corners at a slightly racy speed and not worry about making tossed salad.

But an only grocery bag demanded babying: a front-row seat and kinder, gentler right and left turns.

This had been a quick restocking trip, easy enough to accomplish her first afternoon back in town. Temple loved buying groceries, but she hated lugging them out of the car and into the apartment. She always enjoyed the end product of the food-getting process, but loathed the steps in between, including cooking. On the other hand, she loved the artful presentation of food. Tell Temple Barr that her culinary efforts looked much better than they tasted, and she would not be insulted.

This was one area where context pleased her more than content. Of course, she avoided cooking as much as possible, usually "concocting" instead. Whatever she prepared would be nicely arranged, attractive in color, decently calorie- and fat-conscious, and come in a can or a box or a plastic baggie from the fresh produce section.

At least at the butt-end of December she didn't have to worry about the low-fat yogurt melting.

She parked the Storm between an older custom van and Electra Lark's pink Probe. The van was one of those beige behemoths that are so impossible to see around—or through—on the road. And Temple firmly believed in driving while looking through other people's windshields. She liked knowing what was coming up ahead.

So she was wondering which tenant the annoying van belonged to, and fretting about opening her passenger door wide enough to extract her fat grocery bag from the car without denting the neighboring van or smashing the French bread she had treated herself to. And, of course, she didn't want to scuff her Via Spiga heels on one of the van's nasty big wheels while she was wrestling with the grocery bag and her tote bag, key ring jangling from one hand.

Life was full of small struggles for a small woman.

She set the passenger door to lock and kneed it shut. Not quite hard enough. It had locked, all right, but in an ajar position. She would have to put everything down, unlock the jammed door and re-slam it, once more with more feeling.

Temple uttered one of her rare, unembroidered curses. No "Holy Shish kebob" this time, just the "shish." Besides, no witnesses.

"Can I help you out, little lady?"

Shish! No doubt this was the owner of the van that had hogged the parking spot . . . that had given her no room to maneuver . . . that had made her mis-slam the car door . . . that had forced her to stand here in the parking lot of the house that Electra had built, clutching a bag of groceries to her chest like Louie in his CatAboard Seat.

She turned as much as the space and her burdens permitted, tempted to answer, "Help? Well, you could back your behemoth out of the way."

But even before she had visual contact with her would-be assistant, she smelled stale smoke and sour clothes. Turning further, juggling her old-fashioned brown paper bag, seeing mostly asphalt until she managed to look up, she glimpsed seedy Western wear: scuffed turned-up boot toes, jeans worn white along the wrinkles, some tin belt buckle and a straw cowboy hat. Great, a parking lot cowboy.

"Excuse me," Temple gritted between her teeth, ready to shove past the stranger.

"Nope."

She was so busy doing her balancing act that she hardly could see his face under the shadowing brim, but she knew she was in trouble. Temple retreated, backing up between the two vehicles. All right. She would squeeze around the front of her car.

Or had the man's impinging presence backed her up? Because no matter how far she baby-stepped to the rear, he was still too up close and personal for her liking.

And she needed some distance to get a real look at him because she was beginning to think she'd seen that seamed and crooked face before, but where? In the Las Vegas Metropolitan Police Department mug-shot files? Those photos of the usual suspects she'd had the pleasure of perusing at her leisure the last time she'd been assaulted?

Last time? Yes. It was going to happen again. Her stomach tightened into hollow anticipation and her knees decided to turn in different directions. A sudden sweat felt like a July sun was beating her down instead of the tepid rays of midwinter. Her mind was racing, but getting nowhere, like a revving competition engine.

"Take the tote bag; that's where the money is," she suggested.

The man's unshadowed mouth grinned, revealing neglected teeth, and then she recognized him.

"You're—!"

"I'm flattered, little lady. I guess my reputation precedes me, huh? Let me help you with those big bags."

He followed her suggestion and jerked the tote bag straps off her shoulder. The motion pulled her right arm away from the grocery bag, the key ring in her hand flying. It chimed to a heap under the low-slung van. Temple watched, aghast. Her one weapon out of the picture quite literally.

The man tossed the tote bag to the asphalt behind him.

Clutching the grocery bag like a shield, Temple felt her retreating heels sink into the thick, yellowed St. Augustine sod between the asphalt lot and the wooden stockade fence. The Storm's nose almost touched cedar; no one was meant to walk between the parked cars and the fence, but Temple was ready to tread air if she had to, just to elude this instant dead end.

"You don't want to mess with me," she said, planning to heft the grocery bag at him, ditch the shoes and scramble over the Storm's shiny aqua hood in one graceful, balletic motion. . . .

He grabbed the recyclable brown bag, which ripped from top to bottom, and jerked it away. Groceries pelted Temple's feet and rolled under the vehicles, joining her keys.

Effinger's dingy boot crushed a loaf of fresh, warm French bread in a crackling waxed wrapper. The thick crust, pulverized, sounded like bone shattering.

Temple began scrambling as planned, but Effinger's lizard-skinned hand grabbed her wrist and slung her back against the warm metal side of the van.

No room. No room to run, to deliver a graceful, balletic martial arts kick. Her mind revved in a self-defeating circle: she tried to twist her wrist so she could force it free where his grip was weakest, between his curled fingers and thumb, but her wrist was too slim; his huge hand circled it too tightly for Temple to accomplish more than an Indian burn of effort.

"Why?" she wondered.

"Because if someone can find me, it works the other way, honey. I can find him, and I can find out who he knows. Because he's too big to hurt any more, and you aren't. Tell him that. Tell him to keep the frigging hell outa my business."

"I will," she promised, surprised by how truly scary bad words sounded when uttered by the wrong people. Promise 'em anything, but give 'em Arpege.

Temple struggled to escape with all her Mighty Mouse might. Effinger just wrung her arm and twisted it behind her back. She ducked under his custody, conceding the arm and kicking hard at his knee.

A narrow shadow loomed over her . . . Effinger's arm hauling back as he held her too far away to connect with anything but air. Then his open hand connected with the side of her face.

Perception blurred as her glasses flew off her nose, her teeth snapped into her own tongue . . . just a pinch between cheek and gum, a sharp, pinched feeling. Her head thumped the van's solid metal wall as a thick tang filled her mouth.

"Tell him." Effinger's face leaned close. He desperately needed a breath mint. "Tell him to leave me alone."

Temple nodded. Now was when the dental assistant would suck the mingled blood and spit from her mouth with the little vacuum hose. Drool was trickling out one sore corner of her mouth, and she without a neat clip-on paper napkin to catch it.

Worst of all, she was sandwiched so tightly between Effinger's shabby, smelly body and the dusty van that she could hardly breathe. She wondered how scared—or scarred—Effinger thought she should be to become a sufficient object lesson to Matt. One slap was not enough, she knew.

Still, she wiggled a little, pretending feeble resistance while trying to think of something effective.

"Hey!" someone not far away yelled.

The woman's challenging tone dismayed Temple. A woman witness wouldn't discourage Effinger. He liked beating them up. He grinned again under the shadow of his rancher's hat and brought a hand to her throat, tightening until the dry, hard pressure made choked blood sing a subliminal high C in her head.

The internal scream erupted into an ear-drilling screech. Temple pictured clapping her hands to her ears in self-defense, but her hands didn't move because she couldn't feel her arms, could hardly feel her feet on the ground. She was tacked up to the side of the van like a grade-school drawing, a flat and distorted stick figure with splayed limbs.

Effinger didn't like the piercing screech either, and slapped one hand back to his own ear, to something behind him.

Temple gathered her waning strength both mental and physical in the moment he brushed at the interruption.

Wasn't fancy, wasn't particularly balletic, but Temple got one knee cocked and aimed it for the classic target.

The shrieking stopped.

Wasn't a bull's-eye hit, wasn't that hard a hit, but she was amazed to feel Effinger ease off as he swung sideways against the van, either cursing or grunting or both at once.

She heard something snap beneath his boots again.

A bower of blurry floral fury came launching over Effinger's shoulder.

He yelped like a dog. Temple kicked at his kneecap and connected this time. *The kneecap's connected to the . . . thigh bone* (a higher, harder kick) *. . . the kneecap's connected to the . . . shin bone* (another kick just above the boot top) *. . . the instep's protected by the . . . boot hide,* but, hey, she could try Old Faithful, the knee to the groin again, or just try to escape.

Effinger's death grip on her throat had loosened. She made herself relax and slid slowly down along the van side as if passing out. He released her to attack the harrier at his rear.

The moment his attention ebbed, Temple pulled herself up and dragged her oddly clumsy body atop the Storm's sloping hood. She slipped over the smooth aqua nose into the fence, her churning legs and ankles knocking wood and painted metal. She felt like a cartoon character defying gravity, her moving hands and feet skimming over the car's warm heavy-metal surface like a waterbug skating on a swamp.

The shrieking began again, sustained as an off-key high note, maddening. Now she could cover her ears. Great; see no evil, hear no evil.

Silence brought its own tonal terror.

Temple struggled to rise from the thick grass verge, nearsightedly knocking her abused ankles on the concrete tire-stop of the parking slot next to the Storm.

"Temple, baby? Are you all right?"

This was a voice of ordinary pitch, and bearable. "My glasses," she muttered, finally letting the warm mouthwash flood down her chin.

The moving wall of clematis and hibiscus faded, then swam into lurid focus as Electra leaned over her again.

"Oh, dear God! So much blood. Can you walk?"

One of Electra's hands bore a red licorice-twist of metal and plastic, the other was fisted with the notched steel glitter of keys stabbed between every finger in the approved women's self-defense-tip fashion.

"These won't help much," Electra warned.

Temple managed to hold one unbroken lens up to her eye, rather like a monocle. "He's gone?" She talked thickly, as if still under anesthetic.

Still? There was no anesthetic, or couldn't be with this much pain.

"Gone?" she repeated, sounding drunken and disorderly and unconvinced.

"We gotta call the police. Me, I mean. But first I have to get you to a hospital emergency room."

Temple lifted her hands. *Hold on,* the gesture said.

Electra ebbed away again, but was back with an open roll of paper towels from the spilled groceries. Why hadn't Temple thought of that?

Electra tore fistfuls off the roll and pressed the crushed wads of paper to the front of Temple's clothes, and more tenderly to her face.

"Mouths bleed a lot," Temple mumbled in her new Marlon Brando fashion. The Godsister.

"You think I don't know that? With three grown kids?"

Electra, daubing at the wet places on Temple's face and clothing, sounded angry, like Temple's mother had when she was a kid and had taken a spill on her first bicycle. Why blame the victim?

"Who was that awful man?" Electra was asking between daubs.

"You ever heard of the evil stepmother?"

"Who hasn't?"

"That was the evil stepfather."

"Yours?"

"God, no!"

"Whose then?"

Temple hesitated, trying to sigh and instead drawing a long, low whistle of pain through her teeth, if she still had any.

"I need to see a dentist."

"You need to see some*one*. Whose stepfather? And why is everybody mugging you?"

"It does feel like everybody. Help me up."

"Gosh. Look at your legs."

Temple tried to do that through her makeshift lorgnette, but could only make out the yellow glimmer of winter-dead grass at her feet.

"What's wrong with them besides not holding me up too good?"

"You're scraped to hell and back. And you'll probably have a lot of bruises. Ice. Ice will help that, and your mouth. I'll get you inside, at least for now."

"Thanks."

Leaning on the upholstered trellis of Electra's out-of-focus muumuu-clad body, Temple limped back onto the parking lot asphalt and toward the building.

"Oh, Electra!" She stopped.

"What, dear? Where does it hurt?"

"Key ring. Under the van."

"We'll get it later."

"No. Might remember, come back for it before us."

"Oh." Electra suddenly shared Temple's vision of a man like that with the keys to a female tenant's apartment. She scurried to retrieve them.

Temple smiled to picture the bland beige van being accosted by the fiery floral energy of an Electra Lark muumuu. Or she tried to smile; it didn't feel right. She touched her teeth trying to see if they moved. Sure hurt. The back of her head throbbed too. And the bloody spit was mounting in her mouth again. *Hurry, Electra!*

He might come back. Temple might pass out. She might have dental problems that not even the Tooth Fairy could compensate for.

"I don't know how James Bond does it," she muttered crossly when Electra returned, keys jingling.

"I brought your tote bag too. How James Bond does what?"

"Takes a licking and keeps on ticking."

"Men get used to being injured in school athletics. Besides, real men don't feel pain."

"James Bond isn't a real man. Ooooh."

"You need to see a doctor. Listen! We're in the parking lot. What am I thinking? I'll take you to the emergency room in my car right now."

"No! Just help me back to my place. Not being able to see clearly is my worst problem."

"You're not seeing clearly in more ways than one. Why are you being such a macho woman?"

"Because I was the youngest of five, with a fistful of older brothers. You should have seen me after that toboggan trip down Suicide Hill." And she had to think about *what* had happened, and *why,* and *who* she would tell about it. Lieutenant C. R. Molina was not among the who.

Electra had taken Temple's arm and was guiding her up the single step into the Circle Ritz's side door. She leaned so close that Temple could see the concern curdling her amiable features.

"Electra, all I need . . . is an ice pack, a heating pad, pain-reliever and some peace and quiet."

"Hmmm."

But Electra didn't argue further and Temple finally tottered through her own front door. Hearing the heavy mahogany shut behind her made her feel like a relieved pioneer, as if a barred wooden door would keep out the wilderness and every feral creature in it, man most of all.

Electra led her directly to the bedroom, and Temple didn't object.

On the zebra-striped coverlet, the sleeping Midnight Louie cast a velvet-black shadow. He stirred as Temple's side of the bed sank under her weight. Ever since Max had been gone, she had kept to "her" side; probably just because it was close to the alarm clock and the telephone, or maybe just because hope keeps habits alive.

Seeing the cat's vague outline was oddly comforting. So was hearing Electra bustling around in the other rooms, digging the heating pad out of the guest bedroom-office closet, banging ice-cube trays in the kitchen. Temple half-reclined against the piled pillows as Louie stretched all his limbs straight out, then lumbered up to her side.

"Hello, Mr. Midnight." She stroked his velvet-napped head while he arranged himself against her hip. "Had a rough day at the office? I sure did."

Electra was hovering again, armed with fire and ice and a tepid glass of tap water to wash down a couple pills.

"Tylenol. Two pills shouldn't interfere with anything stronger you might get later. Where's your dentist's number?"

Relieved that Electra was no longer dwelling on the hospital, Temple let herself be packed with hot and cold: ice to the face and lower legs; the heating pad—and Midnight Louie's furred warmth—to her midsection.

Safe in bed, and buttressed into place with pillows and home remedies, Temple allowed herself to drift into the alternate state of injury. Shock blunted the pain, even when Electra pulled her shoes off.

"Are my Via Spiga patent-leather heels okay?" Temple asked, straining to lift her head and see. "No scrapes, no dings?"

"I can't say as much about your legs." Electra moved towel-covered rocks of ice against her ankles. "We should get your knit top off, but I don't want to pull it over your poor face."

"Leave it," Temple murmured, feeling a strange indifference. She just wanted to be left alone, to lay here and recover, maybe for a few days.

Amazingly, she soon drifted into sleep, without even wondering what dreams would come, and who would be in them.

Chapter 3

Nightmare in Red

Temple must have edged into the *Twilight Zone*.

She had a sense of not quite losing consciousness, but of losing track of time, and perhaps space.

She could still hear Electra rustling in the kitchen of her unit, but she felt suspended somewhere else, between two opposite poles, one as fiery and relaxing as hot wax, one icy and full of frozen tension.

Her oddest delusion was that Midnight Louie had swelled in size, as perhaps her face was doing. His warm length had stretched along her right side until he seemed to match her height.

Cats will do that, and Louie could twist himself like a licorice rope to an impossible length, front and back limbs flung to their farthest extremes.

But Louie wasn't panther-size the last time she looked.

So she looked again, cautiously, through her uncorrected vision.

Louie's fuzzy (thanks to her deficient eyes, not his sufficient hair) tail dangled off the California queen-size bed's edge, and his heating-pad-abetted body heat ran alongside her all the way to the top of her head on its mound of pillows.

Louie was large and flexible, but not *that* large and flexible. Not unless he was doing magic tricks these days.

Temple turned her head—far too quickly and far too far for her condition—and squinted into the green eyes that looked as large as saucers in her unfocused gaze.

"Midnight . . . Max! How did you get here?"

Before he could answer, Electra hallooed from the next room. "If you've got everything you need, dear, I'm leaving now."

"Fine. Thanks," Temple managed to mumble.

She heard the landlady's key turn in her door, locking her in, with Max.

His fingers played with her hair, startling her. Seeing through a veil, palely, made even the lightest touch threatening.

"Poor baby. I found your old glasses in the medicine cabinet. Will they help?"

"Yes!" Temple grabbed at the blur dangling from the invisible hand at the end of a black sleeve and shoved them at her face like a mask.

"Ooh!" Even lightweight plastic hurt as it touched the bridge of her nose and curled behind her ears. But at least she could see. Max was clad in magician's black from neck to toe, lying alongside her pillow- and ice-packed body like a human breakwater.

"What are you doing here? How did—?"

"Electra wisely called for reinforcements, especially when you refused to go to an emergency room. I gave her my number when I came back. She was terribly worried, said you had hit your head."

"*Some*thing hit my head. Mainly I got slapped."

She lifted her left hand to her cheek and winced. Why did one have to probe a hurt to make sure it was real? "Ouch!"

"Don't mess with it." Max captured her hand and held it. Her fingers felt icy in his warm grasp, but maybe that was from touching the ice packs alongside her face and neck.

"Temple," he said, "I understand why you want to avoid a medical record on this, but I'm not sure it's wise. It's not the mouth cut and the black eye. You could have a concussion; that's what worried Electra too."

"Black eye! Where?"

"Where they usually are. How are you feeling? Sleepy?"

"No. Just . . . numb. All this ice—" She started to push the packs away, but Max stopped her hand again.

"You need it. That's my job. If you won't go to the hospital, I'm here to see that you don't push off your cold packs and that you don't go to sleep."

"Well, you were always good at that last part—ow!"

"What's the matter?"

"I guess I breathed too strenuously. And how come it feels like my mouth is stuffed with cotton wool?"

"Swelling from the cuts to your inner cheek. When you're stable enough to stand, you can rinse your mouth with warm salt-water. The icepack stopped the bleeding, so you won't need stitches. Lucky you. Inside mouth stitches are pesky."

"Aw," Temple moaned, beginning to realize what an utter mess she was.

"And don't flail your legs. Electra put antibiotic ointment on the cuts and scrapes."

She sighed, and Max sighed soon after.

His voice lowered to an intimate tone she would have called pillow talk except that there was no danger of any hanky-panky here and now.

"Temple, I can't tell you how sorry I am that this happened again. Those first two thugs look like goners by now, and I was complacent enough to assume new goons wouldn't spring up to take their places. Electra thought you hadn't been under attack for very long when she got there, but two seconds is too long, as far as I'm concerned. Damn my past! I've no right to think you can have anything to do with me."

It was a very nice speech, Max beating his breast with copious mea culpas. She was almost tempted to leave things as they were, nurse Kinsella clucking over her, the pet patient, and feeling so deliciously guilty. She deserved pampering and penitence for at least a few more minutes.

"Oh," she commented astutely, making noise more from moral than physical discomfort. "This hasn't got a darn thing to do with you, Max, you conceited ass."

"It doesn't? You were simply mugged? Any self-defense expert could warn you that you're most vulnerable entering and leaving your car, in parking garages, parking lots. . . ."

Temple was even more tempted to leave him there, stubbing his toes on his next half-baked conclusion. But her conscience writhed as much as her oversensitized skin.

"Not exactly any old mugger."

"How can one be 'not exactly any old mugger.' "

"He can be a shady character known to someone of the victim's acquaintance."

Max was silent, translating her reluctant, roundabout confession.

"You knew the creep?"

"Only by description."

"Don't play with me, Temple." Max's lips brushed her unhurt cheek. "I'm tired of half-meanings."

"This had nothing to do with you. At least not directly. It was . . . Matt's stepfather."

"Cliff Effinger? But why would he mess with you? I know that Devine turned him in to Molina. . . ." He moved his face parallel to her mostly immobile features. "He took it out on you, is that it, to get to his stepson?"

Temple swallowed, then regretted it. All the muscles on the left side of her face protested major movement. Even talking was wearing her down. As was Max.

"Was that it?" he persisted. "Just . . . blink your eyes 'yes.' "

She tried to laugh, another painful procedure. "What's 'no,' then? Or don't you want to hear any of those?"

"Effinger went after you in revenge for Devine's tracking him down?"

"A warning, he said."

"Matt Devine." Max savored the name as much as spoke it. His tone was not so much antagonistic as rueful. "His purely personal quest stirred up a hornet's nest, I'll give him that. And now the wasps are stinging everybody in sight. Nobody wanted to see Effinger located by the police. Nobody," Max added in particularly grim tones.

"Your eyes are green again," she said out of the blue.

"What? Oh, I forgot. These are my Las Vegas eyes."

"And your Minneapolis eyes. Maybe I'll try to lose these stupid glasses again, see if I can adjust to contact lenses. Give it another try. I could have kaleidoscope eyes then, too. A new color. A new me. What about . . . violet."

"Lovely." Max's finger touched the tip of her nose. "But not you."

"Who says? Mr. Chameleon the shape-shifter?"

"True. I'm no one to discourage a changed appearance." His fingers toyed with her hair again, as his mouth nibbled delicately at the good side of her face. "You'll be better by morning, Temple, and then you can make appointments with your dentist and optometrist. At least you should be pretty well healed by New Year's. We'll go out, in disguise and dark glasses, someplace extravagant to see the New Year in."

"Ummm," she agreed, distracted from aches and pains and everything else by Max's minor amorous attentions. She was definitely not up for the majors this evening.

Then her sedated memory and its coconspirator, guilt, kicked in again.

"No, Max, I can't go anywhere with you New Year's Eve, not even with dark glasses!"

"Why not?"

"Um, I have an appointment."

"An appointment on New Year's Eve?"

"A meeting."

"With whom?"

"You're so grammatical in crises; I should have known there was something suspicious about you from the first."

"Forget the first, what about the first of the New Year?"

"I'm going out. With Matt."

"Devine?"

"The very one."

If she had not been banged up, he would have dropped her like a hot potato, his shock was that palpable.

"Why? After New York—"

"This is to finish up *before* New York business. Matt asked me as soon as I got back. I haven't heard the gory details of his track-down of Effinger."

"You have plenty of gory details relating to Cliff Effinger your-self. If that's why you were attacked, why hang around the cause?"

"Because. I haven't told him yet."

"About us. Simple. There's a phone right on the nightstand. Call him and tell him."

"Max! I can hardly talk right now."

"You won't be that much better by New Year's."

"You just said—"

"That was before I knew you had other plans."

"I'll feel better if I'm with you?"

"Yes! And you'll be safer too."

"I don't know. You two are about even when it comes to safety factors."

"My wasps are dead."

"Presumed dead. Some of them. Should I, like, tell Molina about this?"

"God, no! Your instincts about the police are dead right. Oth-erwise I'd never let you sweat this out at home."

"Freeze is more like it."

Max sighed at the reminder and drew closer. "I shouldn't agi-tate the invalid."

"Exactly. Especially if you intend to hang around all night."

"I do."

"Whatever happened to Louie?"

"He dove over the side when I showed up."

"Oh, poor guy, he's feeling shunted aside."

"Poor guy is pretty bright."

"He's used to sleeping next to me."

"Funny, I'm used to *not* sleeping next to you. Guess we'll have to work it out."

"He'll think you're moving in on him."

"I wish I could, but it's better I stay under the radar for now. I'm still partially responsible for your problem, Temple." Max rested his chin oh-so-lightly on the top of her head. "Effinger is one of my problem players too. He doesn't just belong to Matt Devine. And neither do you."

"I don't 'belong' to anyone."

"I know. But let's pretend."

"Um, Max. I'm not supposed to do anything strenuous."

"Nothing strenuous," he agreed, as incorrigibly amiable as always.

Chapter 4

The Bum's Rush

I knew something fishy was afoot.

And I am not referring merely to the stocking-clad human foot that has been well aged in Bruno Magli footwear.

I knew it before I was fully awake, when I felt my muscular form being shunted aside by a force dark and vast and as elemental as the universe.

In this case, by the time I opened my eyes to observe the cataclysmic change in my situation, I had identified the Force's current manifestation as the Mystifying Max. (And I was much faster at this elementary deduction than my dear Miss Temple Barr was a few minutes later when she opened her baby blue-grays to the Change.)

I cannot say how it happened, save that I was supplanted in my slumber. Swept aside by mere sleight of hand. Slid out of my accustomed place before I had blinked the sleep from my eyes. Left the lower corner of the coverlet for my reduced lot. Claim-jumped.

Of course I could not accept this vastly reduced territory.

I immediately leaped to the bedroom floor, playing into the usurper's hand, and stalked to a corner of the room to consider my retaliation under the guise of grooming my ruffled fur.

Naturally, no one noticed.

Had Miss Temple been in her right senses, I have no doubt she would have observed my ousting and repaired the damage.

As it was, she was in no condition to come to my defense, having so recently—and so ineffectively—come to her own.

I cannot blame her for this dereliction of duty. Nor can I blame the Mystifying Max for exercising his territorial imperative. That is what we guys do.

I do blame myself for catnapping at a crucial time, when the balance of power was up for grabs. And I do blame that handy goat for all things grungy and inglorious: Cliff Effinger. I am getting sick and tired of this creep messing up the calm domestic lives of me and mine.

Someone will pay for this unseating, and it will not be feline.

Count on it.

Chapter 5

New Year's Irresolution

Temple stared into the mirror over the bathroom sink, looking like a hungover detective from a vintage film noir.

Her small, nineteen-fifties bathroom mirror was made to enhance that effect. It covered a built-in medicine cabinet, and was lit from above by a flickering, buzzing wand of blue-white fluorescent bulb.

Knowing this, Temple never looked in her bathroom mirror. She used the incandescent-lit looking glass on the bedroom wall above her bureau-cum-makeup table. But she needed to pass critical muster tonight, and figured that the only mirror on the wall that would judge her camouflaging makeup job as "fair" enough was this one.

The brutal downlight aged her ten years and even then she barely looked twenty-five. Cruel shadows played pocket-pool with her facial planes, but she still only resembled an unmade bed, not an assault victim.

Temple nodded at herself. Her head no longer ached at such violent movements. Good. Even under this pitiless light she passed for healthy. The only sign of Effinger's attack two days ago was a tendency to mumble. Her cut mouth and sore jaw refused to let her tongue tap-dance at its usual articulate speed.

But this was New Year's Eve, right? They would be eating (mush for her) and drinking, right? She wouldn't be expected to sound like an elocution student with a fistful of glass marbles in her mouth spewing out consonants with spitball precision.

Temple glanced at the dainty bangle of evening watch on her left wrist, blinking while the temporary soft contact lenses floated like dead jellyfish skins over her eyes. The optometrist had said they were close enough to her forthcoming prescription to do everything but drive with, and she was not going out for her gala New Year's Eve date with Matt Devine (during which she would have to confess that she and Max were an item again and good-bye except for some neighborly schmoozing now and then) wearing those groady eight-year-old round frames: yuppie plastic tortoiseshell. How had she ever been hyped into choosing the East-coast owl look? Stupidity of the sweet bird of youth (probably an owlet), she guessed, as opposed to the stupidity of young single adulthood.

Temple stopped her antsy mental monolog, stopped moving. This was all an act, like dressing for the performance of a play. Concentrating on hiding the results of his stepfather's attack from Matt kept her from thinking of the emotional assault she would make sometime tonight on Matt himself: admitting that she and Max were together again. Their own recent relationship had been unspoken, but warm and even tender. Now that would have to stop. She didn't want to reject or hurt Matt, and she knew he didn't approve of Max, just like her family. She put cold fingers to her warm cheeks, feeling like Scarlett O'Hara not wanting to think about it until tomorrow. *Frankly, my dear, I do give a damn. I'd give up Tara not to have to. . . .*

Temple rushed back to the bedroom, grabbed her quirky little evening bag (Temple owned two sizes of purse: huge and lilliputian) and paused before the bedroom mirror. Of course, the brittle Cosmo Girl's number-one ground rule for telling a guy that everything was kaput was to look especially fabulous. The eat-your-heart-out look. But Temple had no need, intention or desire to have Matt cannibalize his cardiac organ. She just wanted to exit from his personal life on an optimistic note, not like a beaten puppy. And she certainly didn't want him feeling guilty about Effinger turning on her, when she was the guilty one for letting any relationship flower between them when her heart, body and soul were still mortgaged to the Mystifying Max Kinsella.

The soft-focus bedroom mirror told her that the foundation caked on her left cheek and eye socket as thick as burn camouflage worked like gangbusters. She practiced a smile. The left side lagged behind the right, but in a dim-lit restaurant that would only look like dramatic lighting.

Otherwise, she was up to snuff: the same silver-beaded dress Matt had seen before, so he wouldn't have any illusions she had, like, gone out and bought something special for this evening to remember, poor man . . . the Midnight Louie heels flashing their Austrian crystal brilliance everywhere, except on the glittering black silhouette of a green-eyed cat atop each high heel.

Temple twisted her torso to view as much of her rear as possible. Silvery gray panty hose covered her bruise-tattooed legs, but too bad she wasn't wearing hose with seams. The way the cat's front paws reached up the back of the shoes, Louie could almost be construed as straightening invisible seams. So forties noir. Too bad Louie couldn't straighten the seams in people's emotional lives. . . .

The real Midnight Louie, in the all too, too solid flesh and fur, lay stretched out horizontally, not vertically, on the bed's Zebra-pattern coverlet.

Temple blinked again. Not tears. No tears. Her sensitive eyes were tolerating the lenses better than they had earlier unsuccessful attempts at wearing soft contact lenses, but she was having trouble focusing through these Saran-wrap windows.

Louie yawned, displaying so much deep pink mouth and tongue that she couldn't miss the gesture.

"I won't be back until late, Louie. Real, real late."

She checked her watch again and grimaced. Eight-thirty. A nine P.M. dinner reservation at New York-New York Hotel and Casino, then hanging out until midnight to see the New Year in. After that, Matt wanted her to stop and view the red sofa in his apartment. She'd said she'd be too rushed before, that they could do it after. So that would be the scene of the coming crime: his place, in the wee hours of the New Year. She would tell him that she was once again previously engaged. Sort of.

"I am a worm!" she told Louie in heartfelt tones.

He did not disagree.

Despite her physical and mental preparations for the coming ordeal, Temple still jumped when her mellow doorbell chimed.

She clattered to the front door over the parquet floor, pausing to look through the peephole first. No more surprise carry-out boys for her!

The tiny convex glass conveyed a travesty of fuzzy, foreshortened image, but there was no mistaking that butterscotch-blond head.

Temple flung open the door, always prone to overreact under stress, and prepared to chatter away despite the risk of revealing her mandibular difficulties. Instead she was struck dumb.

Well. Wow. What could she say? He stood there looking like the perfect prom-date-cum-Greek god, wearing some sort of bronze-sheeny jacket over an ivory turtleneck that turned his hair to spun gold and his warm brown eyes to the richest, smoothest, most self-destructive chocolate mousse you ever wanted to drown in.

And she had thought Max had a certain stage presence.

But it wasn't just the clothes or Matt's always enthralling looks. Matt was different, very different. Somehow, he had changed more than she had over the Christmas holidays, during their separate missions.

He stepped in without being asked. "You look fabulous," he said, as if on cue, and with sincerity.

"Oh, this old thing. You've seen it before. I wore it to the Gridiron dinner."

"It looks even better now."

"Look who's talking."

"Maybe this is a bit much." He glanced disowningly down at his brandy velvet sleeves.

"No. Perfect. But you reminded me. It is January, or almost January. I need a wrap. Rats. Be right back."

Temple retreated to her bedroom to root through her closet. All the best-laid plans of mice and Minnies, and she had forgotten to find a suitable evening wrap. . . . A loose-knit black wool capelet went flying over her shoulder to drape Louie. Too casual. A sheer jacket of black chiffon hit the bedspread next. Too cool.

Finally she pulled out a black velveteen bolero and tore back to the foyer.

Matt wasn't there.

The door was now closed. Had he been kidnapped by his evil stepfather? Had he fled? Where? What?

She turned in a circle while wrestling her aching arms into the jacket. And saw him standing by the French doors to the patio, studying the eternal aurora borealis of the Las Vegas Strip.

"Now I'm ready," she said, joining him.

"Chicago's so cold, narrow, dark. In the winter, at least. Even the streets with the snow piles at the curbs seem to be hunching their shoulders. But Las Vegas is like Camelot in the song from the musical: the weather is wonderful by decree."

"By decree of the corporate entrepreneurs who would pay the sun to shine if they had to; luckily, they don't."

Matt turned from the window, a small wrapped package in his hand. "Merry Christmas."

"Christmas, but that's . . . history. You . . . I didn't get you anything."

"You overlook the sofa-hunt."

"But . . . I only got you to spend money."

"You sure did. I've been on a real jag. It was kind of fun. But it stops here."

He looked a little anxious. Temple finally realized that he had probably never bought a woman a present before, other than a nun or his mother. She desperately hoped she would really like it, although she would like it even if it were a weenie beanie baby from McDonald's.

The soft contact lenses softened even her closeup focus, as if she viewed everything under very clear water. A long thin box said jewelry; her conscience said, please, nothing too expensive. Her conscience had also said to leave off the opal and gold ring tonight, so her hands were bare as she wrestled off the elastic gold cord and the jewel-tone paper and finally had no option but to open the box.

"Oh! Wherever did you find it?"

"I thought it might go with the shoes."

"Oh, it does. Thank you." Temple blinked. "Damn these new contacts! I can't f-focus on anything. It feels like my eyes are watering all the time. Are they watering?" she added, not looking up from the box.

"They look a little dewier than usual. Do you really want contact lenses?"

"I suppose so. Why?"

"Well, you look kind of . . . different without glasses."

"Better, right?"

"No. Just different. Like a stranger. I guess it'll take me a while to get used to the new you."

Was he *righter than he knew!* Temple lifted the delicate gold chain from the box, elevating the central figure of a cat in crushed black-opal inlay, collared in tiny diamonds, with winking emerald-green eyes.

It would go perfectly with Max's ring.

"It's wonderful, Matt! Perfect." She undid the tiny clasp and lifted her arms to fasten it behind her neck. Of course, her muscles screamed, "no fair!"

He mistook her pain for some confinement of the dress and took the chain ends from her fingers.

"Never done this in my life, but I think I know how it works. There."

He sounded proud of himself, but Temple skittered away to the foyer mirror, avoiding one more compromising moment, not that a lot of them weren't forthcoming.

Poor Matt was jumping every gate like a steeplechase champion; he just didn't know that the winner of the race had already been announced.

Temple positioned the exquisite charm in the hollow of her

throat and swallowed hard to keep from bursting into tears. Probably they would float the treacherous soft lenses straight onto the floor as she shrank from shame like Alice into Tiny Alice, at risk of drowning in her own saltwater mess.

"Lovely," she managed to get out as she snatched her purse from the hall table and opened the door.

Matt followed, looking bemused, as if she had really chameleoned into a semistranger.

The mechanics of getting to the New York-New York complex distracted them both from awkwardness, although Temple couldn't restrain a small shudder as they approached the parked Storm.

"Not as cold as New York?" Matt commented, momentarily wrapping an arm around her shoulders.

It hurt, but she dared not wince.

He saw her into the passenger's seat, then got behind the wheel and backed out of the slot.

Every ordinary action, and reaction, was pure torture for Temple. Why had she thought she could let Matt down gently? That leading him on was kinder than letting him down from the first? Women were conditioned to feel responsible for everybody's hurt feelings, especially men's. They were either too hot or too cold, too encouraging or too chilling. They were supposed to figure out what they themselves really wanted and needed, all the while taking the emotional temperature of every soul around them and trying to soften blows and ease reality.

Max had been right. She wasn't here tonight because she needed to prolong the agony. She needed to delay the moment of truth.

Matt finally spoke, his face illuminated like a medieval angel's by the unholy halo of half-light from the dashboard. "I really can't thank you enough, Temple, for what you've done for me."

Mea culpa, mea culpa, mea Maxima culpa . . . and she wasn't even Catholic! She wasn't even a good Unitarian, although she was suddenly thinking of entering the convent.

"Oh, yeah?" As if she were saying, "How interesting."

"Yeah. That's what I wanted to tell you tonight. I bet you're dying to hear how I tracked down Effinger, but that was just the beginning. Going back to Chicago was a revelation."

"So tell me," Temple said, getting a grip on her paranoia and deciding to relax back into the passenger seat.

This is what she was really here for: to listen, to understand. Matt's quest had become more entangled with her life than either he or she would like, but it was, had become, a tandem journey. That, Effinger had proven in the Circle Ritz parking lot not two days ago. That, nothing could change, not even Max. And he knew it. Sort of.

"First, I want to explain the plans for the evening." He glanced at her as they glided under a brilliant swath of street light.

Temple wished her face didn't feel as if it were wearing a plaster of Paris mask.

"I thought New York-New York might be fun, since you haven't been there yet and you're fresh from the real thing. They had this New Year's Eve package . . . a before-dinner drink at the New York Bar at Times Square, dinner at a steakhouse—Gallagher's—and an after-dinner drink at a place called Hamilton's, finishing with a midnight champagne cocktail back at the Times Square Bar."

"We should be finished by then, all right."

"I know it sounds kind of touristy and hokey—"

"It sounds like fun. . . . and what isn't touristy and hokey in Las Vegas. Drive on, MacDuff."

Matt seemed to relax now that she had accepted the evening's program. At least the novelty of visiting New York-New York would distract them both from any misgivings.

Naturally, the hotel loomed on the horizon, its skyscraper skyline lit up like an old-time switchboard on crack cocaine.

Matt parked in the MGM-Grand lot across the street. "I thought walking over would be the best way to see it. Can you walk this far in the Midnight Louie heels?"

"Can a stork stride?" Temple scrambled out of the car before Matt could come around to assist her. "This is so much better than real life. Even for Christmas, Manhattan is granite-gray drab. They should get with the mauve and verdigris buildings."

"Mauve and verdigris, huh? I took them for pink and pale green."

"Well, the green is the aged-copper color of the mock Statue of Liberty. Also the color of money. A very subtle reference in its own screaming way."

Crossing Las Vegas Boulevard was made simple by escalators up to the Brooklyn Bridge, whose light-draped spans glimmered like golden garlands against the night sky.

"Now that does look like the real thing," Temple said.

An escalator on the other side glided them down to the street level and the reflecting pool that surrounded the Lady with the Lamp.

They joined the random current of people bearing left past the Statue of Liberty to the hotel's main entrance. The front of the long porte cochere was a neon litany announcing "New York-New York" against a spiky crown motif borrowed from Lady Liberty.

In fact, a bed of flowers basking in the lurid neon glow repeated the tiara design. Across the driveway, stationed before the brassy row of entrance doors, pulsated a string of stretch limos painted Broadway yellow and striped with checkers to emulate New York City cabs.

Matt nodded to the limos and their vanity plates, which read NY NY 1, 3 and 4. "Wonder how Gangster's likes that?"

"You can't copyright ideas, especially in this town," Temple answered. She looked up at the glittering gold tiara above her, and the gilt art-deco fountain designs of the entrance facade. "Cool."

Matt pulled a glossy brochure from his jacket pocket. "We're due at the Bar At Times Square for a predinner cocktail. I've got a map here—"

"I bet you do. This outing must have set you back a mint."

They pulled on Lady Liberty's torch-shaped door handles and entered the icy, dark interior of the hotel casino.

"It was nothing, compared to the second-hand sofa."

"And the necklace," Temple added in a spasm of guilt (or was that spelled "gilt" in the glittery ambiance of New York-New York?). Her fingertips traced the small feline figure at her throat.

Beneath them, marble inlaid floors sketched out another gigantic version of Lady Liberty's headgear. Around them chinked and chug-chimed and electronically yodeled dozens and dozens of slot machines. Ellis Island this was not.

They followed a marble-paved path past some upscale shops to the Central Park area.

"Oh." Temple paused.

Despite the eternal night sky of the casino interior, they were positioned to enter what she considered a Chinese plate scene: weeping willow trees, autumn trees half afire with fall colors amid the green leaves of summer, stuffed birds beside artistically arranged nests, a bridge over the untroubled waters of a small indoor lake.

And always the undying chatter and whoop of the flocking slot machines.

They crossed the bridge to the Bar at Times Square, its lit red apple poised high above the crowds, ready for the traditional New Year's Eve dip at midnight.

They found a free cocktail table for two, and squeezed into the seats.

"Cozy," Temple observed.

"I'd say crowded. And noisy."

A waiter slouched over with true Manhattan nonchalance.

Matt flashed a green chit and the waiter was gone as fast as he had come.

"The drinks are built in," Matt said. "No choice."

"Another authentic touch of Olde New York."

"You sound a bit jaded."

"Maybe lugging Midnight Louie around Manhattan can do that. So tell me about the Great Manhunt here in Las Vegas."

"Effinger. What a bust. For Molina, anyway."

"She couldn't hold him for anything."

"How did you know?"

"Oh, guessed." Temple wasn't about to admit that she'd seen Effinger on the loose.

Some women, she supposed, would use Effinger's attack as an excuse to stop seeing Matt. But telling Matt that *he* was too dangerous to know, and then hanging out with Max Kinsella was hardly consistent. Not with Max's shady connections having brought a much worse attack down on Temple months before. She suddenly remembered that Effinger was linked to Max as well as Matt. Lieutenant Molina suspected Max of involvement (in other words, murder) with the two dead men found in the casino ceilings of the Goliath and Crystal Phoenix Hotels months apart. The second body had borne Effinger's ID, although it was later proved a decoy when Matt tracked down the real Effinger. Effinger . . . Matt . . . Max, an eternal triangle, but what did it mean? Her thoughts stopped at Matt's continuing commentary on Effinger himself.

". . . pretty funny, I guess. Me trailing dear old stepdad through off-Strip dives and finally nailing him at the Blue Mermaid Motel. I kept remembering you met the flamingo guy there. Blue mermaids and pink flamingos. Only in Las Vegas."

The waiter materialized beside them, whisking two wide-mouth cocktail glasses floating maraschino cherries to the tabletop.

They both leaned over their mystery drinks, puzzled.

"Ah." Temple cracked the case first. "Manhattans, what else?"

Matt sipped his, then frowned. "Kind of . . . sweet. What's in them?"

"Ed Koch only knows! But you can put the cherry aside so the stem doesn't tickle your nose."

"I sampled a lot of strange and undrinkable concoctions on my pilgrimage."

"So what finally gave Effinger away?"

"His drinking habits. Boilermakers. Bartenders remember people's taste in liquor."

"Boilermakers? Yech."

"I agree. Anyway, I waited at the motel until some guy showed up who was wearing a cowboy hat, and I followed him home."

"Wasn't that risky? Nevada's a western state. Lots of guys could wear cowboy hats."

"Well, the first one to come along was Cliff Effinger."

"So you . . . what? Approached him outside his door, asked him to come along to see the nice policewoman?"

"Not exactly. I, uh, invited myself in. At that point I wasn't sure what I was going to do. That room was such an incredible dump. And Effinger wasn't the ogre I thought he was. What? You look . . . skeptical."

"Tell me about it," Temple said swirling the cherry in her sweet, murky drink. She needed to know what had happened between Matt and his stepfather so she could understand why the man had come for her.

"It's not exactly edifying information for a New Year's Eve gala." Matt made a face as he sipped his Manhattan. "But nothing I have to report about my Christmas vacation is what you could call edifying. So. There's Effinger not believing it's me, and me not believing he's Effinger. Such a scruffy old creep. Then he tries to run. Suddenly, I'm Tarzan. I feel like I could fling him around like Cheetah. I cool him off in the shower, haul him out to the pay phone by the manager's office and call police headquarters for Molina."

"That's it? He was just a rag doll?"

Matt nodded soberly, thanks to the foreign taste of the Manhattan. "He just didn't seem so big and dangerous any more. And he was really, really disturbed that I found him."

"Disturbed?"

"Ah, guess I should use the P.I. lingo. Pissed. I never said that to a lady before. Never said that to anyone."

"Heard it, though, I bet. So Molina was duly grateful."

"Not really. She didn't have enough grounds to arrest him, but they kind of . . . coaxed him into going downtown for an interview. Then Molina lectured me for involving myself. I thought that was that, until she called me just after I got home and asked me to come in to watch his interrogation."

"Watch? Like behind one of those two-way windows?"

Matt nodded. "I'm not sure who she hoped to learn more from: Effinger, or me. Molina's tricky. She's always thinking of something you haven't gotten to yet."

"That's just the impression she wants to give. Carmen the Omniscient, always in control."

"Speaking of control—" Matt rotated his wrist. "We're due for dinner now."

"Nice watch."

"Huh? Oh. Christmas present from my mother. That's where the real mystery was solved. In Chicago."

"And I have to wait until we shift tables and settle down again to hear that." Temple struggled upright in the crowded bar and joined Matt on the fringe of the huge, echoing central casino. "Where to next?"

"Uh. Yon butcher shop, I guess."

"Oooh, someplace gruesome to discuss buried secrets." His, she devoutly hoped.

Not hers.

Chapter 6

Should Auld Acquaintance Be Forgot . . .

Gallagher's steak house had an impossible-to-miss gimmick: its window-glass facade displayed massive hunks of meat in the process of aging, perhaps visibly, while you watched.

Temple swallowed, but not in anticipation.

How on earth was she going to chew steak in her condition, even if it was from the five-week-aged tender, flavor-intensified king-size cuts on raw display here? *Oh, what a tangled web we weave, when first we practice to deceive.* Robbie Burns knew about a lot more than true love and red, red roses.

They passed under the red-brick apartment building facade that reminded Temple of Rudy's rent-controlled building, only that dump didn't have three red awnings over arched windows. But the side was trellised in black metal fire escapes. She could almost see a black cat sitting high on some gridlike balcony.

Temple felt as if entering Gallagher's was like stepping into her bathroom mirror: serious forties noir. The wooden floors flowed into dark wood dadoes, with creamy upper walls framing huge black-and-white photo-portraits of long-gone stars: Bogie and Bacall and Barrymore and Bergman.

Diners at the hundred or so tables glanced up at them. Temple realized that she and Matt were the Yvette and Solange of the New Year's Eve crowd, an accidental metallic symphony in silver and gold. Except for her red hair. Always the bad-luck sign.

The maître d' led them to a table beneath Bette Davis and Paul Henreid smoking the farewell cigarettes from *Now, Voyager,* a fitting placement, Temple thought. *Bonjour, Tristesse.*

When the waiter brought the menu, Temple glanced with trepidation through the entrees listed between aisles of famous faces.

Matt unhesitatingly ordered the dry aged New York sirloin.

Temple hesitated.

"You're entitled to any entree except the King Crab legs, ma'am," the waiter prompted her.

"It's just that I . . . went to the dentist today. I guess the . . . red snapper."

The dinner included soup or salad. Temple settled for the gummable beef barley soup; Matt ordered the Caesar salad. Temple took her potatoes mashed; Matt his French fried.

Soon after their orders were given, the waiter returned with glasses of New York wines; red for Matt, white for Temple.

"I thought you sounded a little slurred," Matt mentioned. "I hope the dentist wasn't too bad."

"Actually, making an appointment for between the holidays was the smartest thing I ever did."

"No trouble?"

Temple smiled. "No trouble. Just a temporary discomfort."

"Dentist appointments can be rough."

She nodded and sipped her white wine. "So tell me about Chicago."

Matt shook his head, smiling. "Cold. Snow-choked. What the artists call 'unforgiving.'"

"You mean a demanding environment."

"This time, I demanded back."

"How so?"

"I saw it from a distance, for the first time. I'd avoided going back for years. Told myself it had been blighted by Effinger. But he was long gone, and all that was left were relatives and schoolmates. And I realized that they were a blight too."

"I'm glad I just visited Aunt Kit. Going home for the holiday can be . . . wearing."

"You don't know what you started with that red Goodwill sofa, Temple. I thought the last thing I needed was some extravagant statement, but in Chicago I discovered that's exactly what everybody around me needed. My mother, my cousin Bo and his wife, their would-be punk-artist daughter Krystyna . . . It was like 'Return to Elm Street,' only I was Freddy Krueger."

"You!"

"You've always seen me the way you wanted me to be, not the way I've seen myself. I was a freak. The last one in the family to enter the religious life. These people are descended from Polish immigrants. They live and breathe the Catholic religion and family values. And yet . . . none of my contemporaries and none of their children have made any more commitment to religion than sending their kids to Catholic schools. Which are nowadays taught by laypeople mostly, not clergy.

"I was like the fall of the last knight in a game of chess. I expected to be ostracized. Instead, they were afraid of me, as if *they* had been found wanting, not me for leaving the priesthood. It was . . . weird. And my mother was even weirder."

"How?"

"I hadn't seen her from that distance before. So . . . beaten down. So self-shrinking. I discovered that the anger I thought I'd felt for Effinger really belonged to her."

"But . . . you said you'd learned so much in Chicago. You were so . . . optimistic when you called me in New York."

He nodded. "The *Paradiso*, but first the *Inferno*."

"I get the idea, but not the reference."

"Catholic poet. Dante. The so aptly named 'Divine Comedy.' " Temple nodded.

"I had to go to the bottom of the well before I could bob to the surface again and see the sunlight. Speaking of 'Devine,' that isn't even my real father's name."

"You learned about your real father?"

"Not much. A one-night stand that began with a meeting at a church vigil stand. You know, racks of candles lit to a saint or the Virgin Mary. Or the Blue Mermaid. It's an old-fashioned, an old-country tradition, and the Polish parishes in Chicago cling to the something old, something Virgin Mary Blue."

"Matt. Maybe it's me or maybe it's the white wine, but I'm not following all of this."

He shook his head. "I think it's me, and the red wine. We always use it in the mass, for blood. Don't worry. The point is my mother was one of these foolish virgins schooled to be ignorant past the age of consent. She was nineteen. He was a Romeo with a Roman candle. Bound for Vietnam, a volunteer lighting beeswax to the Virgin and meeting her incarnate in my mother, and leaving the aftertaste of New Testament shame, only no angel excused the carnal amid the spiritual. No Holy Ghost claimed fatherhood. Only Effinger, by default."

"Would you mind translating for an unbeliever?"

"You're no unbeliever, Temple. Quite the contrary."

Their soup and salad came, wafted down from above, like homely manna.

"It's simple," Matt said. "My mother was unwed and pregnant. A source of terrible shame in her community. When Effinger came along and saw her vulnerability, he offered to marry her. Why not? She had a two-flat to rent and was willing to work, even if he wasn't. She . . . used to be good-looking before she tried to become invisible. I wasn't even in preschool. They hadn't heard of it in that neighborhood. Kin looked after kin, unless you were the kind of kin not spoken of. A bastard. My mother married to protect me from that label."

"Effinger was better than single parenthood?"

Matt's laugh was weary. He hadn't really done more than move his Caesar salad around, and Temple was finding even barley too tough to swallow.

"To my mother, in that old-time Catholic neighborhood. Yes. Apparently he became worse with time. And you were right."

"Me?"

"The real mystery, once you see and accept that my mother thought she was doing the best thing for me. She never had any illusions that it was the best thing for her. The real mystery is my natural father. He seemed to be from a well-to-do family. He'd wandered into the Polish section that night on the eve of leaving for Vietnam. She said he could have been exempted, which I presume means he was a college student. But he thought it was his duty. Their attraction was instant. I guess it happens that way sometimes?"

Temple nodded, aware of two times in her own life, neither over yet.

"He died over there. Later, some family lawyers came to see my mom and offered a . . . settlement, I suppose. Either a lump sum or a support payment until I reached my majority. She took the lump sum, only in the form of a two-flat in the neighborhood of St. Stan's. She . . . rooted us in the place that most denied us, for security's sake. Her house made her attractive to Effinger on-the-make, before he contracted gambling fever and Vegas dreams. And that was that. I grew up with lies and concealment and confusion and anger, and sought sense in God the Father. My mother paid her price and suffered in silence and finally grayed into aimless middle age. When I left the church, I left her lies to herself and to me. She's going to have to live for herself now. And I think she might finally be able to."

"Matt. That's a horrible story."

He grinned. "Isn't it? But it's the past. From here on in, it's all waiting to be rewritten."

"And that's what makes you feel optimistic?"

"That, and breaking with my mother's past. We've been at odds. I can understand why she did what she did, but I don't agree with it. She wanted me immured in the safety of church approval, the bastard made man of God. I think you're right; I think the story behind my real father is worth finding out. But first I've got to get free of my false father, Effinger, and I think I have."

Temple nodded, and leaned back as her soup was taken away and a large plate of fish placed before her.

"A very Christian dish, I guess," she noted mischievously.

"You're way ahead of me, as always."

"You give me way too much credit, as always."

"Anyway, that's what I feel like celebrating tonight. My freedom from the past, its lies and half-truths, its benign enslavement, its souvenirs like Effinger. There were so many things I thought I had to be; now there are things I've never dreamed of becoming. I'm not going to cut free all at once, but I think, I think I'm finally loose enough to be human again. I feel like I stand a prayer of having a relationship with a woman without miring it in theological debates. I'm on some sort of brink. I feel like I could fly and not dash my feet on the stones below. It's crazy. It's incredible. Let's toast it."

He lifted his glass of blood-red wine and Temple lifted her glass of pallid hue. Brims touched. Chimed like New Year's bells in miniature.

"I don't know if we can make two more stops," Matt said when they left Gallagher's.

Temple, ever practical, checked her fragile watch face. "If we pace ourselves. It's just after eleven."

"So did my 'At Home in Illinois' story inspire you?"

"I'd sure like a line on those lawyers who bought your mother off."

"You think—?"

"For one thing, your natural father might not be dead at all."

Matt stopped in the concourse, frowning. He looked slightly tipsy, as she had never seen him. She wasn't sure whether it was emotion or St. Emilion. It was one thing to have slain the evil father figure from his past; another to admit the possibility of a missing father in his future.

"The family lawyers told my mother he was dead. Vietnam."

Temple shrugged. "His family lawyers aren't her or your lawyers."

Matt, stunned silent by the possibility, finally shook his head as if renouncing Satan. "Temple, sometimes your imagination runs in overdrive. My mother got a settlement. It's over. And I've hunted missing father figures long enough."

He pulled out the package brochure. Subject closed. "Hamilton's next. For dessert and an after-dinner brandy. They do believe in mixing spirits, don't they?"

"Where's Hamilton's?"

"Upstairs. We'll have to work our way across the Central Park Casino to the Empire Lounge, then take the stairs or escalator up to Hamilton's."

"I vote for the escalator."

"Hard walking in those heels?"

"Hard walking in this swamp of spiritous liquors. Brandy? And it still won't be midnight?"

"We celebrate the New Year back at the Times Square Bar, with champagne cocktails."

"Ooh, my aching head. Put away your brochure, Robinson Crusoe; it isn't even Friday."

Matt took her arm as they threaded their way through the slot machines and their minions.

Temple couldn't object to the support. She'd thought her ten days in New York had been action-packed. Matt's journey from back-alley Las Vegas to secret-laden Chicago seemed the far more dangerous voyage.

The Empire Lounge was hard to miss with its huge rotating mirrored red apple over the stage. They headed in unison for the escalators, Temple leaping gingerly over the first step in her Midnight Louie high heels.

As they rose, the view grew more impressive. By the time they stood at the entrance to Hamilton's, they could oversee the entire first floor gaming area and the distant walls whose painted New York skyline was limned in sunset shades of rose and purple. Twilight time. Very romantic. Except that they reminded Temple of bruises. Beneath them twinkled the trees of Central Park.

As if heaven-sent, Big Band music swayed in the background. Could Guy Lombardo be far away?

A sign outside Hamilton's requested "appropriate attire" after eight P.M. Temple and Matt exchanged a glance. Could they be any more appropriate?

A maître d' again accepted Matt's blue chit. They passed a black-and-red gift shop and a walk-in humidor oozing the odor of expensive cigars.

Another glance was exchanged.

Under their feet lay leopard-design carpeting, and black leather banquettes curled around black lacquer-and-chrome tables.

Art deco geometric fabric covered the central chairs; torchères spiked the walls. Everything was dark and elegant, lit by champagne flutes of light. A soft blue haze draped the ambiance like a feather boa.

Once they were seated, a statuesque female in a slinky strapless gown slunk over with a selection of cigars. His and hers. Temple picked up the tabletop matchbook, whose motto was IT'S ALWAYS MIDNIGHT AT HAMILTON'S.

They both shook their heads, shocked. Soon a decadent cheesecake dessert arrived, accompanied by brandy Alexanders.

"I don't get the dame with the stogies," Matt admitted.

"I think this is a 'cigar bar.' The latest thing on the Coasts."

"But women—?"

"Light up now, too, in trendy circles. Me, I think trying to act like a man is always dumb. I mean, mouth cancer isn't worth it."

"You do have a way of improving the appetite," Matt said, glancing down at his dessert.

"That's just Heart Attack City. Dive in."

Temple did. Her appetite had revived when faced with something smooth and creamy and sweet. The brandy Alexander was equally agreeable, and she'd had just enough liquor to numb the buzz saws of pain grinding at her face and jaw.

"You're enjoying this, really? Despite my personal recital?"

"Personal recitals are my favorite thing. And, yes, I am. This is the way the real New York should be: all fairyland and no hassle. We don't even have to catch a cab."

"True. But I don't know if I can take one more drink this evening. I thought I'd hit my quota during my Effinger chase."

Temple sipped the brandy Alexander, deciding a headache in the morning would be worth it. And it was work keeping her mouth shut about Effinger's attack to save Matt's big evening of celebration and revelation.

As for telling him about Max . . . tomorrow was another day. Her fingers went to the black-cat pendant at her throat. She hated to return it.

"You haven't eaten too much tonight," Matt said.

Only then did she realize how closely he had been watching her.

"The dentist. Kind of yucky. But I've tasted everything, and loved every moment."

"Even the P.I. report."

"The best parts. I wish I knew what Molina was really going to do about Effinger, though."

"What can she do?"

"More than we might think."

"I wish you weren't so suspicious of her. She's really, well, I can't exactly say personable. She has integrity."

"Look what that got you."

He shrugged. "That's the past. I'm finally seeing beyond it. And what I see is—"

"Yes?"

"You."

Oh, my. For a moment Temple felt the room spin. She wasn't sure if she was drinking because she was happy, or because she was not happy. The line was very fine between sober and tipsy, between optimism and despair.

She checked her watch, then changed the subject, which was her.

"Eleven-thirty. Do we need to decamp back to the Times Square Bar?"

"Probably. This cigar smoke is going to get to me soon anyway."

They wandered out of Hamilton's trendy haze, overlooking the ersatz New York below. Temple was suddenly tired, dispirited, guilty with the weight of too much not said.

Matt took her elbow to guide her through the frenetic casino, but her real escort was dread. She pictured telling him the truth about Max and her in his apartment with the alien red sofa front and center. Would he go berserk, as he had once when he had less to lose, both in terms of furniture and expectations? How far had he come since Chicago? Enough to expect an intimate end to an extravagant evening?

When should she say it? What should she say?

The bright red apple hung poised over the New Year's revelers as the Big Band sound lured celebrants onto the dance floor. Matt and Temple were seated at a lilliputian excuse of a table for two, and champagne cocktails in narrow flutes were placed before them. The last libation on the evening's ticket.

They sat silent, not willing to compete with the swelling, seductive music, watching couples swing-dance.

The clock ticked toward midnight, and Temple's Midnight Louie glass slippers would not melt, nor would the Storm in the parking lot turn into a pumpkin, although its owner might be reenvisioned as a rat if the whole truth were known. . . .

"It's almost midnight," Matt said, standing and leaning over her.

He offered her a hand. "I think I can manage to shuffle through 'Auld Lang Syne.' "

It was an offer she couldn't refuse.

Temple stood, aware of a subtle tremor in her frame: fatigue and something else.

They went to the edge of the crowded floor, and then the artificial blue-black sky of New York-New York was the desert's impenetrable dome again, and the music came small and wee from a tape deck and their feet moved like scorpions slow-dancing on the sands of time.

The orchestra segued into "Auld Lang Syne," the boozy, maudlin rhythms whose words everybody knew, and everybody around them was singing and so were they, Temple just humming.

Midnight was announced with a dramatic gong sounding for twelve long drawn-out moments.

And Matt kissed her, a wonderful, searingly enthusiastic kiss on the mouth that hurt like hell, hurt almost as much as half-truths and lies. Bloody lies.

Temple broke away too late and headed for the table, blinded by her contact lenses.

Matt followed. Shocked. Concerned. Contrite. All the wrong, wrong things.

"Temple."

The bells still rang, and around them people celebrated with bad booze and good music as they always did.

He put a hand to his lips. "Did I do that?"

"No!" She scooped some ice out of the water goblet she'd ordered to dilute the effect of all those varied drinks, and wrapped the inexcusably tiny cocktail napkin around it, then pressed it to the inside of her cheek.

"The dentist?" He was using his own napkin to dab at the blood on his lips.

"Yes. The dentist." She moved the ice to the ache on her cheek, unsure what would stop the bleeding, once started.

Matt was watching her with the helpless inaction of the onlooker. "Do you want to visit the ladies room? Or . . . I'm sure they have some sort of first-aid station here."

"I'm fine. Just give me a minute."

He frowned. "What have you got on your face?"

He was staring at her left cheekbone and eye. She knew instantly the soggy napkin had smeared the makeup.

She didn't know whether he read the answer to his question in her eyes, or in his own memories of the past, but his face hardened. She didn't know which devastated him more, the truth he finally saw for himself, or the liar he finally saw in her.

A Cup of Kindness Yet

Temple waited alone under the merciless neon glare of New York-New York's glitzy urban porte cochere, longing for sunglasses. It felt every minute of almost one o'clock in the morning.

She thought people kept looking at her, but maybe the drawing card wasn't her slightly cracked facial facade. Maybe it was her festively glittering dress and shoes. Still, she wished for the concealing offices of her usual eyeglass frames. Wearing contact lenses made her feel exposed. It didn't help that the new contacts, not to mention the blinding illumination all around her, made her eyes tear. She might have matched the surrounding glitz, but she felt like a Black Hole sucking all that light and energy into some vast, hidden and concentrated emptiness.

Matt had insisted she wait for him to bring the car around. His grim fury may have been on her behalf, but it sheathed her in icy isolation. Around her, people came and went, deliriously tipsy or well en route.

Even the hotel's cheery stretch limousines rebuked her. She

watched anxiously for the Storm's impudent aqua silhouette among the upscale flock of precious-metal-colored Infinitis and Lexi.

At last the Storm swooped to the curb, the passenger door popping open simultaneously.

Temple got in, grateful for the privacy if not the continuing conversation. Matt's last, ironic comment still echoed inside the Black Hole: "Maybe you'll finally figure out that he isn't worth protecting."

Neither spoke until the entrance glare of New York-New York was a comet trail behind them, quickly shrinking against the vast inkiness of nighttime Las Vegas.

"I wish you'd told me," Matt said.

"So do I, but, then again, maybe not."

"I don't get it. Why you keep shielding that guy? He's brought thugs down on you, for the second time."

"How could I have stopped what happened to me?"

"You couldn't. It's not your fault. But I'm with Molina. Why do you keep denying that Max Kinsella is nothing but trouble? You're just like my mother."

"That's it, isn't it? I'm your mother and Max is another face of Cliff Effinger. Having enemies may not be Max's fault."

"Letting you play sitting duck for them is."

"What can he do? Kill them?"

"Maybe he did. Lieutenant Molina tells me the first two goons haven't been seen since the parking garage incident."

Temple was silent in the face of that fact, wondering why Matt didn't see the obvious, other than the fact that the obvious is always as mysterious as the hand in front of your face, a magnified surface of such familiarity that it becomes foreign when confronted too closely.

Matt sighed, automatically navigating the traffic stream of the Strip.

"I guess all the martial arts exercise was useless."

"Not useless. But I was trapped between a van and my car with an armload of groceries. All he got in was one good wallop, really, but it knocked my glasses off and I hit my head on the van. Then it was messy while I tried to scramble over the Storm's hood to get away. Electra came to my rescue with a brass knuckle of keys. End of story."

"One guy, huh? And it wasn't either of the missing thugs?"

Temple shook her head. He still wasn't seeing that this attack was nothing like the first.

"They're getting bolder, though," Matt went on, "actually coming to the Circle Ritz. Why? What did the man want? Did he say anything? Any clue why the great Kinsella's ex-girlfriend is being singled out for assault?"

"Could you pull over for a minute?"

"Here? Off the Strip?"

"Yeah. Anywhere."

"There's hardly anywhere convenient to stop. Why? What do you need?"

"Absence of motion, for one thing."

"You're getting carsick? Temple, have you seen a doctor? Don't tell me you pulled the same routine as last time, refusing to go to an emergency room? I can't believe Electra would let you be so foolish."

Temple gritted her teeth. "There's the Hacienda. Just pull into the parking lot."

As the car left the Strip, everything around them dimmed and quieted. Temple exhaled in relief.

"I don't mean to carp," Matt was saying, "but nausea could be a sign of concussion. I'm worried about you, Temple, and I'm worried that you'd still choose to lie to me rather than betray Max Kinsella. Isn't our relationship better than that?"

Temple sighed again. It was as if an internal gag order was in place. She could hardly bring herself to say the truth he was asking for, that his every assumption was goading her into revealing.

"I'm okay," she said. "The attack was two days ago; I'd hardly develop symptoms of a concussion now. I'm sorry. I tried not to ruin your celebration. I know what you've accomplished in the last few days is really important. But I can't have you blaming what happened to me on Max. It had nothing to do with him. Zero. Zilch."

"It was a garden variety mugging? Then why the big act? Were you afraid I'd feel my self-defense tutoring was inadequate? I think my ego can handle that."

"Oh, your ego can handle the truth. I'm just not sure your id can."

"Temple! Just tell me the truth. I don't know why women do this. Suppress and excuse in the name of other people's feelings. You've got to face reality."

"We're trained not to. Okay. My attacker wasn't a common garden variety mugger. He wasn't a mugger at all. And you're right, I do seem to be paying for my associations. It was Effinger. That reality enough for you?"

"Effinger? Cliff Effinger?"

Matt sounded stupefied. Temple had expected a major implosion.

"I ought to know," she added, "I saw the full-size portrait of him before he was memorialized in wallet-size."

"Effinger. Why? Why bother you?"

"Not because he was looking for Max, or you, that's for sure. He was angry because you'd forced him to see the police. He wanted you to know that if you could find him, he could find someone close to you."

"How on earth would he know—? We're not exactly a front-page couple. I can't believe it."

"Maybe he had help. He seems afraid of someone or something. More afraid of whatever that is than he is of you, or the police. His message was, leave him alone."

"That creep! True to form; go for anybody weaker, a woman."

"It worked before. Threatening your mother."

"He's cunning enough to push all the old buttons."

"And desperate enough. You and Molina can do your worst to harass him; you'll never scare him more than who he's been working for."

Matt hardly heard her. He was back exploring some interior maze of memory and emotion.

"You see why I was a teeny bit reluctant to tell you," she said.

"No. I'm not a child to be kept in the dark. My mother thought she was doing that, protecting me, but kids need the truth even more than adults."

Temple debated jumping to the second level of Truth or Consequences. So far, Matt had not greeted her news with the storm she had expected. Still, his abstraction and withdrawal were a tad eerie. He had almost forgotten her.

"I wonder if that woman . . ." he murmured.

"What woman?"

"Huh? Oh, somebody I ran into when I was hunting Effinger. I suppose he's moved by now."

"And he sure doesn't want to be found again, that I know."

"Why?" The question was not posed because he expected an answer.

Matt put the idling car into gear again. "I don't suppose you'd let me tell Molina about this."

"Molina? Why not? Better for her to meddle with Effinger, if he's going to take being tracked down so personally. But I'd appreciate a day or two more of recovery before I have to face her."

"She doesn't need to see the damage, just needs to know how he reacted. God, I never dreamed he'd hurt you."

"At least we know he's afraid of you."

"And what good is that if he lashes out at people I know? All I've done is make him more dangerous."

"Maybe you've made him expendable to his overlords. Maybe he's fighting for his life."

"You mean, my finding him could get him killed?"

Temple nodded.

Matt considered that. "So I might have accidentally played Judas. There's some justice in that."

The Circle Ritz parking lot looked deserted when the car turned into it, headlights flashing the darkness.

They exited the car warily, stopping, looking, listening for lurkers.

But it was fifty-some hours and a New Year later. Effinger was a ghost visible only in the hollows of Temple's face.

Matt herded her inside like a guard dog.

Waiting for the lobby elevator, Temple said suddenly, "I'm tired."

"Seeing the sofa can wait," he agreed, still abstracted, still fitting together the puzzle of Effinger and his shadowy associates.

He saw her to her door and insisted on searching the rooms be-fore he left her.

"Take care of yourself," he said at the door before leaving, putting a palm to her face so lightly she barely felt the touch. He kissed the top of her head and was gone.

Temple locked the door, deflated.

Where were the funny hats and the streamers? Where had Matt's good mood gone? Why did she have a sense of having faced only half the music?

She moved slowly into the bedroom, taking the shoes off as she went.

And where was Midnight Louie? So far she hadn't seen him.

A shadow moved in the bathroom. He'd probably been sleep-ing in the tub again.

She went to greet him, but Max stepped out of the room on quiet cat feet instead.

Chapter 8

Mr. Mystery

"You look like hell," he said.

"Happy New Year to you too."

"Come on. Let's wash off that unhappy face."

Max boosted her onto the pedestal sink's generous edge, then opened the medicine cabinet, pulling out the cotton pads and makeup remover.

When she'd patted on the concealing makeup, Temple had thought of how uncomfortable it would be to rub off, but Max, veteran of greasy stage pancake that he was, whisked it off with featherweight strokes.

"So." He ran warm water over a washcloth in the sink. "How did he take it?"

"I can't believe you were sitting here waiting up for me like an overprotective parent. What if he had come in for more than a quick look around? And where were you then anyway?"

"Outside. Prepared to make like a human fly if he checked out the patio. You're avoiding the question. Why would he come in if you told him that you're . . ." Max swathed her face in the warm washcloth.

"That I'm what?" she asked through the muffling terry cloth.

"How can I put it so you won't take offense?"

Temple pushed the washcloth away. "You can't."

Max grinned. "Never could. How *did* you put it?"

"I didn't, exactly."

Max backed away from her and leaned against the opposite wall, a study in black-clad disappointment on washroom-white tile. Temple used to take his all-black attire for Magician Chic; she suddenly realized it was Sable Second-story Man.

"My masquerade didn't work, Max. So we got into the Effinger incident instead. Telling Matt that finally finding his stepfather had made me into a target was bad enough; I didn't see any way to add on, 'Oh, by the way, Max and I did the wild thing in New York and I can't talk to you any more.' "

"You're just avoiding the inevitable, and insulting us both."

"I know. But it feels like I'm sparing somebody's feelings, like mine."

Max pushed off the wall, relaxed again. He dabbed at her cheek with the lukewarm washcloth.

"I think you'll like the contact lenses, but why did you chicken out on getting a wild and crazy color?"

"Don't be so sure I did. These are temporaries while I'm waiting for the prescription."

Max looked intently into her eyes; she wasn't getting sleepy. He took her hands, held them up like Exhibit A on the strong tented surface of his fingertips. The ring he had given her was missing.

"Temple. I know you wouldn't be waffling on telling Devine the truth if you didn't have deep feelings for him. I'm not putting a name on them, but they're there, and they won't get out of our way until you tell him that we're together again."

"But are we? One night doth not a relationship make. Or mend."

Max reached behind her neck to undo the tiny black hook at the neckline, then ran the back zipper open to her tailbone, his fingers tracing the route with the same featherweight touch.

"Why don't you slip into something comfortable and sleep on

it? Tomorrow evening, when you've had a chance to rest up and concoct a new set of waffles, I'll pick you up so you can come on over to my place," he whispered into her ear in a bedroom voice. "I could use an amateur sleuth and an editor in the worst way."

Then he grinned and left her sitting on the sink to jump down on her own.

She followed him as far as the bedroom door, shouting after him as he vanished onto his favorite exit, the patio.

"Max, you want to lure me over to your place for editorial services?"

He didn't bother answering, so she shut the door, pointedly, and did as he suggested. Amateur sleuthing at the former Orson Welles house? Editing? Curiosity killed the cat, and apparently it had driven Louie out for the night as well.

Temple felt relieved to drop her glittering carapace of a dress and peel off the concealing pantyhose. She actually felt relieved to be alone at last, bereft of all masculine company, human or feline, passionate or purely platonic.

Sometimes you, yourself and I were all the company one could stand.

Chapter 9

Flamingo Memories

Temple only needed a liquid powder foundation by the next day to disguise what the old-time gumshoes called a "mouse."

As black eyes go, it was a fading charcoal gray; her mouth only felt like it had been to the dentist, and she was beginning to simmer in anticipation of Max's forthcoming mystery night out . . . in.

And entering the Crystal Phoenix's understated entrance drive was like returning to Manderley again, sans Max de Winter.

Van von Rhine had insisted that a New Year's Day appointment would not intrude on family or business plans. In fact, she had added over the phone yesterday, the holiday was especially appropriate to the renovation project and the wonderful . . . donation that it had received.

Donation in Las Vegas? Temple wondered. Money was wagered and lost and—occasionally—won here, but rarely was it simply given away. And never to commercial projects.

So Temple crossed the Phoenix's navy-and-camel casino carpeting Tuesday morning and barely heard the frequent chimes of slot machines as she headed to the executive offices behind the reception area.

Lines of registering guests snaked obediently through the roped-off maze in front of the long front desk. Apparently the Phoenix wasn't suffering despite lacking some of the latest gimmicks on the Strip, such as a Jurassic Park theme park or a roller coaster shaped like the Loch Ness monster. They could have a baby Nessie for the kids. Hey, not bad ideas, either of them, although a bit pricey for the Phoenix.

She kept an eye out for lurking Fontana brothers, Nicky's nine darkly handsome littermates. They were touchingly protective of her but rather overwhelming en masse, both sartorially and for an undeniable air of Gangster cologne. Fontana Inc. was always impeccably tailored and accoutered by Cerutti and Beretta, though somewhat rough around the behavioral edges.

She spotted neither the Fontana brothers' Armani-suited silhouettes nor their less conventional post-romance-convention attire, Elvis jumpsuits. No doubt they had rung in the New Year until their fine Italian heads had also rung.

Nicky Fontana, though, sleek as a black Maserati with camel-colored leather interior, was waiting in his wife's outer office to usher Temple into the inner sanctum.

"Sorry to have played hooky over the holidays," Temple told Van, who rose from behind her glass-topped desk to join her husband in front of it.

They were living proof that opposites attract and make an attractive couple: Nicky with his sienna skin and vibrant dark eyes and hair; Van a Nordic blond with a demeanor as cool as her husband's was heated.

Nicky leaned against the thick glass and crossed his arms. "So how was New York? Did the cat take it by storm?"

"He took the advertising agency by storm, though that was all of Manhattan he saw, except for my aunt's glamorous condominium in a miniature flatiron building. Oh, and a railroad flat in a part of the Village where only the lonely live."

"Uptown, downtown," Nicky said. "That's what makes New York exciting. Sophistication and sleaze side by side."

"Thank God our hotel isn't going for the New York-New York look, then," Van put in, shuddering genteelly.

Nicky liked to scratch his discreetly manicured nails across the blackboard of her fine sensibilities. Van had been reared in the hushed, hothouse atmosphere of the European luxury hotel industry and found Las Vegas trying at times.

"So what is this surprise?" Temple asked, not feeling up to spending too much time at the Phoenix today, despite her fondness for Nicky and Van.

Van, wearing one of the exquisite Escada suits that were her trademark, stepped dramatically away from a long side table.

That's when Temple spied the cityscape-in-miniature of an architect's model.

She edged toward it, taking in a jumble of shapes and color. The thing looked like a Miro or Matisse painting in 3-D. And it was fully accoutered with . . . flamingos. Lots and lots of flamingos.

"But . . . this is Crystal Phoenix Hotel and Casino. Shouldn't they be phoenixes?"

"Not when Domingo himself has designed the new children's petting zoo. It will be partly a permanent installation of his recent headline-grabbing conceptual art hit with the plastic flamingos, and partly a zoo."

"I think they're both the same," Nicky muttered in Temple's ear, donning an angelic expression as Van shot him a suspicious glance.

"And Domingo is giving us the free use of his design, 'if his friend Miss Temple Barr approves.' Isn't that wonderful? You must have made quite an impression on him."

Temple shrugged modestly.

"And all he wants," Van went on, "is that we dedicate it to 'Brother John.' "

Temple let her jaw drop. And instantly regretted it.

"What's the matter?" Van looked concerned.

"Saw the dentist yesterday. She was open half the day and I'd booked the appointment before I knew Louie and I would be the toast of New York during the holidays."

Van nodded, still admiring the colorful model. "I don't know who Brother John is, but I'll put his name up in neon if it's adequate thanks for getting a children's park designed by an internationally renowned artist."

"Brother John," Nicky ruminated. "It must mean something. I don't have a brother Gianni, hard as that may be to believe, but I'll adopt this one gladly."

"A simple flamingo-pink plaque somewhere should be all that's needed," Temple said demurely.

"I suppose it could be a Brother, as in order of brothers," Nicky speculated. "Domingo could be Spanish."

"Or Italian," Van put in.

"Or Incan," Temple added.

"He is . . . international, isn't he?" Van asked, looking dazed. "But study this layout. It's an Alice-in-Wonderland sort of maze, a children's sculpture garden. And the animals will be displayed in this most unnatural environment quite naturally. He's even specified a Wonderland croquet vignette with the plastic flamingos as mallets."

"And the Mushroom Maze is a prairie dog town," Nicky added.

"Amazing," Temple agreed. What wonders, she wondered, would Max produce this evening to compete with a Domingo Original. "It lends itself to all sorts of tie-in products."

"Wonderful idea, Temple." Van's tranquil face glowed. "I've been so stupefied by Domingo's offer that I hadn't considered the spin-off possibilities."

"We'd have to cut Domingo in on the product profits," Temple added, "but it would be well worth it."

"Absolutely," Nicky agreed. "I'm sure we can work out a good deal. The guy was like Santa Claus with an American Express platinum card. He brought his wife and kid with him, and of course Van had to bring them up to the penthouse to see Cinnamon."

"How is the baby?"

"Cinna's just terrific, Temple."

"She has actual hair now," Nicky put in.

"She always had hair," Van retorted. "It was just . . . baby-fine."

"Louie will like her a lot better with more fur," Temple said. "I can sympathize with the state of parenthood now that I've lugged him all over Manhattan in a cat knapsack."

"So how did everything go?" Van sat down behind her desk.

Temple gratefully collapsed into one of the upholstered Parsons chairs paired before it, while Nicky played on the sidelines with the moving parts of Domingo's model.

"How did it go? You could consider it an existential Christmas, I guess. Santa was dead."

"Santa . . . died?"

"At the advertising agency Christmas party, no less. Louie tried to warn us something was up, but they wouldn't listen to Lassie either."

"You're kidding!" Nicky said hopefully, from the sidelines.

"No, I'm not. Put quite a crimp into the selection process for the Allpetco spokescats and spokesperson. I don't know who will get the nod, and, right now, I don't care. I'm eager to get going again on the Phoenix project, especially now that this bonus has dropped into our laps. I think I'll go gaze on the real estate out back, try to envision Domingo's park as a part of it."

"Go. Gaze. Graze a little in the restaurants, if you like." Nicky waved her away like an Italian mama shooing schmoozers out of her kitchen. "You're always on the house at the Crystal Phoenix."

"Not a bad advertising slogan," said Temple, only recalling a moment later why the phrase sounded familiar: *It's always midnight at Hamilton's.*

Midnight at New York-New York on New Year's Eve would always be a miserable memory. Trying to carry on as normal had been the worst possible move for everyone.

Temple smiled a wan good-bye to Van and Nicky and made her long, solo way to the hotel's rear courtyard, which housed the pool, some tennis courts and a lot of undeveloped Las Vegas scrub that was worth its weight in sand.

Visions of sugar plums and plum advertising contracts vanished before the bright, palm-decorated vista. Not only was the surface land waiting to be morphed into a new fantasy recreational area, but the Crystal Phoenix lay above a network of underground tunnels that could be exploited for a delightfully dark Disneylandish Jersey Joe Jackson mine ride, complete with the old coot's holographic ghost. Temple thought about Jersey Joe building the Joshua Tree Hotel here in the forties, then squirreling caches of his ill-gotten goods all over the wastes of Las Vegas and the surrounding desert. Maybe excavation would unearth more treasure, like the highjacked silver dollars discovered a few years ago. And maybe not. Today's coveted treasures were multimillion-dollar state lotteries.

She glanced up at the hotel, now transformed into the elegant Crystal Phoenix, trying to pinpoint Jersey Joe Jackson's seventh-floor ghost suite. Even if his shade didn't actually haunt the suite that had been his home in good times and bad, it would holo-graphically prowl the underground mine ride. That was more than Howard Hughes's ghost could claim, for all that his estate still owned most of Las Vegas.

So it wasn't just expensive mania, which seemed to drive New Las Vegas these days, it was history!

Temple actually felt one warm brown bubble of optimism ex-plode on the top of her brain. She was perking up, quite literally. She thrived on ideas, on linking strange odds and ends, and on get-ting her brain bubbling until it overflowed into her demeanor and that flooded into the enthusiastic public relations pro personality.

That side of her had been dormant of late, she realized, dragged down by personal conundrums like Bachelor Number One or Bachelor Number Two. God forbid a Number Three should show up on the scene. She'd lose all momentum then.

Some of the palms would have to go. But they wouldn't be re-placed with the ersatz reconstituted palms that lined the entry to the Mirage. Domingo was right: better the genuine fake than the trumped-up substitute. Neon palm trees painted metal-sculpture pink, and green-and-blue palm fountains. But not instant freeze-dried palms.

And the carp pond. Louie's beloved former hangout. That might have to be relocated. . . . Temple wandered in its direction, toward the thicket of canna lilies not now in bloom.

She stopped, surprised. A black cat sat in elegant relief against the broad canna lily leaves. Of course. Midnight Louise, aka Caviar. She was the Crystal Phoenix mascot now that Midnight Louie had moved in with Temple at the Circle Ritz.

Louise sat statue-still, perhaps staring at an exotic goldfish doing a pas de deux, fins in the water. Koi in kinetic motion. Even the cat's shadow didn't stir.

And then Temple blinked the mushy contact lenses into better focus.

The cat's "shadow" wasn't a shadow, but another black cat, this one hunched on all fours, gazing fixedly into the pond.

Temple edged nearer on her dainty red-and-purple-and-pewter Manolo Blahnik snakeskin pumps.

Neither cat stirred, but they simultaneously turned their faces toward her, one gold-eyed, one green.

"Louie! Is this where you've been? I missed you last night. Well . . . this morning, really."

He blinked, as if clearing his new contact lenses. Then he stared down into the water again.

Temple felt distinctly snubbed, but she supposed that returning from New York to become, in short order (a) an assault victim, (b) an invalid and (c) a New Year's Eve gadabout did not endear her to her loyal feline friend.

Besides, she had thought that he and Midnight Louise did not get along.

Temple approached the cats until she too could see into the water.

But no fish schooled there. The pond was empty, perhaps vacated for the coldest part of the winter. Maybe the koi had gone south to winter at Phoenix, Arizona. What were the great feline hunters watching, then, waterbugs?

Temple could have sworn they were brooding.

Was she in a funk! Attributing her own downcast emotions to a pair of sunning pussycats.

"Well, feel free to come home whenever you feel like it, Louie."

A party of passing tourists stared at her.

Temple talked back in her mind: *Hey, some of you people talk to dice! At least cats are sentient, and sometimes a whole lot more.*

These cats were mostly indifferent to her. Temple left them, feeling deserted by Louie's return to the Crystal Phoenix.

She got over the perfidy of cats by the time she stopped at the optometrist's, who had opened up briefly despite the holiday just so her "emergency" client could literally "see" New Year's Day in.

"The black eye's so much better now," noted the young woman sympathetically. "With these new lenses you won't be walking into open doors anymore because your glasses slipped down your nose and you nearly dropped your groceries. You'll see so much better with the exact prescription."

Temple underwent the icky process of peeling out the old lenses and putting in the new. "Out with the old, in with the new" reminded her of the recent disastrous holiday celebration, only her personal motto could be: "in with the old, out with the new."

But . . . the optometrist was right. The glittering environment of the shop, including ranks of traditional glass frames, was in much sharper focus now.

Temple fingered the narrow brochure she had picked up on her first visit. "About these colored lenses."

"Ideal for someone with your mid-range correction."

"Yes, but . . . color." She would never have speculated on rotating eye color with a male optometrist.

"Green would be the obvious choice. Or a deeper blue."

"Not . . . violet."

"Well—"

"I've always thought violet eyes would be . . . electric."

"Whatever you like. The whole idea is to play with your image, right?"

Or maybe play with your identity, maybe fool someone hunting a redhead with light blue-grey eyes.

But Temple could tell that her favorite color, violet, didn't strike the optometrist as the most flattering disguise for her rampant coloring.

Max would tell her to do what she liked. *Do what thou wilt.* That was the motto of some long-dead magician, she remembered from her exploration of the profession during Halloween week. Alistair Crowley, that was his name. Only he had been more than a magician, more like the leader of some decadent cult. Something metaphysical and creepy and a little silly.

She thrust the brochure back into her tote bag.

Violet eyes.

Maybe another day.

Chapter 10

The Mysteries of Gandolpho

Louie was still boycotting the Circle Ritz when Temple greeted Max at the patio door at seven that evening. She had tried calling Matt earlier before he left for work at the hotline, but got no answer. She had an edgy feeling that he was taking Effinger's attack far harder than he had let her see the previous evening.

But tonight was Max's and she'd get really schizophrenic if she kept mentally bouncing between the two of them.

In honor of her New Year's Day's night with Max, she had donned loose knit pants and top, in burglar black, and tennis shoes.

Max seemed please to find her waiting, but glanced at her feet. "What are those?"

She looked down at her $7.88 discount-store black velvet tennies. "Stealth tennis shoes. I assume we'll need to slink into your house, as usual. Things are rough, Kinsella, when you have to break into your own place."

He looked around the condominium. "Yeah. I know."

An awkward caesura killed the chitchat. Midnight Louie wasn't even around to serve as a conversation piece.

Temple joined Max on the uncontested couch, offering him a mug of coffee. She expected this to be a long evening, one way or another. "So, seriously, what's at your place that's so fascinating, besides you?"

He lifted an eyebrow at her concession of interest. "I've been poking around Gandolph's computer files and his inventory of magical appliances."

" 'Magical appliances'? Sounds kinky."

"Magic has always had a kinky undercurrent, and a metaphysical one. Confinement, release. Death, rebirth. But I'm running into traces of more than the usual baggage. Something . . . sinister."

"Does it have anything to do with Gandolph's death?"

Max hesitated. "It could."

"Well, now that we're hyped up on caffeine, I suppose we're ready to face anything. As least I won't crash at ten P.M."

Max put her half-drunk coffee mug on the glass-topped table. His long fingers suddenly framed her naked face. The expression in his eyes was so intense she felt she was listening to the profession of a vow.

"No more 'crashes' for you. Not from that quarter. I doubt that Effinger will be anyone's problem very much longer."

She was afraid to ask him what he meant, just as she had been afraid to tell Matt what she meant to do with her personal life. It wasn't lost on her that Max would escort her to and from his house; she was not to be on the streets alone.

Max's house, previously occupied by the late Gary Randolph—Max's magician mentor known professionally as Gandolph—and before that by the late Orson Welles, gave Temple the creeps. And it wasn't just the ghosts of the two dead men.

Maybe the house felt eerie because they were always having to creep up on it. Max wanted—needed—to conceal his residence there, so every entry was clandestine.

Temple was also intimidated by the house's heavy oriental furniture, especially Max's opium bed, a sort of fretwork pagoda, inlaid with cinnabar and mother-of-pearl. It exhaled the scents of exotic *parfums*, forbidden substances and irresistibly unnatural acts.

Add to the house's outré appeal a spare bedroom crammed with Gandolph's and Max's magical paraphernalia, and now his computer cockpit, and you had a juxtaposition of the mystical and the technological that was positively bizarre.

Sneaking into the place was the usual blast.

Once inside, Max led her to the world-class kitchen.

Even here she was uneasy. It was so clinical—so stainless steel/wine cellar/walk-in freezer perfect—that it unnerved her. You could hide a body in that freezer, in that climatically controlled walk-in wine cellar. Maybe even in that microwave.

"You look better." Max brushed a thumb over her bruised cheek. "Or is it makeup again?"

"Light foundation. Cover Girl if you're interested in the brand."

"Don't talk so tough in your Material Girl way. None of it's real but the act."

"True. How real is your act?"

He leaned against the stainless-steel-fronted refrigerator to consider it. Temple remembered the poster that Lieutenant Molina had commandeered from the inside of her bedroom closet wall so many months ago. That preserved the Max of two years ago: big hair, laser/razor cut. All eyes, like a cat. Mystery his middle name. Sex appeal his secret code.

Today he was otter-sleek, simpler. Dark hair pulled back into the low-profile ponytail made his face all elegant bone and nerve. Lots of nerve, but not nervy, like a spooked horse.

He was stripped down, bereft of stage props, boiled down to muscle and bone and a hank of hair.

"Where were you when you were gone?" she asked.

He smiled. "Where do the politically awkward always go? Canada. I worked as a corporate magician."

"You? A company man?"

"My role was subversive. I was supposed to make people laugh, relax, screw the boss. It worked. Actually, I liked it a lot. Even Canadian companies are so structured . . . I was a deconstructivist, and well paid for it, which is more than most real artists can say."

"You should have met Domingo."

"The Flamingo Man?"

She nodded. "I think his secret sin is that he really is a rather good artist. Don't you miss being a magician?"

He wrapped his arms around himself, made himself into a matte-black mummy against the steel-colored sarcophagus of the freezer.

"Did I ever leave it?"

"Your performance dates. Your venues. Your agent."

His hands mimed emptiness. "Magic is smaller than that. Much smaller. Thumbelina. In your hand." His empty palm opened to her in the mime's classic gesture.

"Is that why you like little women?"

"You're wrong. I love little women."

Temple blinked. Contact lens trouble again. Or something.

"What about your family?"

"What about them?"

"What did they do for Christmas?"

Max pushed off the refrigerator, moved to the huge stainless-steel-sheathed island unit.

Once, under his spell, she had envisioned that kitchen accessory as a stage prop, and herself as an accessory to magic upon it. The little lady who may be sawed in half, or who may just be feigning truncation. Now it looked like an altar.

The magician was part actor, part policeman, part priest. She remembered Professor Mangel quoting Edmund Wilson on the subject. Part deceiver, part detective.

"My family." Max declaimed the words like the title of an essay; an exercise in school. Something distant. Academic.

"I went back for Sean's funeral. Have your ever been the One Alive when you should have been the One Dead? We went as two on our teenage jaunt to the Old Country. One came back dead, one came back alive. Or did he? Everything that appalled me, that killed Sean in the Old Country became instantly real in the New Country. Why him? Why not me? His family never said it, my family never said it. But they both felt it. I felt it. I saw then there was no place for me here."

" 'Here?' The U.S.? With your family?"

"Both."

"But you were barely seventeen years old."

"I was a hundred years old. I'd survived, and he hadn't. And there was no way to explain it."

"So you've never gone home for Christmas since then?"

He shook his sleek head as if tossing off invisible droplets. Of water. Of blood. "It would have stirred up the blame."

"Do you blame yourself?"

"For surviving when he didn't, yes. For doing what I did at the time, no. We were ignorant boys. But we died as men. That's what Ireland, north and south, does to you."

"Died? Both died?"

Max nodded.

"That's why you retreated back to Europe; you had brought the Troubles back to your own home town."

"Back to my own family. I saw in a nutshell how four hundred years of strife had divided a whole population. And . . . I was dangerous to those closest to me, even if some of them hated my guts."

"Dangerous because you were in danger?"

He nodded again. "From the IRA, from the government forces. When I turned in the IRA men who had bombed the pub and killed Sean, I was an instant wild card no one wanted. Except those who deplored all terrorism. Gary Randolph was my first mentor. I began as an apprentice to Gandolph the Great, but magicians have a perfect cover, and our European appearances were always more than magic."

"Why are you letting me interrogate you?"

"You ask good questions. And you deserve any answers I can give you."

"Okay. Enough for now. What have you got to show me?" A pause, a very long pause. "Not *that!* I mean the advertised mysteries. What was hidden in Gandolph's magical mystery supply of tricks? What did the computer files reveal? Where is the hidden staircase?"

Max grinned and took her hand. "Follow me, and all will be revealed."

The room, or rat hole, in which resided the new object of Max's affections, the computer and its attachments and various arcane guides to them all, was as crowded and messy as when Temple had last seen it. Only someone who knew the extreme, catlike meticulousness of Max Kinsella, as Temple did, would have been surprised by that.

The glowing computer screen was a window into a lurid Halloween world inhabited by squadrons of bats flying over haunted houses and graveyards.

"The Halloween screen saver is still on," he noted. "Would you care for something Christmasy? Flying Santas?"

"No. No, thank you." Temple hadn't mentioned the Santa slaying in New York. She thought she probably never would.

"You're right; it's a little late for Christmas. I suppose I could find something for Martin Luther King Day."

"Flying freedom marchers in outer space, no doubt. No thank you. So. What's to see here?"

Max sat in the swiveling office chair, swivelled, and plucked a two-inch-high stack of papers from the top of a pile that leaned like the Tower of Pisa.

Temple hefted the stack. "Half a ream. Impressive. What is it?"

"Gary's book. My book. I hope, your book."

"Really? You finished a draft of Gandolph's exposé on false psychics? Already? He must have been an interesting man, always a secret crusader. Did he die because of what you two did in your common past, or because of his late-life campaign to expose psychic fraud? I wonder if his mystery will ever be solved, or how much you can reveal in a book. I realized why you wanted to finish his book, but for a nonwriter to actually accomplish it. . . ." She regarded Max with respect. "I'm . . . amazed."

She flipped through the neatly typed pages, surprised and somehow gratified to see Max dealing with a process she had always understood; not special effects and illusions, but ideas made into the flesh of words. Paper work. Writing.

"Gary's part of the story was mostly written down already. I tried to give it context. I don't know if I succeeded."

"Modest Max."

"Yes. You know I'm hoping that you'll read it. Make suggestions. Edit. Cut me to ribbons, if you like."

"Oh, not ribbons. Whose byline?"

"I don't care, personally. Gary's, I suppose. And yours if you want."

"Pity he wasn't as well known as David Copperfield, or even you."

"Gary gave all that up to follow his quest. He really was a knight in shining . . . drag, I guess. It's almost hard for *me* to believe. I added some sections on disguise to explain his success."

"Makes sense. I'll read it and give you my expert opinion, buttressed by the publishing observations and consulting opinions of my aunt the historical novelist."

"Really? That rather elfin lady writes those big heavy tomes of yesteryear?"

"Er, yes." Temple would be damned before she'd clutter the discussion with that put-down word of all put-down words, historical "romance."

Why was every novel in the nineteenth century considered a "romance," and in the twentieth century a "romance" considered "a bodice ripper?" From what she had heard of mid-twentieth-century popular literature, male writers were the main practitioners of bodice-ripping scenes.

"I'll take the manuscript home and study it assiduously."

"Manuscript. That has a nice sound."

" 'Book' is even better, but the jury is out on that."

Max's long fingers hit some keys. The screen saver vanished as if swallowed by Dracula's inky cloak. Temple recognized the Windows program, but Max's fingers flitted from screen to screen too fast to follow.

"I've come across traces of unauthorized entry."

"In your computer?"

"It was Gandolph's. From what my long-distance friends can determine, someone has been watching Gandolph's literary progress and mine."

"Looking at the book?"

Max nodded. "I've been given safeguards and procedures. But

sophisticated defenses beget sophisticated offenses. I take it as a given that this computer is not fully secure."

"And . . . this house?"

He shrugged. "Any house is vulnerable. It depends on who wants to break into it how badly."

"You said something about Gandolph's illusions."

"Illusions. Always the best place to attack. In this case, quite literally. Can I take you to a scene of the crime?"

"Fine." Temple left her tote bag by the computer and followed Max out into the single-story home's bedroom hallway.

He led her to the room filled with magic, with painted boxes and curtained mirrors and other arcana.

"You know how valuable these artifacts are?" he asked.

"I guess. They must be custom-made."

"Temple! They are magician-made. They're worth literally thousands and thousands of dollars. Each magician's tricks are his stock-in-trade. When he retires he can sell them to one inheritor. Never more than one. It's the professional code. We never betray each other. We perfect our signature acts in solitude and keep their workings secret. We're worse than the Masons used to be."

"Sounds creepy."

"It is creepy. But I inherited Gandolph's equipment, and I've been exploring it. In this—," Max pressed an elaborately painted upright box, a sarcophagus shape again. A small drawer in the base snicked open. "—I found these." He presented her with a hand-written book bound in heavy parchment, thongs of suede tying it together.

"What is this? The Necronomicron of the mad Arab himself?"

Max managed to look both intrigued and mystified.

"Never mind. Just jump out of the way if drops of blood start dripping onto the text from the ceiling."

"There's nothing up there but crawl space."

"Crawl space is named that for a reason, trust me. Can I sit down somewhere with good light and look at this?"

"Of course, Madame Detective. May I interest you in my parlor?"

"As long as the ceiling doesn't drip blood."

Max's "parlor" was what every good female fly would fear it would be: in his case, an opium bed.

Just the name of the thing carried a freight of exotic superstition. It was the size of a latticed garden gazebo, a lacy carved wooden structure meant for the swooning upper classes of China as they inhaled from the elegant sterling opium pipes curling around their thumbs like ophidian rings.

Temple knew the artistic provenance of the piece; she just didn't like its social history. Or maybe she didn't like the fact that one was likely to start living up to that history once reclining on the cushioned fabrics within its architectural boundaries.

But she had to admit it was the perfect site to sit, propped up by silk and suede-covered pillows of every shape in a geometry book, gazing on mysterious papers by the warm light of the craftsman-style floor lamps hung with fringed brocade shades.

"This setting reminds me of Fu Manchu's brothel," she complained while settling in after kicking off her black velvet tennis shoes.

Max bent down and wordlessly presented a tiny pair of embroidered satin Chinese slippers.

"Your feet could get cold."

Temple curled her toes into the silken mules and focused her new custom lenses on the thick calligraphy.

" 'Sacred secrets shall never be shared,' " she quoted the first page of parchment. "Well, the author has an overdeveloped sense of the poetic. Not only four instances of alliteration, but the first two are a simple 'ess' sound and the second two are the 'sh' sound so dear to librarians. Pretty hokey."

"It gets hokier." Max leaned on one elbow, settling beside her like a warlord being entertained by a favorite geisha. No, that was Japan.

Temple frowned and read the second sheet, identically penned on identical paper.

" 'The Synth is like a battlement, safety. The aberrant brother is like a match, fire.' Were all the sheets folded in quarters?"

Max nodded. "Why?"

"It's an odd, old-fashioned way to fold messages, as if they weren't sent by mail."

"I found no envelopes."

Temple moved to the next crackling sheet of heavy paper. "Sherlock Holmes would no doubt have something enlightening to say about the paper source."

"It's handmade, high rag content. No maker's markings. A labor of love by a skilled craftsman."

"Or craftswoman."

Max nodded solemnly.

Temple recited the third message. " 'The aberrant brother shall be declared anathema. The price upon his head shall be death.' "

"Or her head?" Max wondered.

"This is a brotherhood," Temple pointed out. "I think we can take that literally. No need for equal opportunity pronouns. They were sent to Gandolph, presumably."

"Presumably." Max committed a private smile. "It's taken me more than a month to find and figure out how to open that particular hidey-hole, so I doubt anyone else has been paging through them. Gary was a talented magician long before he was a talented psychic debunker."

" 'Anathema.' That almost sounds like . . . excommunication from the Synth."

"Is that your broad liberal arts background talking, or your hard-headed Unitarian ancestors, or a touch too much of Matt Devine?"

"Maybe a little of all three."

Max took her hand, her left hand. He turned it so the lamplight caught the opal in his—her—ring and turned it to pale fire. "Do you dress for the part, or for the partner of the moment?"

"Max, I am not going to bang anybody over the head with our relationship. What if Lieutenant Molina should spot this ring and ask about it, and she would, believe me. She's like a hawk looking for any trace of you in my life."

"Maybe she should get a life of her own."

"And maybe you shouldn't worry about controlling mine when I'm not with you."

"But you're so often not with me now, not like before, when I was foolish enough to think we could live together openly."

"So I don't wear my ring openly."

He nodded. "I know. I just don't want to know." He lifted her hand and kissed it. "Let me take those tacky illuminated threatening notes away before they give you a headache."

"A headache was never a reason to say no in my book."

"No. But why take any chances, when we've so few of them?"

Chapter 11

Midnight at the Oasis

Midnight. Murder. What's the Diff?

When one is short, short of cash, and persona non grata at most of the establishments in town (through no fault of one's own except accident of birth, I might add), finding entertainment in Las Vegas is still as easy as even odds. There is no more democratic town than Vegas when it comes to playing to the rabble of any species.

One just has to get there early enough to ensure a good seat.

So it is that I find myself perched upon the lip of an ancient-looking wharf, gazing into the rippling waters of an ersatz Mediterranean Sea. No doubt my Egyptian ancestors sat in just such a pose to contemplate the mighty yellow delta of the river Nile.

My dubious descendent, one Midnight Louise by popular acclaim but no input of mine, sits beside me currying her tail with her tongue.

She makes a great deal of this common beauty routine, rather like a human female applying fresh lipstick at a dinner table in the

Paris Ritz. No doubt the grooming fetish is meant to remind me that she has Longhair on the one side of the family—not mine—for my rear member is long, but bears a buzz-cut rather than a ponytail. This suits me fine.

Not that I am admitting any paternity here. I was not born yesterday, and the Esquire I use after my name on occasion is not just for show: when they use the phrase "street legal" they are thinking of my gaming-house-lawyer nose for what is permissible, performable and preferable.

Although the New Year has not quite turned, I am still in a holiday mood. Thus I attempt a gesture of reconciliation with my namesake.

"These are pretty cheap seats, Daddio," she sniffs once she has deigned to lift her face from her rear quarters to regard mine. My *face*, that is, not my rear quarters. Miss Midnight Louise has been "fixed" so that her only interest in the aft of the male animal is to see it walking away from her.

"The Midnight Show at the Oasis is not exactly a prime ticket," she adds. Her petite black nose strains out over the water, sniffing again. "This man-made swamp does not even support any game fish, just a lot of rusting underwater gears and tracks."

I resist the opportunity presented by a lonesome stretch of water and an empty wharf; I allow the mouthy Miss Midnight Louise to mince back from the brink with distaste. Were she any spawn of mine, I am sure that I could not resist a disciplinary whap with my despised shorthair tail.

"I thought we could dine later," I reply, unruffled. "At Chef Song's private table at the Crystal Phoenix."

"The Crystal Phoenix is my beat now, and I eat in it all the time. I am sure that Chef Song gives me a higher quality of leftover than he would give you. You do not turn your pockets inside out when you spring for a meal, do you, Daddy dearest?"

"Stop using that dreadful misnomer. We are no relation. I much preferred your shelter nom of Caviar. I cannot understand why Miss Van von Rhine had such a lapse in taste as to rename you 'Midnight Louise.' "

"She was a new mother at the time," Louise returns sourly.

If I had been grooming that longhaired vermin trap of a tail, I would be sour too.

"But, then," she adds for good measure, "what would you know of new mothers? You are the type to hit on, and run."

"Ah, but I am no longer offspring-enabled," I point out.

"No thanks to any doing of yours."

"Circumstances have deprived me of parental expectations, it is true, but I will make the best of it."

"I am sure you will, but not with me."

"Louise! I am shocked. You insist that I am your father. Although I disagree, I must respect your misapprehension. I would never make unfatherly overtures toward you."

"No, you never would, because you know you would get a five-claw salute to the kisser." She shrugs the rusty black fur-piece over her shoulders into neater order. "I do not know why you suddenly wish to share my company, since you deny being my father to the death and you know that I would lacerate your lousy hide to the bone if you tried anything funny with me."

"With my luscious little redheaded roommate, Miss Temple Barr, working on a long-range project for the Phoenix, I feel we should get to know each other better. Bury the hatchet. Cooperate like the trained professionals we are. We will no doubt be seeing more of each other."

"I am professional. You are a blot on the seedy Las Vegas landscape. A very large blot."

Just because the streetlight behind me flares like a setting sun and I cast a long shadow that blurs the edges of my true, muscle-sculpted form is no reason to affront my size. I do not call *her* a "puny, anorexic pip-squeak."

By now the foot traffic behind us has picked up. Human feet and legs and body odor crowd us to the brink. Everyone in Las Vegas knows that the Oasis Hotel's "Battle of the Barges" occurs on the hour around the clock.

Being the thoughtful escort I am (even of an ungrateful brat), I have arranged that we see the more dramatic night-time spectacle, held at my signature midnight hour.

"It was thoughtful of you," Midnight Louise admits after turning and delivering a blood-curdling snarl to an encroaching human ankle, "to invite me to the show held at the time that celebrates my new name. Much as I hate to bear a version of your name, at least 'Midnight Louise' is a hair better than just plain 'Midnight.' Humans have no imagination when it comes to naming black individuals of other species. Where did the 'Louie' in your name come from, anyway?"

I fan my nails, which bear an ebony sheen that would do a Steinway concert grand piano proud.

"Some suggest I was named for my distinctive singing voice."

"You do sometimes sound like Louis Armstrong with a tracheotomy."

"Others say I was plucked off the street as a kit and gotten drunk on beer by a group of frat boys, so the name of their song got pasted onto me."

"The infamous 'Louie, Louie,' " Louise growls. "I wish I had been there. I would have signed, sealed and nailed those creeps for introducing alcoholic substances to a helpless minor of another species."

I am touched by her concern, but cannot let a misapprehension linger. "These were Eastern frat boys, my dear. I was not named after that low-brow drunken bar chorus you mentioned, but rather after 'the Whiffenpoof Song' so dear to Yale University undergraduates."

" 'Whiffenpoof!" Louise practically rolls over the wharf's edge laughing. "Whiffenpoof? What a wimpy name."

"I believe the line is: 'and to the place where Louie dwells, to dear old Temple Bar.' "

"If so, it certainly was a prophetic naming. I believe that your Miss Temple is a female of accomplishment worthy of admiration despite her inexplicable association with you, but isn't she a little young to be celebrated in song by drunk undergraduates of Eastern educational establishments?"

"I notice a distinct improvement in your vocabulary level from associating with me, but unfortunately not in attitude. You are leaping to the erroneous conclusion, as usual. The 'Temple Bar' in the song is not a person, any more than 'Temple Bar' landing on Lake Mead is. It is a bar."

"Aha! I might have known."

"And 'Louie' is the esteemed proprietor of same."

"Are there any esteemed barkeepers?"

"Apparently in song."

"Speaking of keepers, you are right at least that Miss Temple will be haunting the Crystal Phoenix more of late. Groundbreaking has begun."

I cannot let Miss Louise's latest gratuitous dig go unplumbed. "Miss Temple Bar is not my keeper. I allow her to consider herself responsible for me—though that often entails odious or even torturous visits to the vet—but the fact is that I am the one who keeps her from disaster during her forays into crime and punishment."

Now that I have put Miss Louise in her place, I can inquire into the tidbit of news she has dropped like a guppy into a Great Lake. "So what ground are they breaking at my dear old stomping grounds?"

"They are tearing up the back lot for the latest theme scheme in town," she says, wetting a foremitt to stroke her airy eyebrows into place.

"Oh, yes. The Jersey Joe Jackson memorial ghost town and mine ride."

"The construction site is attracting the usual lowlifes."

I nod. Construction sites mean construction workers. And construction workers mean brown-bag lunches and fast-food wrappers and leftovers.

"I do not mind the homeless making discreet forays into the daily garbage, but the pickings also attract scavengers that cannot be tolerated at an upscale place like the Crystal Phoenix."

I nod again, as the foul word finally slips my lips. "Dogs."

"The occasional dog is all right as long as it does not whine and beg excessively. I am talking about packs."

"Dogs tend to congregate in cowardly gangs."

"I am talking wild dogs."

I lilt my luxurious brows without bothering to groom them first. Miss Midnight Louise is a petite thing, for all her big mouth, and I cannot see her facing off a pack of wild dogs.

"If you mean coyote clan, I could put out the word on the sand that they are to steer clear of the Crystal Phoenix."

"Like they would listen to you."

"Hey. I handled a tricky case for them. For the head coyote, in fact. Mr. Big."

"I have not heard of a Mr. Big in the coyote clan around here."

"This was the Big Mr. Big. The one the Paiute Indians call The Trickster God. He can take on all shapes and all colors and all species. Believe me, he is one awesome dude."

"Oh, Daddio. You and this New Age kick of yours. Cats of your generation are such an old-fashioned and superstitious lot. Coyote clan is a gang of nervy, nomadic scavengers who may be pretty wily, but are basically garbage collectors and public nuisances. My sole problem with them is that the only cat they have the sense to respect is a desert puma. I have to make my point—" here, she flicks out a set of dainty but razor-sharp shivs "—with them over and over. They are beginning to regard four tracks across the snout as some sort of gang initiation rite and are sending all their young toughs to me. You would think I am a tattoo service."

"You need not act like a puma to make your point. They will listen to me without me lifting a shiv. I tell you, they owe me. I will come over some night and tell them to get lost."

"No! I have enough to patrol with all the construction mess without looking out for you too. Besides, are you not going to be bouncing in and out of town as a fast-food endorser?"

"That remains to be seen. Miss Temple unmasked a killer at the advertising agency that is deciding the spokescat sweepstakes."

"Not good PR." Louise's jet-black brow frowns. "I hope she does not find any dead bodies in the Phoenix's construction ashes. We do not need the bad publicity."

"She cannot help it. She has a natural affinity for murder."

"Hmm," Louise purrs unhappily, hunkering down for the show.

I settle down beside her. One by one the torch-topped poles lining the opposite shore in front of the Oasis Hotel's Karnak Temple facade are whipping into gas-fired life, the flames rippling and snapping like scarlet flags in the night.

The staffs of firelight play over the thirty-foot-tall statues glimpsed beyond the tall, fat pillars. Naturally, I have selected a viewing spot on the wharf directly opposite my patroness, Bastet. She is a tall stately woman with arms crossed upon her proud bosom, and the dignified head of a Somali cat. The flames reflect like a wink from the gold earring in one erect ear tip.

"You realize," I comment to Louise, "that if you are my daughter, and I make no concessions by speculating, you are descended on the female side from Pharaoh's Footstool."

"Shhh! The show is starting!"

Louise is gazing ahead as if stalking prey, and I see why. Something low is glinting through the water. It looks like a crocodile, but it is the size of the Loch Ness monster. In the flickering torchlight, the head lifts out of the water, a predatory beak on an epic scale. We are talking a bird-headed reptile here. This particular combination of totems is very dear to the feline heart, especially the heart of the desert-dwelling feline. Consider it a feast of Godzilla with feathers.

Of course the entire show is an ancient-world version of the Mirage Hotel's famed pirate ship encounter in a man-made moat farther up the Las Vegas Strip. Let us face it; with all the fresh construction here, it is hard to come up with a new shtick.

Speaking of shticks, long gilded oars are beating the water into ripples, like on sand dunes. The torch flames skim along every moving surface, turning the lagoon into a black bolt of moiré taffeta that rustles with chilling movement.

Behind us, onlookers have crowded into a solid wall, despite the late hour. I would be nervous to have all those human feet straining toward my rear member, except I too am caught up in the spectacle.

Then drums erupt like the distant strikes of a giant. Hollow, echoing beats simulate the heart of the monster barge as its oars cut through the water like dull sheers slicing ebony silk.

A gasp in unison turns all heads in the opposite direction. Another low, dark gilded beast of the submarine night is surging toward its opposite number. Oiled galley-slave arms writhe like pit vipers as they propel the oars in their lumbering rhythm.

Suddenly a fireball erupts in the black sky over the lagoon. I am highly doubtful that the Egyptians had fireworks, but they could have had an unsung Chinese advisor . . . or perhaps a well-traveled cat who had the ear (and foot) of Pharoah, a cat who had preceded Marco Polo to China by several hundred centuries, a Midnight Marco, so to speak.

While the fallout of sparks showers down upon temple and water and wharf, Midnight Louise stirs beside me. "Hmmph. You would think with all the money for foolish spectacle in Las Vegas they could get a better carver for the figurehead."

Much as I revere Egyptian art, I would have to admit I find it a bit wooden, so I am not surprised that this mockup does not pass Miss Louise's connoisseuress's standards. Meanwhile, I am gazing left at the incoming barge as on-board torches flap into life like tethered birds of prey.

I recognize the jeweled glow of a splendid throne, and sitting on it is that splendid dame of Old Egypt, Miss Cleopatra herself, decked out to make any chorus girl take notes. Her barge boasts a busty figurehead with a jackal head that reminds me of the one at Cleopatra's Barge restaurant at Caesars Palace (the bust, not the jackal head). Since the Oasis is owned by the same lot that run Caesars, it is no surprise they reinforce each other's theme.

By now two sets of tom-toms are striking enough tympanum to raise the dead, which is not to be unexpected in an ancient Egypt-inspired spectacle. The jackal-headed god Anubis strides forth between two pillars, a limp human form dangling from his extended arms. Gore has been selling since Moses was knee-high to a Neanderthal.

I take a quick peek at the statue of Bastet to see if she is undergoing any changes, since not even statues in Las Vegas are permitted to just stand there anymore, but must do parlor tricks, or at least vaudeville turns.

Now Anubis's voice booms out, and he sounds an awful lot like the hairless fellow who does voice-over advertisements on TV ever since he quit captaining a starship. I guess the Brits had their sights on north Africa even back in ancient times.

"Beware the wrath of Osiris," Anubis hollers in hoity-toity tones. "Your kas will walk upon water before they sink beneath the anger of Cleopatra's warriors."

"Our 'whats'?" Louise hisses next to me.

"A 'ka' is a spirit. A soul. The animated remnant of a dead person."

"Oh, come on! The only thing animated about a dead person might be the parasites it attracts."

"Please! Must you be so graphic? Remember, we plan to eat dinner after this."

"People food," she spits with disdain. "You are getting too soft, old man."

I refrain from my usual reply to such lip: a smack in said lip. In this case, given our foggy genetic connections and gender differences, it could be construed as kit abuse, and I could be sued. It is getting in this country so that you cannot defend yourself against even your own (maybe) kin.

I avert my gaze to the forthcoming flash. The intruder barge lobs a fire-bomb over the low-slung bow that explodes above the water and sinks into it like a cargo of shattered stars.

By now the topside fireworks are shooting off in streaks of red, blue, green and pink. Those do not strike me as particularly Egyptian color schemes, except for the blue, and neither does the matching-hued neon hieroglyphs that light up the temple pillars and begin flashing on and off. I expect at any moment to read a neon crawl circling a pillar that advertises "Cleo's Dreadlocks Braided While You Wait" or "Ramses the Bookie" or "Sethos the Cabbie Charioteer." Though I suppose it would be the *Book of the Dead* that Ramses would be hawking.

How very odd that when one thinks things Egyptian, one dwells on death. But, then, the culture set great store by death . . . or, rather, by ritualizing the aftermath as well as the afterlife.

I find it also odd that only the figure of Bastet remains in the dark, so to speak. Except for the fugitive passage of the surrounding neon blinking over her stony, sarcophagus-shaped form, she lingers in the shadows, calm and dignified.

Then a vagrant shower of fireworks falls upon her shoulder, and her earring burns like a circle of molten lava.

"It is sinking!" an onlooker shouts behind me.

I glance to the water again. Of course the intruder barge is sinking. These water fights always end with the loser taking a bath in the briny deeps. By now the barge is a fiery pyre that slowly douses as it sinks. The galley slaves in their striped, sphinx-style headdresses dive into the spark-showered water like rather decorative rats.

Not long after no trace remains of the sunken barge, Cleopatra's majestic ship glides through the glittering water where it foundered, the queen herself nodding regally to the witnesses, her barge now ablaze with fire-lit gilt and tinsel.

The drums have reached a pitch that makes the wharf's heavy timbers shiver. I shiver myself in the cool January night, despite my heavy fur coat, despite the press of human body heat behind me, cheering the victorious queen, forgetting the fallen crew.

I eye Bastet again across the gaudy gulf of showboat and fireworks and agitated water.

She is shadowed and dark and calm. And ominous, very ominous. My whiskers twitch. I may not yet have a ka, Ra be praised, but I have a feeling that the other services of Pharaoh's Footstool will soon be called into action.

Something is rotten in the Middle Kingdom. And I think Midnight at the Oasis is about to become Murder at the Oasis.

Chapter 12

Moral Bankruptcy

Temple woke, aware that she had cold feet.

The graceful Chinese slippers had long since gone the way of her wrinkle-resistant black knitwear. She was tangled with snakes of exotically patterned linens, a naked wrestler of the night.

Above her, the opium bed loomed like a tree turned into a carved cinnabar box.

Stained-glass night-lights glowed just above floor level, like safety beams establishing perimeters, or votives marking the presence of altars.

She had worn no watch, nor wanted one.

Yet now she had a sense of time suspended, and she knew, as she had finally known in New York, that Max was no longer there.

But she was afraid to make sure, like someone awakened from a nightmare with a horrific vision still in fine-focus in her head. Temple suddenly perceived something odd about her night vision: she had not removed her new contact lenses. The optometrist had said that was fine, although not too often. She could *see*. See the razor-sharp halos of light around the plug-in night-lights. See highlights in the mother-of-pearl fretwork, see sheen on the silken pillows.

She couldn't see Max.

Wouldn't see Max?

Dreaming?

Seeing too much? Or too little?

All she had to do was reach out and find something besides twisted bedlinens and scattered pillows and satisfaction.

After New York, she didn't dare.

Chapter 13

The Mummy Swims at Midnight

"I smell a rat," Miss Midnight Louise observes as the wall of human feet, legs and foot-powder odor behind us disperses among the Oasis's neon-scrawled temple pillars.

"That would not be unusual for the vicinity of a wharf, even an ersatz one."

"I did not like the cut of the figurehead on the intruder barge."

"Well, if it offends you, it will remain underwater and out of sight until the sunken barge is reeled back on its underwater track to its berth behind the hotel. So you need not trouble yourself about it."

"I saw it move."

This gives me pause. Wait! I already have paws. Rather, I should say, this makes me blink. And think.

Now there is not a species on the planet that is better equipped to detect the infinitely small motion than ours.

I would not be boasting to say that I can spy the tremor of the forward feeler on an ant at thirty paces. I would be only modest to claim to see the winking facets on the eye of a fly perched atop the MGM lion's three-story-tall, noble leonine head. I could even spot a beauty mark on the heaving, er, pastie on the Tropicana's lead chorus girl from the back row.

But the problem is, I did not notice any unsanctioned movement on the wooden figurehead leading the doomed barge to the bottom of the vasty deeps of the Oasis watering hole. Granted, I was more interested in making sure . . . seeing that Bastet kept her magnificent likeness carved in stone than in eyeing prow decorations. So I think that Midnight Louise is all wet, but I see that her curiosity has been aroused, and since she has so little in her life of an arousing nature, I take pity on the poor thing and decide to humor her. I can at the same time impress her with my awesome knowledge of how Las Vegas works behind the scenes.

"Very well, my little chickadee. We can stroll around to the staging area to inspect the disturbing figurehead. I am sure that close up it will prove to be as wooden as any figure on the burial chamber wall of a pyramid tomb."

"Now that you mention it, the figure reminded me of a mummy."

"I doubt the folks behind this display would use something as mundane as a mummy for a figurehead. Mummies are extremely featureless and pale."

"Like a ka?" she asks as we stroll toward the moat of desert landscaping that surrounds the Oasis Hotel.

"I have never seen a ka. You would have to ask Karma."

"Karma?"

"Have you never met Karma, Miss Electra Lark's reclusive associate?"

"I spent as little time as I could at the Circle Ritz."

"A pity. Karma is worth consulting, especially when the Unknown rears its indeterminate head." Actually, I am picturing the territorial dispute if these two headstrong babes should meet. No doubt it would be amusing.

"I do not need consultants," Miss Louise says as we trot over the cool, shifting sands trucked in from Mexico. "My senses are sharp and reliable."

Of course I understand the unspoken insult: Midnight Louie is over the hill and too slow to sniff, see and strike these days. Miss

Midnight Louise has a lot to learn, but I let her lead the way for the moment.

The launching area is hidden from public view by a high stucco wall and a swaying conga line of palm trees. A knothole-ridden wooden gate offers our only peek into the area. In the checkered illumination of low-intensity work lights we can see the backstage crew readying the two barges for the next show in fifty minutes.

"I'm over the gate. See you later, Pop."

Miss Midnight unsnicks her shivs and is soon scaling the knotholed boards like a feline fly. Quite an impressive demonstration of athletic ability and youthful enthusiasm. I watch her plummet to a patch of sand on the other side like a stuntcat. She strolls toward the activity with tail high and not a backward look.

Too bad. She misses me scaling the gentle slope of a palm tree, thumping down a couple feet atop the stucco wall and then lofting down from oleander bush to wheelbarrow to ground. At no time did I tax my limbs or tender pads with a jump of more than two feet. In addition, I was pretty much invisible most of the way, unlike Miss Strut-Your-Stuff Midnight Louise, who is ankling in and out of the work lights like a stripper playing peekaboo with a spotlight.

There is one additional sense to the sight, sound, touch, smell and taste Miss Louise is relying on, and it is not that vaunted sixth sense that our breed are often credited with. It is a sense that must be aged, if not pickled. It is called "common sense," and there is nothing common about the way I use it.

So I follow in the shadows, hearing a worker or two comment on my darling daughter's passage. Luckily, none of them is a perverted cat-hater, so she makes her way unmolested to the dock where the vanquished galley is rising slowly from the dead depths thanks to the services of an automated winch. The technology here is so up-to-date that nothing human is hanging around to watch the Good Barge Bathyscope come afloat again save us two cats.

Miss Louise does not turn when I slip from the shadows to sit beside her.

"This is more interesting than the show out front," she comments. "That rat I smell is even ranker back here."

I nose the air several times, until my white whiskers wave like semaphores. I inhale the scents of stale water, chlorine, grease, wet wood, spent fireworks, human sweat . . . and fresh kill.

Fresh kill is barely detectable, except to the natural-born predator's nostrils. I may be semiretired when it comes to slaying for my supper, but old instincts never die. Miss Louise is revoltingly right. The resurrected barge has brought up something dead.

There it sits, unattended, barely riding out of the water more than eight feet at the prow.

Miss Louise trots around the side to board it.

I eye the jump and decide to supervise from the dock. Someone needs to play lookout anyway.

She looks like the cow jumping over the moon as her form is silhouetted briefly against an aureole of light as she leaps aboard. I watch her lithe bounds from oar to oar. She moves like the daughter of a Mexican jumping bean, showy but not subtle.

Luckily, the area remains deserted. I watch her make like a wire-walker as, foot crossing before each foot, she minces out over the prow.

Sure enough, the figurehead is not only mum, but swathed with gauze like a mummy. Not just painted gauze, real gauze. I know this because Miss Louise reclines at the prow's very tip, then catapults over the edge.

I shut my ears, my ears flattened back, waiting for the flying water-drops that betoken her imminent midnight dip in the mighty Nile of the Strip.

I hear a muted growl of annoyance, and peek.

Miss Louise is dangling from the mummy's head like a mouse from an alleycat's jaws, her sharp little shivs clinging to mere gauze.

Her tail works wildly, trying to compensate for her unbalanced position.

But, sure enough, the gauze is giving, ripping away, stripping off the mummy's anonymous face.

I squinch my eyes half closed. I do not like to see the dead violated, especially if the dead in question is maybe a couple of grand old in years. Is there no respect for age anywhere? Even if this is just a mock mummy, I expect the unseen face to be the usual freeze-dried skeletal mess that plays so well on TV late shows. Cannot an old dude even be allowed to rot in peace, if not rest in peace?

But I am wrong.

There is plenty of flesh on the face so slowly being revealed by the weight of Miss Midnight Louise's hanging form. Fresh flesh. Fresh kill.

Miss Louise claws upward to avoid losing her grip and swags down more of the material. I glimpse open eyes, like cueballs with black leeches on them.

Speaking of black leeches, that is what Miss Louise herself looks like dangling from the deceased.

Finally, even one of the lazy-faire workers around here wakes up enough to spot her swinging like a bell from the prow of the barge.

"Hey!" he shouts originally. "Get off that prop."

I do not see an airplane propeller anywhere in the vicinity (although if you would wind up Miss Louise and swing her by the tail she might resemble one), but she evidently decides that she has done her duty in attracting human attention to the obvious scene of a crime.

She climbs the poor dead dude's face like he was chopped liver and scrambles over the prow-top to repeat her tap dance down the oars and to the dock.

Without a word, we act as one and dash back into the shadow of some shed.

Meanwhile, yon worker shambles over like the man with the hoe in the famous painting.

He stops where I had sat to observe the unveiling, and stares long and hard at the prow and the tawdry figurehead.

"Mummy," he mutters, but he is not calling for his maternal parent. "We didn't have no mummy up front. It was an Egyptian mermaid. With great boobs." He edges toward where the dock meets water, and looks harder.

I was not aware of such a thing as an Egyptian mermaid, although, judging from the figurehead fronting Cleopatra's Barge Restaurant at Caesars Palace, great boobs appear to have been a classical human theme. That asp must have had a field day.

Anyway, yon slow-witted witness suddenly straightens and hollers. "Hey! Guys! There's this stiff on the prow. Get over here!"

A stiff on the skiff. Finally, the light dawns. Louise and I eye each other in the dusk of our cover. Are we going to make a night of it and see what happens next? You bet your best sarcophagus!

Bedtime Max

"Bedtime snack?" he asked.

"Hmm?"

Temple struggled awake, still worrying about intact contact lenses.

"Sweet and sour sauce. Try some."

"Chinese? In the middle of the night? What time is it?"

"You need your energy."

"My energy is history."

"But not for long."

The sweet and sour was not on the pointed ends of a pair of chopsticks, but on a tongue.

"Oh, Max."

"What?"

"What . . . what."

"What do you mean by that?"

"Who knows. You're impossible."

"I'm a magician."

"Former magician."

"Retired magician."

"This is retired?"

"You're not very retiring, I know. In fact, you seem wide awake now."

"No thanks to you."

"Thanks."

"You're welcome."

He was.

The Unkindest Cut

"I made it through Christmas," the raspy voice on the phone complained at 2:45 in the morning, "and it was a jingle-bell bust. Why should I hang on any longer?"

"Because you made it through Christmas. Now you can make it through New Year's."

"Aw, just shoot me now, Brother John. I got no money, no friends, no one who cares. What am I supposed to do, drag through one holiday after another? Next you'll be telling me to live for President's Day."

"You're the one who's attaching your survival to holidays. What did you expect from Christmas?"

"I don't know. Some kind of . . . high, I suppose. A lucky run at the craps table. A handout from some big winner. I came here because I thought Las Vegas was always up, you know? And I'm still down."

"Time of year and location don't have the most to do with highs and lows. You do."

The caller sighed. He spoke in the slow, flat-liner tones of the chronically depressed. Matt didn't think he was suicidal, but he was certainly toying with the possibility.

"You need a helping hand, but not a handout," Matt told him. "Maybe some short-term medication. I can refer you—"

"Refer me, schmer me."

But the man finally took down the information.

"Call right now," Matt said.

"It's too late."

"Nope, not in any sense of the phrase. Call, and someone will get right back to you. Someone will even keep you company until you can get in for an appointment tomorrow."

"Appointments to make life worth living. It's a crock."

"But you'll call?"

"Yeah. Thanks. I guess."

Matt hung up, shaking his head.

Bennie in the adjoining cubicle scuffed his chair back to see Matt.

"Another happy, dancing holiday depressive, huh? Jeez, I hate pulling these holiday shifts. Everybody who calls is so down. But you seem okay, buddy. You seem more than mellow."

"I thought I was always mellow."

"Uh-huh. Quiet, but not mellow. You are new-minted mellow, dude. So what's happening?"

It was almost three A.M., when Matt finished his shift. Bennie had another three hours to go, until dawn's early light. They were alone.

Matt shrugged, then smiled. "I took care of some old family business. Took my own advice and confronted and buried the past, or at least some of it."

"So that's why you took off over the holiday. What did you do New Year's, then, more family business?"

"Uh, no. Just . . . fun. I had a date."

"A date! Fun's okay too. Oooh, I bet Sheila will be sorry to hear that."

"Why should she be?"

"She's interested in you."

Matt shook his head.

"Hey, yeah, man. Listen. Old Bennie knows these things. So tell me about your New Year's date."

"Not much to tell." Matt found himself unwilling to get into a roll call about Temple, their relationship. "Yet."

"Oh-ho!" Bennie wiggled his bushy eyebrows and made hand signals like a baseball pitcher that Matt couldn't decipher, except they implied a male camaraderie.

He realized his "yet," meant to indicate that the outing hadn't resolved the relationship, had been interpreted as a prediction of lascivious things to come, of scoring. He hated to disillusion Bennie, but if anyone in his and Temple's relationship this far had cherished hopes of scoring it was more likely Temple. Matt himself was still experiencing fear of flying.

The line rang, too late, given Matt's shift, for him to pick up.

Bennie scooted his chair back into his phone cockpit.

"See you another night, amigo."

Matt grabbed his sheepskin jacket from the battered wooden coatrack by the door—all the office furniture was donated—and pushed the glass door open into the Las Vegas dark.

Here, away from the Strip, you'd never know you were standing in Neon City, Nevada. He shrugged the jacket on while rounding the building corner for the side parking lot. The night was cool but hardly cold. His fingers prodded the jacket pockets for his gloves.

The parked Hesketh Vampire leaned into a Mercurochrome pool of streetlight, looking like a motorcycle from an Edward Hopper nightscape painting. Matt rounded the lime-green trunk of Bennie's ancient Volkswagen, digging for the key in his pants pocket.

"At least *that*'s not yours."

The low voice was close enough to make him freeze. Low in tone and intensity, but contralto.

Matt turned to find a lithe dark figure moving into his orbit, eclipsing his view of the Vampire. It reminded him of a martial arts movie ninja, as much a part of the night as a black alley cat.

Matt remained alert, but not alarmed.

"I haven't got much money."

The figure shrugged, its back to the light, a silhouette that blocked but didn't threaten.

"The engine on that cycle takes more babying than it's worth, even for a joy ride," he added.

Silhouetted elbows lifted as fists rested on hips.

"This is no joy ride," the voice said, but he recognized his accoster more by the posture.

"I suppose you want a reward," he answered. "Thanks to you, I found my man."

"Thanks to you so did the police."

"Not what you wanted?"

"Not what I wanted."

"It's a little late to worry about it."

"For me maybe. Not for you."

She stepped closer. The woman who called herself Kitty was wearing black denim jeans and jacket and what looked like combat boots.

"I'm disappointed in you."

"You sound like a homeroom teacher. Look. You told me where I could find Effinger. What happened afterwards was my business."

Her head shook slowly. "It was always my business. I just thought you'd take care of it—him—for me."

" 'Take care of?' I did, I took him to the cops. He was wanted for questioning. What else did you think I would do with him?"

"You said that it was family business. You said that you might kill him."

"Yeah. I was angry enough to wonder about that. But I didn't. I was fine. In control. Grabbed the sorry sucker by the nape of his greasy jacket and trundled him off to the police. Maybe I got him a little wet first; he needed cooling off. But I didn't."

Her silence made him feel like a truant inventing excuses.

"It's not like you *wanted* me to really kill him . . . Did you?"

"You said it was Family business," she accused.

"Oh, my God. You thought I was a hit man?"

More silence.

"Do I look like a hit man?"

"That's why I took you for a hit man. You think they run around looking like Joe Pesci nowadays? They look like junior accountants."

"Me, kill someone for money? Good God, woman, until less than a year ago I was a priest."

Silence. She moved closer, but also more aslant to him. Oblique, she was, like a rattlesnake. Now he was alert, and alarmed, thinking defensively, countering her slight adjustments in position.

"Priests can kill," her husky voice answered at last. It wasn't husky like Temple's, a funny, foggy-bottom edge that showed up now and then, it was tension-husky. Dead serious.

She came closer, and he didn't dare back away, back down.

"I knew one priest," she said, "that killed five people."

"I'm sorry you knew such a bad priest."

She came closer, her boot soles scraping across the parking lot grit.

"I've slept with six priests."

"I don't do confessions anymore."

"Sacrament of Reconcilation," she corrected him.

"You seem to be more up-to-date on it than I am. I said I'm an ex-priest, but the vast majority of priests I knew were faithful to their promises. All their promises."

"Six priests, and an Islamic imam. And a few dozen other good men."

"I don't do confessions. Unless you want to call me in there. There I'm paid to listen to whatever . . . confessions, fantasies."

"It's not your fault."

"Thanks."

"I should have known better, seen better. You seemed pretty cold."

"Just . . . careful."

"I bet you are pretty cold, living in a dream world all those years. You were never among killers, or fornicators or pedophiles, only the good and the true, isn't that right?"

"It's impossible to see into every soul."

"Especially your own."

"I wouldn't like to see into yours."

She stepped back, angry. "If you were a good priest, you'd have to. Were you a good priest?"

He'd been asked that before, by whom? Not Temple. She didn't know or care about that, only what kind of human being you were.

"I was a mostly honest priest."

"Didn't screw women, children or domestic pets?"

"You're so mocking, but you're mocking yourself, not me."

"You are such an innocent, too innocent to live."

"It sounds like you know someone who could take care of that."

"Would you fight? For your innocent life?"

He nodded.

"For the right to be tainted?"

"For the right to be human."

"And I am not human."

"You're not acting much like it."

Closer again, a threatening closeness, not intimacy, unless intimacy is hate-driven seduction.

"How am I acting, former Father? You tell me."

"Like an angry teenager. Cynical and hate-filled."

"Teenager! You son of a—"

Her rage was a wave cold as ice water. He braced for it to break upon him in some physical form.

But she contained it, and half-circled him again, pacing as if caged.

Matt considered brushing past Kitty, but he didn't like to expose his back to her. He had diagnosed her too well. If she was as volatile as an angry adolescent, she could be as impulsive and violent too.

"You've never met anyone like me." Like a hostile teenager, she demanded tribute to her uniqueness, her self-centered ego.

"Likely not. The Light and the Dark are extremes and most people live among the shades of gray."

"I'm not gray."

"No. But the world really isn't as dark as you see it. If you sat inside and listened on the hotline for an hour or two, you'd see. The people who call are troubled, but they're trying to find the way to the Light and dealing with the Dark in themselves."

"You deal with the Dark in me, and you'll be dealing with the real world. You need to taste the real world, see it for what it is, feel it. You need to feel failure."

Her hand came up fast as a striking snake. She slapped his face, hard and open-handed, the way women in old movies slapped sneering men who questioned their sexual virtue. It was as if he had questioned her essential badness.

He couldn't resist catching her wrist as it passed. The bones were thin and hard and he held them so she couldn't twist out of his grip without hurting herself.

"What are you?" Her anger outclassed his, even gave him a sense of wonder.

What made a person, a woman, so truly eager to embrace evil? One man's death, other men's falls from grace.

The moment he touched her, the violence between them shifted. Her attitude, physical and mental, changed. She stepped closer, her free hand curling into the lapel of his open jacket,

"You want me?" she asked. The voice was a throaty croon. "Is that your weakness, ex-priest?"

He had to let her go, even if it left him defenseless. "No. But I almost want to hurt you back."

"So that's your dark side, Father. War, not love. Thanks for the information. You've just killed your first man tonight."

She stepped closer again, the final approach, so he could feel her body heat radiating against the chill air.

She pulled his face down into a kiss, a hard, ugly Judas kiss that made him rear away in disgust. What did she mean, he'd killed his first man tonight. *First* man. *Tonight.*

He heard her boots scraping away like a sidewinder snake's scales whipping across desert sand. What did she mean.

Then he saw that his right hand had automatically gone to his side and he felt melting warmth flooding his fingers, oozing between them. The night air held a sudden, tungsten tang.

Blood, Matt thought. His blood. She had . . . cut him.

He finally heard the words Kitty has breathed into his ear as tenderly as a mother to a sick child as she departed. "Remember me, you bastard."

He had killed his first man tonight. Did she mean . . . himself?

Chapter 16

Dead Again

"Hell of a crime scene."

"That's why we called you at two in the morning, Lieutenant."

Molina pulled her attention away from the body grotesquely attached to the Roman galley's prow. Sometimes she was a camera, and now she was panning back into a long shot.

The worklights glaring down on the dock and the water made the death scene into a stage set.

"Hair and Fiber is bitching about their technicians having to hang upside down like bats," Detective Morris Alch went on.

He was a dapper, low-key man on the cusp of fifty, whose graying mustache existed more to hide a sense of humor than add distinction, which it also did.

She nodded, stifling a yawn. "We'll lose a lot more than bat droppings if we don't do this right. You talked to the crew?"

"Gaithers did."

"Do they use any kind of small boat to clean or touch up the ship?"

Alch nodded at a uniform waiting near them, who disappeared into the corona of spotlights.

That was how, in ten minutes flat, two rowboats lay poised in the water before the galley's gently bobbing bow, a fresh plastic dropcloth stretched between them. A third boat waited in the shadows to receive the body once the technicians were through and it could be detached.

"Bizarre," Alch commented.

"This is Las Vegas. What do you expect?"

Molina watched stoically, which was more than the Oasis crew boss could do. She also serves who stands and waits in larger-than-life scenes with her ID tag clipped to her lapel.

The hotel crew boss paced soft-shod in Nikes, a wiry, worried man in his fifties.

She had to credit the work crew; they snapped to like a Navy detail to man the boats. The crew boss, clasping his walkie-talkie to his mouth like a seventh sense, muttered reports and encouragement to the crew manning the other galley on a distant dock.

The evidence technicians cut the body free, sparing all knots for later analysis and fighting to keep any fragments from falling to the jerry-rigged plastic net below. Suspended from the barge's decks by ropes, two technicians eased the body bag over the lower limbs of the now-dangling corpse. If only the tourists could see this.

So far the Oasis had only canceled one show, but Molina figured she wouldn't be able to release the barge until after dawn's early light.

"The show must go on," Alch muttered, not disapprovingly.

"The real show will be on the autopsy table. This body won't be talking until the ME's report."

"You think he was dead before he was bound to the, uh, front lady here?"

"It's called a figurehead. Wonder if that means something?"

"We're hardly into the New Year and we land a freaky stiff."

"Freaky, yeah. Reminds me of those casino bodies last year."

"But those were interior death scenes, with the bodies stuffed up in the ceiling."

"They were still found publicly, in the heart of Las Vegas attractions. Somebody thinks this whole damn city is one big set for murder."

Molina walked to the water's very edge to squint into the corpse's garishly lit face. It resembled a ghost of olden days with cerements meant to hold its jaw shut obscuring its features.

"If the guy's hands weren't bound to the carving at his hips," she said, "I'd say he had tried to tear at the face wrappings while the galley was being submerged. He was alive, and I bet there's a gag in his mouth under the gauze."

"You mean they weren't just trying to make him look like a mummy?"

Molina shrugged. "It fits the ambiance."

"Ambiance, Lieutenant?" Alch mocked.

"This is Vegas, Morey. It's all ambiance, including us."

"Yes, ma'am." But his mustache grinned.

An hour had passed before the plastic had been folded and stashed in the evidence van, before the rowboats were off the water, and the body lay in its garbage-bag-green body bag on the dock.

Molina stared down at the hidden face in its soggy carapace of ordinary medical gauze. The man's wet clothing was unremarkable: jeans, shirt. He had died with his boots on. Someone had stage-managed this; and more than one person had executed it, had executed the victim in a particularly cruel fashion.

She could finally snap on the latex gloves, crouch like a kid over some gruesome find, and work back the waterlogged gauze. She felt a bit like an archeologist as the rigid features were exposed to the worklights.

Nose, mouth, fish-eyes. It was enough. She wasn't aware of having frozen in thought until she realized Detective Alch had stopped searching the dead man's face to study hers.

"You know him, Lieutenant?"

Molina sighed, and stood. "Know his kind. Let me know when

the ME schedules the autopsy," she told Alch. "And it better be soon."

Her features sharpened. Contrary to TV crime shows, cops seldom ventured into the autopsy room; reports said it all, or should.

"Hey." Molina offered one of her rare smiles. "We don't often get to see a mummy unveiled."

She turned to go, to go back home and hopefully not to wake up Mariah. To free Delores to return to her house and her own family two doors down. To try to sleep before getting up again to another administrative day. Being a cop and a single mother was hell on hot wheels, dragging her out with little notice in the dead of night to commune with the dead. To interrogate the silence. To speculate about the living. But it had been worse before she had made lieutenant. Now she was only called when the case was particularly puzzling, or politically delicate, and, luckily, most murders were depressingly routine. But she doubted she'd sleep much tonight, even if she got home in time for a couple of hours rest. Too much to think about.

The dock felt exotic in the chill of a Las Vegas winter night. She could smell wet rope and dank water, could barely hear the disturbed water's slight slap against the pilings. She could have been standing on any exotic shoreline from Lake Mead to Lake Titicaca in the Andes to Lake Victoria in Africa.

At the fringe of the spotlit space she noticed a couple of upright objects.

Not objects, figures. Feline figures.

One was big and muscular with a low-pile coat. The other silhouette, half the size of the first, was blurred by frills of longer hair. They sat like Egyptian statues, still as the massive figures girding the Oasis facade, watching with eyes that changed to UFO-green as she walked away and the light illuminated the eerie night-time neon of their irises.

Leaving the bizarre crime scene, for the first time that evening, Lieutenant C. R. Molina felt a chill of apprehension, even though she wasn't superstitious.

She knew those cats, and, if so, she certainly knew they meant trouble. But who could interview a cat? Luckily, there were plenty of Homo sapiens around to do the talking, or the not-talking.

"Round up the usual suspects," she muttered.

And, she added mentally, *maybe some very unusual ones.*

This was Las Vegas. A cop could bet on that, and win every time.

Chapter 17

A Beached Barge

"It is most interesting to observe a police crime-scene team in action," Miss Midnight Louise says once everything human—and formerly human—has left the death scene.

We are alone, for the barge crew has finally accepted that the show must not go on until Lieutenant Molina says it can. Only the dead-in-the-water barge remains, nudging the dock like a whale calf cozying up to Mama.

"Now it is time for the real experts to swing into action," I respond. "And I do mean 'swing.' Think you can get up to the brow of that prow again pussycat?"

"Do not call me 'pussycat.' I find the term demeaning."

"De meaning was not meant to be anything personal. I believe I would be best suited to observing operations from the dock, like Lieutenant Molina."

"You mean you are too paunchy from sucking up free cat food in New York City to make like an acrobat. Do not sweat it, I will be up and at the scene of the crime in two shakes of a spaniel's tail."

She follows through on this promise before I can object to her parting remarks, none of which are true. And only humans sweat. I watch her balance on a cable as thick as Miss Temple's wrist as she uses it like a tightrope to the bridge, if a barge may be said to have a bridge. Despite my sire's oceanic adventures and current lakeside residence, I am woefully uninformed about maritime matters. Frankly, unless it is shallow and there are fish in it, or Miss Temple's damp clouds of bubbles, I do not care for water except for drinking purposes.

Midnight Louise is soon hanging by her fingernails from the stolid wooden countenance of a sea cow, which is the figurehead to which Mr. Cliff Effinger, whose ugly mug I was close enough to see unveiled, was bound for his final dip-and-ship. It seems that a blue mermaid of sorts has helped to do the dirty dude in.

Although the regular crime-scene team has been all over the area to which the body was bound, Miss Louise tries to rake up what clues she can, running her streetwise nose over all the surfaces.

She sneezes.

"Be careful that you do not catch your death of cold," I advise her from the sidelines. "Damp sea airs can be contaminated. And watch out that you do not fall into the water."

"Yes, Popsicle. I know I do not have your vast experience of drooling over the Crystal Phoenix koi pond."

She twists her petite frame until she is arranged over the sea cow's head like an oddly chic black fedora. "The cops seemed to have nailed most of the hair and fiber on the scene, including mine. But—"

"Do not be coy. Spit it out."

"I sniff the somewhat soggy traces of a foreign substance."

"What is it?"

"If I knew, it would not be a foreign substance. It reminds me very slightly of my favorite blend of catnip, which Miss Van von Rhine dispenses on an old sock of her husband's in her office when we are both working late."

"Miss Van von Rhine plies you with nip? I was never allowed to tipple on the job."

"Perhaps Chef Song's koi supply was the perquisite when you

were house dick at the Crystal Phoenix. I had enough of sushi when I was on the streets, so Miss Van's offering is more than sufficient. And a little nip only sharpens my senses."

"Not to mention your tongue, I bet."

"What was that?"

"Nothing. I was just saying you were a little *young* for too much nip."

"Suit yourself, but do not try to dictate to me. All right, I have done this scene. Until I can identify the trace odor, there is nothing new here to report. I need to get back to the Phoenix to make my morning rounds. And I suppose your human will be waiting up for you at the Circle Ritz."

I sigh while Midnight Louise scampers back down the taut cable to my side.

"What is the typhoon for, Daddio-not? Did you expect to identify the perp in one go?"

"No. I just do not know where I will go. I am afraid that my Miss Temple is considering upheavals in my lifestyle."

"A waterbed?"

"Something even more disagreeable, I fear. But do not worry about me, I have survived turmoil before. Better get back to the job before some dog takes advantage of your absence and does a Dumpster raid."

She takes my advice for once and trots off without making the further, solicitous inquiries the female gender is noted for. What are these modern dolls coming to when they are so involved in their careers that they do not have time for being understanding of the male gender?

Then something dreadful occurs to me. Could Midnight Louise have a gentleman friend? Is that why she rushed off so eagerly? True, she is sterile, but that does not mean she could not overcome her missing hormones and at least be up for a little mush and slush.

I shudder. I am glad that I am not a victim of my gonads.

Chapter 18

Cut to the Quick

"Jesus, man. Jeee-sus, man."

Bennie's leathery skin had gone cocaine-white when Matt staggered back into ConTact.

Bennie ran for the bathroom, and came back, fists full of the crummy beige paper towels they were usually out of.

Thank God for small favors, Matt thought. Maybe prayed.

Blood soaked through the flimsy paper like water. His blood.

"Jezzzzzusss, man."

"My jacket," Matt said, for some reason concerned about blood getting on it.

Bennie worked off the left sleeve, dialing Leon, the supervisor, on the one-button dial key. "We gotta get you to an emergency room," he was muttering half to Matt, half to his headset, which he had jammed back on, crooked.

Matt found himself noticing details like that as he watched his own actions and Bennie's panic through a numb veil of emotional anesthetic. Nothing hurt. That was the odd part. He didn't feel a thing. Just a disbelieving wonder at all the blood that was pouring out of him.

"Yeah." Bennie had connected. "We gotta close down now. Matt's been mugged in the parking lot. He's bleeding—all over the place. I can take him, yeah, if my damn bug still runs. Right. We'll go now. If the lines are down, hey, we got an emergency here."

Bennie tore off his headset, looked at the wadded paper towels at Matt's side. "I bring the car around and come in for you. Or, hey! Nine-eleven. They come here."

Matt shook his head. "I think it's . . . slowing. Bennie, I can't go to a hospital. Do you know somebody else?"

"Alternative medicine, man? Now? You're *loco. Loco, loco, loco-motive.* You need help pronto."

Matt laughed weakly. "Thatsa Italian, Bennie. Pronto. Look, there must be someone in the neighborhood."

"You think I do drugs anymore? You think I'm still some sixties wild and crazy guy. *Loco local?* I don't know anybody. Well, maybe. Jesus, man. I'm gettin' the car, that's all I know."

Matt waited under the bright fluorescent lights, feeling as if the light itself was draining his color into a blue-white skim-milk pallor. He never knew he had so much blood in him, and so little pain.

Everything felt unreal. Kitty. Her charges. Her attack. His wound. Bennie's panic.

The building door banged open so hard he thought the glass would shatter.

Bennie helped him up and out to the Volkswagen chugging at the curb.

"It's a heap. A junker." Bennie raced around to the driver's seat and put the car into gear. "No smooth ride. Sorry."

"Better than my motorcycle," Matt got out.

"Jesus, man."

Bennie drove like a demon through the deserted side streets. Matt was relieved to see they were heading north, into the Hispanic area. No nosy big-hospital intake rooms, no sirens and bright lights. He was scared but mostly he was scared of

who/what/when/where/why. He couldn't risk the authorities finding out. Not for his own sake, but for his mother's. What was
Effinger involved in, that it had come to this?

The small car forced his knees up into a semifetal position.
Every jolt made more blood well over his fingers through the
damp and reeking paper towels.

Finally the car stopped on a dark street lined with low houses
and bristling cactus plants.

Bennie escorted him inside the house, knocking, not ringing a
bell. By now Matt was wondering if he'd made a fatal mistake. If
he'd killed his first man tonight all right.

He caromed off of doorjambs and shuffled through dark cubby-
holes and finally was guided to lay down on some hard cold surface. A bright light glared down on him.

An old man leaned over him, skin as sun-seared as the camel-
colored leather upholstery in an abandoned junkyard convert-
ible. The paper towels fell away. Gauze pads swabbed the wound.
The old guy nodded and squinted, pressing scorched-earth wrinkles into an already time-seamed face.

Matt heard the murmur of Spanish, like prayers, felt a gnawing
and pulling at his side as if scavenger animals tore at him.

Bennie's face hovered momentarily before the old man's, smiling like a harvest moon. "Tape," he was saying, nodding.

Or glue too? They would glue him back together with horses'
hooves. Dead horses' hooves. Wasn't that stuff in gelatin? He
would come back as Jell-O-man, maybe lime-green all over, able
to ooze into any form.

Bennie lifted Matt's head and forced a white glass bottle neck
between his teeth. White fire seared his lips and esophagus, spilled
down his chin and neck like antiseptic.

He passed out.

He awoke to people talking about him in a language he couldn't
understand. The rhythm of the speech was like background
Muzak, some orchestral samba in an elevator.

He was leaning against the elevator's back panel, its sleek ungiving surface supportive. Too tired to open his eyes, he listened, soothed by the steady basso murmur.

Only gradually did he notice the bundle of scratchy newspapers he was holding at his side, did he feel the burning disagreement of a bad stomachache.

"Mateo," someone said, but that wasn't his name.

"Matt," someone else said, in English.

His eyes disobeyed him and opened.

Light off to the side somewhere and cupboards all around, all he could see as he lay there. The cupboards with their medical supplies.

No. Kitchen cupboards. What the heck—?

"Get up slowly, man. Let me help."

Bennie spun Matt's legs off the smooth surface while the other man pushed his back upright.

A terrible tearing sensation in his side took his breath away.

"Julio says no pulling those muscles for two, maybe three days. *Nada.* Not at all. So watch when you sit down and get up, lie down and get up."

Matt nodded instead of speaking. Bennie translated instructions that seemed more practical than medical: take ibuprofen for pain, keep the wound clean, the tapes tight; avoid physical strain. If it breaks open or becomes red and infected, plan to see an establishment doctor. The man kept only two of the crumpled twenties Matt thrust at him.

Bennie helped him out to the tiny Volkswagen, Matt regarding the act of getting in as one of the more demanding of his life.

"Sorry," Bennie said. "Seat don't go no further back. Maybe we should hit an emergency room, after all, huh?"

"Don't you trust that doctor?"

Bennie hovered over Matt. Car engines tuned to a deliberate growl prowled the distance like roaring lions. Dawn leaked like skim milk through the stunted desert trees.

"Listen. He's an illegal. Has been for thirty years. Never learned the English, never had to. He tends people who can't go to regular clinics. He takes you down from highs, patches you up when you've been stuck, he even used to fix the girls when their periods wouldn't come."

"An abortionist? That old man was an abortionist?"

"Not any more. Now there's clinics for that, even if you have to pass the protesters to get there. What's the matter? You sure ain't been in 'Nam, man. There ain't no political correctness in foxholes, or in gook tunnels."

"The same guys who called them 'gooks' would call you 'wetback.' "

"Yeah." Bennie had come around to pretzel himself behind the Bug's steering wheel. He grinned at Matt under the faint moonglow of the dome light. "But we're winning this war. Come the millennium, we wetbacks are gonna outnumber you all in a lot of places."

Matt shook his head, too tired to answer. "What about blood loss?"

"Doc says you lost some, yeah, so take it easy. I'll call you in sick. Told Leon you were mugged, but all he has to know is you were beat up. I'll get you home as fast as Chiquita here can take you."

"Chiquita, huh?"

"The belle of the barrio." Bennie jerked the shift into gear and the car leaped forward like the bug it resembled, a hard-shelled little booger with no grace.

"So. I'll take you home, but I hope there's someone there to look after you."

Matt received this hint in silence. He now had reason to understand Temple's reluctance to report her assault. He couldn't rely on her, and Electra was just an extension of Temple.

For a moment the bitter aloneness was more cutting than the pain. Then he remembered something—someone—else.

"I'll tell you where to go. It's not too far."

"Hey, Matt. Distance don't matter to me. I just wanta make sure you're okay. I'm a counselor, remember? Can't leave a client in the lurch."

Matt grimaced as the car did just that: lurched around a corner. Every little motion (and the bug didn't have any subtle moves) seemed like teeth tearing at his flesh.

That damn woman, Kitty with claws. Why him? Why this? He shook himself alert. Time to worry about that later. Now he had to guide Bennie, and get ready to explain himself when they got where they were going.

The street was dark, and street lights in this neighborhood seemed placed to aid predators more than victims anyway.

"Our Lady of Guadalupe." Bennie nodded behind the wheel. "I use-ta live near here. Go to church here."

"This is the convent. They're not expecting me."

Bennie's well-worn face added new wrinkles of concern. "We crashin' on a set of nuns at, um—he squinted at the uselessly tiny dashboard clock—five A.M.?"

"Who's more likely to be up for early mass, huh? Can you . . . see me in?"

"Hey, I don't surrender you to just anyone, *compadre*."

The friendly form of address both reassured Matt and made him aware of how ironic the "padre" part of it was. Here he was, fresh from the healing hands of an ex-abortionist, wounded by a wild woman, about to throw himself on the mercy of a group of elderly nuns.

"You feelin' kinda green, Matt? Wouldn't blame you. Been a bad night."

"Then it's got to be a better morning." Matt grunted as Bennie worked to extract him from the Beetle's passenger seat. What about the motorcycle? Who could he trust to rescue it? No one. It would just have to survive—or not—on its own.

They made it to the door, Matt nearing collapse.

When Bennie rang the bell, they heard its interior echo, but no one came for a long time.

"In this neighborhood, man," Bennie began.

Matt shook his head. They would answer or not. Meanwhile, what else was there to do, but wait?

But a couple minutes later the big wooden door creaked, then opened a slit. A flashlight probed the predawn dusk and their faces. Then the door swung wide.

"Father Matt!" exclaimed the smallest of the three of them: insomniac Sister Mary Margaret, she of the deaf ear, even to the obscene phone caller. But there was nothing wrong with her eyes, even if her memory was anchored in long, long ago.

"Matthias!" said Sister Mary Seraphina, shocked and angry.

The third woman he had not met.

"*Father* Matt," repeated Bennie Cordova, beginning to sound both confused and illuminated.

"I need a place to rest," Matt said.

"He's been cut to shit," Bennie put in, not trusting the two negotiating parties to cut to the chase in any decent amount of time. "Mugging at the hot-line parking lot."

"You need a doctor," Sister Seraphina said even as they all swept back before the wide-open door.

"Saw one," Matt managed to say. "Just can't make it home."

"My dear boy, you have."

When a Body Meets a Body, Part II

January Second dawns bright with the kind of chill that sits well on a martini glass.

I am making my way home from a murder scene that has turned into a long walk down the Las Vegas Strip past scenes of my past triumphs both personal and professional. There is a time in a dude's life when he has to question why he is finally wending his way home, sleepless, at some abominably cheerful hour of the morning like ten A.M., when all others have risen gladly, breakfasted cheerily and headed off to decent, daytime occupations.

If twilight is the Children's Hour, the late morning is the Rascal's Hour. It belongs to the debauched of the world, the all-night gambler and rambler, the person who has reason to wonder who has been sleeping in his or her bed because he or she certainly has not been there.

I keep my natural sunglasses slitted against the bilious morning rays and swagger into the parking lot of the Circle Ritz, planning to make a discreet entrance at the rear. Perhaps Miss Temple has even missed me.

This thought so cheers me that I lash my pace to a medium slink. The lot is usually deserted at this in-between hour: residents gone for the day, and visitors not yet come.

So as I slither around the shed used for housing Miss Electra Lark's Hesketh Vampire motorcycle (now ridden routinely by Mr. Matt Devine), I am shocked to stride snout-first into a dawdling pair of human legs and feet clad in black slacks and tennis shoes.

Imagine my surprise to find that it is my very own roommate. Though she is usually clad in ladylike skirts and shoes of an ambitious nature in the heel department, today she looks like a nightcrawler: rumpled, disheveled and disreputable.

I cannot believe my eyes, and neither can she.

"Louie! Where have you been all night? You look awful."

As if I were not wont to roam of an evening! She is the one who is supposed to stay put and be waiting when I return from my nightly business. And a little more perkiness would be in order too.

"Come on," she says, "let us hurry inside. I am hungry enough to eat hors d'ouevres. Or maybe even Free-to-be-Feline."

This threat to my ever overflowing bowl of dried spaghnum moss (or whatever it is) is no skin off my pads, but I fall into step with her, aware of exotic new scents radiating from her person. This reminds me of the strange scent Midnight Louise detected at the Oasis barge. She let me sample some on her paw before we parted company in the wee hours.

I notice that Miss Temple is practically tiptoeing. I never have to worry about making undue noise when I come and go, but I can see that she is not eager to be spotted in her casual getup looking as if she were up to something not casual at all in the past few hours.

Surely she cannot have discovered her own dead body?

She opens the side door into the building and we ankle inside, discreet as cockroaches.

The lobby is shining and empty. Miss Temple sighs her relief and scuttles to the elevator to push the Up button.

"No Electra," she is muttering while she fidgets before the closed elevator doors. "No Electra, please! No awkward questions. Just a quick fade into my own little home, sweet home."

I do not know what unseen force she is addressing. It cannot be Bast; as far as I know, Miss Temple Barr has no cat-headed goddesses in her personal pantheon, unless she has converted recently.

We are standing there, her impatiently, myself with my usual air of unshakable calm, when the front door whooshes open and shuts with a decided thump.

Miss Temple gives a little scream, and I am so startled by her nervous behavior, that I arch my back and hiss at the intruder.

Who, it turns out, is not an intruder in the ordinary sense, in that he lives here, but who certainly seems to be the last person on earth Miss Temple Barr wished to see, to judge by the winding-cloth pallor of the skin between her freckles.

Speaking of pallor, Mr. Matt Devine is setting some records of his own in that department.

He has always been a modestly attired and behaving person, but now he seems to have faded to a shadow of his former modest self. His clothes are wrinkled and disheveled, as if he had slept in them (which, come to think of it, is the exact condition of Miss Temple's garments), and he moves with great delicacy, as if unsure that the marble floor beneath us might remain solid.

His jacket is carried over one arm, which is crooked before his midsection.

"Matt!"

It is hard to tell if Miss Temple is more shocked by his appearance than his . . . er, appearance on the scene.

"Temple!"

It is hard to tell whether Mr. Matt is more shocked by Miss Temple's appearance than her presence here and now.

No one calls my name. That is what happens when you are vertically challenged. You are invisible. I sit down and lap my coat into order, having been so recently reminded of the importance of neat outer garments.

"Are you just . . . getting home?" Miss Temple blurts out a question she would probably kill another person for asking her.

"Ah, yes. There was an emergency at the hotline. I had to stay on, overtime."

"Oh. Suicide or something?"

He winces visibly. "Something like that. But you—?"

"Ah, still so tired from my trip. I overslept and ran out to get . . . a New York newspaper, got used to reading it, but they were all out."

Mr. Matt Devine frowns. "You shouldn't be going out alone like that, not after what happened. I thought I saw a black car pulling out of the back. You-know-who could be lurking."

"I'm fine."

He frowns more deeply. "Don't you need a . . . that big purse when you go out?"

"Not for a run to the convenience store. Just a few dollar bills in my pocket."

Mr. Matt Devine studies her outfit, which even I can tell is a clingy black two-piece affair with not much evidence of pockets.

Meanwhile, she is staring rather fixedly at a dull brown stain on his crumpled sheepskin jacket.

Neither one, it is clear, believes the other's explanation of their atypical presence in this time and place and atypical condition. But they are so busy trying to fool one another that they hardly notice where their own stories go wrong.

What this means and what it will lead to, I have not a clue. But I can tell you this: my Miss Temple is the more inventive liar in a pinch, if that is any sort of recommendation.

Chapter 20

Postmortem Post-it

Lieutenant C. R. Molina studied the waterlogged scrawl through the clear plastic bag that contained it.

"Traces of adhesive on the upper edge. Probably a Post-it note," Detective Alch said.

"We're lucky to get anything off this scrap."

"He used a ballpoint. A felt-tip wouldn't even have left an impression. But you can see the hardest strokes retained some ink. Good thing the Good Ship Suicide never goes underwater more than ten minutes a performance."

"Good thing the crew noticed something extra bound to the figurehead in the dark."

"Some fighting cats on the dock drew the crew's attention to the prow of the boat. Barge. Whatever."

Molina kept her face deadpan, but it wasn't easy. Those damn cats. Every Las Vegas homicide cop needed a couple of fairy godmother cats, right? She squinted her eyes at the smudged writing in a dead man's messy hand.

Six little words. The lab interpretation suggested: "deadhead at Circus rich." And something "on Hyacinth."

"We figure it was a tip-off to some easy mark at Circus Circus," Alch added. "From every indication, the dead man was a petty criminal. Just the type to be scamming some big spender."

Molina only nodded. She didn't agree, but she had inside information. Cat magic. Who would she hit on first? That was the question.

Maybe Matt Devine. He was the most vulnerable, the least guarded, the most intrinsically honest. Knowing that made her job easier, and his life harder. Too bad. For a cop, a conscience is a terrible thing to waste.

Chapter 21

Viewing Time

Matt was collapsed on his single bed, in his mostly empty bedroom, the small portable television blaring some impossible talk show featuring sluts, cross-dressing motorcyclists and other American family stereotypes. All it needed was a Publishers Clearing House Prize Patrol surprise appearance.

The wound throbbed and burned. The tape around his ribs itched and pulled. His head felt spacey. When the phone rang he jumped as if they'd just pumped the juice into him in some prison execution chamber.

Getting up took a while. He knew the phone would stop ringing just as the greatest effort had been expended. But it didn't stop. He got it on the seventh ring.

"Yes?"

"Lieutenant Molina. I need you downtown right away."

"What? Listen. I can't possibly come."

"Why not?"

"The, uh, motorcycle's on the blink. I don't have transportation."

"How were you going to get to work tonight?"

"Cab, I guess."

"Then take a cab downtown. Or I can send a car to pick you up."

"That . . . urgent?"

"More than urgent."

"It'll take me forty-five minutes to an hour."

"Fine."

His heart was pounding as if considering arrest. Arrest. You never would have known from her tone of voice, or conversation, that they knew each other.

Clipped and to the point.

Just when he didn't need this. Just when he had some guilty knowledge to conceal. Matt considered several unpriestly expletives and settled on one.

An hour and fifteen minutes later he was deposited before the blond curved slab that passed for Las Vegas's entry into the Stonehenge sweepstakes.

The cab driver sped away to other fares; no hop was long in Las Vegas, so cabbies had to settle for quantity rather than quality. And the occasional winner's tip.

Matt walked across the street and into the concrete courtyard. The glass-fronted reception area reflected him and he studied the image like an egoist.

The jacket had brushed clean. He had shaved, combed and slapped some color into his face. He was walking almost normally.

Halfway through the door, he wondered why he needed to keep Kitty and her bizarre attack such a secret. Matt stopped in midstep. He couldn't explain his instinctive reticence, but he suddenly knew it was the same motive that made Temple try to go through a gala evening out with a half-smashed face.

Matt blew out a regretful breath, and regretted the gesture as his rib cage contracted, stretching tape and taped skin.

He signed in at the front desk. Molina was called, and an officer came down to escort him up in the cramped elevator.

Molina sat at her desk in her tunnel of an office. When she invited him to sit on one of the meagerly upholstered side chairs he eased down slowly, as if thinking the move over, as if puzzled by her summons and moving in four-four time.

Which he was.

She looked up, her extraordinary blue eyes flat and cold. "Effinger's dead."

"Dead?"

She watched him.

He didn't have to feign slow motion now. "Recently?"

"Last night."

"Killed?"

"Where were you, say, around eleven-thirty?

Matt's head reeled. "At my job. At ConTact. You don't think—?"

"At this stage in an investigation, you're right. I don't think. I gather. And, from what you say, what you ask, I gather that your stepfather's death is a surprise."

"Hell, yes!"

She smiled at his expletive. That's when he knew that everything he'd done so far had played into her police officer's scenario.

"How did he die?"

Molina's face was surveying her desktop and its accumulation of papers and photographs.

"You have any idea of where Miss Temple Barr was at that time?"

"Eleven-thirty last night?" He cringed to remember them meeting in the Circle Ritz lobby this late morning, both of them looking like they had been for a long time somewhere they oughtn't admit to.

Molina didn't bother nodding, just looked up and regarded him like a schoolteacher waiting for the right answer.

"No. I can't say where Temple was." Why was Molina so interested in Temple's whereabouts, Matt wondered. She couldn't know about Effinger's attack, could she? How? Lying, he was finding, made him sound as stiff as any bad actor. "I assume she was . . . safe at home."

"You have witnesses for your own whereabouts?"

"Witness." Defending his own partial truths gave him second wind. "There were only two of us on last night," he answered with brisk candor.

"Despite the holiday rush?"

"New Year's is an upbeat holiday. People begin again. They usually don't end it, although I did get one despondent caller."

"I assume the calls are recorded."

He shook his head. "Privacy violation in our business. The callers' identities are sacrosanct."

"Seal of the confessional, huh? So all you have to put you in the clear is one witness?"

He nodded. He was in the clear until three A.M. and the encounter with Kitty. Apparently that was enough. Matt's relieved exhalation seared his ribs again.

He tried not to let his breath catch as he gave her Bennie's name and the name of the ConTact supervisor who would have Bennie's home phone number and address.

Molina wrote it all down with the precision of a secretarial school graduate. Then she swerved into a totally unforeseen subject like a Mack truck into a bridge abutment.

"I would suppose the only witness to Miss Barr's nighttime whereabouts ordinarily would be Midnight Louie."

Matt suffered a mental stuttering fit. Did Molina mean to imply he would know about Temple's nocturnal habits? Did she know where Temple had been coming from this morning when he and she had crossed paths in the Circle Ritz lobby? Was that knowledge incriminating? To him? To Temple? Matt managed to shrug. Even that hurt, but he tried not to show it. "Cats can't testify."

"They can, actually. Midnight Louie was not with Miss Temple last night," Molina went on crisply, shuffling autopsy photos.

Matt guessed that she had wanted him to glimpse them, especially the sawn-off cranium.

"How do you know where he was last night?" he asked, playing straight man to her crookedly devious cop.

"Because Mr. Midnight Louie was at the crime scene."

"Temple's cat? Come on!"

"I've seen that big bozo often enough. He was accompanied by a smaller black cat. I recall being present at the Crystal Phoenix last fall when she was renamed 'Midnight Louise.' Now what would a pair of cats from two such different locations be doing at midnight, at the Oasis?"

"The Oasis?" Matt clung to the one fact she had given him, besides the falderal about the cats.

"Never mind. You up to a visit to the ME's?

"ME's? Oh. Medical Examiner's office."

"Righty-ho." Molina stood. She was wearing navy today, like a good Catholic schoolgirl, if said schoolgirl stood almost six feet tall and packed a rod. "Let's go over and eyeball the dear departed."

"Do I have to?"

She cocked a Mr. Spock eyebrow.

Matt remembered a distracting detail, that Temple always fussed about Molina needing to pluck her strong dark eyebrows. He decided that she was more effective unplucked.

"Don't you want to know for sure?" she prodded him.

"I guess I'd take your word on it. You saw him alive for yourself. But I'll . . . identify the body, if you want." He rose slowly, trying not to wince.

"Perhaps condolences are in order; he *was* your stepfather."

Matt smiled. "Not quite condolences. Sorry I'm a little slow in reacting. It *is* a shock, and . . . I pulled a muscle a couple days ago working out."

"Those martial arts will tear you up every time."

"Not every time, thank God. Just now and again."

Driving to the morgue had a feeling of arrest to it that Matt suspected as being deliberate. He rode in the back of the capacious Crown Vic, Molina in the passenger's seat with a uniformed officer driving.

Her attitude was brisk, ultra-professional and bored. Routine, it implied, when he knew damn well it wasn't. But he was grateful for the Crown Vic; a big car with a marshmallow ride, it saved him a lot of pain in transit. Physical pain, anyway.

He was glad the ME's facility was familiar. By the time they arrived he had managed to ape Molina's attitude inside and out. Only a small twitching nerve near his left lower eyelid told him this was the real thing: he would gaze upon Cliff Effinger dead. The man would hurt no living thing again.

In the viewing room he and Molina stood side by side, like a bizarre honor guard, silent, at attention, stiff. He was quiet because he hurt; she was stiff because she was on duty.

The curtain jerked back in increments. Matt gazed down at Effinger's closed-eyed face. Pale, gray, still.

"No identity doubts this time?" Molina asked.

"No doubts. And you?"

"I always knew the answer. I just wanted to watch your reaction to the actual corpse."

"And?"

"You're too guarded. You're not telling me squat, except what I know, that the dead guy is Effinger. Now I'll tell you something. He had something in his pocket. A reference to Temple Barr. Think about it. And does the word 'Hyacinth' mean anything to you?"

Matt shook his head. "Hyacinth? No. But Temple . . . what kind of reference?"

"Do you know of any reason why Temple Barr would have motive to kill Cliff Effinger, or to know it was done?"

"No!"

"Well, I know of a reason a straight-John citizen might have grabbed Effinger a week ago and turned him over to the law. It's called precedenting. You could have alibied yourself by being a restrained citizen, then gone back and offed the asshole. He was an asshole, wasn't he?"

Matt met her eyes, on a level with his own. "Maybe. Maybe not always. Life isn't only black and white, Lieutenant. Effinger wasn't the Ogre of All Ogres."

"Really? And how long have you felt with charity toward all, malice toward none, Mr. Lincoln?"

"Since I went to Chicago for Christmas, and found villains other than Effinger."

She read the truth in his eyes, and didn't like it. She made her living looking for lies.

"Outa here, choir boy. And do tell Miss Temple I plan on talking with her."

Chapter 22

On Hyacinth Lane

As soon as Matt got home he unearthed his map of Las Vegas. Under "H" in the street directory he found Hyacinth Lane.

A short residential street just west of downtown, Hyacinth Lane's neighborhood sheltered in the fork made by U.S. 95, the principal east-west highway in town, crossing U.S. 15, the north-south highway that roughly paralleled the Las Vegas Strip.

Matt located the Oasis Hotel on the map, down the Strip from Hyacinth and near the Stardust. From there he pinpointed the Circle Ritz. The three locations formed a right triangle, with the Strip as its hypotenuse.

Matt sat back and gave the throb in his side free rein for a few minutes. He felt his face crease into a mask of total feeling, which was a much better fit to his inner state than the mask of total unfeeling he had been wearing.

He supposed that crooks and cops both had to adopt that deadpan survival guise, becoming more like each other and less like the citizens they preyed upon and protected.

Alone, he could wonder why his every instinct had screamed that Kitty's attack must be concealed.

Shame, he supposed. Hurt, he was a child again, struck unmercifully by a callous world. The woman was, in a way, evil incarnate, an embodiment of everything he had never stood for. She hated good, or what the church defined as good. She hated him for trying to live up to that ideal. Basically, she hated, and it wasn't personal, even when the hatred expressed itself in such a deeply personal way: outright attack, verbal and physical.

Temple had concealed Effinger's attack to spare Matt guilt and anger. Now Matt himself concealed his injury to . . . learn more. More about Kitty, and more about himself. Also to soothe his wounded manhood. Falling victim to a female mugger was a loss of masculine face. His Adam had been betrayed by an Eve who had also played the role of the snake. And perhaps she had also aspired to a prerogative of the Almighty, taking Matt's life and his integrity in her hands and twisting slowly. She was the Tree of All Knowledge, and he had a lot to learn. About her, for sure. Maybe especially about himself.

And maybe he had a lot to learn about Temple. Where to start? First he called Electra.

After exchanging the usual pleasantries, Matt explained that he'd had a martial arts injury and couldn't ride the Vampire for a while.

"It's safe, Electra, locked on the ConTact lot. But that's not the best neighborhood in Vegas. Could we drive over in your car and you could ride it back? I really have to avoid . . . vibrations."

Electra laughed that earthy laugh of hers and agreed to everything. "Just let me collect my 'Speed Queen' helmet, honey, and we'll glide off into the sunset together. Yeah, fivish would be fine. See you in the parking lot in two revs of a Vampire's wail."

Matt hung up, pleased. That abandoned motorcycle had been weighing on his conscience. Couldn't lose anything that had belonged to Max Kinsella. That would tip the balance between them, which was too unbalanced to begin with. Max and his carnal knowledge of Temple.

The phrase was as lurid as his thoughts sometimes became lately.

Temple sounded both relieved and worried when he called.

"Matt. Are you all right?"

In view of what had happened the night *after* their date, Temple's question was ultra-appropriate.

"That's debatable," he answered. "Could you stop by my place in a couple minutes? I have some news you'll want to hear in person. Besides, you can see the Big Red Sofa in position."

"It's all right, isn't it?"

"Better than I am."

He knew that sign-off would set her internal rescue sirens keening. That's how Temple got involved in everyone else's business, she was a one-woman cleanup detail. "Murder scenes and emotional wrecks tidied up while I agonize and you watch," could be her motto.

She was ringing his doorbell before he could get the instant coffee made.

Her face fell when she saw him. "What's the matter?"

Matt was glad he had news shocking enough to explain his pained look.

"Sit down."

"Hey! Who could resist this free-form settee." Temple put her fists on her hips and stared at the sofa, or rather the sofa's current user. "And what's Midnight Louie doing up here, sprawled on your Vladimir Kagan like he owned it?"

"He's been showing up at my door, rubbing back and forth on the frame and my legs. I finally decided to let him in this afternoon. He headed for the Kagan as one to the biomorphic born."

"He'll get black cat hair all over it, though he does look like cover boy material posed there."

"I'm not sure this sofa is very practical, Temple. Louie can mold his feline form to the thing, but a person would have to have scoliosis to sleep against that ess-curved back support, such as it is."

Temple perched on the sofa like a pixie, oblivious to a serious clash between her sunset-orange-red hair and the sofa's deep lipstick-red color. She was as determined to stake her claim as Midnight Louie.

"On the other hand, it's sure cheerful," she decided. "Like those red-painted free-form steel sculptures they put up in every downtown in the seventies. Where'd you get the cool little tables?"

"Goodwill." He returned from the kitchen, setting their coffee mugs on the silver-gray melamine-covered ovals. "And just in time. I don't want you holding that coffee cup over the suede sofa seat when I tell you what Molina told me this afternoon."

"You've seen Molina? Matt, you didn't report Effinger's—?"

"No. I'm no tattletale. *She* reported on Effinger."

"And?"

Matt watched her. "He's dead."

"Dead?" Temple held her coffee mug over the laminated table with both hands, then lowered it very slowly. "But . . . that was fast. How?"

"Molina wasn't saying. She did drag me over to the ME's office to identify the body. Wanted to make sure this time."

"That was all she wanted with you? Identification?"

He shook his head. "She wanted to know where I was before and after midnight on New Year's Day."

"Last night? Before midnight?"

"And after midnight. I was at work, of course. She asked if I thought you had an alibi for that time."

"Me? Why me? I can see why *you* might be suspect if Effinger's death was suspicious, although why collar the guy and turn him in to the police, then knock him off a few days later?"

"Illusion. Misdirection. Turning in Effinger might make me a less likely suspect when something happened to him later."

"Why would she suspect me, though?"

"I don't know. She sure wants to know where you were last night."

"Safe in bed."

Matt cleared his throat. "Not exactly an alibi, for a single person. Louie was on the crime scene. She may think you were roaming around too." His eyes refused to ask where she had been coming from that awkward morning after.

"Louie?" Temple excelled at misdirection herself, her newly naked eyes avoiding his. "Matt! You didn't tell Molina about Effinger's attack, that would explain her thinking I had a motive."

"Of course not! But Effinger had something on him that pointed to you. Something about the word 'Hyacinth.' She asked me if that meant anything."

"It's a flower."

"And a street name." Matt lifted the map tented over the sofa back. Its loud crackle made Louie, nose and tail in the air, leap to the floor. Matt found it odd to see Temple examining tiny type without glasses. "That highlighted area there, just west of downtown."

" 'Hyacinth Lane.' Sounds like part of an old Nancy Drew title: *The House on Hyacinth Lane.* You ever been near there?"

Matt shook his head as he reclaimed the map. Wrestling with an unfurled map stretched his muscles a little too far. "Mmmfh," he muttered before he could catch himself.

Temple eyed him anxiously. "You look awful, Matt. Pale and wan. Learning of Effinger's death so soon after learning about his last dance with me must be a one-two punch."

"One-two punch is right." He tried to sound rueful rather than pained.

"You were so angry with me on New Year's Eve. I thought . . . I've been trying to tell *me* why I took it upon myself to keep you in the dark for your own good. That is awfully condescending."

"Never mind. Forget it. I mean that, Temple. I overreacted that night. Pride had to go for a roundabout ride. I was so pleased with myself for digging up Effinger and not tearing him apart that I never considered I might unearth some nasty consequences. I hate that you had to pay for my hubris, but at least Effinger will never do that to anybody again. And . . . I see things differently since New Year's Eve. I do understand why you tried to soldier through. I guess that's what people do; try to protect each other."

"Well, that's a turnaround. I was prepared to writhe and crawl on my belly like a snake for at least twenty minutes."

"No time for self-obeisance. Sorry. Can you drive me past Hyacinth Lane and get me to work on time?"

"Sure. But . . . we could take the motorcycle."

"No, it's in the shop."

"Oh. Okay. I'll get my car keys and meet you in the lot."

"In the lobby."

"All right, the lobby. But with Effinger gone, safety might not be as much of a concern."

"Or more of one. If Molina's involved, someone killed him, if not me or thee."

She paused at his door before she left, tilting her head to eye him curiously. He could tell that she sensed something more than Effinger's death bothering him.

But she decided not to press it. Now.

"Nice couch!" Temple exited on a wink.

He was getting used to her without eyeglasses. He was even beginning to like the contacts. Her eyes were a subtle blue-gray that reflected every shade of clear and stormy weather in her emotions. He had a feeling the outlook for the next few days was definitely stormy, and not just because of the name of Temple's car.

Chapter 23

Unholy Trinity

After cruising by the disappointingly nondescript Hyacinth Lane, Temple dropped Matt off at ConTact and headed for an opposite side of town: the upscale housing development where Max was hiding out, maybe from more than she knew.

On the way there, Molina's question, delivered through the fiendish medium of Matt Devine, repeated in her mind like a TV advertising slogan: *Where were you at midnight on New Year's Day?*

Not curled up in solo sleep in her Circle Ritz trundle, but sharing an exotic opium bed in Orson Welles's former house with her former—make that previously former—boyfriend/lover/fiancé. Who of course was in deep cover, and possibly even denial.

Great. Her alibi, should she need one, was the Invisible Man.

Temple knew that Max would probably disapprove of her impulsive drive-by consultation, but should she trust her phone lines now? Besides, she had masqueraded as a real estate lady in this neighborhood before, and could do it again.

Temple did balk at leaving her aqua Storm parked in Max's

always-empty driveway. She parked on the lot line three houses down and went in on foot.

After ringing the doorbell in the shadowed outer courtyard, Temple assumed some sort of surveillance system recorded her approach. That hummingbird feeder could be a camera. Then again, a recording device could have been built into the soffit under the eaves.

Paranoia was a terrible affliction.

The door opened of its own seeming volition, as usual. Temple was beginning to suspect it was automated, like a haunted house door. All that was missing: the scream of creaky hinges.

"Is this a raid?" Max's voice asked darkly from the dark within.

"This is a retreat."

"What's wrong?" He clasped her wrist and drew her inside.

"It seems that we are each other's alibi in a murder case. If we can trust each other's testimony. But it doesn't matter because we *can't* testify."

"Come into the computer parlor; the light's better."

He led the way through the tangled house plan. Homes of a certain age in hot climates were shaded mazes designed to foil the sun's daily invasion.

Just before they crossed the threshold into the glow of the computer screen, Max surprised her with a steamy soul kiss in the dark. "Nice *not* seeing you again, so soon."

Temple was almost ready to deep-six her mission; their reunion was bringing back all the many advantages of a steady relationship, including myriad possibilities for the private display of affection at the most inapt times in the most unexpected places, and therefore all the more exciting.

She sighed as they emerged into the subdued light of the computer-cave, a cable-lined cavern whose boundaries were piled printouts and stacked volumes of endless documentation.

"Did you have a chance to look over the manuscript yet?" Max sounded boyishly eager, a new role for him.

"Not yet. Didn't get home until mid-morning, you know, and then I crashed. I am a recovering invalid."

"Sorry. I've worked on it night and day all through the winter.

So." He sat on the big swivel chair and pulled Temple onto his lap. "Whose murder rap do we have to dodge?"

"Effinger's."

"You're kidding."

"Never about Cliff Effinger. He's the evil genie who's stalked us from the time you disappeared after the body was found in the Goliath casino ceiling, to the dead Effinger lookalike who plummeted down onto the craps table at the Crystal Phoenix, to the fist sandwich I ate in the Circle Ritz parking lot four days ago."

"I'm glad you didn't say 'evil genius.' I would have had to take exception. But how do you know about this? And why do 'we' need an alibi?"

"Well, it certainly looks like I need one, and since we were supposedly together at the time in question, you'll have to be it. Except that I woke up several times during the night and you were not necessarily here. You know how often I wake up at night."

"And a convenient habit it is too." Max took a stab at giving her a hickey on the nape. "You know how often I get up to roam around at night. Usually a case of the hungries."

"Great. So we agree. We both have erratic nighttime habits and who knows when, and if, we really were here."

"But I don't understand. How did you hear about Effinger's murder?"

Temple extricated herself from the distracting nibbling. "From Matt. Molina had him downtown to identify the body, for real this time. From what she asked him, the critical time is around midnight last night. And she asked him if he thought I would have an alibi for that time period."

"Naturally you immediately told Devine exactly where you were and what you were doing."

"Naturally . . . not! Matt doesn't know much about the murder or any evidence, but he thinks Molina has something concrete that relates to me and to the word 'Hyacinth.' "

"Hyacinth. Pretty word. Pretty flower. Why don't I print out a new version of my manuscript and you can give it a quick read while I do my best to distract the editor from typographical errors."

"How can you be so calm? Matt may be home free . . . though I get the impression there's something he's not telling me."

"How dare he? The cad!"

"Yes, I know we're all a hopeless bunch of liars at the moment, at least by omission. But what are we going to do? Our mutual alibi is hardly ironclad and, anyway—"

"And you don't want to use it, anyway, because you haven't screwed up the courage yet to tell Mr. Devine that you are seeing me in a very committed fashion."

"Dammit, Max. I need some time on this."

"Molina may not give it to you."

"Yes. That's freaky, Effinger dead so soon after mashing my face."

"Nothing in the evening paper. I skimmed it already." Max spun the chair and began clicking computer keys.

"You're consulting the Millennium Swami?"

"The local paper's on-line. Maybe they posted a story that won't make print until morning. Ah."

"What?"

"Bizarre."

"Max! I can't read the screen very well while still adjusting to these contact lenses. Please!"

" 'Unidentified man drowns at Oasis barge attraction.' Sounds like Molina's got the information on this case wrapped tighter than steel wire. Hmm. Man caught in the barge sinking mechanism and drowned. Not a member of the work crew. No theories on how the tragedy happened."

"Hmm." Temple was suspicious in turn. "I know media fudge terminology. They always call it a 'tragedy' when they're not sure if it's an accidental or deliberate death. He could have just gotten drunk and fallen in the drink."

"Not likely. Remember, I told you that I didn't think his well-being was a good bet in this town for long."

"Yes, I do remember, and is *that* a sterling piece of evidence for the prosecution, in case you hadn't noticed! 'Did Mr. Kinsella predict that Mr. Effinger was not long for this world three days before the man's death? Answer the question, Miss Barr.' "

"But you will turn a cold ear, as you did to Molina for all those months, and bravely go serve an open-ended contempt sentence, your lips sealed until the bitter end.

"Max." She put her hands on his shoulders and gazed deep into his eyes, which she could do a lot better without glasses in the way. "Did you kill Effinger?"

He shrugged, then shook his head. "I was beginning to be as enthusiastic about the idea as Devine, especially after his last . . . transgression. I did suggest that he be watched, and that may turn out to be a very good thing."

"Who? Who would watch him?"

"Associates of mine."

"Not the Brotherhood?"

"No. No capitalized pass-names. Only discretion. Wait a second. I'll do a search for the word 'hyacinth' on Gandolph's system."

Max's "second" stretched into a few minutes, which they managed to occupy quite creatively. Matt Devine's effect on Temple's heart might be ambiguous, but there was no doubt what Max Kinsella did for her hormones.

"I wish you could move in here," Max said after a while.

"Well, now that Midnight Louie has deserted me, there's not much to keep me at the Circle Ritz. It is nice being together again, isn't it?"

"It is. More than nice." A pause. She knew where he was going next, and that was nice too. "It's paradise," he sang softly.

That you belong to me. But the old standards fell short of modern realities. "Belonging to" was not a politically correct notion nowadays. Temple rested her forehead against Max's, happy she no longer had glasses to steam up. That was one thing she owed Effinger: losing the eyeglasses.

"Four references."

"Huh?"

"To hyacinth."

Temple blinked and leaned forward to study the screen.

"Hyacinth Lane. Matt found that on the map."

"Hooray for Matt and his electric map."

"Hyacinth Bowling Lane?"

"And the Hyacinth Cleaners. Also, Shangri-La and Hyacinth."

"An intersection? But who would name a street 'Shangri-La'?"

"In Las Vegas, dollink, anythink is possible. 'Hyacinth Halo Escort Service.' "

"I bet they're no angels."

"I doubt it refers to anything we'd find on here, Temple. It may have been some lucky phrase. Effinger was a gambler, above all. Or Molina may have just thrown it into the mix to confuse matters."

"She's a cop. She has to tell the truth."

"Not to suspects. And look where she went. Not to you. To Devine. He's the weakest link. Don't sputter defense and protest, Temple. I'm being totally practical here. Molina's already had several go's at you on my whereabouts and didn't get anywhere. But here's Devine, fresh from an authoritarian system in which he examined every shade of motive and meaning. He's not good at dodging the truth, Temple. He's had very little practice. He'd crack before you or I would."

"So Matt's a target because he's honest?"

"Being straight is a weakness in a crooked world, Temple."

Temple stared down at the keyboard, unhappy with the truth Max had spoken.

"I *know* Matt's hiding something, something he hasn't told Molina."

"Then you had better find it out first. And in the meantime, don't tell him anything that might be . . . distracting."

"Now you're telling me to *not* tell Matt the truth about us at the earliest opportunity?"

"I'd love to see this unholy trinity busted up, but not just yet. It might make the difference in saving all our skins if we work together despite ourselves."

Chapter 24

Hunting Hyacinth

I am astounded.

I express my minor annoyance with Miss Temple's altered domestic arrangements by steering clear of her for a few hours, and not only does she not notice my dereliction, but she ends up suspected of murder.

Some people simply cannot be left to go through this world unshepherded.

Although I had hopes of muscling in on Mr. Matt Devine's bachelor pad whilst I was expressing my severe disapproval of Miss Temple's new nocturnal habits, he is pretty much a bust too.

As soon as the roommate formerly known as mine skedaddles the premises, Mr. Matt Devine makes a face and heads for the bathroom. I follow, as he needs to learn to leave the window open at least seven inches so I can come and go as I please.

But he does not go to the spare bathroom on the building's outer wall, but to the master bathroom, which has no window. It does not even have a litter box yet, and if Mr. Matt does not tumble to opening my usual window, he had better tumble to a litter box, or he will step into a significant surprise on his bathroom floor in the morning.

But while he does not seem inclined to consider my needs, I am fascinated by his. For when he strips off his bulky sweater (and I know Miss Temple would love to be here to see this, even if she is dallying with the competition), I find that he is either wearing one of those new-fangled wide-body cat harnesses, or a half-mummy wrap.

When he strips the item off (and I do not think this part would interest Miss Temple), I see that he has been in a cat spat and slashed by a critter either the size of one of Siegfried and Roy's six hundred-pound white tigers, or by a human with artificial shivs.

I am no sissy and have nursed my share of festering nicks, scratches and punctures without medical attention in my career, but I do cringe at the sight of this nasty gash, taped together as if by Dr. Frankenstein in the dark.

Right now two of the significant others in my life are bearing marks of another's antipathy. I pause to muse that it is too bad Mr. Max Kinsella has not received his licks, so far as I know, but an attack on him might backfire and engender Miss Temple's ever-ready sympathy. This is the only reason he and I did not go mano-a-mano in her bedchamber the other night. Also, I consider it tacky to get blood on the bed linens.

I also note that the lines of communication between the humans of my acquaintance are getting tangled and dangled and mangled. They are so busy hiding things from each other that they will never find anything out.

I see it is up to me, and I will begin by tracking down the mysterious meaning of "hyacinth."

To do so, I will have to leave. I tell Mr. Matt Devine so.

"What? Food? Out? You'd better go back down to Temple, who knows what you want."

If she knew what I wanted, the magician would never darken her door, and vice versa, again.

Mr. Matt sighs and leads me to the front door. "You want to leave?"

I rub on his legs twice before I go, hoping that public display of affection will encourage him to run out and purchase a litter box and a better class of cat food than Miss Temple keeps on hand below. But my hopes are faint. Mr. Matt Devine is not tuned into the animal world and will take much patient educating before he knows how to offer the proper tender, loving care.

Once in the hallway, I am stuck, being barred from Miss Temple's place and my easy exit to the outside world. I will just have to deal with the inside world.

I trot for the stairs and shove a shoulder into the swinging door. It opens just enough, long enough to allow my body and most of my—ouch!—tail through. Then I take the stairs to the penthouse.

Hyacinth Lane, indeed.

That is too easy. There must be a dozen other hyacinths in Las Vegas, and I intend to find every one, by every means available.

But first I must figure out a way to break into Karma's joint from inside. I am used to being an outside operator. Inside is nothing but hallways full of door knobs. Now I know how these door knobs work, and I am certainly big and strong enough to reach one. I just do not carry the proper equipment to move the silly thing.

So I resort to the ancient technique of my kind, which I have mentioned before. The Stare. The Stare is usually more effective if there is a human within sight, and up here on the penthouse level I do not stand a chance of even being spotted by a helpful tenant.

No, all I have is the solid mahogany wall of Miss Electra Lark's door, the only one in the place that is not numbered.

But I have faith, if not hope and charity. I sit and give the door the Stare. I just pretend that there is one tasty mouse behind that door and that eventually something will have to come out of it.

"Eventually" is not as long as I fear it will be.

The door opens and I lift my head. I expect to be looking Miss Electra Lark in the kisser, but there is no one there.

Chagrined, I lower my gaze to my own level.

Sure enough, Karma herself is sitting there, doing the compulsive washing bit with the white gloves on her forelimbs.

"What do you want, Louie?"

"Two things: a way outa this place, like your patio, and a lead on something in this town called 'hyacinth.' "

"The first part is simple, Louie. I am always ready to show you the door. The second is complicated. A hyacinth is a flower. There may be thousands of them in Las Vegas and neighboring communities. And that is just counting by the plant, not the individual bloom."

"Enough with this blooming conversation! I am not looking for your ordinary posy. The hyacinth I am hunting has something to do with a murder and with my Miss Temple."

"My, my. You certainly do like to push a big paw into business that is none of yours, do you not, Louie? Well, as long as your crude powers roused me from a nap, come in. Miss Electra is out, fortunately. I will think about hyacinth as other than the obvious flower while we make our way to the patio doors. It will be up to you to open them; I used my current energy reserves to unlock and open the front door just now. You certainly are a bother."

"You certainly are a bother," I mouth behind her long fluffy tail as it fans back and forth before me on the way to the patio.

Once there, Karma turns, sits, and allows her baby blues to go slightly cross-eyed.

"Hyacinth." She begins to purr. Actually, it is a sort of hum. Actually, it sounds a lot like that phoney baloney eastern meditation chant: "Om." Most of our kind are content with a simple, down-to-earth purr. We need not do it in a foreign accent.

However, since all of Karma's creamy hairs began to stand out in a disheveled halo, and since for a second it seems to me that she is, er, elevated slightly off the floor (although that may have been a misleading side effect of the sudden Static Attack), I am not about to mention my skepticism to her.

"Oooom," she purrs. The ear with the gold ring twitches. (My ear would twitch on cue too, if it were pierced by some alien object.) "Hyacinth. I detect an odor."

"Why not? Flowers do stink."

"Fragrance, Louie. Flowers have fragrance. That is your key problem in this life, Louie: you do not discern the difference between scent and stink."

"I know when I smell a rat, and that is all that matters in my business. And I not only smelled this stinko rat, I saw it."

"I see that you must, as usual, deal with the crudest element first. Very well. So shall I."

"Welll," she hums, purrs. "Shallll."

I shrug. You have to put up with a lot from sources, sometimes, in my business.

"I smell water. Rats indeed. Death by drowning. Bastet watches with her ancient eyes."

My own ancient eyes blink. Take away the falderal, and Karma the Kute is describing the scene of the crime pretty darn well.

"The mummy bears a hyacinth in his dead, bound hands, but he knows not what he harbors. And you are not alone, Louie. I glimpse a softer, feminine side. Is it possible?"

"Nix on that. And if you are referring to my alleged daughter, Louise, you would know she has got the soft, feminine side of a buzz saw."

"I see you are proud of her, Louis."

"Louie! And she is no spawn of mine."

Karma hums. Karma purrs.

"I smell a house of flowers, not too far away. Such an outpouring of blossoms. Quite, quite profligate. Even sinister."

"Profligate? Hey, I do not do that anymore!"

"Poor Louie. The subtle is lost upon you."

"So what else does Your Worshipfulness sniff?"

"I smell . . . the scent of a woman."

"Human female?"

"That is . . . debatable. Feline, certainly, but of more than one species, I believe. Magic. I smell magic at all four corners of this sphere."

Oy, boy. What a bunch of gobbledygook.

"The magician pulls a bouquet of . . . hyacinth from a long, flowing sleeve."

I have never seen Mr. Max Kinsella in long, flowing sleeves, but then I have never seen him perform professionally. Only as an amateur, and very amorous indeed, on Miss Temple Barr's living room sofa and more recently on her California queen-size bed (which allows me plenty of room at the foot to stretch out). It does occur to me, with a wince, that the reason Miss Temple has one of these extra-long but not excessively wide beds is because of her once (and possibly future) relationship with the attenuated Mr. Max. I am ashamed to admit that yours truly may be benefiting from being an afterthought.

"Beware the sorcerer, Louie! Beware the dead man whose pale face rises wreathed in hyacinth blossom. Beware she who bears thorns. Beware the alchemist! I see dying petals on a whirlpool. I see blue eyes. Not mine. Beware, Louie, beware."

Ho-hum. Ho-omm. More vague predilections. I should have known better than to come to Karma for real enlightenment. I see my only course is to consult my encyclopedic stooge. Just show me the exit, honey, and I will be outa this joint and back in the real world.

"I see you are as blind as always, Louie. Go. Seek your fate. The patio and the palm tree await."

Just to show her, I crack the French door with two precisely placed bounds. The lever snaps open. I jump up and depress it. The door pops ajar, and I am out in the crisp winter air, inhaling a scent of . . . polyurethane. Trust Miss Electra's patio furniture to clear a guy's head of metaphysical mumbo-jumbo.

I leap to the overweening palm tree and then ratchet down its length, claws out. We are talking murder most foul here. We are talking death by dread. We are talking much bigger stuff than a few fishy smells on the whiskers of a Sacred Cat of Burma!

There is one place that can answer all my questions: the Thrill 'n' Quill bookstore, overseen by its tiresome mascot, a feline who is long on book-learning and short on sense. I head off down the street, trying to figure out how I will roust Ingram after hours.

Chapter 25

Relativity

Matt was glad that Bennie was his front man with ConTact. He had five precious days off. He didn't care what Bennie told them; he didn't care if he was supposed to have been mugged into a bloody pulp. He needed this time to deal with Effinger's death.

And one thing he couldn't put off much longer. He dialed Chicago.

The phone rang for a long time until his mother, breathless, answered.

"Matt!" She sounded relieved that it was him. "I was out."

"You were out?" He shouldn't have sounded so shocked.

"Well, I'd promised to go. Otherwise I would have been here. Did you call earlier?"

"No, Mom. And I'm glad you were out. Can I ask where?"

"Oh. That Krys. She wanted to see a movie for the third time and no one else would go with her. Harrison Ford. I haven't been to a movie theater in years. They're so loud."

"I wouldn't know. I haven't been to a movie theater in years myself."

"Well, no wonder. It's all so . . . violent. And the trailers. So . . . immoral."

"Probably. Did you have a good time?"

"Well, the audience was very noisy, not like when I was a girl. Then, it was like you were in church."

"So the outing was a bust, huh?"

"Not . . . exactly. It's like a video game, that's what it is. I've seen the boys playing those things. Bang, bang, bang. You've got to pay attention every minute. Harrison Ford. I don't see what the excitement's about. Now that Brad Pitt, maybe. You even, God forbid. But a young girl like that shouldn't fixate on such an old man."

"Mom, Ford's probably a little older than you."

"Oh. What did I say? An old man." But she laughed.

There was no easy segue into the next topic. Matt stepped into it flat-footed.

"I've got news."

"Oh?" The old wariness.

"Cliff is dead."

Silence.

"He was killed."

"By who?"

"I don't know." More silence. "Maybe me. Maybe by tracking him down, I brought him the wrong kind of attention."

"That's crazy, Matt. If he was killed, it was because he drove someone beyond endurance. Not . . . you?"

"Not me. I'm past that. I don't need that. I'm almost sorry he's gone, because I'll never have a chance to prove how much I'm beyond him now."

"That's what I was trying to tell you when you came home. I got beyond him a long time ago. Maybe I'm bitter, but I'm not . . . trapped with him in the past. Okay?"

"Okay. I love you, Mom."

"Oh, Matt. You know . . ."

That's as close as she could ever come.

"It was a pretty good movie," she conceded. "Krys isn't so bad. Maybe Harrison Ford isn't either. So don't spend time worrying about . . . him. He's gone. He's been gone a long time."

"Yeah. Thanks. Bye."

Matt hung up, thanking heaven for banal conversations. For starch, for fattening filler that avoided the meat of the matter.

Sometimes evasion was the best coping skill.

So when the phone rang twenty minutes later while he was reading Thomas Mann on his new red sofa, under the light of his new floor lamp, he thought maybe his mother was calling back with something more to say.

"Molina," she said, sounding like a mother superior.

"Oh. Isn't it . . . after hours?"

"I don't think cops—and priests—*have* hours. So. What do you want to do with the body?"

"Body?"

"We got lucky; no pileup at autopsy central. The medical examiner's ready to release it to the next of kin."

"Carmen—"

"Lieutenant Molina. This is a murder case, Mr. Devine. You are a suspect."

"Oh—"

"Yes?"

"You're saying it's up to me to bury the body. Haven't you people got a potter's field or something?"

"Sure 'we people' do. It's called the county. Wooden crate et cetera. That's okay with you, it's okay with us."

"Wait. Ah. Suppose I think it over . . . what does it involve? A funeral home, some kind of casket?"

"Conscience. My best weapon."

"I know. But I just finished telling my mother about it. You got me at a bad time."

"What did you tell her?"

"Not much about how he died, since you didn't tell me. I told her I may have drawn the wrong person's attention by tracking him down."

"What did she say?"

"Not much."

"Well? I'm going out of my way on this."

"Why?"

"Because I figured you wouldn't have thought of it, and then you would have when it was too late. Conscience. A cop's best friend."

"Thanks. Who do I talk to if I decide to claim the body?"

"The ME's office. Don't thank me until this is over."

"Will it ever be?"

"It's my case, Devine. You better bet that it will be."

"That sounds like a threat."

"Only if you're guilty of something."

"You know I think I'm guilty of everything. What does that make me? A very unreliable source."

"No. It makes you more reliable than you know."

She hung up without farewells. He was beginning to realize that was because it wouldn't be over, until it was over.

So he made a call, one he'd been putting off.

He had an appointment so fast it was almost embarrassing: ten the next morning. It was one he both looked forward to, and dreaded. He was beginning to wonder if conflicting emotions could be addictive.

Finally, he called Temple and told her about Molina's amazingly considerate offer to return the dead departed to his custody for the good of his immortal soul.

Chapter 26

Buried in Cyberspace

From:	Flack@neon.net
Date:	1/2/98 9:45 PM
Subject:	Re: Roadkill
Address:	To Hattrick@ginjoint.net

Can you believe it? What Lady Copperhead has offered the recent Roadkill to his Poor Relative? What is she up to? I mean, should Poor Relative have to pay for burying a rotten relative?

From:	Hattrick@ginjoint.net
Date:	1/2/98 9:52 PM
Subject:	Re: Roadkill
Address:	To Flack@neon.net

I hope you don't mean "rotten" literally. Of course the Lady Copperhead is just exerting pressure. But this might not be a bad idea. Think about it.

From:	Flack@neon.net
Date:	1/2/98 9:54 PM
Subject:	Re: Roadkill
Address:	To Hattrick@ginjoint.net

Poor Relative can't afford to be magnanimous in this maggot's case. And, yes, I do hope I mean "rotten" literally.

From:	Hattrick@ginjoint.net
Date:	1/2/98 9:58 PM
Subject:	Re: Roadkill
Address:	To Flack@neon.net

No, but Hattrick can afford to be magnanimous. He can even spring for a nice announcement in the newspapers' obituary pages. What if we held a funeral and watched to see who came?

From:	Flack@neon.net
Date:	1/2/98 10:03
Subject:	Re: Roadkill
Address:	To Hattrick@ginjoint.net

Nobody would come to watch that worm go to his long-delayed last reward. It would be a waste of money.

From:	Hattrick@ginjoint.net
Date:	1/2/98 10:07 PM
Subject:	Re: Roadkill
Address:	To Flack@neon.net

Maybe. But it's my money. I say, let the games begin. Tell Poor Relative it's on the house.

From:	Flack@neon.net
Date:	1/2/98 10:11 PM
Subject:	Re: Roadkill
Address:	To Hattrick@ginjoint.net

Some consolation! Poor Relative would have to put up with seeing the worm treated like a real human being, and he would hate being indebted to you.

From:	Hattrick@ginjoint.net
Date:	1/2/98 10:14 PM
Subject:	Re: Roadkill
Address:	To Flack@neon.net

He need never know if you come up with an inventive story. Shouldn't you be in bed with someone?

From:	Flack@neon.net
Date:	1/2/98 10:20 PM
Subject:	Re: Roadkill
Address:	To Hattrick@ginjoint.net

I am. He has shiny dark hair, big green eyes and a world-class tail. Nighty-night.

Chapter 27

Remembrance of Things Passed Up

The cab dropped Matt at his ten o'clock appointment at five to the hour.

Knowing he was the first customer of the day, he dawdled his way to the front door. The first and only time he had sought this woman's services, it had ended with him jumping to an awkward conclusion and bolting. He owed her an explanation, but what he thought had happened between them had been so unspoken that explaining himself was a sure road to embarrassing them both. Killing time allowed him to anticipate the worst, and the best.

When he rang, the bell was answered soon enough that he didn't feel too early.

"Hello again." Janice Flanders stood in the shadow of her entry hall, sounding like an old friend. Everything about her was easy and earth-toned, from her short ash-blond hair to whatever subtle makeup she wore, if any.

"Come in. I can't wait to get to work on this. You said the other sketch had 'borne fruit?' "

"Yes."

He followed her through shadow and sunlight from the sky-
lights to the same completely cozy sunroom in which they had
worked last time.

"Take your jacket off; I'll hang it up. You know the routine: get
comfortable. Then we go to work."

He winced writhing out of the jacket. "Pulled a muscle working out."

"Oh. What do you do? Weights?"

"No. Tai chi. Other stuff like that."

She nodded. "I run, do free weights and yoga. The price of living in the physically fit nineties. Would you like coffee? Decaf? I
forget what I gave you last time."

"Ah, lemonade, I think. I don't remember either. Coffee's fine."

She vanished into the adjoining kitchen.

"Kids back in school?" he asked to make conversation. Then
wished he hadn't. He might sound . . . hopeful.

"Yes! Time for me to play at my own work. So." She came back
with the mugs and set them down on glass-topped metal tables
near each of their chairs. "Tell me about your success with the first
sketch."

He sipped the coffee first, aware of her relaxation and his stiff-
ness. She was wearing tight-fitting leggings this time, not jeans,
and an oversized knit top that emphasized her trim legs. Earrings
must be a signature with her. Today they were huge beaded iridescent circles that ricocheted the sunlight like stained glass.

Her sketch pad lay tilted against the corner of the sofa. Daybed,
it was called, he thought. Stacked with small pillows of all shapes,
infinitely programmable.

"You seem . . . stiff today," she noted.

"A bad muscle pull. Every move I make reminds me."

"Tough. You want a back support?" She lifted an oblong pillow
covered in some flowered purple fabric. Hyacinths? he wondered.

She tossed it to him and he stuck it behind his back. It did re-
lieve the strain, actually.

"So. Mr. Effinger."

"Simple really. I reduced the sketch to wallet size copies and
laminated a bunch to show around town. Then I had to trail him
through a few sleazy bars." Her eyebrows lifted. "But I found him

and reported him to the police, who questioned him and let him go."

"Got your man and they put him on the streets again. Typical." She shook her head. "Well, I'm glad my sketch worked. Maybe now he'll be nailed for something else."

"Oh, yes."

She picked up her sketch pad. "You had a lot of emotion toward the last subject. Who's the next one?"

"A woman. I've seen her only twice, but recently."

"Hmm." Janice was in her interviewing mode. Abstracted, impersonal, as acutely attuned to his unspoken testimony as a Geiger counter is to buried uranium.

Getting up the courage to see her again, letting her draw conclusions from his description was like going to confession, Matt decided. He expected another ordeal, but he was grateful she was as good as she was at it.

"A woman." Her mouth quirked into a tiny smile. He saw that she was curious about this "wanted" woman, almost as curious about her as she was about him. "For an ordinary citizen, you require an extraordinary amount of police services."

"Yeah." He wanted to adjust his position, but realized it would dislodge the tapes, which itched constantly now, marking his skin more virulently than the healing gash. "She's hard to describe. I guess it's because she'd be considered beautiful, and that's so vague."

"You're absolutely right. Regular features have no character, but even the most perfect face has its quirks. Start with the shape of her face, her coloring."

"Her features were very sculpted, but pointed."

"Good bones."

"Her head was small, her neck rather long and thin. Snow White coloring, but not wide-eyed like Snow White."

"Not looking for a handsome prince, huh?"

"Not looking for anything predictable. Black hair. Thick, with a harsh sheen. Not pretty hair, not pliant."

Janice nodded, her fingers sweeping over the porous paper. Her pencil hissing soft as a serpent on each long stroke.

"Odd eyes. Blue-green. Could be contact lenses. The only

other creature I've heard of with aqua eyes is a purebred cat. A shaded silver Persian."

" 'Creature.' An odd thing to call her."

Matt considered it a compliment, under the circumstances. "Chin?"

"Small, like everything else about her. Nose, ears small. Tidy, neat. Even her teeth were unusually tiny. Made you realize why people used to compare them to pearls."

"Nose straight, or turned up?"

"I . . . didn't notice. Straight, I think."

"Lips?"

"She wore little makeup, or maybe little noticeable makeup. I'm not an expert, but I'd suspect she had on more than I thought. *And her lipstick hadn't rubbed off when she'd kissed him.* He'd noticed that hours later in the bathroom mirror when he was changing his dressing for the first time.

"She made you distinctly uncomfortable."

Matt laughed, though it hurt. "That was her intention, but I think that's her intention with everyone. Every man, anyway."

"A femme fatale?"

He nodded slowly, pleased that she was putting his impressions into words as well as pencil strokes. "So focused. So . . . manipulative."

"Weight and height?"

He understood now that she needed to visualize the whole person before she could finish the face.

"I'd say she was about five-six. And about fifteen pounds more than a model would be at that height."

"But not plump or blowsy."

"Lord, no! Sleek as a carnivorous otter, if that makes sense."

"Aha! *Now* I can see her. Smug, too, I bet."

"Smug? Certainly . . . knowing."

"Feral. Tidy. Lovely to look at in a self-involved way. We girls have another name for her than femme fatale."

He merely looked puzzled.

"Bitch," Janice said sweetly.

Matt, serious, weighed the term. "Actually, in her case, I think that's too mild."

Janice lifted both eyebrows without comment. She was expertly drawing out his feelings about Kitty to imbue her image with his emotions.

"Perverse," he said suddenly. "She is the most perverse human being I've ever met."

"Do you mean sexually?"

"How could I? I've only seen her twice."

Then he realized that, yes, if he were a man with an ordinary background, he could very well have known her sexual inclinations in two meetings, especially in this town.

A blunder. He felt he ought to blush, and not too long ago could have. But not anymore. Not over such a minor faux pas. He wasn't trying to impress Janice with anything about himself, only to give her all she needed to work with.

"Scarlett O'Hara," she suggested again.

He had seen endless clips of the film's various TV "events" through the years. He thought of Vivien Leigh's pretty, pointed, feral face, and nodded.

"Not a double of Leigh, of course. But very like Scarlett herself."

"Someone who lost something once, long ago, and has never forgotten it."

"Exactly! And she's Irish. Or at least she gave an Irish name."

"Black Irish."

Janice's pencil fairly flew now, her face a mask of satisfied intensity.

When she turned the pad to face him, he was stunned. "That's it. That's her."

Janice shook her head. "No, not yet. Maybe close. But look again. Examine each feature. Eyelashes. What were they like? Thick, black, mascara-coated? Insignificant? That space between the upper lip and the nose. So crucial to good likenesses. The 'blind spot,' I call it, because so few people observe it. Should it be wider? Narrower?

Under her relentless interrogation, Matt found himself nagged into refining the image until, the last time Janice turned it around for his approval, he had to repress a shudder.

Janice noticed. "What did she do to you?"

"I can't go into it."

"You know—," Janice rested an elbow on her bent knee, then braced her face on her hand. "You pay your money and you get the best sketch I can do, but I'm really curious about what you need them for and why these people mean something to you."

"You're too good at what you do."

"Thanks. That's the first time I've been accused of being an artistic overachiever." She smiled until he caught the virus and smiled back.

"I really appreciate your art skills and interviewing technique. Gosh!" He took refuge in his watchface. "It's after eleven-thirty!"

"And you have to be going."

The wry assumption in her voice made him bristle. She was so good at summing up people; he resented being one of her easy reads.

"I was going to say, it's almost lunchtime. Could I treat you?" Then he realized he was in no position to offer anything. "But . . . my motorcycle is out of commission and I don't know any restaurants in this neighborhood—"

"How did you get here then?"

"Cab."

"Say no more. You buy lunch, I'll drive, and I'll drop you wherever you want to go. Fair enough?"

He nodded, pulling out his checkbook and wishing she took credit cards. His account was getting decidedly flat and would deflate a little bit more with lunch. Having a social life was expensive.

"Give me five minutes to freshen up," she said as she took the check. "Just look around. I'm an artist. *Mi casa es su museo.*"

He was too strictly reared to wander her house at will, but he did some minor exploring. More photos of two carefree-looking preteen kids, always a dangerous assumption with kids. Conch shells and other seaside salvages that looked found, rather than bought. Everything bright and somehow California. He wondered suddenly if she would appreciate his Vladimir Kagan sofa . . .

"Ready." She'd switched to one of those long, pleated dark velvet skirts so popular nowadays, topped by a patchwork bomber jacket in brocade and velvet and denim. "We won't go any place too chi-chi. Good southwestern chow. If that's all right."

"Sounds wonderful. I haven't been in Las Vegas that long. I can always learn about a new restaurant."

The red Jeep Cherokee he remembered took them to a strip shopping center about a mile away and a small unpretentious place with lacquered tabletops and pottery napkin rings.

Water glasses came with lime slices, the lunch menu didn't offer an item above ten dollars, and the blackboard listed an awesome number of Mexican and foreign beers. The joint was jumping with a decibel-level so high that it gave you the false sense of a privacy bubble around your own table.

After they'd ordered tasty melanges of salsa, black beans and pico de gallo over the dish of their choice, Janice folded her arms on the tabletop and leaned closer to be heard.

"That woman I just sketched is a piece of work, in the worst sense. What does she have to do with you?"

"You know . . . Effinger was my stepfather."

"Was?"

"You're very quick." Matt sipped the Bohemian beer he had ordered. "I didn't want to tell you. He was found dead early Tuesday morning. The police are proceeding as if it was an unnatural death."

"You're saying he was murdered?" She whistled between her teeth when he nodded. "And the woman?"

"She's the one who told me where to find Effinger. Where to start seriously looking anyway."

"Wow." Janice sat back, away from him, unaware of her withdrawal. "I've sketched the faces of a serial killer or two. But this is the first time that someone has died *after* I've drawn him. Usually my portrait subjects get put away for crimes against other persons."

"Effinger was guilty of that, believe it."

"But you're not a cop, you're not a private detective, right? So why are you hanging out with these unusual suspects? I can't place you. My work has brought me into contact with lots of people in police work and associated professionals. You just don't track. You could be a social worker, or a shrink, or maybe a bounty hunter. I don't know. I'm at a loss, I admit it. If I sketched you again today, you'd be a different man, and that was just—what?—a month or so ago?"

Their food arrived, but Matt didn't feel like eating. He was remembering the awkwardness of their first meeting and last parting, at the door to her bedroom, when he'd sensed he'd be welcome there and had found himself hesitating on the brink of a very fine moral line for the first time in his life.

He'd always owed her an explanation for bolting like that.

"Sure, I strike you as a mystery," he said. "How many ex-priests do you know?"

That floored her. Her plate was going to go home in a Styrofoam box, too. The kids would love it.

"I'm Episcopal," she answered. "Closest thing to Catholic around. But our priests marry and have a families, so there aren't too many exes. You're . . . you were the other kind, right?"

"Right. Roman Catholic."

"How long? Or, I should say, how long have you been out?"

"Lord, it must be . . . ten months."

"So a month ago, you were just coming full term, as it were, newborn at nine months."

Matt looked down at his utterly unappetizing plate, through no fault of its own. "Yeah. Pretty raw."

She nodded, getting the message. "Thanks. You didn't have to tell me. But I . . . need to understand. I must have scared the hell out of you. Oops."

"Hey, priests talk too. Yeah. You did."

"But you came back."

"I needed to."

"I've been good this time, haven't I?"

"Like gold."

"So, do you date?"

"Well, I took my neighbor out for New Year's Eve."

"An eligible young lady, I take it."

"Oh, yeah. I'm beginning to think: aren't they all?"

"Umhmm, I bet you're a real drawing card. Women must be real torn between not knowing whether to mother you or seduce you. Well, if you ever want some company without the pressure—"

"I could do with less pressure."

"Me too."

Suddenly, his hand was pushing the fork around his plate again. "Not too many people know about me. It's not the kind of thing you lay on new acquaintances. Nobody talks about religion much, except born-again Christians, so you don't know who will know what, or even care."

Janice was nibbling at her corn-and-pimiento side dish again. She paused to lean her face into her palm.

"Now I know why I liked you so much. Just think of it! You've never taken out an awkward girl and denied it all around school the next day. You never slept with a woman on the first date and then told everybody what a slut she was. You never had sex without a condom."

He was seriously in danger of blushing again, just when he thought he was permanently cured.

"I've never had a chance to commit any of those social sins," he reminded her. "But I've committed others. And I'm so anxious not to make a mistake in the . . . area you mention, that I'm practically paralyzed. Inaction is not a virtue. You can't resist temptation if you don't expose yourself to it."

"Well," she said, suddenly ploughing into her entree like a lumberjack, "you're just going to have to put yourself in harm's way to find out if you're as good as you look, aren't you, Matt?"

She winked at him over her frosted beer mug.

Chapter 28

A Forced Bulb

A lone security forty-watt lightbulb beams inside the Thrill 'n' Quill, Las Vegas's only bookshop devoted to the mystery and thriller novel, which also has an extensive section of used books on a variety of subjects.

Despite the tepid illumination, I can still spot the familiar but contemptible forms of the stuffed versions of Baker and Taylor, the eponymouse Scottish fold cats who represent a major book distributor also known as B & T. There is little Scottish about these so-called cats, though their tightly folded and crimped ears show a certain characteristic stinginess, like that of a pursed-mouth purse.

I am looking for another and more animated stuffed shirt, this one reputedly among the living: Ingram, the bookstore cat. This dude is one of my regular sources, to both of our regrets. But the Danger Game makes for strange bedfellows. Ingram is of the domestic feline stripe, and far too domestic for my taste. He would not touch a tootsie to the mean streets to save Bastet herself from a mugging. Yet I must that admit that Ingram's bookish habits (he sleeps on them incessantly) come in handy at times, for he has absorbed much arcane knowledge.

I have never tried to roust him after hours, however, and am not sure he has the basic street smarts to open a locked door or to find another means of communication with a visiting client.

I scratch the display window glass, my sharp nails making the high-pitched screeching sound that humans associate with blackboards rubbed the wrong way. There is no way of rousing Miss Maeveleen Pearl, owner of the Thrill 'n' Quill. Unlike her official layabout Ingram, she never sleeps on the premises.

Pretty soon Ingram's tweedy little form is tiptoeing through the tomes. I study some of the mystery titles through which he must thread his circuitous way. One grouping requires mirror shades to take in: it is a neon-covered oasis of books in the new Florida noir genre, each cover boasting various shades of hot pink, slime green and Caribbean turquoise. Then there are the usual darkly dingy covers whose titles begin with "Death in" and "Murder at." And there is, I am happy to note, an attractive assemblage of four-footed sleuths: a rapidly spawning pile of books featuring furry friends from armadillo to zebra, no doubt, although I approve the predominance of my own species among them. Someday I will have to write a book, like Miss Kit and Mr. Max and Miss Temple.

Once he has navigated the window display's bookish obstacle course—and Ingram does not disturb a whisker or dislodge a book during his prissy pussyfooting approach—he sits opposite me and makes with the silent meow. The effect is like watching pheasant under glass yammer at you before you eat it.

So I go into my charade routine: walking to the front door, stalking back; leaping up at the door's glass inset; even disappearing around the corner as if visiting the back of the building.

Have you ever noticed that the most overeducated individuals are often the slowest on the uptake when it comes to deciphering real life? Ingram is one of these fogbound fellows, so wrapped up in his good opinion of himself that he would not wake up and smell the espresso if the entire supply of beans in Columbia erupted like a volcano right on top of the Thrill 'n' Quill.

But finally he manages, with an extremely complicated crick of his neck, to indicate that I might do well to go back and see about scaling the building's north face.

When I get back there, I am not enamored of his suggested entry route. I will have to go straight up a brick wall to get to a ventilation grille, which I will have to work off while clinging to the aforesaid sheer brick.

Well, what the hell. I have not had a good hangnail in weeks.

One would think that Ingram, being the visitee, could at least manage to kick the door open for the visitor, but I do not have much faith in Ingram's ingenuity quotient. That is what you get for being confined to quarters most of your natural life: stunted imagination.

So I baby-crawl my way up the mortar, and find my naked fangs can work out the cheesy aluminum vent that was installed up here a few years after the Flood. Then it is a dark, dusty crawl through a horizontal tunnel that abruptly turns vertical. Luckily, I am well padded and soon am butting one of those lightweight ceiling panels off its metal gridwork. I hop down atop a bookshelf and then down into the artistically cluttered interior of the bookstore. Unfortunately, Ingram is part of the clutter.

"I hope you did not dislodge any spiders," is his greeting.

"Only a few snakes and lizards," I answer, just to watch his back twitch.

"I like to get a solid twelve hours shut-eye," he adds. "So tell me what you want now, and I will do my best to satisfy you and get back to my beauty sleep."

Twelve hours. What a nonlife!

"I need to know about anything called hyacinth."

"I did not know you were interested in horticulture, Louie. Are you perhaps developing some refined interests in view of your upcoming retirement years?"

"Gumshoes do not retire, especially for twelve hours at a stretch. No, I need this dope for a case I am working on."

Ingram shakes his head until his rabies tag chimes; then he leaps atop a desk, following it to another section of the store. I follow the leader, such as he is.

"Hyacinth is a flower, Louie, a lovely fragrant growth with massed blossoms of curling petals. I always think of them as pale blue-purple, but they can be white or yellow as well. They are also of the interesting family of plants that develop from bulbs."

"They need light bulbs to bloom, like shrinking violets or something?"

"Your botanical knowledge is sadly primitive. No, they grow from bulbs, underground self-contained food-storage systems. Remarkable, really."

"What I am looking to find out about hyacinths is how they would figure in a murder."

"I cannot imagine that they would. A more delightful, benign flower cannot be found. But here is the plant section. Look for yourself."

I scan the shelves, seeing a lot of titles mentioning roses and violets. Only one title reads "Bulbs," so I leap right for it and soon have it spread open on the floor.

First I run across a mug shot of the perp I am tracing: a closeup of a field of purple hyacinths on the loose in a garden. A handy rap sheet in the book's back lists the breed's salient characteristics: short (under one foot), partial to hanging out around gardens and rock gardens, sun worshipers, but can also be found in a potted state in ordinary homes. Blossoms from one-to-two inches, but some run over two inches, so these can be swell-headed types. Cocky, you might say. Known for a distinctive body odor.

By now I figure I would recognize one if I found it, but I am still in the dark.

"Other than a tendency to hang out in dark nightspots at certain times of the year, what would these bulb-type characters have to do with a murder? Are they toxic?"

"Not that I have heard, Louie. Your oleander is, of course, and all sorts of common yard and house plants. But I have never heard the hyacinth so described."

"Well, you got a poison how-to book in this place? I thought mystery readers went for that sort of thing."

"Mystery writers certainly do."

"So there are some local ones?"

"Some would-be local ones."

"Hmm. Maybe I could find a partner to write my memoirs with.

My roomie would ordinarily be right for the job, but she is lavishing her talents in another direction at the moment."

Ingram is uninterested in my domestic wrinkles. I secretly suspect that he does not approve of me living with an unmarried woman. He leads me back to the mystery section, but to a series of shelves weighed down with nonfiction. I peruse such titles as *Deadly Doses, Preferred Poisons, Planted Evidence, Murderous Mushrooms,* and the elegantly titled *Spiders and Spitting Toads and Snakes, Oh, My!*

Although I knock off several of these venomous guides, and although I learn that many innocuous plants are thoroughly poisonous, the hyacinth is not among them, although the hydrangea and the heliotrope are. Close, but no cigarette.

When I express my frustration, Ingram sniffs before replying.

"You certainly are a bloodthirsty fellow, Louie. I am afraid that your line of work leads you to look for the worst in everything and everybody. I for one am glad that the fragrant hyacinth has been cleared of wrongdoing despite your best efforts."

This sanctimonious speech is highly irritating. I desperately peruse the shelves one more time until the initials "AMA" leap out at me. We will see what the croakers have to say about this in their guide to "injurious" plants.

I hit pay dirt in the index at the rear. Several citations for hyacinth all lead to a startling conclusion: the hyacinth is not only poisonous, but every cell of it is lethal, and this occurs in a species called "Hyacinth-of-Peru." (To confuse matters, it seems that hyacinth is also referred to as jacinth in some places.)

What is not confusing is the particular toxin the plant dispenses when administered in sufficient quantity: digitalis. I am not a chemist, but it has not escaped me that digitalis is a drug of choice in simulating—or stimulating—heart attacks in victims.

I am not a medical examiner, either, but I would love to see the autopsy report on Mr. Cliff Effinger. Did he die of drowning, or did he die of cardiac arrest in anticipatory fear of drowning? Did anyone look for traces of hyacinth digitalis in his system?

"Is there anything else on hyacinth in this bookstore?" I ask Ingram, letting the AMA book fall shut with a triumphal slap.

"Only a 'hyacinth glass,' which is a two-tiered bulbous bibulous vessel for containing and rooting hyacinth bulbs."

"I do not believe I am interested in 'two-tiered bulbous bibulous vessels,' which in my book are dim bulbs indeed."

I stare at Ingram so that he realizes I am obliquely referring to the biggest dim bulb of all, Ingram himself.

He clears his throat, confounded that my slapdash search has unearthed information he was not privy to.

"I can do no more for you," he concludes.

He is right, except for one thing. "You can find me the key to the front door. I do not plan on making like an earthworm and wiggling my way back up the ventilation shaft."

"You cannot unlock the door and then open it! And what will Miss Maeveleen say when she finds the shop unlocked tomorrow?"

"Watch me. And . . . as to what she will say, maybe she will get a watchdog."

So I leave Ingram gibbering over his botanical texts. He reminds me of that famous mystery dude of old, Brother Caedfal. Ingram is not only celibate in the extreme, he is more at home flipping through the photographs of flowers than tiptoeing through the tulips in person. What a sad lot, who never stop to sniff the snapdragons.

Since Ingram claims he cannot remember where the door key is kept, I am forced to retrace my entry route. While writhing through the duct, I review what I have learned. Although the hyacinth/digitalis connection is interesting, I do not see what good this outpouring of information on flora large and small is going to do me. I amble toward the Strip, hoping that a little noise and naughtiness will clear my overburdened brain.

And then I look up and see it.

Right before my eyes. A billboard advertising a Downtown lounge show. The main attraction is some shady lady in a chiffon robe that looks as though it has been through an accountant's shredder on April 14. She is no doubt some piece of cheesecake worth lingering over if you are on a human diet, but my eyes are riveted by a smaller, furrier figure in a corner of the billboard.

This is an Oriental dish wearing a skintight custom-fitted catsuit of custard-colored velour, with lavender velvet gloves, racy hock-high hose and a kinky velvet mask covering her eyes and ears that matches the pronounced kink in her lilac-velvet tail. Her eyes, seen through the purple haze of her mask, are a piercing china blue and slitted thinner than the steel-blue of a straight-edge razor blade. She is obviously used to being in the bright lights.

Of course I have already read the words two feet high above the preening females of their respective species. This is what they say: SPICE AND SPECTACLE! TAKE THE RISK AND TASTE THE MAGIC. SHANGRI-LA AND HYACINTH. NIGHTLY AT THE OPIUM DEN.

Here is a bit of Hyacinth any gumshoe worth his unfiltered Lucky Strikes will burn rubber to rush right over and investigate extremely closely: a lilac-point Siamese who moonlights as a lady magician's assistant. Is this babe up my alley, or what?

Chapter 29

Confession Time No. 9

"Here's my dirty little secret."

Matt Devine, not waiting to be invited in, or asked to sit down or offered coffee, tea or vodka, set the rolled sketch on Temple's kitchen counter.

"The original sketch of Effinger?" Temple unrolled it delicately. Matt's call advising of his imminent arrival had been businesslike, terse and so very unlike him.

"No. It's a new one."

But Temple wasn't listening. She was literally struck dumb by the compelling portrait of a beautiful woman.

"Who on earth is this?"

"Good question. Two weeks ago I would have said my guardian angel. She was the woman who gave the lead on Effinger."

"And now you wish she had never pointed you in that direction?"

"Right. But you're concluding that for the wrong reason. She nails down my alibi for Effinger's death, quite literally."

"But you no longer think she's your guardian angel?"

"Now I think she's the devil." He sighed. "Temple, I gave you hell for hiding what Effinger did to you. But ever since the very next day, I've been hiding what this Kitty O'Connor did to me."

"What?"

Temple couldn't take her eyes off the sketch. The face was schizophrenically hypnotic. Perfectly symmetrical at first glance, then oddly off-kilter the more you looked at it. Despite her best efforts to be impartial, Temple probably felt she was seeing an ideal female face someone had dreamed up from anything but life. If this woman really looked this good . . . the competitive clutch in Temple's stomach was nothing that Max Kinsella's girl-friend should be feeling.

"This," Matt said, referring to his hidden truth.

She turned to see that he had pulled up his beige sweater on the right, and that a piece of paper adhered at an angle to his ribs. Not paper, a huge gauze pad.

"Matt—?"

He was pulling off tabs of white tape with no regard to tape burns, revealing a long, puffy dark scab imbedded in red, infected flesh.

"Oh, my God." Temple, like all gawkers at other people's accidents, was repulsed, awed and felt obligated to interfere. Her fingertips touched the hot pink skin, but Matt jerked away.

"It's pretty much closed now," he said. "The infection isn't spreading. I avoided going to an emergency room so I wouldn't have to explain myself. No stitches."

"My God! She stabbed you? Why?"

"We think a razor slash. I didn't feel it at first. And why? Apparently I wasn't as dangerous as she thought. Apparently she gave me Effinger's location because she took me for a hit man."

"We?"

"Bennie. One of the hot-line volunteers. He's a sixties grad and knew an . . . alternative doctor. Stereotypical Hispanic. Lots of knife cuts in that culture, right? Bennie saved my life, or at least my sanity."

"New Year's Day night."

"Right."

"The night Effinger was killed. Oh! Listen, Matt, maybe you better sit down."

"I've been sitting down—and getting up—very carefully, ever since it happened."

"Do you want . . . something to drink, eat?"

"I don't need nursing. I need . . . absolution."

"From whom?"

"You."

"Me?"

"I bit your head off for concealing Effinger's attack, ruined our evening out, even went home to pout. Then I got attacked, by a woman yet, and I did the same thing. Let's say I understand now. I got angry at you because I've been there, done that, and didn't know I was about to do it again. It's hard to admit you were taken advantage of like that, abused like that. It's . . . embarrassing."

Temple nodded. "You said it when I was cornered in that parking garage last fall. If you've been victimized, you'll react like a victim. You'll run, you'll hide, you'll try to pretend it was nothing. Can I at least persuade you to sit down? You probably need the practice."

He slapped the tape ends back into place, pulled down the sweater, and followed her into the living room.

Temple carried Miss Kitty in her extended arms, as if they were waltzing together in a weird way. "I want to examine this baby under a good light." She turned up the floor lamp before sitting next to the sofa arm. "This the same artist who sketched Effinger?"

Matt nodded.

"She's good. Caught that unpredictable edge behind the dropdead looks. Did this Kitty O'Connor, if that's her real name, really look this gorgeous?"

"I suppose, but I don't see looks; honestly, I see past them, because I wish other people would see past mine. . . . she made me uneasy from the first. I suppose a really fine pistol is beautiful

when it's pointing right at you, but you'd have to have a very detached point of view."

"What was her connection to Effinger?"

"I don't know. I know now that she's driven by intense
hate. She told me I'd killed my first man just before she cut me.
Obviously, she was referring to Effinger. She wants me to feel
guilty for his death, because I *didn't* kill him. Perverse philosophy,
isn't it?"

"If she was there to attack you, then she couldn't have killed
him herself."

"Why not? She caught me at three A.M. just as I was leaving
work. According to Molina, Effinger was dead by then."

"She could have come from killing him. I wish we knew how he
died!"

"You're thinking he was slashed to death? When I saw the body
I didn't notice any marks on what I could see of it."

"You didn't see his ribs, I bet."

"No." Matt's hand reached for his side, an unconscious gesture
of the past few days. Breathing still hurt, but he was getting used
to that. At least he was still breathing. Effinger sure wasn't. "I
don't know what we can do to find out Effinger's manner of death,
other than asking Molina. She talk to you yet?"

"Not yet. Probably wants me to squirm. Maybe I can pump her,
but there is another way to find out how Effinger died."

"How?"

"Max."

"Keep him out of it. And don't tell him what happened to me."

"It might be important. Max knows a lot of . . . strange things.
And Effinger is his business, too. The first casino-ceiling death is
what forced him to run and hide."

"Because he did it, or because he didn't?"

"Naturally, I assumed—"

"But has he *said?*"

"No. But I don't believe his involvement in these deaths is any
deeper than knowing more than he should about them."

"While we don't know enough." Matt reached for the drawing.
"But keep Miss Kitty out of this. She's my problem."

"Don't want to lose face with Max, huh?"

"This has nothing to do with him. But it's obvious that you still do."

A perfect opening, Temple thought, at the absolutely worst time. While she dithered over his comment, he left, and nothing had changed.

Chapter 30

Love Potion No. 9

I am not one to dilly or dally when a real dilly awaits me.

I hie over to the Opium Den to find that the eight P.M. show is still running, with an "adult" eleven P.M. show up next. I assume the "adult" part is a human euphemism for female upper frontal nudity.

I cannot understand this human male obsession with mammary glands. In my species, the glands in question come in quadruplicate, span upper and lower torso and are of no particular interest to anyone but a litter of kits.

Ah, well, it takes all kinds to populate the planet, and fortunately, some of them are endangered species. I often think the human is the most endangered species of all.

Certainly, when it comes to murder, it is.

I slip backstage. How can I lose? The lights are dim; I am low and dark and soft-footed.

Luck is with me; Miss Shangri-La's dressing room door is indicated with her name over the image of a wing-extended bat.

(The bat is not a figure of blood-sucking in Asian mythology, but one of good fortune. To this I say: good luck!)

I nudge my way within to find the usual dressing room. Among the strewn costumes and magical props I find the dressing table, and find upon it the remnants of a woman: false fingernails as long as staple guns, hanks of jet-black hair, hair picks sharp and long as daggers dangling decorations; open makeup tins.

And, among it all, extending long, red-painted nails to roll a tin makeup cover over the dressing table edge, is the lady of the billboard, said Hyacinth.

I manage to catch the tin circle before it hits the floor.

She is long, lean and lithe. Looks like she was painted by that cretin who got a Spanish nickname: El Greco. Someone has affixed pixels of purple glitter to the lilac-tinted mask surrounding her arctic-blue eyes.

She hisses at me. "Give that back! It belongs to me."

"It belongs to your mistress, the lovely Shangri-La."

"At least you can see. What are you doing here? We have bodyguards. They will break your bones and serve your tail to a monkey's bastard."

I blink. This lady is not like any I have met before.

"I take it that you are Hyacinth."

She sweeps a clatter of makeup tins off the dressing table with a swish of her angry, crooked tail. "I am also called Shanghai Showblossom and Blood Orchid. I have many names, for the line of my ancestors is long and noble and sometimes infamous. Who are you?"

"The name is Louie. Midnight Louie."

"This is it? What is your bloodline?"

"What is written in my shivs." These I flick out, fast. I do not normally flash my assets, but I feel it is important to impress this unimpressed but impressive lady.

She leaps to the floor like a falling cut-velvet scarf: half air, half illusion, all pussycat.

She is writhing around me, brushing the elegant buzzcut of her short fur against me. "I have not heard of you in this town before."

"How long have you been here?"

"Two weeks."

"Well, then. And I like to keep a low profile."

"A low profile is not always possible in Las Vegas."

"Particularly when you are a world-famous performer. I had no idea Siegfried and Roy's royal white tigers had such lissome competition."

"Have you seen me perform?" She is purring now. Flattery is a weapon too.

"Not on stage, Sister Showblossom, but I bet it is a treat."

"I can get you a free pass."

"All my passes are free."

"You are so bad." She flicks her tail-tip in my face.

I can tell she likes me, and try not to sneeze. Sneezing is not noir.

"Hyacinth is such an unusual name. How did you get it?"

She sits, wraps that warped tail around her slim ankles and eyes me from under glitter-dusted lashes. "Actually, it is only one of my names, and it is due to something naughty."

"I am always in the mood for something naughty."

Her purr intensifies. "A man was threatening my mistress. He did not know I was in the room, high atop a chiffonier."

I refrain from asking what a chiffonier is.

"I leap down upon him, all claws extended, screaming the battle cry of my kind. He died of a heart attack, but his face was a star sapphire of scratches. Since that time, my mistress continues to dip my nails in curare whenever she repaints them."

She flexes the blood-red shivs on her forefeet. Remind me not to encourage this tootsie to slap my face.

"I still do not understand how that admirable deed got you the name 'Hyacinth.'"

"It refers to an attribute of hyacinth to deal death that few know about."

I do not tip my hand. "The name suits you," I say. "How long have you assisted your mistress, on stage and off?"

"Since I was a tiny kit weaned from mother's milk onto bat's blood."

Yech! They eat some strange things in the Orient. In Asia, excuse me. Asia Minor and Major. Yet who am I to sneer at a true carnivore? I used to be one myself when I did not know better or realize that ready-made food was to be gotten for the begging. I am sure that this dame would not eat Free-to-be-Feline to save her soul, if she had one.

"Your mistress is a magician. That is an unusual profession for a lady, and for a lady of the Asian persuasion."

"She is a most unusual lady. But you will meet her in a moment."

I turn. I am not sure I am ready to reveal my uninvited presence.

"There are no secrets between us," Hyacinth hisses behind me. "She will be most interested that I have attracted an admirer."

"That cannot be an unusual occurrence."

She purrs again, and boxes me on the face, curare-dipped claws in. I have managed to dodge just enough that her shivs only stir my whiskers.

"Louie. Midnight Louie. You are fast for one of your venerable age and weight."

"I am no sumu wrestler," say I modestly.

And then the dressing room door opens. Perhaps thunder and lightning drive it back against the wall. I cannot be sure.

A figure stands motionless in the doorway, but the diaphanous garments shrouding it like a ghost's cerements move constantly, as if in a wind.

The face is a demonic mask in the manner of a Chinese ghost: rice-powder pale complexion with rose-petal blush from cheeks to temples. The eyes and eyebrows are drawn in kohl, a stylized stage makeup that tilts these facial features into a piquant exaggeration.

Her lips are red, and her hands are tipped in scarlet-enameled mandarin nails a full four inches long.

Shangri-La. An ambiguous name. Not Chinese, not Japanese. Not Siamese, any more than Hyacinth is.

"A black cat," the lady magician declares, regarding me with pleasure. "And still alive, despite intruding. Hyacinth, you must introduce me to your new friend."

Hyacinth screams and leaps toward Shangri-La.

I expect to hear chiffon rent, at least. But Hyacinth has landed feather-soft on the woman's shoulder, and rubs her face against the ruddy cheekbone as if confiding a secret.

Shangri-La strides to her dressing table, scratching Hyacinth's chin with her truly awesome shivs.

"You naughty kitten!" she chides. "You have been playing in my paint boxes again. Mei!" she calls.

A young woman in black satin pajamas bustles in from the hall beyond, as if she had been waiting there, or had been summoned like a demon.

"My makeup." Shangri-La gestures theatrically with her shiv-heavy fingers.

The woman bows and scrapes along the floor, retrieving Hyacinth's playthings.

"Up here, cat!" Shangri-La's endless nails tap the dressing table top.

I leap in a bound that lands me amid the clutter without disarranging anything.

"More agile than you look." The painted face smiles at me. "Hyacinth is not usually so tolerant." Her shivs scratch me behind the ears until I purr despite myself.

She nods. "A good show tonight. And another to do. Hyacinth, if you must entertain friends, make sure they are gone by eleven."

Hyacinth listens sagely, her incredibly narrow head almost nodding.

It is as if I see the lithe Hyacinth in a funhouse mirror; her entire figure is a distortion, as the extreme leanness of human fashion models elevates malnutrition into a virtue.

I do not like these lean and hungry ladies from the East. I do not like their screeching voices and imperious manners and lethal shivs. If this is the Hyacinth referred to in Effinger's pocket, she might even be a trained assassin. What is the difference between nails dipped in curare and the digitalis concentration of hyacinth oil?

I may be looking at a murderer, and it is not human: it is purely, inescapably feline.

Hyacinth regards me with slitted eyes, both horizontally without, and vertically within, and purrs. In her content at my successful introduction to her mistress, her painted nails contract. In and out.

In and out.

Chapter 31

Nigh Noon

At high noon the next day, Temple's phone rang.

She wasn't surprised that Lieutenant C. R. Molina was on the line's other end, requesting an audience.

Actually Lieutenant C. R. Molina was demanding an interrogation.

"Here? In half an hour? Sure. I appreciate curb service."

Temple hardly knew what to do with herself while preparing for a visit from the local constabulary. She took a white-glove stroll through her rooms. (Actually, she darted through, picking up newspapers and straightening gewgaws.)

She decided she needed a pizza for lunch. She decided her nails needed doing, but there was no time. She concluded that it would be easier to get her story straight, if only she knew what part of it she needed to embroider: the part where she had no alibi for Effinger's death because she was sleeping with Max at the time (and she certainly couldn't admit that to Molina), or the part where Max had no alibi for Effinger's death because he was sleeping with her at the time (but she was awake and Max was not necessarily there at the time).

Temple was a wee bit nervous. Ordinarily, Molina couldn't do that to her. But ordinarily Temple's future did not turn on sleeping with Max (whose very presence and location in Las Vegas were sacred trusts for her) and being able to prove it.

Even the doorbell sounded paranoid instead of mellow when Molina punched it. Temple just knew Molina punched it. She was the type to abuse even a vintage doorbell. A doorbell that was probably older than Molina was. Bully!

In this state of anthropomorphic snit on behalf of her doorbell, Temple opened her door.

She had forgotten how bloody tall the lady lieutenant was, or how thick and uncompromising her eyebrows were.

Molina entered without invitation, but only advanced eight steps into the room before turning on Temple.

"Where are your glasses?"

"I've switched to contact lenses. Sorry. Is that a crime or misdemeanor?"

"Neither. You just look different. Why didn't you wear contacts before?"

"Simple. My eyes were too sensitive to handle all those chemical baths. But I guess they've come up with new formulas. They're working so far."

Molina stalked into the living room. What else could she do in those clunky-heeled oxfords so popular now?

"You know Effinger is dead, of course."

"Of course." Temple sat down, but Molina didn't.

"Can you account for your whereabouts around midnight the night of January one?"

"New Year's Day night?"

"Right."

"Ah, yes and no."

"Yes first."

"I was here asleep in my condominium."

"The no?"

"I was here solo."

"No witnesses."

"Sadly, no."

"Midnight Louie?"

"Out on errands of a peculiarly repellent nature."

Molina's midnight-margarita eyes narrowed to catlike slits, it seemed. "You speak truer than you know."

"What do you mean?"

Molina only smiled, meanly, as she circled the love seat. "Where's Midnight Louie now?"

"I don't know. He does come and go. I have to ask: why do you associate me with Effinger? Or his death?"

"I don't do it; he did."

"Effinger? How? He said something before he died?"

"Now that's interesting. What would he have to say about you at any time?"

"I don't know. But you said he implicated me."

"Not personally." Molina smiled. It was not a reassuring expression. "I must say that coming here to see you personally was an inspired idea. I ran into your landlady in the lobby."

"Electra."

"The very one. She was happy to see me."

"Oh?"

"She was delighted that you had decided to report your assault in the Circle Ritz parking lot."

Temple fell suddenly silent.

"She was happy that the evil stepfather wouldn't be allowed to get away with it. I'd say he wasn't."

"It wasn't much of an assault. Most of the damage came from getting away."

"Then you weren't too disabled to get out and about New Year's Day night."

"But I wasn't out and about. I was . . . home."

Molina smiled too tolerantly to indicate belief. "Assault aside, a note in his pocket implicated you."

"A note? To me?"

"Not precisely."

"Could you tell me, precisely?"

"No."

"Could you at least tell me how Mr. Effinger died?"

"Mr. Effinger. I imagine that's a new one for him, even dead. His death was bizarre, to say the least."

"I read the item in the newspaper."

"He was . . . affixed to the prow of the fatal barge and was sub-merged with it."

"So he drowned?"

"Not necessarily."

"He was already dead, of course, before the barge descended."

"Not necessarily."

Temple considered the options. "I don't look like someone who could 'affix' a grown man to the prow of a barge."

"You could have had an assistant, or vice versa."

"You don't really believe that."

"All I know for a fact is that the deceased carried a reference to you in his pants pocket. And now I learn, not from you, that he had assaulted you recently. And I know that you have friends very capable of teaching him a lesson."

"What was on the note? My name and phone number?"

Molina shook her head.

"Then what?"

"I can't say. I can only ask if you still insist that you were nowhere near the Oasis dock that night."

"I swear to God, I wasn't there."

Molina nodded, finished, if not satisfied. She headed for the door. There she paused for a parting shot.

"Then why was your cat, Midnight Louie, on the scene?"

Temple was speechless.

"Accompanied by the Crystal Phoenix mascot, one Midnight Louise."

"I . . . I'm not responsible for where cats go, or when."

Molina left. Leaving Temple to ponder her earlier question: where was Midnight Louie now?

Chapter 32

Checkmatt

Matt thought nothing of answering his doorbell, even though it seldom rang, perhaps because it was always either Electra or Temple, and he had just seen Temple, so it had to be Electra.

He couldn't have been more surprised if it had been Kitty O'Connor.

"Just a few questions," Molina said, walking in uninvited, and looking around even more uninvited. "My, my."

She stopped in the foyer to survey his new living room suite.

Matt eyed it past her shoulder and admitted to being impressed. The fifties sofa snaked through the room like a red upholstered highway, islands of lamp and table to either side.

An especially effective touch was the black cat sprawled on the sofa end.

"Who's your decorator?"

"Mr. or Ms. Goodwill. With a little push from Temple."

"And the cat is on loan to add to the ambiance?"

"I didn't think 'ambiance' was in your vocabulary, Lieutenant."

"Every time I visit the Circle Ritz, I add new words to my vocabulary. Like genius loci."

"You've got me there. And it's even in my native Latin."

Molina nodded at the cat. "You know the literal meaning: a local deity; you just don't recognize the avatar. What's he doing here?"

"Louie? What does any cat do anywhere? He's been showing up lately; so often that I've taken to leaving the bathroom window open, like Temple does."

"From her house to your house." Molina flashed him a bolt from her medicinal-strength baby blues. "Wonder what cat snit is driving him from his former home, sweet home? Maybe a territorial dispute?"

"With a man rather than a mouse, you think?" Matt shrugged, even though it pulled like a steam burn on his taped bandage. "None of my business."

"Mine, though." Molina grinned. "And you're my business too. My official business."

She pulled a narrow reporter's notebook from her jacket pocket, along with a pen. "Don't worry. I'm not going to sit on that thing with Midnight Louie. But you can."

Matt did.

"Bienvenido," she announced ominously. "Nice name. Welcoming name. Nice fellow. A little anxious about the fuzz. Sixties reflex. Tends to say more than he has to."

"He did verify that I was hard at work from seven to three?"

"Oh, yes. You are a sterling worker." She flashed him a smile. "I would expect no less. Just as Bennie Cordova is a sterling witness."

Matt shifted on the sofa. It was an unyielding architectural form, elegant but unforgiving. He tended to slump when sitting on it, and that didn't help his taped-together wound.

"So what did Bennie say?"

"Way too much. One of those watched pots that starts out impossibly slow to come to a boil, but then bubbles over and over and over when it gets there."

"I know Bennie."

"Then you know what he told me, all in the effort of clearing you of possibly being anywhere else not only around midnight but well into the next day."

Matt sighed.

"Why didn't you tell me in my office?"

"What?"

"The assault. Why didn't you report it to the police the next day? Why didn't you get to an emergency room that night, or a private physician the next day? Why suffer in silence, other than you've had the training for it?"

Matt laced his fingers together and studied them, the secular form of prayer.

"It's not anybody's business."

"With Clifton Effinger dead, it is."

"Clifton. I'd forgotten that was his full name."

"Clifton."

"Obviously, I couldn't have had anything to do with it."

"Still, you turn up wounded at around the same time the Effinger killing went down."

"Then it *was* murder. You're not fully candid with me, either."

"I don't have to be."

"Look, this was a private—"

"Private what? No attack is private. If it was just a mugging, why not race to the ER, run to file a police report, list the missing money?"

"Nothing was missing, except my blood."

"So you frightened the mugger off before he got anything?"

Matt was tempted to agree, but he always had trouble lying to Molina. Maybe she reminded him of the younger Sister Mary Seraphina.

"Martial Arts Matt to the self-defense?"

She was actually teasing him, which made him feel even guiltier.

"No, I didn't do a damn thing to defend myself. I didn't even know I'd been hit until afterward."

"Ah." Molina sat down, notebook on her trousered knees. "That's why the big secret. Plain old macho mania. You didn't want to admit you'd been sucker-punched."

Matt remained silent. There was a lot more he didn't want to admit.

"So now you're stonewalling: nothing happened. Nothing the police need to know about. Sounds familiar. You're starting to develop unpleasant habits from associating with Miss Barr, such as keeping things from the police."

Matt resisted the impulse to lift his hand to guard his side from her probing. "It's not something you easily tell even your confessor."

"So what's a mugging? I get unlikely confessions all the time."

His slow sigh of surrender pulled each of the tapes taut, like tiny thorns. *Remember me, you bastard.*

"If you want to call it macho anything, I guess it might support your theory if I tell you the mugger was a woman."

"A woman? Knifed you? Street person?"

Matt laughed. "Like Elle MacPherson is a street person."

Molina frowned, but not at what Matt expected her to react to. "How do you know who Elle MacPherson is?"

"Got a TV. Got a remote control. Sometimes don't get the news turned off fast enough to avoid *A Current Affair.*"

"It's hard to keep 'em down in the rectory, once they've seen MTV. So. Your mugger was a chic street person. I can see you might be a bit chagrined to report a female mugger. Big, strong martial arts expert like you. So that's it. You swear that this incident had nothing to do with the Effinger death?"

"You'd make a good confessor. What do I get for withholding the facts? Six Hail Marys and an Our Father?"

"You get off the hook."

"Put me back on."

She had been stuffing the notebook and pen back into her side pocket, but now she stopped. "What?"

"I can't swear it had nothing to do with Effinger. It had a lot to do with him. I just don't know what."

"Speak," she barked, as if addressing a particularly intelligent dog.

So Matt told her of Kitty O'Connor's miraculous appearance by the Circle Ritz pool ten days ago, with a location for him to begin looking for Effinger.

"You felt from the beginning she was challenging you?"

"It was as if we were talking on two different planes, or from two different planets maybe. Like she wouldn't give me the info on Effinger unless I passed some test of hers. So I let her see my anger, I . . . played it like she wanted it. Maybe meaner than I was."

Molina nodded.

"Then, when she came back—it was like I had betrayed her, her expectations. I asked if she had mistaken me for a hit man, and when I told her that I hardly would kill anyone, that I had been a priest until recently . . . she reviled priests. Called them murderers and fornicators. She said I was like that too, that I'd just killed my first man tonight. And then she cut me. I told the truth. I didn't feel it, didn't understand it, any of it, until she was gone."

Molina had stopped taking notes, and was sitting rapt, spell-bound. "Fascinating." Matt doubted that she often slowed to a complete stop over the mystery of anybody's behavior. "What a psycho."

"Is that what she is? I kind of took her for a demon of some kind, maybe just a minor one, but she sure raked me over the coals."

"How?"

"She was so taunting . . . so personally taunting. As if she thought she knew me. This is a woman who would have respected me if I was a killer, but loathed me for having been a priest."

"How did she taunt you?"

Matt hesitated. The details were deeply disturbing. He would never tell Temple. Molina was far less on his side, but she had been reared Catholic; she knew the ambiance. She knew the lingo. She would understand the implications.

"She mocked me. Mocked everything that's sacred to me. Knew just how to do it."

Molina considered the implications. She wasn't stupid. "So she didn't mock your manhood—"

He wasn't going to confess.

She inhaled the insight like pure oxygen. "—but your priest-hood."

Trust Molina to understand that they were, and were not, the same thing.

"And then she stuck you." She frowned. "Let's see."

He lifted the shirt and pulled away the already loosened tapes, feeling exposed far more than skin-deep.

Molina was as clinical as any battlefield medic. "Straight edge. Not deep, but deep enough. Long, but not that long. Just about right." She looked away as he dropped the sweater back over the wound like a curtain.

"You, my friend, have been the victim of a hate crime. I can pursue that."

"The weirdest thing was, she kissed me while she did it. It was a kind of farewell."

Molina stood, snapping her notebook shut as if it had jaws. "We'll get the bitch."

He blinked, and she laughed. "I can do squad-room rap as well as the next cop. I've just got an impressionable preteen daughter to think about. Look at it this way. You did not suffer in vain. We can swear out an assault complaint on . . . the little darling."

"An assault complaint? A woman against a man? I don't think—"

"Now we get to the manhood part, right?"

"Not exactly. I just don't think it sounds credible. This is a woman I've never met before except in answer to a missing-person quest of mine. It doesn't make sense."

"It's a crime. It doesn't have to make sense. Listen, Devine, don't go wishy-washy on me. Effinger's dead. You're a prime suspect in any cop's rule book. This lethal lady and her razor could get the heat off you. Don't let her get away with hit-and-run."

"You're really ticked off about this."

"You bet I am. She's a sicko, at the very least. And she smells of out-of-town interests."

"You think *she's* a hit woman?"

"Don't sound so incredulous. Women can do everything nowadays, you know, hunt as well as be hunted. But, no. You'd be dead if she was, which was one of the messages she was sending. She kiss as good as she cut?"

He shook his head. "It was symbolic, like the razor."

Molina nodded. "A sicko. Although how you would know the difference, I'd like to know."

Sardonic was her hard-bitten style of humor. Interrogation over.

"Think about swearing out a complaint. You have a name, for what it's worth, and a description," she added. "You might find it to your advantage. Statute of limitations doesn't run out for some time, and you'll be scarred for life."

"So what's new?"

She shrugged. She was done probing his wounds. Like a deliberately lousy surgeon, she had left a scalpel sewn in to irritate the site until he came back for corrective surgery. Maybe.

Matt wondered if he should have revealed the sketch of Kitty O'Connor and let Molina really go to work. He wondered if he should have repeated, and recorded the final humiliation, the words the woman had breathed at him as she departed, when he first felt the liquid warmth oozing onto his fingers and hadn't yet grasped what it was.

Remember me, you bastard.

Was that a symbolic attack too? Or worse?

Because, as few people outside a very small neighborhood in Chicago—and the late Effinger—knew, he was indeed a bastard.

Quite literally.

Chapter 33

Forbidden Plant

"Yo, Sherlock!"

"Temple?"

Max sounded surprised by her gung-ho tone.

"I've read your manuscript and I've spent far too many hours at the library looking up forms of hyacinth. Does Gandolph have any books there that might pertain to hyacinths?"

"Nothing flowery. But what about the manuscript?"

"What about it?"

"Can it be saved?"

"Modest Max. Perhaps. What are you going to give me for dinner?"

"What can you bring?"

"Boston Market?"

A pause. "Home cooking isn't my style, but beggars can't be choosers. Just don't spill anything on the manuscript."

"You can always print out another one."

"I know, but it doesn't feel that duplicatable."

Temple smiled. Max was used to making magic out of transient impressions and other people's blind spots. The concrete power of words awed him. Maybe he understood her bailiwick better now.

"Be over in half an hour."

Temple packed her tote bag and took an uneasy tour of the apartment. Louie was certainly making himself scarce lately. She wondered if he were trying to send a message.

But she had another message to decipher. Hyacinth.

She tucked a couple of flower books from the library into her tote along with Max's manuscript, checked to make sure one last time that Louie's bathroom window was ajar, and then locked the condominium on the way out.

She had to admit to a snare-drum rattle of excitement. Going over to Max's place felt like Minneapolis all over again. Just meeting Max, going out. Okay, not exactly going out. The only times recently she had gone out with Max it had been a major undercover operation, or a breaking and entering.

Still, they were working on things together. They were working on being together. Temple's red two-inch Cuban heels did a castanet click over the Circle Ritz marble lobby floor. The ghosts of Fred and Ginger and that happy, chattering rhythm followed her to the parking lot.

Even cocking the pepper spray on her keyring as she neared her car couldn't dampen her spirits.

Her long red corduroy skirt refused to dampen its folds to fit into the Storm on the first try. So she collapsed it like a recalcitrant umbrella and then locked herself in, after checking the back seat. Then she sighed. Twilight time. A beautiful January night, with the sun hanging over the western mountains like a bloodshot moon.

It was dusk by the time she pulled into Boston Market's car-jammed lot and inched through the crowded line, buying everything hot and homey, so it would drive Max bananas: corn and meatloaf and mashed potatoes and all that midwinter, Midwestern comfort food.

Loaded with one brown bag, and sure this time that no bogeyman would be lurking by her car, unless he was an escapee from *Night of the Living Dead*, gruesome thought, Temple clicked out to the car, stowed her goods and revved the Storm away from the sun sweltering into a burnt-orange puddle behind the mountains.

The sky was still the faint, pale blue of the madonna's cloak when Temple carefully parked on the border of Max's lot line and carried her burdens to the house.

This time the door was infinitesimally ajar and she glided through without having to shift her packages.

"What?" she asked the darkness inside. "Am I Midnight Louie, with an automatic entrance/exit?"

Max shut the door behind her, and closed her mouth with a kiss as he off-loaded the food bags.

"Editors can be snakes, I understand," he said. "So I left the door open just wide enough to accommodate one."

"Not all editors," Temple protested. "Just a few bad ones. I thought my literary skills were going to be respected around here now that you're an aspiring author."

"I don't know what you think of my opus; until then, I'm prepared to consider you the enemy."

"Ridiculous." Temple followed him into the awesome kitchen. There was something charming about eating fast food in such an intimidating atmosphere of haute cuisine. "You want my opinion, then you shrink from getting it. Listen, if the manuscript stank, I'd return it in a plain manila envelope marked 'Illiterate, irrelevant and immaterial,' so all the neighbors would know."

"Sensitive soul, aren't you?"

Max was pulling out Styrofoam containers and frowning at the contents. "This is like Sunday dinner on the farm, Grant Wood edition."

"Isn't it fun?" Temple didn't wait for an answer, but pulled plates and silverware from drawers and cupboards she had checked out on previous visits.

The baronial breakfast table was of burnt oak, with captain's chairs burly enough for Bluto.

Max was laughing by the time he brought the food to the table, along with a thin elegant bottle of wine from the walk-in wine cellar.

"The sublime and the ridiculous," he announced, setting the bottle on the table with a marked emphasis.

"Who's the sublime and who's the ridiculous."

"We both are both."

The cork teased out of the wine bottle, releasing a dry pungent scent. Temple guessed that this one bottle would have paid for a month's worth of fast-food dinners, but she didn't know, and didn't care.

She searched for her tote bag and found it by the side of her chair.

"Thanks. I suppose you can't wait for this fine cuisine to digest before I get to the manuscript."

Max was staring at the meatloaf as if wondering what to put on it. Perhaps a wig.

"Here's the sauce. It's good, really! Pretend you're having a nice hot meal at home, and dig in."

"That's what this is about, hmm? My missing family dinners. You don't exactly go in for them yourself nowadays."

"No. But I had deli with my aunt in New York. Besides, my taste buds are on Minnesota wintertime, no matter the climate. I've got that squirrel-it-away-for-the-winter mentality."

Max dished up servings from the various steaming boxes.

"All right. I'll load up on starches while you critique the starch out of my manuscript."

"Gee, I wish I had my glasses. I have an absolute craving for frames balancing on my nose as I make my pronouncement."

"I prefer to see your unadorned eyes, all true blue and absolutely honest."

Temple sampled the meatloaf, corn and potatoes before pulling the stack of white pages to her side.

"Well, it's pretty seamless where Gandolph's part ends and yours begins. I like your history of magic and psychic phenomena intro. You need more contemporary examples. And why don't you exploit the Houdini séance?"

"That's . . . still under investigation. I prefer not to give anything away."

"Don't hold back. Put in what you have now. You can always update it later. Houdini is your thread. He should bracket the entire book: the mystery of his magic tricks, the mystery of contacting the dead. He's still the most famous magician of all time, and he ended up fascinated by the hope of contacting the dead, then disgusted by the fraud that passed for psychic power then . . . and now? What would Houdini think of the Russian ESP experiments? Et cetera, et cetera."

"I'd have to . . . rebuild the whole book."

"You've sawed half-naked ladies in two and put them back together again."

"Not since I was seventeen. That's much too obvious to be real magic."

"So's the book as it stands now. It needs more personalization. Maybe you could parallel Houdini's development as an escapologist with your own development as a magician."

"But Temple, a good magician is always both front man and unseen operator. What you're talking about would expose my life, and you know how dangerous that would be."

"Didn't you say the best disguise in Las Vegas is loud? Maybe in magic, it's naked. And you said that revealing yourself as 'just' a magician might disarm all those nasty terrorists out there that don't want to believe you're not an active counter-terrorist."

"It's true. The more I put myself into this book, the more I blow my cover, the less useful I am to anybody."

"Besides, any book is written on water. It can always be changed. Until you sell it, of course."

Max was cutting the meatloaf Continental-style—with his fork in his left hand, his knife in his right—into neat cubes as if it were the finest steak. He didn't seem to be aware that this was no way to treat a nice, mushy, down-home meatloaf.

"And," Temple added, not hampered by having to excessively chew anything on her plate, "it would be really nice to add Orson Welles and this house as a bracketing element too."

"That would really blow my cover!"

"Maybe, by then, you wouldn't need it anymore."

"By . . . when?"

"Oh, the three to four years you'll need to finish the book and find someone to publish it."

"Three to four years?"

"Didn't you say a good illusion takes years to develop?"

Max gave up on the dinner and devoted himself to the wine. "I had no idea you would be such a stern taskmaster when it came to the book."

"You could always publish it yourself, of course."

"I could?"

"All it takes is a little money, and then you wouldn't have to worry about it blowing your cover. It would probably print about twenty-five hundred copies to be sold to a very exclusive readership."

"That's not what I wanted for Gandolph's book."

"Then you must make it yours and Gandolph's book."

"I'll have to think it over."

"Of course. I wouldn't expect to sit down to dinner with you on virtually no notice, throw a major, life-altering proposal your way, and have you fall for it hook, line and signet ring right there and then."

Max winced. "I get it. You accepted my proposal in a spirit of game impulsiveness. I can do no less. Now. What is this about hyacinth?"

"That, you'll be happy to hear, I'm at a loss on."

Max lifted his wine glass so she could mirror his gesture of conciliation.

"Sometimes ignorant women can be very reassuring."

Temple chimed rims with him, watching the opal ring on her finger glitter under the overhead sparkler of light. Everybody had a bailiwick.

First they attacked Gandolph's computer.

"I seem to remember encountering the word 'hyacinth' somewhere in this house when I first came back here," Max said. "Since I've been messing so much with Gandolph's files, I'm wondering if I didn't see it in here."

But a search turned up nothing but a spell-check definition: "any of various bulbous herbs."

"Hyacinth is an herb?" Temple was amazed. "That's news to me."

"What's so special about an herb?"

"Nothing, except that herbs usually have a long history as folk remedies, and I've never heard of hyacinth in that context."

"I've got a dictionary of toxins on hard disc. I'll check that."

"A dictionary of toxins, Max, why?"

"For emergencies?"

He grinned as the file came up and the search program box obscured the regular screen. He stopped grinning when an entry came up.

"Digitalis. It's a potent toxin, our friend the hyacinth plant, though probably in unwieldy amounts if it's to be fatal."

"Max! You're putting down the poor hyacinth because it would take too much of it to kill someone?"

"Efficacious poisons require minute amounts for morbidity, and, of course, the most useful ones are also the least detectable. And perhaps the least well known."

"Like hyacinth, in that regard?"

"Like hyacinth."

"What now?"

Max looked up at her, his narrow face uplit by the computer screen and looking utterly sinister. "Now we consult the magician's grimoires."

"Grimoires," Temple said on the way to Gandolph's storage room, her heel taps far too gay on the hardwood hall floors for this grim errand. "Such a nice, nasty word. What does it mean?"

"A book of spells, of herbal knowledge, of incantations. It sounds better than it is. Any grimoires I've seen were either obvious frauds or benign and boring compendiums of dubious home remedies."

"Did Gandolph really have any?"

"No, but he has 'many a quaint and curious volume of forgotten lore.' "

"Poe man."

"I assume you have suddenly developed a Southern accent."

"Assume your worst. I assume these three open bookcases are it."

"Indeed. I'll skim the top shelves; you do the lower ones."

"Thanks. My knees needed that."

Max suddenly sank to the floor beside her, his joints collapsing like hinges. "We'll start at the bottom and work up, sharing all the way."

"Why does that sound like an indecent proposal?"

"Because it is," he whispered, opening the first book and setting it on her lap. "I suggest we check the indices under H."

"Elementary, my dear Datsun."

Gandolph's books were indeed a fascinating stew of offbeat and even eerie subjects. Rasputin. Judge Crater. Alistair Crowley. Numerology. ESP. Psychics. Freak shows. Graphology. Spirit knockings.

Temple and Max sped-read indexes by the dozen. "Hy" words were at a premium.

"Hypatia," Temple caroled out once.

"Early Christian woman mathematician and martyr," Max mumbled back, absorbed in his own search.

"I wish all mathematicians *would* be martyred," Temple muttered.

"Then who would do your taxes?"

"Jimmy the Greek?"

"I think he died."

"Doesn't matter, according to this book on revenants. He could come back, better than ever."

"I think he died politically incorrect."

"Oh. Then he's beyond any human help."

"Hyperbole," Max suggested hopefully.

"A literary term. It means exaggerated overstatement."

"Like 'you are absolutely too delicious to resist with meatloaf on your breath.' "

"Oh, ick, Max! That sounds like one of those awful mispronounced foreign language sentences that's supposed to say, 'Where is the meat market, onion breath?' "

They laughed so hard that the third shelf of books fell into their laps.

"Oh, this is interesting."

"What?" Max asked.

"Just a book of gemstone lore. I'll look up opal."

"Don't. I can tell you that they're considered unlucky."

"And that's the ring you gave me?"

"I'm not superstitious."

"But *I* might be! Especially after I read this book."

Max's big, bony hand covered the open pages like a shroud over the face of the dead. "Then don't look."

"Call me Pandora. I have an aggravating need to know."

Temple bent her head over the small-print index entries. A check of the copyright page revealed the book to be a 1913 first edition.

She found a string of entries under "Opal," and flipped to the major section.

"Maybe that's why I can finally wear contact lenses," she announced after a couple minutes of silent reading.

Max looked up from his reference book.

"Your opal ring," she explained, waggling the finger it decorated. "According to this book, in the middle ages wearing an opal was regarded as beneficial to the sight. Some even said wearing opals conferred invisibility."

"I could use that."

"Maybe that's why it's the patron stone of thieves."

Temple nodded, already paging through the old volume. She was a sucker for any book title that began *Curious Lore of . . .* and this one, with its frequent footnotes, engraved illustrations and lists of gemstone attributes was a particularly addictive example.

Under "Planetary and Astral Influences" she stumbled across (appropriately) acrostics formed with stones. Acrostics were linked concepts whose first letters spelled out a meaning. Thus,

> Feldspar
> Amethyst
> Idocrase (Huh?)
> Topaz
> Heliotrope

. . . spelled out F-A-I-T-H with their first letters. Eighteenth-century French and English women would wear rings, bracelets and brooches set with these gems in order to give the secret message. However, change one gem and you had quite a different saying. Temple's larcenous mind invented a new quintet:

Topaz
Heliotrope
Idocrase
Emerald
Feldspar

Thief. Or a slightly twisted Feith.
Hope looked a little harder to come by than Faith. She smiled at the obscure or antique-named gems listed:

Hematite
Olivine
Pyrope
Essonite

Luckily, more common alternate gems were given for each motto:

Hyacinth
Opal
Pearl
Emerald

Hyacinth was a gemstone? Be still her beating . . .

Hyacinth
Emerald
Amethyst
Ruby
Topaz!

. . . HEART!
Max looked up from the massive tome table topping his knees. "Something you ate?"

"Heartburn. You're right. Did you know there was a gemstone called hyacinth?"

"Never in a million years."

Temple was fumbling through the index for citations on the gem called "hyacinth."

Max watched her with amusement. "You'll excuse me if I rather doubt that Effinger was carrying the name of a rare precious stone in his pocket."

But Temple was immersed in the long description of jewels in the High Priest's breastplate from the book of Exodus.

There it was, *hyacinthus*, listed among the twelve foundation stones of the New Jerusalem in Revelations as well as on the High Priest's ritual body armor. Granted, various translations from the Hebrew, Greek and Latin through the centuries varied on just what the stones were: sapphire seemed a popular substitute for the more obscure hyacinth or its apparent twin, jacinth.

And lists of birthstones for the various months included hyacinth as a second choice on more than one month.

And in the Sanskrit of India, the hyacinth was a jewel dedicated to a mysterious "dragon," the cause of the periodic eclipses of sun and moon. As such—the embodiment of the evil genius of a great, unseen power—it was a potent talisman against misfortune.

Temple devoured these arcane info-bits and finally spat them out undigested to Max.

"Fascinating," he said in his best Mr. Spock manner. "But I just can't see any of this falderal having anything to do with that animated piece of pond scum called Cliff Effinger."

"No, I can't either. Yet. I'm just happy to find out that the word has some other history than as the name of a boring and innocuous flower."

Max had neglected to drop his eyes to the book he was studying. Instead he was staring into the distance as if much enamored of it.

"On the other hand," he murmured.

Then he was up, so smooth and fast that the abandoned book eased itself shut with a whisper of slick pages.

"What?" Temple sprang up like a raspberry-topped Pop-Tart.

"On the other hand," Max repeated in a more energetic tone, taking hers, "maybe that's where I ran across the word on Gandolph's files. Not in the general folders, but in the directory he labeled " 'Shan.' "

"Na-na?"

He dragged her back to the computer room, scooted a wheeled steno chair under her, then sat down in the computer chair to play the keyboard like piano.

"I didn't think to check the files involving that magician league hocus-pocus."

Temple refrained from offering Matt's definition of the origin of the phrase "hocus-pocus" from the Latin of the Roman Catholic mass: body and blood.

Some info-bits were unwelcome, even in an information age.

"Hmmph." Max sounded grouchy.

"Couldn't find it?"

"Oh, it's here all right. But as vaguely mentioned as the mysterious 'Synth.' "

"What's really bothering you?"

"Heartburn?" he asked wryly. "Meatloaf? Really, Temple."

She shrugged.

Max shook his head, his dark hair as sleek and glossy as Midnight Louie's—Max's long, back-gathered hair serving as the tail to finish off the comparison.

Won't you come home, Midnight Louie? Temple sang inside her head. She already did the cooking, such as it was, and she paid the rent.

"I don't like it." Max pushed back, making the chair squeak for mercy. "What does this mumbo jumbo of Gandolph's have to do with what lowlife Cliff Effinger was carrying around in a note in his pocket?"

"I was also mentioned in that note, somehow."

"How do you know?"

"I forgot to mention it. Molina paid me a surprise interrogation today. Unfortunately, Electra thought she was there to follow up on Effinger's assault on me, so Molina now knows that I have plenty of motive to wish him ill."

"And me more motive."

"And Matt even more motive than you."

"All right! We're all motivated to death! What about the note mentioning you?"

"She wouldn't say exactly how I was mentioned, but admitted to 'hyacinth.' And she did tell me how Effinger died."

"Forgot to mention that too?"

"I *was* coming to see you."

"Awwwww. Couldn't think of anything else, poor baby. So . . . how did he die?"

"Via barge. Only he was 'affixed' to the boat and sank with it during the programmed descent."

" 'Affixed?' That was Molina's word for it?"

Temple nodded glumly. "Would I forget a weird description like that? Plus, Louie and his little friend from the Crystal Phoenix were at the scene of the crime."

"Louie? And . . . who?"

"This black female cat that showed up at the Phoenix after he moved on. I didn't think they got along."

"They're both cats; of course they get along. But why at the Oasis, on the very scene of Effinger's dramatic demise?"

"I don't know. Molina seemed a little spooked by it, though."

"Molina? Spooked?" Max snorted.

"I know it's hard to believe. Maybe she has personal pressures. Or maybe she's tired of Louie and me showing up in every case she supervises . . . and you never showing up at all."

Max's smile was surprisingly mellow. "Not always 'never.' I want to see the autopsy report. I can try breaking into the computers for it, or I can have some real fun and ask Molina for it."

"Max, no! You can't! If she got ahold of you, she'd never let you go."

"We could negotiate."

"How?"

"By phone. By computer."

"Those are traceable."

"For a while."

"You like darting into the lion's mouth."

"I'm used to it."

"I'm not."

"Oh yes, you are. And speaking of that, when are you going to tell Devine?"

Temple squirmed until her unstable chair tilted.

"I can understand you didn't want to ruin his grand night of reporting the triumph of nailing Effinger," Max went on. "Hey, I'm glad he did it. Otherwise, I would have had to. More power to him. He's got a G-man cereal-box badge in my book. So he's a big boy now. He deserves to know, Temple."

Yes, but. She couldn't tell Max about Matt's newest secret: Kitty's bizarre and disturbing attack. Temple sincerely wished she could. Kitty was a wild card. Max would understand wild cards as no one else would.

They were an eternally stymied trio right out of Jean Paul Sartre's play about Hell, *No Exit.* Only instead of being held in stasis by conflicting sexual preferences, they each held different pieces of a jigsaw puzzle long in the making. And the game board upon which the disparate parts were coming together was called "Effinger." If only they would compare enigmas. Or the two men would allow her to move between them without each demanding her utter confidence and loyalty.

But no. Each tolerated the other's existence, at a distance, only so far. And the battleground became, not Effinger, their common enemy, but Temple, their common friend. And in one case, lover. Past. Present.

"When the time's right," she finally said.

Max said no more. The time was right for him now.

They adjourned to the kitchen for a final glass of wine.

Hyacinth, they agreed, was presenting as much of a stalemate as the issue of Matt.

"Maybe it was meant to be a distraction," Max suggested. "Maybe Effinger wanted to pick out a roll of toilet paper with that brand name. I think it's a dead end."

"It was for Effinger," Temple said.

Max was determined to pursue what he called "official sources" on Effinger's death, but they also were in accord that Effinger's passing should not go unnoted.

They plotted his funeral. Temple agreed to walk Matt through it, and Max made no unseemly comments about their continuing partnership in death. Max needed to stay out of plain sight; as much as Max wanted Matt out of Temple's life, he needed him.

Stalemate.

Max leaned across the kitchen table to jiggle Temple's wrist.

"You're looking tired."

"Sweet-talker."

"Let's go to bed. No?"

"Why can't this house have one regular bedroom?"

"You don't like the opium bed?"

"Oh, it's great for lounging around in when you're feeling decadent. Fine for foreplay. But . . . when I was little—no wise cracks; I mean when I was *really* little, a tiny kid—my doting grandmother got me one of those stupid Colonial beds with a white eyelet canopy. And pink satin ribbon twining through the eyelets.

"I was only five or six. I hated having to climb up into that bed using a stool, like I was a baby. I hated the pink satin ribbons, and I hated that canopy that hung over me every night like an eyelet spider web. I kept thinking about all the creepy things that might be hiding up there. Spiders and bats and snakes, all waiting for me to go to sleep so they could fall down on me."

"You're afraid of enclosed beds. But the opium bed doesn't have any concealing curtains. The frame is pierced."

"But all those carvings. Those hidden faces in the shadows, watching."

"Now the bed's a voyeur! Your romantic imagination always takes a Gothic twist. All right. We'll sleep in 'my' bedroom, on the futon. Should be good for our backs."

"Yes, therapeutic."

But when they got to the room Temple had glimpsed only once, she was struck by its stark opposition to the excesses of the opium bed.

"Now here I could be agoraphobic instead of claustrophobic! This looks like a monk's cell." She eyed the low black-lacquered tables, the huge red ceramic vase sporting one stalk of driftwood, the black-and-white fabric on the futon. "I wish we could live at the Circle Ritz like we used to."

Max adjusted a panel installed on the wall and low music infiltrated the simple "cell." Vangelis, like the dusty CDs in Temple's bedroom.

"Magicians are addicted to extremes," Max said with a smile. "We love the elaborate for the illusion it offers, but the underlying tricks are all deceptively simple."

"So the opium bed is the set dressing—"

"The futon is the basic necessity. I suppose I could be really simple and revert to the floor."

"Or the cave floor."

Max shrugged, dimming the lights. "You're hopelessly domestic."

"Domestically hopeless," she said, laughing. "But I guess it doesn't matter where, or when, or on what. Only with whom."

"As long as," he added, "there are no hidden spiders, snakes and Chinese bats."

Temple eyed the room's pristine white ceiling from the starched comfort of the futon a few minutes later. She would never tell Max, but too much blank simplicity overhead turned into an empty movie screen for the horror show of her anxieties and worries.

Excess or simplicity. Neither distracted her from the ever-present, encroaching Gothic all around, twining toward the unwary like kudzu. Danger and death and things that go bump in the night, like conscience. And secrets.

Chapter 34

Siamese Twins

I am most sorry to leave the backstage scene of the Opium Den and the presence of the lively Hyacinth, but I have a mission to accomplish.

So I make a lightning run back to the Circle Ritz. This is some trek to undertake in a hurry. If I am not careful, I will be in need of an undertaker, all right. So I try to hitch a few rides, but the Strip does not usually offer the sort of working vehicle that is best for clandestine hitchhiking. The delivery vans and panel trucks usually take Highway 15 to avoid the crush and the hordes of tourists on foot crossing every intersection.

I must admit that I am spotted now and then, and my obvious sense of purpose is duly noted.

"Look, Craig. That cat looks like he knows where he is going. And what is he carrying in his mouth?"

"Probably a dead lizard. Or a long tongue. How can he know where he is going? Everyone knows that cats do not think. And I am not too sure about dogs, either."

Imagine crediting dogs with an evolutionary edge, however

slight, over cats! Ridiculous. Another sign of the jealous nature and weak-minded stance of those who disdain feline virtues.

Of course I do look rather silly with the object of my mission flapping from my mouth in the dry desert breeze, but I am singularly short of pockets in this skin-tight catsuit I wear (and the Mystifying Max thinks he invented black velvet Spandex for *his* act!).

I do not know if my Miss Temple (and I do consider her *my* Miss Temple even though she has developed a wandering eye of late) is still pursuing the floral angle on Hyacinth, but I think the feline angle in the angular person of Miss Hyacinth Curare-tips (and probably lips, for all I know) is a far more promising lead. At least it sniffs that way to me, but I may be a bit prejudiced. "Cherchez la femme" strikes me as stellar advice in all cases.

Do you know that I am also wondering if Miss Temple has perhaps had a bolt backed out in her brain since Mr. Cliff Effinger slapped her silly against a van side? Also, her conversion to contact lenses could account for her strange lack of vision in selecting her male companions lately. She should know from experience that I am always hot on the trail of evil-doing, and am also very cuddly and undemanding—except for my territory, which has been our bed, our bedroom and our suite of rooms all these past months, with visitors allowed at my discretion and with my approval.

I am not surprised when I get home that the bathroom window is ajar in welcome but the place is as bare as a stripper's bottom at the All-nite, All-nude Bar on Paradise and Flamingo, Las Vegas's least classy junction.

I sniff for unwanted scents and they are all over the place: Mr. Matt Devine, Mr. Max Kinsella, Lieutenant C. R. Molina . . . the only one not present of late in my digs seems to be the late Mr. Elvis Presley. I even dig up the faintest sniff of hyacinth in bloom, which I recognize from sniffing the plant on Miss Shangri-La's dressing table, that Miss Hyacinth of Siam almost knocked to the floor in one of her frequent fits of peke. (That is another snot-nosed breed of dog I cannot stand, the Pekinese, and it is an Asian import to boot.)

Well, I drop my offering on Miss Temple's coffee table, which lately, according to my expert sniffer, has held only libations of a more bibulous nature. (I believe this bibulous liquid is something found in the Bible, as in admonitions to not get drunk. Liquor is a kick, but I only lap a little up at a time.)

I certainly hope Miss Temple's contact lenses can spot a clue as big as a brochure. But I have done all a little fellow like me can.

So I skedaddle and make my arduous way back downtown. Every instinct in my body tells me that the Opium Den is where all the action is in this case, and I do not think this solely because a sinuous lady with sapphire eyes and ruby-red claws awaits my return with bated breath.

Chapter 35

Mum's the Word

"Maybe this will be therapeutic," Temple suggested to Matt in her living room the next morning.

"You mean, my literally burying Effinger?"

She nodded.

Matt consulted a small notepad he'd brought down from his place.

"I asked my mother about any relatives. She said she didn't know of any." He slapped the notepad against his knee. "Sad, isn't it? To be that isolated. Must have hated his family, for probably the same reasons I hated him. Sound like therapy to you?"

"Absolutely. So what can we say in the newspaper obituary?"

"Cliff Effinger. Lowlife around Las Vegas. No survivors, no mourners, no loss."

"Is 'bitter' therapeutic?"

"No, but it's fun. You're the press-release writer. Come up with something."

"Okay. Um." She commandeered the notepad and turned to a

clean page. "Cliff Effinger, starting with the name is good. Died January second. Formerly of Chicago."

"That's good!" Matt encouraged her.

"Longtime Las Vegas resident."

He nodded.

"Ah . . . what can we say he did?"

"Small business man."

"Very small. Okay, put that in. And what you suggested. No survivors. Visitation at 1 P.M. at Sam's Funeral Home on Charleston Boulevard. Interment private."

"Fine. Good. I'm glad Electra knew someone with a funeral home. Now what?"

"Now we visit the funeral home, buy a suitably modest casket and decide what clothes to put on the corpse and all that fun stuff."

"I guess I've finally got control of the creep, haven't I? I could even have him buried in an Elvis jumpsuit."

Temple giggled. "Talk about a picture to remember. Just keep laughing. Think of this as theater, not burying someone."

"At least we can just cremate the body after this charade is over. Do you really believe it will lead to anything?"

"Somebody bothered to give Effinger a very public and outlandish death. Maybe they can't resist attending a good funeral. Maybe somebody hates him even more than you do. I wouldn't rule out that Elvis suit, if I were you."

Sam's Funeral Home was a typical Las Vegas operation. Its pillared white facade echoed the grandeur of Tara, the O'Hara plantation house. Inside, acres of plush pastel carpeting were discreetly marked by the shuffles of respectful feet, or at least of pallbearers weighed down by the usual sloughed-off mortal coils.

The hush, though, was deeper than that in the exclusive baccarat enclaves of the finest hotels. Death was in permanent residence here, and was more exacting of tribute than money.

Sam himself saw them in an office furnished tastefully in mahogany Queen Anne pieces with chorus-girl-curvy legs.

"So nice to meet friends of Electra's. My deepest condolences at this time of loss," he added in a voice that would pomade barbed wire.

His own hair had ebbed from the Gibralter of his pate, reduced to a silky fringe from ear to ear that ended in a fluster of pewter-colored curls, which gave his shiny pink-granite skull and face a jolly look.

"Who is the bereaved?" he asked gently.

"I suppose I am," Matt said.

Sam's eyebrows, a riot of overgrown gray curls alternated like weather fronts in extremes of high and low. Matt's waffling answer had plunged them to the depths of polite concern.

"Then the deceased has no close relatives."

"Not that we know of," Temple put in. "If one, or more, should turn up, we would be most interested in knowing."

"I understand. Now . . . Mr. Devine. What about clothes for the deceased? Did you bring any to select from?"

"It's difficult." Matt exchanged a glance with Temple.

He was thinking of the Elvis jumpsuit and trying not to laugh. Laughing would not be taken lightly at a funeral parlor. And the rooms eerily recalled parlors from another era, reminding him that "in my Father's house there are many mansions." Funeral-home operators appeared to have taken that to heart, and to have spent much effort in preparing anterooms for mansions.

"We don't know his last place of residence," Matt explained. "So we don't know where his clothes might be, and I suppose the police kept what he was wearing when he died, as evidence."

"Oh, *that* kind of death, was it? Well, we have a fine selection of garments made specifically for such occasions. Well made, in excellent taste and yet reasonably priced."

"Where do you get this funeral-wear-to-go?" Temple wondered.

"There are businesses that solely supply clothes for such purposes."

Dressing the dead seemed an odd business, like making costumes for life-size dolls.

"These clothes," Sam added, "are designed for easy application and to be seen inside caskets."

The notion of clothes being "applied" was truly creepy.

"Now," Sam asked, sounding like a used car salesman. "May I show you a few models of our excellent casket line?"

The showroom reminded Temple of the Liberace museum not far distant.

Bulky caskets on pedestals stood around the showroom like a pod of marooned whales, or open grand pianos whose interior harps had been replaced by pleated satin fabric.

The satin-lined maws waited to received the dear departed on upholstered waves—of coral or pink, or palest blue or ecru—that reminded Temple of said whale's yawning soft palate.

Then the casket's open upper Dutch door would snap shut out of sight and sink all those lost Jonahs deep in the belly of the earth.

Matt must have been more familiar with funeral rituals than she, but he sleepwalked through this macabre duty. Temple supposed that as a put-upon child he had wished Cliff Effinger dead. To be an adult in charge of postmortem arrangements for this man would try the integrity of a saint. Did he secretly rejoice? Or despair, to see the bane of his life consigned to the rituals of burial?

Temple had never had to participate in a burying before. She saw how bereaved relatives could escalate costs in the name of respect. The low-cost caskets, wooden or metal, were so obviously cheesy that only a merciless person would consign anyone they knew to such ignominy.

"Remember," she whispered to Matt as they solemnly snaked single file through the marooned caskets. "Max has lots of money."

"I'm not going to spend the money of one man I dislike to bury another man I despised."

"You don't like Max?" Temple was genuinely surprised that her charmer had failed, even with a rival. "You don't know him."

"We've talked."

"This isn't a simple burial; it's a trap. You have to bait it properly. I say, get a middle-of-the-road casket."

Sam, keeping a decent distance that precluded eavesdropping, paused to smooth his silk-blend suit jacket, a pleasant smile sending his eyebrows heavenward.

They ended up consulting like a couple buying a first car. Wood was obvious. Effinger would be cremated. "Isn't that against your religion?" Temple hissed fretfully when Sam had withdrawn to let them make their decision.

"Not any more. Besides, I don't think Effinger was any religion. I vote for the oak."

"Then can I have the tacky sea-green lining? It should make him look sallow."

"I think death has taken care of that for you."

When it came to clothes, it was one dark neutral suit or another. Temple voted for the plain black over the navy pinstriped. With a yellow shirt.

"Why?" Matt asked as they left the showroom following the funeral director, who was no doubt used to intense, hushed consultations.

"He'll look like an after-dinner mint. You know, those dark chocolate lozenges with pastel fillings, green and yellow. Terrible taste in every respect. Serve him right for making us miserable while he was alive."

"Dressing a corpse wrong is the best revenge?"

"Matt, it's the only revenge you can have on a corpse. Unless you want to go in for grave-robbing or desecration or some-such."

"No. No thanks. Dead and buried is all I ask, and unable to harm anyone else. I'm even getting used to the idea of him getting a decent send-off ceremony."

Temple threaded her arm through his as they returned to the director's office. Her voice assumed a melancholy Eastern European accent.

"The road you valk is thorny, my son, but as the sun rises in the east, you vill find a kinder path."

"I'm not even going to ask where that's from."

"One of those dreadfully wonderful Wolfman movies from the forties."

"It almost goes with my new sofa, then."

"Right. Just get yourself an old TV with a round screen in a blond cabinet and settle back to enjoy yourself."

"Isn't there one of those in the Ghost Suite at the Crystal Phoenix?" His voice lowered as he bent to her ear. "Maybe we could reserve it someday."

No. No, they couldn't.

By the time they had resumed their overstuffed chairs in front of Sam's huge mahogany desk, Matt was mellow and Temple was cast down.

"Now I understand that the expenses are being assumed by an anonymous donor." Sam smiled like a JP at a pair of newlyweds whose parents had paid for the ceremony. "Fine with me. Just okay the items you've approved, folks, and I'll take payment later. Any friends of Electra Lark's are friends of mine."

Nodding, smiling and stunned by how much even their modest choices added up to, Matt signed on the dotted lines. Then he and Temple escaped the whited sepulcher world of funeral homes and pastel plush carpet.

"I'm not sure about the piped-in music," Matt said.

"Irish dirges are always appropriate, believe me."

"Effinger isn't Irish."

"But our 'sponsor' is."

"I see, the piper pays, he gets to name the tune."

"What would you have chosen?"

"Perhaps the medieval chants."

"Toney, but a bit much for Effinger."

Matt nodded. "I'm not looking forward to the visitation Monday morning. At least there'll be no religious service. I couldn't have stood that."

"I just hope something happens Monday."

"Like what?"

"I don't know. Something odd and revealing. Something sinister. Something that points an inescapable clue toward Effinger's murderer, or murderers."

"Plural?"

"Now that Molina has 'fessed up that Effinger was bound to the barge and sunk with it, it's obvious it took more than one person to do it. And something else is also obvious."

"What? I guess I'm too close to him, his odious history. All I see is that someone stamped out the life of a vile bug."

"Nicely put. No holy moly stuff excusing the poor sod. But . . . you've got the wrong species."

"Bug?"

Temple nodded seriously. "The way Effinger died was a broad hint about why he died."

"Temple, don't hint. I'm tired, I'm hurt, I'm having to treat this creep like a human being now that he's dead, which is probably good for my soul but does nothing for my instincts. Just tell me what you mean."

She took a deep breath. "He died by water, knowing he would die for at least twenty minutes before it happened. It was a mean, sadistic killing. It was sending a message, to Effinger, and to everyone who ever knew him. It said: this is the end of a dirty rat. A drowned rat. A man who spilled his guts. Who talked to the police."

"Jesus, Temple."

When Matt swore, it always struck Temple as a prayer.

"You're telling me I killed him. I found him, I took him to Molina. I made him a marked man."

"You couldn't have done him more dirt than that, if you had wanted to."

"Oh, I wanted to. I just thought, at the time, I wanted justice more."

"Maybe you got it. Maybe this was the only way you were going to get it."

"Through killers, instead of the law?"

"The law kills legally. What's the difference?"

Matt couldn't answer her.

The visitation Monday afternoon was the height of what passes for civilization among the funeral-home set.

Keening celtic pipes set the tone as visitors to "the Effinger observance" were funneled into the tastefully accoutered viewing room. A gilt-lettered volume, open like an angel's book, recorded visitors' names. Discreet white envelopes and cards the size of cocktail napkins accepted cash, check or spare chips in the name of good works in the name of the deceased.

In return, donors acquired gilt-edged cards embossed with the nondenominational image of a dove.

Matt and Temple were the first to arrive, both a symphony in black. Matt was probably the only man in Las Vegas who wasn't dead and who possessed a black suit.

"I just realized that look is ultrachic," Temple commented as they left the car.

"Please. I can't take being chic at the moment."

"*Men in Black,* the motion picture. All you need are the vintage shades."

"I missed that one."

"You miss a lot of them."

"And I don't miss them at all."

Matt paused outside the antebellum facade of white pillars.

"White is the Asian color of mourning."

"And it was the favored color in eighteenth-century France, I believe."

"So why are we in black?"

"It's always chic?"

Temple didn't own much black, but this long-skirted loose dress with its row of tiny buttons seemed appropriate for the occasion.

Low-volume music piped them into the proper viewing area. Spencerian script on a white card announced the name "Effinger" by the open double doors.

Inside, a scene both sweet and cloying overwhelmed them.

"Did we order piped-in perfume?" Matt asked.

"No way." Temple scrawled her name and Matt's in the ornate book.

No one else had signed in yet, but the day was young.

They advanced across the empty quicksand of too-thick plush carpet to the front, where the plain casket was bracketed by banks of flowers from floor to six feet high.

Unlike the usual large, showy funeral blossoms and wreaths, these were diminutive flowers that impressed by mass rather than bulk or size.

Rank on blue-purple rank of curlicued blossoms. Hothouse flowers forced into bloom afore time. Hyacinths breathing saccharine scent into the room, enough to overlay the sickly sweet odor of the dead.

"What is this?" Matt stopped dead in midroom.

"Let's see if there are any cards."

But Temple probed among the spear-shaped leaves to no avail. These flowers were truly anonymous, a legion of delegates from nowhere and no one.

"This is bizarre." Matt stopped before one of two padded kneelers set in front of the casket. Temple knew he would never kneel here. "Hyacinths, right?"

"Hyacinths. Let's see who comes to visit them."

First they passed by the casket. Matt's hand tightened on Temple's forearm.

Effinger lay there, wearing the healthy tan of a department-store dummy, his features stapled into a sharpness they had never mustered in life.

He did look pasty in the black suit and yellow shirt against the gag-green-colored satin. Yet all that tawdry glory seemed to elevate him to the station of an effigy. A symbol more than a man. A murdered man.

Matt moved on, retreating to a rose brocade settee along one wall. "Now what?" he asked Temple.

"You should know."

"Not here. At visitations I attended, the Rosary Guild would come to tell the beads. Or I would read from the psalms. There were crowds of parishioners. Everyone knew everyone. Everyone felt a personal loss. This is . . . a mockery. No community. No religion. Only empty ceremony."

"And hyacinths by the hundreds. I wonder why?"

"I don't think I care, Temple. No one will come. This practical joker who says it with flowers won't show up. We won't learn anything, and Kinsella will have spent his money for nothing."

"Let's wait and see."

Waiting and seeing involved the next two hours.

Two nuns came in. They wore civilian dress except for the vestigial headdress: a shoulder-brushing navy veil with a starched white rim at the hairline.

They were heavyset and middle-aged, performing an act of charity by mourning the unknown dead who had no survivors.

After a glance Matt ignored them. He hated to see the good sisters waste their sincere prayers, but even they could not save

Effinger. He knew that every soul was salvageable, by the lights of his religion. He just couldn't believe it in this case, his most clear crisis of faith since he had left the priesthood.

A few itinerants drifted in as the second hour ticked away. Street people looking for diversion, perhaps someone worse off than they were to shake their heads over.

Matt was always struck by street people's kinship with dust-bowl nomads. He had thought those starved, asymmetrical, suffering faces no longer existed outside of Depression era or postwar Europe photographs. He could hardly restrain himself from handing them cards with donations as they left, except that the poor have a dignity that cannot be violated in their few sanctuaries, and apparently funeral homes were one of them.

"Sad," Temple commented. "It's an event, like a wedding chapel ceremony. That's why Electra put the dressed-up soft sculptures in her pews. So many people in cities don't belong anywhere nowadays."

Matt nodded, checking the watch his mother had given him for Christmas. Somehow it was appropriate that it be here, ticking away Effinger's last moments as a physical body on this planet. He'd had about all that he could take, and his pierced side throbbed like a grandfather clock, pain and time swinging back and forth on the pump of his blood through taut veins.

"There's nothing to learn here," Matt mumbled to Temple, turning to go.

At the double doors they met Sam himself, who suggested softly that they adjourn to his office.

Once seated in comfort—and not a seat in the house was other than cushy—it was impossible for Matt and Temple to fidget, though they both felt like doing that, given the restless swings of their feet along the plush carpeting.

"Were all the arrangements satisfactory?"

"Completely," Matt said.

"Who sent all the hyacinths?" Temple asked.

"Is that what they were! We usually see gladioli and lilies, mums and roses. Funny you should ask. No card was found."

"But you have a record of the delivery service?"

"Of course." Pages turned in his plump, uncalloused fingers.

"Well, that is odd. The flowers were found in the delivery area this morning. No, I guess we don't have a record of the delivery company.

"But you folks aren't to worry about any of the details. Your anonymous donor showed up in person first thing this morning and paid for everything, in cash."

"Did he say anything?" Temple was shocked into asking. Why would Max personally inspect the visitation scene?

"*She* was very soft-spoken. Wore a hat with a true mourning veil, utterly impenetrable. And black leather gloves. Quite a dramatic figure."

Matt and Temple exchanged a long glance. Max's hoped-for visitor was a dramatic one.

After leaving the director's office they loitered restlessly in the foyer, about to conduct a hushed postmortem of speculation on the Lady in Black.

At that moment a black-suit-clad assistant rushed out of the viewing chamber.

"Thank heavens I caught you," he said. "There was a windfall among the offerings. I don't know where these all came from, but I had to find a stationery box to hold them."

Temple took the box, surprised when it weighed her arms down.

"Bingo," she said in a daze, staring into a mound of small square envelopes.

Matt pulled one off the top and opened it. Only the usual folded note card and inside . . . he elevated a silver dollar like a glittering metal host.

"No note, just this."

"Silver dollars are . . . collectibles these days, worth more than face value."

Matt shrugged and pulled out some other envelopes. Each one contained a silver dollar.

"Bizarre."

"Just like the veiled lady who came to pay the bill," Temple noted. "Veiled lady! Can you imagine anyone but a funeral director swallowing that?"

Matt chuckled. "They do thrive on ceremony."

"The Lady in Black has forestalled us," Temple observed as the last visitors plodded toward the exit.

"Yes. The veiled lady in black. Oh, no!"

Matt made himself focus on his surroundings and the unconsciously observed guests. The trio of nuns were just trailing out the double doors.

Trio?

Matt's memory counted wimples, pared-down contemporary wimples, but wimples nevertheless. Only two when they came in.

"Come on!" He grabbed Temple's black-knit-swathed arm at the wrist.

Outside, the sun blared like rock radio music but the temperature was only a steady sixty degrees. Two nuns were getting into an ancient Toyota compact.

The third was nowhere to be seen.

Chapter 36

Madder Music and Stronger Wine

They left the funeral home with the addition of the guest book, thanks to another rescue mission by the assistant. The lined pages were empty except for the names of the pair of nuns and a couple of strangers.

"It looks like a wedding photo album," Matt observed, tucking the padded cover embossed with designs of doves, crosses and lilies under his arm.

Temple used both hands to carry the heavy cardboard box of offering envelopes, the ones stuffed with silver dollars that shifted with every motion, clinking dully through the muffling paper.

Matt was glad that Temple usually let him drive the Storm. He needed to go through the motions right now; any motions. Driving back to the Circle Ritz, going to her place. It had been easier to see Cliff Effinger's bare body in the morgue than tricked out at a funeral visitation.

The mockery and mystery of the event had put him into the numb withdrawal the shell-shocked must feel after a long battle. Matt also felt the underlying weight of death, and the death of his old life. So, he imagined, a long-term penitentiary inmate would feel to know the hated place had been razed at last: a numbing sense of triumph, freedom and resentment at this loss of an institutionalized object of fear and loathing. And, perhaps, the loss of a negative motivation toward seeking a better life.

"You're quiet," Temple commented in the car, the shimmying box of envelopes chiming on her knees like a tambourine.

Matt only nodded, lost in thoughts that shifted like a kaleidoscopic image.

He finally glanced at her. Not surprisingly, she wore the black cat necklace he had given her as a late Christmas present. For the perennially thoughtful, wearing someone's gift in their presence as a sign of appreciation is second nature. And the necklace, subdued enough to befit a visitation, complemented her long black-knit dress; also sober enough for funeral duty.

Temple seldom wore black, he realized. He had found himself watching her sober silhouette against the funeral parlor's determined pastel palette. The dress hung like a ballerina's costume in a fifties musical fantasy, graceful and girlish. The round neckline didn't crowd the throat, but circled two or three inches below, a perfect setting for the necklace.

The simple black dress reminded him of an old-time nun's habit. It reduced Temple's normally busy appearance to a James Whistler study in chalk-white, black and rusty red.

He wondered if the black dress, or unplumbed emotions in the face of Effinger's death, made her look so pale today. Who could blame her for rejoicing in the elimination of a tormenter? Yet Matt doubted that Effinger's attack on Temple had stirred any strong personal feelings against him. His blows had been a lightning bolt from a virtual stranger. To her, Effinger was first-cousin to a random mugger, a bad experience to be forgotten.

The silence between them was contented, rather than awkward. They knew where they were going, although not what they were going to say or do when they got there, but that didn't bother them by now.

Temple's rooms held a tranquilizing familiarity for Matt. He felt relief, even sanctuary, here when Temple admitted them.

She put the box on the coffee table. "Drink?"

"It's only—," wearing the watch his mother had given him made her a silent witness to Effinger's end, even if by proxy "— one o'clock."

"Feels like five," Temple said, coming back. Two glasses of red wine shimmered against her servant-black bodice with its fussy row of tiny, shiny, round black buttons from collar bone to hemline.

She sat down and kicked off her black pumps.

Matt's tense muscles welcomed the wine, but he could have wished for a drink less reminiscent of his ceremonial priestly past than red wine. No funeral mass for Cliff Effinger. Not with Matt officiating. Dust to dust and ashes to ashes quite truly. The ashes in their tasteful receptacle suitable for any location would be mailed to him, he had been told, though the funeral home would have preferred to present them in person with appropriate ceremony. Matt thought not; mailing would do fine.

What the hell he would do with them was his business.

Temple shuffled through the odd collection of envelopes. "I suppose we should turn these over to Lieutenant Molina, along with the news of the expensive outpouring of hyacinth plants and the mystery woman who paid for the whole thing."

"I'll contact her." Matt's head lolled against the cushy sofa pillow while he stared at the snowy arched ceiling dappled with light like not-quite-still water.

He felt Temple settle into the adjoining cushions.

"Visitations are exhausting, even when hardly anybody comes," she said. "I haven't figured out yet what all this means. Hyacinths and silver dollars."

"Somebody's playing with us. Or Effinger."

"After he's dead? That's such a . . . carnivorous thing to do. Like a cat with a mouse or a bird."

"Or a catnip toy," he reminded her. "Louie's not around?"

"He's in a wandering mode. In and out. I noticed the topping on the Free-to-be-Feline went down since we left."

"Why do you bother to set that stuff out for him? He'll never eat it."

"It's good for him, and maybe he accidentally gets some when he goes for the gold on top."

"I doubt it." Matt laughed softly. "You're such an optimist." He turned his head without lifting it; mental lassitude now made his entire body leaden.

Temple slouched on the sofa cushions too, her face only inches from his own, he realized with a shock. As if they sat with their backs to the same tree someplace peaceful, near a running brook.

The moment was a million miles away from everyday Las Vegas and the regular rituals of their relationship.

"I was wondering," Matt said, "at the visitation, if your face still hurt from Effinger's attack. If you still felt the aftereffects. If he went to his grave with someone, somewhere, still hurting from his violence."

She shrugged and smiled. "I'm almost as good as ever. Pain doesn't have a half-life unless it's chronic."

He sipped wine, feeling a floodgate of blood loosening in his shoulders and arms, tension dissipating through dilated vessels.

"It's over. Thank God it's over." He bestirred himself to set the glass on the table before he lethargically let it spill onto the paper-pale cushions.

Temple looked equally exhausted—white, black and red against the ivory cushions, her mouth glossed by a deep burgundy lipstick, a mere brush stroke on the white-linen canvas of her face. No bruises shadowed her features. Even her freckles seemed to have paled and winked out, like twilight stars. They dusted her cheeks and just-visible collarbones, but not one touched her bare neck.

"I'm sorry I ruined New Year's for you," he found himself blurting. "You did it all for me, and I was an ass about it."

"Women hiding hurts pushes your buttons. I should have known you can't protect anyone from the truth, least of all yourself."

"I was so . . . up about everything that night, and it seems to have evaporated. Why? It's more than Effinger striking back. It's like something between us turned into smoke and blew away. You remember how high I was when I called you from Chicago a couple days after Christmas? It was like I'd solved the family mysteries. I'd confessed my nonpriestly state. I knew who the villains were and I could finally start forgiving them. I was ready to look into a new life, a new job, ready to—"

Temple was listening, as she always did, attentively, intelligently. Somehow that calm, accepting presence irritated him, frightened him.

"Temple. What happened?"

"You were on a holiday high," she suggested, "and then the post-holiday reality hit."

"No, it's more than that. It goes back farther than that. What happened? We were . . . getting together, you were taking me through all the high-school hoops I missed. That . . . wonderful dance on the desert, the times we kissed ourselves silly. When did it stop? It all seems like fifteen years ago. Like it really was high school."

Something stirred her placid features. Puzzlement in the eyes maybe. Now that Temple no longer wore glasses, Matt could see the true shape of her features. She looked almost stranger-like at times when he glanced at her and noticed a plane of cheek or forehead he had never seen before.

In a way, it intimidated him. In another way, this made her attractive to him as she never had been before, though she had always been attractive to him.

He needed to touch that blurred Impressionist-painting face, to make sure the oils were still wet, that the image might yet change under his fingers.

He touched the black opal cat figure at her throat instead.

"You should wear black more often. It becomes you."

His other hand stretched to test the right side of her face. "The bruises are gone." But he wasn't really playing doctor, he just wanted to feel the subtle hollow beneath her no-longer obscured cheekbone.

Temple kept as still as a rabbit on an endless swath of lawn, suddenly aware of the mixed emotions that were overflowing in him. Uncommitted, waiting, yet completely complicit. Wary and waiting. Anxious. Yet excited.

Matt trembled on the brink of expressing an intimacy he had never dreamed of, so earth-shaking that he avoided her eyes, studying her instead as a disjointed Cubist portrait broken into isolated planes and features: the notched curve above her lip; the hollow of her throat that cradled the black cat charm; her long, white and graceful neck, which he had found himself noticing at the funeral home.

He could still taste the shock of fresh blood in her mouth on New Year's Eve. Maybe it was behavior modification, but he shied away from her mouth. Not for him the traditional lover's kiss. He wanted to touch, to kiss, to taste her neck and throat.

And there was nothing to stop him, except wondering if this was weird. So he did what he felt, swept up by an odd wave of overwhelming desire and . . . reverence.

He leaned forward until his lips touched her skin, and then he placed a phantom circle of kisses around the base of her throat. His lips found the faint, fast pulse of her carotid artery and caressed it. This was the kiss of life far more than the neighborly ritual of greeting in every mass celebrated.

His sense of smell sharpened: he could taste the tang of green apple in her shampoo or soap; her skin was satin-velvet to his lips and fingertips. He wanted to devour it, soothe it, seal every centimeter of it as his; the ridges of her collarbones required tracing with kisses. Her hands suddenly twining in his hair agreed with him. Then there was no stopping him.

His fingers found and fussed with the slippery beads of buttons, releasing them from confining loops and kissing the hidden hard escarpment of her chest bone. How could bone be so sexy, highpoint and hollow? It was. What was he doing? Who was he becoming? Vampire. Cannibal. Lover. Devourer. Worshiper. What was he making of her? Icon. Object. Aphrodisiac.

Emotion and desire were building to a pitch that vibrated in the very fork of his being, achingly physical yet as correspondingly spiritual as any meditation in which he had striven to penetrate the mystery and touch the face of God.

The buttons were parting before him like gateways. His lips followed the trail his fingers had forged until his cheek brushed the soft bare swell of what he knew must be breast.

The piercing jolt of pleasure stopped him cold. Primal memory? Or just too many years celibate? Matt pulled his face back, saw the sexy chasm of skin he had exposed between the gaping buttons and loops, the pair of hard hidden buttons beneath the fabric.

Fascinated, he dragged his palms lightly across them.

Her torso surged upward like a body revived by electrical current. Her low moan echoed through his nerves.

A concurrent shock through his own system pulled him back even further, to hover above her and finally dare look at her face.

It was a face he had seen on dozens of billboards around town, the quintessential sexy female face thrust back on an exposed neck above an exposed chest, the eyes mostly closed, the lips parted and slack.

Now he understood the power of the image and also its utter poverty. Its mean, commercial, pornographic parody of the full physical and emotional range of eroticism.

The beauty of her face, the fact that his touch had brought that beauty there, took his breath away, made the demanding vice in his groin tauten further. To see that transformation in a face he loved, to know he could bring it so much pleasure, made him feel omnipotent in an almost blasphemous way. But everything metaphysical was also paradoxical. He had never felt so powerless.

He bent to finally kiss her mouth without fear, tasting nothing but mutual desire and a depth unimaginable.

He was convinced that there was only one sane way to live his life, and that would be doing this with her forever, eternally, in every way imaginable, no food, no sleep, no time, no talk, no stopping, over and over again, amen.

Their touch would never break, their eyes would never open except to look at each other; no serpent, and no punishing god, would ever intrude on their earthly eden, and pleasure would be pure and private forever.

She stirred as if waking from a dream.

The first time she said his name, it was a moan, and thrilled him. The second time was a murmur.

The third time her eyes opened, and tears covered them like crystal cataracts.

Matt watched the serpent slither into his eden within those eyes of dawning regret. Silver-blue eyes, like sunlit water.

She struggled upright a little, then tried to redo a button.

But there were too many and they gaped too wide. It would have been ridiculous to sit there and do up buttons like a Victorian maid after the intense intimacy they'd shared.

Matt watched her with dread, and a reflex of rising shame he hated, and a silly stupefied adoration.

"You're going to be disappointed in me again," she said, her voice thick.

"Never." He sounded besotted and liked it.

"Yes, you will. Matt, I can't."

He didn't need to ask what she couldn't. He started to backtrack, to preserve what had been, at least. He had to salvage some part of this.

"I . . . I don't know what came over me," he said quickly. "The stress of the funeral, maybe. Death makes you want to live. I forced this on you, didn't ask—"

"There are some things you don't need to ask, and this was one of them."

"Is it . . . always so sudden like this?"

"More or less." She was trying to restore normality, but her voice was shaky. "Usually less."

"I'm . . . the feeling's incredible. No wonder so many people get in trouble with it."

She smiled, faintly.

"Temple, whatever you're going to say—"

"I'm going to say it right away, before you go any farther in any way, and hate me worse than you will anyway."

"Hate you—"

"I almost told you earlier a couple of times, but it never seemed the right moment. Now it's the really wrong moment, but I've got to do it."

She hugged her arms around herself, creating a subtle swell of cleavage that made him understand why a man "couldn't keep his hands off" a woman.

Whatever she said wouldn't pierce the sensual, doting haze that wreathed him like smoke and mist.

"Max and I are together again."

The words were gibberish; the moving lips that said them were irresistible and he needed to kiss them.

Her head tilted as if to find him inside his emotional and erotic maze. "Matt?"

"Together." His voice sounded slow, drugged.

"Not living together; we can't. But we're trying to rebuild our relationship. See if it stands a chance at being permanent."

"Together. You're sleeping together. You can't be. This wouldn't have happened if you were."

"*Shouldn't* have happened. I ought to have told you sooner. I was trying to save you a shock at a bad time, but now it's worse than ever for both of us."

"For you and Max, or for you and me?"

"I'm talking about us."

"How can there be an 'us' if you're with him?"

She didn't argue, only picked at some lint on her skirt. The stretchy fabric dipped between her legs. He had neglected undoing the buttons all the way to the bottom. Now he never would.

"How long?" he asked. "When? How?"

She didn't tell him it was none of his business.

"Since after Christmas. In New York. Max showed up at Kit's to take me out to dinner. He gave me a ring. No, I haven't been wearing it."

"After Christmas? That day I called you, was it after—?"

She nodded in super-serious slow motion, like a naughty child admitting to eating all the cream puffs.

"God." The timetable was driving home on hammer blows of irony. "I was so . . . high after that trip home, after settling with Effinger and declaring my independence from the past with my family. You know, I thought about flying to New York just to tell you all about it. Only it seemed kind of impolite and . . . impractical. Guess Kinsella isn't polite and practical."

"Nope."

"He who hesitates is lost. And now I've embarrassed both of us by jumping on you like a—"

"Shut up!" Tears were still refusing to fall from her eyes. "Don't you dare. It was one of the erotic high points of history, and we were there, okay? Both of us. We just can't do it again."

"Why not? Temple, I know I'm supposed to care about things

like this, but I don't care how often you slept with him, or how recently. I want you now and for the future. You don't have to honor the past."

"But I do! Max and I really had something. It wasn't his fault that he had to leave. I can't tell you why, but it wasn't his fault. We owe it to each other to try again."

"Is he in the witness protection program? Is that the reason for all the secrecy? I've wondered."

"A performer? A Las Vegas magician?"

"You quoted him as saying that brazen is often the best disguise."

"Not the witness protection program, but something . . . similar."

"Temple, you've known love, you've known sex. I haven't, until now. I'm not going to give this up. I'm almost ready to suggest that you don't tell Max about us, but I wouldn't mean it, and I know you couldn't do it. But that's how far I've fallen."

She put a hand to the side of his face, a touch almost as comforting as the tenderness in her eyes.

"Max knows I have deep feelings for you. It's horrid that he was gone just long enough for you and I to connect. But I'm going to try as hard as I can to make it with Max. Nobody knows the man behind the magician. He's had pain, he has a past. We have a mutual history that's worthy of saving. If Max had met someone else while he was gone, I'd still try. And he loves me."

"Too."

Matt got up, surprised that his knees still locked when necessary.

A picture of Temple branded itself on his mind and memory: her sitting there as demure and delicate as a ballerina in a Degas sketch, except for the erotic touch of her undone buttons. He loved her for not dishonoring their intimacy by trying to cover up her exposure, he loved her for giving him an erotic snapshot to treasure.

"I suppose we'll talk, see each other, when it's necessary."

"Of course."

The tears still stood in her eyes. If they hadn't fallen yet, they weren't going to fall in his presence, ever. He imagined them glistening on her collarbones and breast, himself lapping up the salt-water drop by drop . . . desire was dementia. Love was delirium.

"Do me a favor," he asked. "Don't ever get rid of that dress."

He didn't say goodbye, and outside the unit, he only got a few steps down the cul-de-sac before he had to stop and lean against the wall.

The erotic charge still shook him. He felt possessed by a power greater than himself. He saw this as one more evidence of the Creator's incredible, indelible omnipresence, something to be celebrated, not stifled. And he couldn't stop an idiotic smile from crossing his face, despite his having heard the worst news of his life. Idiocy looked to be his lot for a while; he was in love and finally knew it.

He started when he heard a click down the hall. It had taken Temple a long time to get up and lock the door after him. He wondered if she suffered from the same weak-kneed condition. If she stood with her back to the wall on her side of the partition, reliving the ecstasy and grinning like a lunatic. Like most serious matters in life, sex also seemed to be a healthy though heady mix of the sublime and the ridiculous.

Chapter 37

Ms. Cellany

Temple poured what was left of Matt's wine into her own glass and took a deep swig.

Then she absently ran the cool, smooth brim over her lips, back and forth, over and over. Amen.

She was huddled in a corner of the sofa, knees jackknifed, arms clutched around them, as if she were cold.

But she wasn't cold at all. Temple balanced her glass on one kneecap.

Lesson number one: sparing other people's feelings is usually a euphemism for sparing yourself the pain of telling the truth.

Lesson number two: playing with fire will give you blisters. You might get to like blisters.

Lesson number three: expletive deleted.

Somehow she'd managed to be disloyal to everybody in this eternal triangle, including herself.

Including even Midnight Louie.

She really could have used a comforting feline presence right now. That sagacious furry face; those wise, slitted green eyes; that warm, solid body against her side.

But even Louie had deserted her. Even? Max and Matt had not, more's the pity.

She chugalugged the rest of the wine and un-corkscrewed herself to set the empty glass on the tabletop.

Not on the tabletop.

On top of a glossy brochure.

Temple saw a flash of color and motion, a sexy female, an exploding firework. The usual Las Vegas come-on for everything from soup kitchens to nuts to celebrity-impersonator revues.

How had this piece of trash gotten onto her coffee table? Maybe someone had stuffed it into her tote bag as she'd rushed by. Las Vegas was always foisting fleshly delights on oblivious passersby with more elevating issues on their minds. Like gambling.

Fleshly delights, oh my. Oh, Matt. Oh, Max. Oh, Midnight Louie. Maybe she should stick to cats.

Except that one word caught her attention as it was about to drift to sea.

Hyacinth.

"Shangri-La and Hyacinth. Hyacinth is also a *cat*, for heaven's sake!"

Well, she would have to ask Max about this lady magician and her magical disappearing cat called Hyacinth.

She would have to see Max, soon. And say? Nothing. Sparing people's feelings, including one's own, could become a very bad habit.

Matt had hours to go before he could go to work and lose himself in open-line jive. He would listen with a whole new third ear now, to lovesick Romeos and Juliets, to suicidal rejectees, to women haunted by obsessive stalkers.

But first he would call Lieutenant Molina. She had handed him a body. He had run with it. Now she could chase down the implications: hyacinths by the truckload, an anonymous donor, fingerprints on the silver dollars.

He needed to call Temple.

No, he really needed to call her, to ask her something.

To hear her voice. To imagine her.

He called.

She answered, and sounded surprised.

"Silver dollars? How many? Sure, I can count them."

She was back at the phone after too long a while.

"Thirty."

"Exactly?"

"Exactly. But you knew that."

"Yes."

Silence. Necessity was over; the gray area stretched between them.

"I'll tell Molina," he said.

She said nothing. He said good-bye. He wondered if she sat there listening to the dial tone for as long as he did. War was hell, but libido was hell with a flamethrower.

Temple called Max.

"Hi. How many lady magicians do you know?"

"There's one in Vegas. Melinda downtown.

"Now there are two. Downtown. Shangri-La and Hyacinth."

"Hyacinth?"

"Apparently a cat is part of the act."

"Cats and magicians go together like Siegfried and Roy."

"Then how come Midnight Louie doesn't like you?"

"He must not be a real cat. I take it you want to take in this show."

"It seems like a good idea."

"Consider it done. But not until tomorrow. I'm doing clandestine research on some of our current conundrums. We'll probably have to hit the late show. Okay with you?"

"I don't think I'll be able to sleep until then anyway."

"Come over for dinner tonight. You can tell me what happened at the visitation."

She couldn't. She couldn't quite do it right now. But she couldn't say why, and therefore couldn't say no.

She certainly couldn't tell Max what had happened, and had *not* happened, *after* the visitation.

Temple sighed as she hung up. How had she maneuvered herself into lying by omission to everybody?

C. R. Molina hung up after taking Matt Devine's call.

A bank of hyacinths. A woman in a long, black veil. Thirty silver dollars left in little square envelopes.

The homemade funeral for Cliff Effinger couldn't have gone better.

She pulled the photograph of the note found in Effinger's pocket toward her. She had expected Temple Barr to figure more prominently in the unfolding scenario, but the mysterious lady in black was usurping her place.

Devine had sounded strained on the phone, like a man under intolerable pressure. She had a feeling he was holding something back.

She had a feeling that he was about to release the always-hidden spring within himself.

She tapped the chewed end of a pencil on her glass-covered desktop. She wanted to push him, but she didn't want to push him into a place where he had nowhere to go except to jump off.

She liked Matt Devine. She didn't like most people she met through her job. As a policewoman, she was in trouble.

Chapter 38

Tight Places

"Rough day?"

Max swept Temple into the house, haunted by the late Gandolph the Great and Orson Welles.

He gestured to push a stray strand of hair off his face, although his hair was swept back into a sleek ponytail, and nothing about it was stray. Could Max Kinsella be nervous about something?

"Homemade dinner," he said, making a face. "I wish I could take you to restaurants here in Las Vegas."

"You're taking me to a magic show later tomorrow."

"A second-rate one."

"Because the magician is a lady?"

"Because the show is at the Opium Den, a third-rate venue if there ever was one. So tell me about the funeral while I whip up dessert."

Max was good at anything that required assembly, but whipping out the perfect chocolate mousse did require more serious attention.

"Thirty pieces of silver dollars. A trifle obvious," Max pronounced, after he heard the funeral-goer's tale.

"Is that what you're making, a trifle?"

"It's a mousse, and it'll be in your hair if you don't quit harassing the cook."

Max lifted her up to the large kitchen island so she'd be out of his way.

"You know," she said soulfully, "you'd make someone a wonderful wife."

"You know, you've had a little too much before-dinner wine. When did you start today? Noon?"

"Not till one," Temple said virtuously. "I guess this is really good stuff."

Max eyed the level left in her glass on his next pass through. "Too good to spoil the broth, the salad, the main course and the dessert."

"You've really put yourself out."

"What else can I do, cooped up here?" Max paused before her, grinned. "Actually, I've already traced the flowers by computer."

"Really?"

"Sent from all sorts of places far and near by the dozens. Cost a fortune. The person who ordered them was named Trudy Zelle in every case. The scent of a woman. Does that name ring a bell?"

"Yes, it does. In some foggy, burgundy part of my brain."

Max stopped, clasped her hands. "You're a little reckless tonight. I like it."

He kissed her, and he did it quite well.

"Was the funeral charade too awful?" he asked, still searching for the source of her odd mood. "I suspect that the cashier's check for the whole thing will be signed by this 'Trudy Zelle.' Do you suppose her first name is a play on the word, 'Truly?'"

"I'm lost," Temple admitted a little tipsily. "I just came here to eat and be dazzled. Why are there so few women magicians?"

"Male mystique," Max answered promptly. "Magic has been a classic escape route for boys too smart to get stomped in football and too optimistic to give up on girls until they get rid of glasses and zits."

"Do you need a correction, or do you just wear contact lenses to dazzle women?"

"My eyesight is twenty-twenty, Temple darling. And I can see that you're in a very funny mood tonight."

"Do you love me, Max?"

"Of course I do. You're the first person I could afford to love, the first woman I could count on *not* to be someone or something else than she seemed."

Temple nodded. "Not like this Shangri-La, or Kitty the cutter."

"Are you a little drunk?"

"I should hope so, if I've been working on it since one P.M. in the afternoon. I like to think of myself as a high achiever."

Max tsked like a schoolteacher as he took her empty wine glass away. Probably the T-bird would be next.

"The chef requires a sober palate, Madame. I suppose seeing Effinger laid out was a rather chilling sight, for you as well as for his stepson. How's he holding up?"

Temple giggled. She was more than tipsy.

"Tell me, Temple."

"He's . . . holding up. I'm . . . tired. What do you make of it? Hyacinths and Ladies in Black, nuns even? And then the Cat-woman—"

"That movie has come and gone; Michelle Pfeiffer has unglued her cat ears and peeled off her wetsuit and licked off her whiskers. You'd better have something to eat, and I hope I've made it right."

So Temple sat in one of the huge captain chairs and toyed with sirloin tips on spinach noodles with peppercorn béarnaise sauce. She teethed on tender-crisp asparagus spears and tried not to wash down everything in sight with the dinner wine.

The chocolate mousse was sheer velvet, softer than Midnight Louie's ears, should she care to devour them, and Temple was growing sober despite herself.

She felt full and more peaceful, and guilty as hell. She got up from the kitchen table and wandered into the kitchen proper, with its sleek sacrificial altar masquerading as an island work surface, while Max cleared the plates.

"Should you go out in public?" she asked Max.

"Downtown should be all right. It's still an off-price venue, despite the glamorous new dome that overarches it. I wish I could understand what's bothering you."

"Maybe it's this mystery," Temple said. Not only magicians could use diversion to good effect. "What's the link between Effinger and those two casino deaths? And now his own death, wrapped in the scent of hyacinth and the aura of mysterious Dark Ladies."

"Ladies, plural?"

"You *are* quick, and too quick for me when I've got molasses in my veins."

"What did you mean, 'ladies.' "

"Oh . . . hyperventilating hyacinths!"

"Temple, you only get inventive in swearing when you're really stressed."

If she couldn't confess the scariest secret of all, maybe she could offer a less vital one.

"It's . . . confidential."

"Everything worth knowing in this town is confidential. Tell me."

Max had followed her into this clinical kitchen so like a surgery of gastronomy. He was doctor; she was patient. She badly needed a nagging thorn to come out. Any thorn.

"There's this woman who's . . . appeared to Matt."

"Virgin Mary, huh?"

"Hardly. Bloody Mary, more likely. I hate telling you this . . . but she's the one who told him where Effinger was likely to be found."

"Bloody Judas, maybe?"

Temple nodded. "You don't know how right you are. She appeared to him again after Effinger was murdered. Within a couple of hours, before it was discovered practically."

Max began pacing, listening, absorbing facts into his very bloodstream with a magician's eerie concentration that could hear locked tumblers clicking, audiences holding their breath, and glamorous assistants scratching their high-rise chorus-girl panty lines.

"She attacked him, Max."

Max stopped. Grinned. "He's not *that* good-looking."

"With a razor."

He sobered so fast the mocking figure of a moment ago seemed like ancient history.

"Sorry. That's serious. That's psychotic. What was her problem?"

"Matt thinks—," Temple felt like a traitor for betraying Matt's confidence, but if she offered Max this truth that he might be able to do something about, perhaps it would atone for withholding the truth that none of them could do anything about.

She was exposing Matt, but not where he was most vulnerable. She hoped. She was using the old magician's trick, creating glittering contrails with one hand, while the real work was being done by the other.

"Yes? You were saying. Matt thinks?"

"It's ridiculous, but Matt thinks this woman thought he was a hit man. That she told him where to find Effinger because she thought he would kill him."

"Interesting. What made her take the ex-priest for a killer?"

"Matt sensed she was one mean mama. He felt he had to take a hard line with her. She asked what he would do with Effinger when he found him and he admitted he didn't know, that he would 'probably kill him.'"

Max nodded. "There are some people I'd 'probably kill' if I found them."

"Some people? Max!"

He shook his head. "We never kill the people we need to. It's something we tell ourselves we could do, but we don't. It's a way of admitting we've known people who deserve killing."

"Never kill them? Even in your line of work? Whatever that is."

Max laughed. "Suspicion becomes you, my lovely sleuth. I'm glad we can talk like this finally. Frankly. Temple, this can be better than before, because I can be more honest with you."

He stepped closer, and she was comforted. Too bad *she* had to be less honest than before. Were relationships always comedies of bad timing? Or tragedies of off-tempo truth?

Temple realized that she had never needed Max's love more than now, when her own feelings were subdivided into searing confusion.

"I know it's hard for you to betray confidences." Max wrapped his endless arms around her. "But this is for Devine's own good. I'd be willing to bet that the woman who turned over Effinger and accosted Matt later for not killing him is the very same woman who sent the hyacinths and paid for the funeral. I just wish I knew her game. Or her identity." Max tilted up Temple's chin, regarded her with a smile that softened his sharp features. "I give your neighbor credit for his Devine forbearance with Effinger. It's obvious that Effinger was a family abuser who deserved a lot worse than he got from Devine, if not the killer. It takes a lot of moral courage to outgrow the past, even if you were trained as a priest. He's all right. And he'll *be* all right, Temple. You'd don't have to mother him."

Wonderful. Max the magnanimous. Max the consoler. Max the idiot! Defending the competition because he couldn't imagine any competition worth worrying about. Poor Max!

Max shook her lightly, as if rousing her from a trance. "So let's forget the personal issues and look at the facts, ma'am. Just the facts. Want to hit the computer room? I can show you a graph on the hyacinth orders."

Temple nodded. She could use graphs and cold, hard facts right now. She could use Max's bracing form of self-confidence. She could use distraction.

But the computer revelations were far more interesting than she had thought. She squinted toward the glowing screen.

"The flower orders are amazing. So many little florists, all over the country. One even from Canada. All on telephone credit-card numbers and all shipping every winter-blooming hyacinth they had. It's like a battle plan. Hyacinths in formation. And it must have cost a mint."

"Seventy-six hundred and eighty-nine dollars. And the credit card numbers are all from stolen cards. From all over the country, by the way."

"What? How do you know?"

"I've access to the latest lists of reported lost or stolen cards."

Temple leaned back in the secretarial chair, her accessory to the more substantial throne that Max occupied in front of the computer.

"Sometimes I don't know whether you're Us or Them."

Max grinned again, fondly. "And who are Us or Them?"

"I don't know. Government or insurrectionist. Police or crook. Spy or seditionist. Human or alien."

"You allow for an incredible range of deviation. I admire a lively imagination. But let's stick to the problem at hand. Does this mystery woman have a name?"

"Kitty, according to Matt."

" 'Kitty the cutter,' you called her."

Temple nodded. "If it was the same woman at the funeral home, she called herself Trudy Zelle then."

Max just grinned.

"Why are you laughing at me?"

"Not at you. At her audacity. I just remembered who Gertrud Zelle was."

Temple shook her head. "Yeah, the name does sound vaguely familiar, like I heard it on a PBS station. An opera singer?"

"Only tragic opera, if so. But dance was her ticket to notoriety. Gertrud Zelle was the birth name of the woman who performed as Mata Hari."

"Then this woman is a spy too!"

"Or wants us to think she is. How badly did she slice Devine? I mean, he's still walking among us. Apparently he can still function."

Oh, yes. "A three-inch wound, to the side."

"Interesting. How did she get that close?"

"She intercepted him after work in the parking lot. Obviously, he never expected an assault."

"Why would she do it? Out of pique? This woman is attracting attention to herself. That makes me suspicious. Who or what is she concealing behind the obvious?"

"Effinger is the key. He's the bridge. Not only to Matt's personal life but to your disappearance and now this whole 'hyacinth' puzzle. The word was on a paper in his pocket, along with some sort of reference to me. Molina won't get any more specific than that."

Max nodded, absently pulling the discreet ponytail at his nape.

He had never made love to her with his long hair loose.

Temple realized that she wanted him to. That she needed time to fully experience the change in his appearance, to see him as the lover in an erotic Japanese woodcut, flying hair and robes and elegant masculinity that didn't need Western overstatement, suspended in time.

He had changed. So had she. They needed to settle down and explore those differences.

Since their reunion only a week ago they had behaved like all forcibly separated lovers: coming together again at every opportunity to prove that nothing had changed when everything had. Their sexual chemistry had always been satisfying, but it had been tempered by the small realities of daily life that gave its fiery heights a more static, solid base.

Now they seemed characters in a spy-thriller, meeting clandestinely, conspiring, conjoining and slipping away into shadows again. These stolen moments had an exciting, frenetic sensation, but also felt fevered, desperate, disjointed. They needed time-out, leisure, a time to make love and a time *not* to make love. They needed everything the current situation was least likely to give them.

"Let's adjourn to someplace more comfortable," Max suggested. "You don't like the opium bed, and I doubt the futon is your cat's pajamas . . ."

"Is there a living room in this place?"

Max smiled, and pinched her cheek. So they went there, to sit in matching Chinese black-lacquered chairs and talk.

"I like to think these date back to Orson Welles's day here." Max ran his hands over the ebony-smooth armrests. "A man his size would have welcomed the width as well as the elegant understatement. A misunderstood man. Not the overweening genius they made him be, but a titanic talent who spent himself too soon. He fell in love with fame at an early age, and never escaped it. Not even in death."

"What did you fall in love with at an early age, Max?"

"A woman named Kathleen. A land. A heritage. Danger and death. Caring so much that nothing mattered, which is the greatest self-deception of all."

Max looked at her across the formal room's gulf.

"So now you're a counterterrorist," she said. "Who are the head counterterrorists?"

"Shadows, even to me."

"Who do you 'counter?' "

He sipped the wine he had brought with him. Temple had abandoned wine. *In vino veritas.* And she had imbibed too much *veritas* for the time being.

"At first I was anti-IRA," he said. "An odd position for an Irish-American. But they had killed Sean. I was off courting a Green colleen when they did it; they weren't Orangemen, but Greens-men, or else there, but for the grace—the gratuitous cruelty—of God, went I."

Guilt, Temple thought. The glue of the human jigsaw puzzle. Guilt made people more than angels, and far less. It made them human. Confession was not always good for the soul. Conceal-ment was sometimes a mercy, even from oneself.

"Tell me about the dead men in the casino ceilings."

"The Goliath management was worried about their security being breeched. Nothing they could put their finger on, just un-ease among the staff, as if they glimpsed something wrong out of the corner of their eyes but never could focus on it. I was asked to penetrate their system, if I could.

"I found the secret watching/listening post in the ceiling, clev-erly placed just back and below one of their eye-in-the-sky cam-era installations. Empty, of course.

"It was cramped even for a midget, but it gave an overview of one of the blackjack tables. I reported it and volunteered to in-habit it one night to see what I could see. My profession involves getting myself into spots that are physically impossible for one of my size . . . or length, at least. I had to belly-crawl down an air-conditioning vent to get there and when I did, the hidey-hole was occupied. Just my opening the panel to it dislodged what turned out to be the body that fell to the blackjack table. Of course there was no way to turn around without entering the now-exposed hidey-hole. I had to belly-crawl backwards to get out, and when I reached the mechanical annex, three armed men were waiting for me. *Not* hotel security forces."

"Max!"

"I fought, I hid, I ran. I knew that I was iced either way. Ex-posed as a spy if I admitted my hotel assignment, and liable to be in the sights of the setup crew for as long as it took to get rid of me. So I ran as far as I could go."

"Where *did* you go?"

"What's the place so obvious and predictable and taken for granted that no one ever thinks about it?"

When Temple shook her head, Max opened his empty hand as if presenting something magical. "Canada, haven for draft protestors and rogue magicians."

"What did you do there for so long? How did you survive?"

"I became a corporate magician."

"You? A house . . . wand-waver?"

"I kind of liked it actually. My job was to build morale and encourage creative solutions to problems. Production problems, personnel problems. I was a human resources wizard. I was expected to be the odd man out, and was paid for it."

"I bet you were good at it."

"I was. Surprised me. That there was something legitimate I could do in this world. Could bring home a salary like all the other wage slaves. People told me I helped them."

"An entertainer helps people too. Probably more than a publicist."

"What about an amateur sleuth?"

Temple gave one of those sighs that sounded too large for a person of her small size. Sighs, and size. Homonyms. A crucial clue in her first "case."

"It's just congenital meddling."

"Or congenital caring," Max suggested gently.

"Either way it's a female failing, isn't it? It's not macho like going out every day in a uniform with a gun and a billy club, or in civvies with a gun. It's listening to people. It's 'arranging' things. It's putting the little details together. I let a killer go."

"Whoa!" Max sat up in his handsome chair. "You and Sherlock Holmes. Talk about an 'amateur.' How? And why?"

"The situation was so muddy. The misunderstandings so tragic. The ultimate victims were so very young. I played God. I decided *not* to judge. But the killer knows I know. I wonder if paranoia will set in, and I'll pay someday."

Max balanced his forearms on the Chinese chair's alien curves.

Not Chippendale, not Duncan Phyfe, not Queen Anne, quite. He seemed like a mystic aiming at elevation, as if he could float off the physical plane. He was just thinking.

She was struck by his grace, which was mental as well as physical. She awaited his verdict.

"Everything is a choice. Good or ill. A choice. Every day brings events, people, that narrow choice. Sends us down a chute like an animal to the slaughter. We twist and we turn. We buck like hell. And we always wonder if we should have broken for freedom sooner, or appeared tamer and less threatening, or been born an amoeba. My choices separated me from you when it was the last thing I wanted to do. I don't know if I'll ever overcome that.

"You let a murderer go. Your choice will make you look over your shoulder for the rest of your life. Not only for the one you think might mull it over and come after you, but for the one you don't realize you let go, and who will never let you go. I know."

Chapter 39

Opium Den Dreams

You know me: I will take the scent of a female over the scent of a flower every time.

Miss Temple Barr and her cohorts are clearly on the trail of the lonesome flora called hyacinth. It is obviously my job to make sure that the lady of the same name is *not* lonesome, especially if she is in the mood for making any startling revelations.

Some would say that my habitual interest in the female of my species is blinding me to the true clue in this conundrum. Be that as it may, I know where my particular talents are best applied, so I hie back to the Opium Den as soon as I deliver my missive to Miss Temple Barr's coffee table.

By then the late show is underway, and Miss Shangri-La is joined on stage by an array of petite Asian ladies all draped in exotic robes missing their tops. Miss Shangri-La, being the star of the occasion, does not need to go topless, but her black-clad ninja-boys have peeled down to a streamlined version of a sumo wrestler's diaper, only theirs are stretch black satin that leaves nothing to the imagination but X-rated speculations.

I do not understand the difference between family and "adult" entertainment in Las Vegas. Come the late show, skin breaks out like a raging ebola epidemic.

Perhaps if humans were fully furred, they would avoid this obsession to shed their clumsy clothes in increments. The fair Hyacinth is on stage with her mistress, lithely leaping into and out of various boxes. Except for a ruby and sapphire dog collar, she is dressed only in the hide and hair nature gave her. I am beginning to think that it is this bizarre custom of wearing clothes that has made humans so strange about the rules of taking them off.

I know that I most dislike the discomfort of having hats and collars affixed to my body parts for commercial filming sessions. But now I am utterly unfettered, so before settling down in Miss Shangri-La's dressing room to wait for Hyacinth, I decide to explore the area beneath and behind the stage.

At times like these, I regret that I was not on the Circle Ritz scene when Mr. Max Kinsella was plying his profession and living there with Miss Temple. Perhaps I could have visited him backstage and learned the secrets of the magic trade. All these painted boxes that are wheeled on stage lie around like mummy cases behind the scenes.

I nearly jump out of my hide when I spot a pair of fire-breathing dragons glaring down at me in the backstage dimness . . . but these are merely painted on the doors of a wheeled cabinet.

I am so incensed at being taken in by a pair of painted mythical monsters, that I fiddle with one door until it pops open. I leap inside. The interior is plain black, an excellent camouflage color for me. I sniff around, detecting no more than a phantom odor of sulphur. No doubt this is a trace element from the dragons on the door, who probably blow their stacks on cue when some shill vanishes and then appears again inside said cabinet.

From what I can see, everything here is from the same old bag of magician's tricks. Nothing new, nothing truly magical rather than merely mechanical, nothing to write home about or call the police for. I am very disappointed, but do not have long to languish in this state.

Suddenly my painted shelter rolls into rapid motion. We are

wafted up together, the dragons and I, on a stage elevator and then rolled swiftly across the hollow-sounding wooden floor of the stage itself. The wheels clatter like a Brobdingnagian baby rattle, but I doubt that they can be heard over the swell of Oriental music, as crisp as water chestnuts and as atonally high-pitched as a tortured water buffalo.

I flatten my ears to my head, then squint my eyes shut as the dragon doors burst open and the spotlights and the whole world glare in at me.

"As you can see," Shangri-La's lilting voice is announcing, "the cabinet is as empty as a gambler's pocket."

Well, I am cowering in one corner of it, but with my eyes and mouth shut, I hope I am taken for the black background. It is all I can do. I never intended to crash a magic act in mid-performance. I keep still as paint and hear the show go on.

"Hyacinth and I will step into this box, and only one of us will emerge."

I hope that three of us will emerge. Also I hope that I am not stepped on, being so at one with my background. Perhaps there is something to this zen stuff after all.

A swirl of flower-imprint chiffon fills the black box. The door shuts, assisted by the ring of an offstage gong that makes my ears sit up and take notice, but by then their red interiors do not show against the black box, because the doors are shut and it is so dark in here even I cannot see my nose before my face.

Therefore, when a spidery drift drags across my whiskers, I get my back hair up. I am not sure if my vibrissae have been impinged upon by an errant fold of chiffon, or by something more chilling.

I do not have long to contemplate the Stirrer of My Whiskers.

The whole bottom of my world drops out so fast that I am plopped with my keister cold-concrete down. Phantom touches web me like spider weavings.

I avoid a shudder, and then one last, airy stroke across my nose pauses to tickle my chin.

"Louie?" a silken voice inquires. "Are you trespassing on my territory? Naughty boy!"

Four at full extension swipe through the blackness, but my trusty vibrissae sense the blow and I rear back.

A hiss tells me the striker knows she has missed.

"I am not angry, Louie. Just reminding you that I am queen of this stage. No unauthorized walk-ons allowed. Follow me."

A nice thought, but it is still darker than the inside of water buffalo's belly down here (no doubt the same water buffalo whose tortured bawls serve as the music still faintly heard from the stage above).

A pair of slanted red eyes glow from the dark. I understand that I am to follow these demonic torches, and do.

Soon we are slipping silently up a narrow staircase, and then it is a short trip down a dim hall to the dressing room I had visited earlier.

Hyacinth turns the instant we occupy the dressing room, shutting the door by stretching up against it until her lean weight pushes it shut.

Her lilac-hosed forelimbs touch the dressing room's concrete floor for only an instant. She lofts atop the dressing table to gaze down on me through heavenly blue eyes.

"What a dump," she says. "We usually play far better venues than this."

A perfect opening for the alert private operative. I jump up to the empty chair seat. This is a wooden affair with a round seat and rounded back, dating from perhaps the 1930s.

"What kind of establishments are your usual venue?"

"Convention centers, major hotels." Hyacinth lofts her tail left and right as if pointing to these unseen but fondly remembered palaces of entertainment.

"Then why have you been shunted to this joint?"

"I cannot say."

Hyacinth's slightly crossed eyes have a sly and dreamy look. I do not know if she is being coy, or she actually has been forbidden to say.

"A pity that you and your mistress must put up with such second-rate accommodations when you offer a first-rate show."

"Oh, you think so, Louie?"

"Indeed. I have been in Las Vegas for more years than the rings on the tail of a tiger-strip, and I have seldom seen a magic act of such elegance and amazing illusions. It reminds me of the Cirque du Soleil," I add, mentioning one of the top acts in Vegas, a combination of acrobatics, mime, circus, ballet and magic. "No doubt Your Grace's . . . I mean your supremely graceful presence accounts for the uniqueness of the act."

"My mistress is rather good, too, do you not think?"

"Oh, she is fine. For a human."

"I think so too, Louie." She tilts her head. It is as narrow and bony as a serpent's, and I cannot say I care for her hyper-elongated looks, but there is no denying their elegant power. "We have much in common, considering that you yourself are so common. I must mention our vastly different backgrounds. I am a descendent of show cats. You are . . . a street person of no notable antecedents."

"Not true," I say, idly grooming a mitt.

"Oh?"

"My ancestors go back to the time of Pharaoh."

"I am sorry, Louie, but your common, coal-black coat; your squat nonaristocratic body; your clubby, ordinary ears and thick, unkinked tail all betray none of the aristocratic qualities of a feline of ancient lineage. That is why there are papers to document such things, not to mention the physical requirements. This is so usurpers cannot claim royal blood."

"Sorry. I heard this news from Bastet herself, during a power-séance to call up Houdini last Halloween. I did not *want* to be the last in line of Pharaoh's private operators—I am not a snob myself—but I cannot duck my destiny. Especially when Bast herself is the message-bearer."

"You do not bear the mark of Bast."

"Oh, the old dame wanted to hang her signature earring on my clubby, ordinary ear, but I do not go for these sissy accouterments. I do not care how many supposedly macho dudes affect earbobs nowadays."

Hyacinth gasps. "You know of Bastet's earring?"

"Nobody punctures one of my extremities and lives to tell of it."

Hyacinth narrows her morning-glory blue eyes and hunches down. She resembles a pile of furred antlers in this position. A guy could commit hara-kiri on her hipbones trying to do the wild thing. I do not go for earrings, nor do I endorse this human fetish for females so skinny they become lethal weapons of the edged variety. However, when I am on a case, I cannot allow my preferences to get in the way of cadging information from a source. The fluffy furred images of the Ashleigh sisters flash before my memory. I guess I go for the pneumatic types. But they are not here and the subject before me is the sinewy Siamese called Hyacinth.

"So where did you two last perform?" I ask casually.

"Hong Kong."

I am impressed and allow it to show. "That must be some flight from here to there."

"Oh, we stopped over in Paris first."

"Paris."

"Have you been there, Louie?"

Yeah, sure. Every other day. "Not . . . recently."

"It is a bit overpopulated with poodles, who are allowed an extraordinary freedom of the city, but it is a lovely metropolis. I have been to Caracas, Quito, Katmandu, Rabat, Singapore, Tokyo, Sydney and Amsterdam."

My flattery has gotten me everywhere, I see.

"Quite an itinerary. I just got back from New York myself."

"Oh, New York! We never stop over there. Too dirty, too noisy, too American."

"I can see that you are an international kind of girl."

She hunches down, leans her narrow face toward me, hisses through her fangs, "You ever had any Panama Purple?"

"Not to my knowledge."

"I have some in my treat bag. Want to try a sniff?"

Doing hallucinatory substances is not a requirement of my job, but I am curious about what this dame is into. And I can sniff the best of them under the table, if I have to.

So I look the usual curious and follow her as she leaps down to the floor and minces over to a purple-velvet bed. Sure enough, there is a drawstring bag beside it, a silk-floral affair (I believe the flowers are hyacinths), and Hyacinth herself is soon sticking her long aristocratic nose into it.

A whiff like medicinal marijuana puffs into the room. I am not much for either medicine or marijuana but it is not polite for a guest to turn up his nose at his hostess's best dishes.

So soon I am rolling in it. It is the weirdest nip I have ever encountered, and the dried leaves do indeed have a purple cast. Panama Purple, huh? I am not about to admit my ignorance of this primo stuff. But it is strong. Soon my head is in the clouds and my feet are in the air.

Miss Hyacinth is in the same state, but I am sorry to say it is not shared by her mistress when she comes into the dressing room.

I am aware of a cloud of floral chiffon floating above my eyes— my slightly crossed eyes—of a perfume of distilled hyacinth that is distinctly floral and human, not feline. Long, daggerlike nails probe my underbelly under the guise of scratching my stomach.

"What have we here, Hyacinth?" a honeyed voice inquires.

Human voices, when honeyed, are more dangerous than the growl of a mountain lion.

"I believe that this pussycat was at the scene of a recent crime. Perhaps we should hold him as a material witness, hmm? Would you like that, my little beauty? Your very own personal playfellow?"

The four-inch-long blood-red shivs jab into my gut. "Of course you may keep him, my darling girl! What else are these foolish boys for? But we will put him away for the moment. We have work to attend to. Playtime later, my pet. Playtime later."

Everything here is dark, but then there is nothing here.

I am flat on my back, in utter blackness, on a hard surface.

My ears and toes buzz. Actually, my ears ring and my toes tingle.

That Panama Purple stuff was more potent than a bull matador in mating season.

Of course I wake up alone. You can be sure that the treacherous Hyacinth is coming to in much softer circumstances, although the idea of being caressed by those artificial shivs that last I felt makes my skin crawl.

In fact, my skin crawls so much I almost think I could slip right out of it and through some crack in this box like smoke. But that delusion is just an aftereffect of the alien catnip. I stand, shakily, and nose the limits of my prison. As I suspected, it is one of these breakaway magician's boxes, but that does not mean I can wave my way out using my tail as a magic wand!

These devices are meant to deceive witnesses with their apparent integrity. I am well and truly trapped. It is a nasty feeling. Usually when one of my kind is trapped, we worry about the bored bean-counting ways of the local animal pound. (The beans they are counting are no doubt the heads of the doomed departing as they are admitted into their doors. I also think that they are called "pounds" in honor of the multitudinous pounds of flesh they do away with. Do you know that they actually keep track of how many victims they dust off in a year?)

But evil as the animal pound is to all my kind, I fear I face a greater evil: the unknown villainies of Hyacinth and her magician mistress.

Chapter 40

Command Performance

Matt's doorbell rang.

He rushed to answer it, thinking it might be Temple. Somehow he expected she would have to be as drawn to him as he was to her.

"Oh."

"You were expecting the Avon lady, maybe?"

"No. Just someone I knew. Better."

"And how many people in Las Vegas do you know better than I?"

She had him there. "Oh, about four."

"May I come in?"

"Uh, yeah."

"Sit down?"

"Uh, please."

"I can see you're really connected today. Something happen I should know about?"

"Probably lots of things."

The element of surprise had lost its sting. Matt pulled one of his

second-hand chairs to the sofa table and gazed at the police lieutenant expectantly, a good student.

She wore her usual neutral clothing as a wall does its paint. It
was hard not to see her and think of business, except when she
sang at the Blue Dahlia, and that incarnation was such a 180-de-
gree turn from her daily persona that it seemed a mirage.

"What can I do for you?" Matt asked.

"A lot maybe." Molina bit her lip, a tentative gesture he'd not
seen in her before. "I need you to finger your attacker."

"You've got her in custody?"

"No. But we've got a lead on her, and she may be involved in
a lot more than razor cuts."

"You make her sound like a barber."

"Barbers got their starts in medieval times as surgeons, blood-
letters, do you realize that?"

"I've heard some history of the red-and-white striped barber
pole. What does that have to do with what you want me to do?"

Molina laughed. "Nothing. Just a little social history. You'll
need to get off work, I'm afraid. You can have your supervisor call
me, if necessary."

"Night work?"

"That's your police force at their best. I want you to accompany
me to a show."

"Is this like a date, Lieutenant?"

"It could look like that. We'll be undercover. Look normal.
Nothing fancy."

"And what do I do at this show?"

"Point out this woman, this Kitty O'Connor, if you see her."

"You know she'll be there?"

Molina shook her head.

"Has this something to do with Effinger's murder?"

Molina shook her head again, shocking Matt.

"If it isn't about Effinger's murder, what on earth is it about."

"He was a little man in a big world. Maybe he loomed larger in
your smaller world, but the police have other things to worry
about."

"And you think this Kitty O'Connor may . . . also . . . be involved in these larger things?"

"Maybe." She stood up. "Tomorrow night at ten. I'm afraid it has to be the 'adult' show. Sorry."

"I think I can survive a little frontal nudity nowadays."

"Especially after the Blue Mermaid." Molina grinned. "You living in this town has got to be one of God's biggest jokes."

"What do I wear?"

"Whatever fits a night downtown. Not to worry. I'm bringing my weapon. And reinforcements. All you have to do is keep your eyes open and point out the suspect."

"That's what they told Judas Iscariot."

"No kissing. You had your chance, and apparently you blew it. And you've already collected your thirty pieces of silver, plus a little extra interest." She glanced at his side as delicately as a doe. "Feeling okay?"

"It only hurts when it rains." He suddenly remembered Temple's unshed tears. Eternal rain.

"Lucky you live in Las Vegas, then." She smiled as she left, her Mona Lisa smile, which was not warm, not amused, but somehow mocking, and especially self-mocking.

Should he tell Temple? he wondered.

No. She had enough to worry about without adding Molina's authoritarian games to her burdens.

Chapter 41

Louie Among the Hyacinth-Eaters

Catnip dreams weave in and out. I am a Chinese junk adrift on the Yangtze River.

Hyacinth petals float like soap slivers on the dark water, and death barges pass, skeletons at their oars and corpses for figureheads.

The cat head of the statue of Bastet turns slowly as I drift by, reclining on a petal-strewn deck.

Her eyes are the color of faience beads, both blue and green. Her fangs are capped with beaten gold. Blood drips from the tips. A wide Egyptian collar extends to her human breastbone.

She does not appear at all friendly to dudes who have had a little too much nip through no fault of their own, but then nobody much does.

I lurch upright and wander to the barge's edge. Water lilies, white and purple, float upon the river, and the low, wart-ridden forms of drowsing crocodiles crowd the shoreline bulrushes.

But I am not here and they are not they. The water lilies open to become bloated drowned faces, and the floating crocs are really human bodies that roll over among the reeds to reveal the face of . . . Effinger.

How would I know this dead dude's face, the astute among you might ask. A good question. I never encountered him face-to-face. Even at his death, his features were veiled in bandages of gauze. He never assaulted me with his ugly mug.

However, his mug shot was flaunted before me more than once in Miss Temple Barr's and my former apartment. (This is not her former residence, mind you, and it is only not fully mine now, unofficially. Got that? I thought you would not.)

Who could blame me for being haunted by a dead body of Effinger's very sketchy acquaintance only a few days after witnessing its assumption back into the Land of the Living? Especially after I have inhaled the deadly Panama Purple?

I know I am in a box, and a box devoid of any softening factor. I lie on wood with the smell of paint soaked into its every fiber. I suppose I should be thankful that no funereal upholstery lines my prison. On the other hand, I am not sure that a cat casket would be lined by anything grander than a hand towel.

Of course there are no facilities here. No food. Only darkness and the occasional hiss of voices heard through a keyhole of time. Perhaps I imagine the voices. Certainly I imagine much else, such as softly swirling movement, which would kill any appetite should I have it.

I cannot understand why anyone at the Opium Den would wish to keep me prisoner. Unless I am not a prisoner . . . but a slave.

Methinks the potent pussycat who goes by the name of Hyacinth is used to having her way with males of all species, a characteristic she no doubt learned from her rapacious mistress.

Am I captured to be a sort of plaything for this sharp-shivved feline femme fatale? Will I be expected to perform at her pounce and yowl? She is of Oriental persuasion, and I have heard of harems in the East. Of course, usually the harems are in the proper proportions: hundreds of lissome lovelies to one virile dude. But it is possible that these renegade ladies from Hong Kong have reversed the proper order of things, such as one finds among a few (thankfully) rare insects, where the female of the species bites the male's head off once the mating ritual is over.

I cannot blame these foreign females for coveting my unique masculine features, especially now that I am both "safe" and salacious, but I must be a free agent in these matters, not subject to some feminine whim. Why, if too much performance pressure is placed upon my delicate masculine psyche, I might even refuse to play ball.

What would they do then? Behead me?

Oops. I do believe that this is an ancient form of execution in the mysterious East and Near East.

Well, I will be ready when they storm my cage, planning to tear me from my refuge for unconsenting sessions of who-knows-what. I will fight tooth, nail and tail. They will get bad cases of whiplash trying to pin me down for their foul purposes.

If only I could get all four on the floor, clear my head and dredge up the energy to unsheath my claws. If only I could determine which side *is* the floor.

But the effects of the Panama Purple drag me deeper into uneasy dreams. Where is Miss Temple? She would defend me against these unnatural females of her species and mine. Has she found the message I left her? Interpreted it correctly? Come to save me from a horrid fate of forced enslavement to the most debased urges found on the planet?

Will I be forced to wear a metal collar and a nose ring? Fed soporific foods so that I become a passive tool of their warped desires? Kept in a kitty harness? My drugged imagination conjures the worst that might befall an alleycat who has been shanghaied into an alien world via an alien state.

The idea of breaking out of my box passes through my mind, but a strange lassitude has crept over all my limbs. I suddenly know what narcotic has been slipped into my nip: it is the dreaded date-rape drug. These imported females will stop at nothing to have their way with me! Truly, this is a fate worse than death. Maybe.

On the other hand, it might be interesting.

Chapter 42

Cabinet Meeting

"Where's my sparring partner?" Max asked when he arrived at Temple's condominium.

There was no question of the unit being "theirs" anymore, not with Max camped out at the house he had rented to Gandolph, not with their new arrangement of not quite living together, not quite living apart.

Louie's obvious umbrage at Max's impinging on territory the black cat regarded as his own was just the final fillip to the situation.

"Louie has been hard to reach lately. I've seen him at Matt's—"

"Have you?" Max asked with bland interest.

"Just in passing," she answered. "And I know Louie's dropped by here from time to time, but he's mostly been out and about. A pity you let him scare you off so fast; apparently he has better things to do than hang around here."

Max had wandered over to the bookcase, selected a volume and was smiling at the pages.

"What have you found?" Temple asked.

"Nothing mysterious. Just my favorite collection of Isak Dinesen. I thought you might throw me out when I came back, but I knew you'd never get rid of my books."

"You did *not* think I'd throw you out. You thought I'd be waiting here like an unplayed CD or an unread book, frozen in time until you came back to remind yourself of what I was like."

"Maybe I used to be just a little overconfident. But I got over it, didn't I? Now I'm just as insecure as your average guy. Suspicious, paranoid, jealous. Happy?"

Temple rolled her eyes and replaced the book. Show time was looming.

But Max exchanged the book for her left hand. "You're wearing my ring tonight."

"My ring." Temple flared her fingers to admire the opal. "I put it on after Molina left."

"Molina was here?"

"Oh, yeah. She just comes to call on her favorite all-around suspect any old time. After she left, it suddenly dawned on me that I was letting what I was afraid other people would think run my life. I never used to do that. I've caught your habit of concealment, and I don't like it. Besides, how many million years will it be before I run into Molina again?"

"Obviously you're a dead end for her on this case."

"This case—" Temple picked up her small evening bag; only bag ladies kept tote bags on their laps in theater seats. "—is a bust. If the only clue to who killed Effinger, and why, is the word 'hyacinth,' it's a lost cause."

"Then you don't think Shangri-La and her performing cat Hyacinth at the Opium Den are our last, best hope for resolution?"

"No! Do you?"

Max hesitated, then sleeked the hair back at his temples and laced his fingers contemplatively behind his head.

He gazed at the ever-fascinating arched ceiling that acted as a movie screen for the play of evening shadows.

"I've tried to trace the act," he said, "having never heard of it here or abroad. I can't."

"You said this Opium Den was a low-end venue."

"But even second-rate acts have a history. And then there's the magician's name."

"Shangri-La? Kind of Eastern mystical. Not bad for a lady magician."

"Shan-gri-La," Max repeated so slowly that she could have read his lips.

"Shang-ri-La. Kind of like frangi-pangi, I guess. I think of *Lost Horizon* . . . Shanghai . . . shantung. Chinese stuff mostly." Then she got Max's meaning. *Shan!* The directory name for the files involving mysterious brotherhood on the parchments."

Max smiled, as if a slow student had finally managed to withdraw an elephant from a top hat. "It struck me as interesting. I have a vivid imagination."

"Max, Effinger isn't worth all this mumbo jumbo."

"Maybe it isn't about Effinger at all. Maybe it's about someone else."

"Who?"

He shrugged. "Let's go see a magic show."

Temple snaked her beringed hand through his right arm (his sport coat was baby-soft black cashmere), caught her knit jacket collar together against the evening chill, and they left the unit, as they had so many times before in less uncertain days.

"My God, wait!" Max ordered in the cul-de-sac.

"What's wrong?"

He clapped a hand to his forehead. "How could I have forgotten? I *have* been a selfish beast. I didn't check out the shoes."

Temple spun to exit the Taurus, admiring her strappy magenta suede Via Spiga pumps with the radical heel to which Max had given his highest seal of approval in the hallway. Shoes were wearable sculpture; they satisfied something in her sole . . . probably the endless kid years when she'd been too little to be seen, heard or even blinked at. Not until she'd acquired literal stature with her grown-up lady shoes. Somehow, one could face anything in the properly spirited shoes.

The entrance to the Opium Den required facing. Max dropped the car keys into the valet's waiting hand with a stern expression that somehow conveyed, "Park it six blocks away at a respectable establishment. And don't strip the gears."

Despite the valet parking, necessary because of virtually no on-street parking and no adjacent lot, the Opium Den's entrance canopy smacked of third-string Mann's Chinese Theater.

The sidewalk outside was gritty with refuse, including crushed private-dancer flyers picturing scores of vacuous pouts. In the entrance facade, missing neon bulbs lent a gap-toothed grin to the garish dragon hanging over all who entered.

Yet tourists poured in, the ladies clad in spike heels and glitter-threaded sweaters with faux mink collars, the men in sports coats over knit golfing shirts. Going out to a show was Las Vegas's most gala event, even if the show wasn't a top ticket like Siegfried and Roy, Cirque du Soleil or Lance Burton.

"Why do the women magicians get the short end of the wand?" Temple wanted to know.

"It's a cruel sexist world," Max answered lightly. "I admit that I'm curious to see her act."

He was gazing at a poster of a woman with a ghostly white face and the dramatic, drawn-on features of Asian drama, strands of flat-black hair whipping around her like a cat-o'-nine-tails. Her quasi-Oriental robe was slashed at implausible points to reveal sinuous white arms and legs up to the firm white thigh muscles.

"Dragon Lady," Temple murmured. "With kick."

Max laughed as they entered the lobby and that's how they came face-to-face with Matt Devine and Carmen Molina.

Stupefaction would not have been a strong enough word to describe the general reaction, which was no reaction, because everybody froze as if suddenly playing the children's game "Statue." That was where one was spun around by the hand and suddenly released with instructions to freeze in whatever position one could stop in.

Temple was caught stepping forward on her right foot with her left hand reaching up to brush the hair from her face, a pose which highlighted her ring like a de Beers diamond ad.

Max had been guiding her ahead of him so the crowd wouldn't smash into her, as it was wont to do with one of her short stature.

Matt had been checking his watch, left wrist raised and twisted, a comment on his lips iced into a sudden silence.

Carmen Molina had been turning her head to scan the crowd, and had spotted them both in one eagle-eyed sweep, had eagles ever been blessed with morning-glory blue eyes.

Like a camera, Temple took in the entirety of the pair before her. Matt's bronze velvet jacket (*how* could *he? So soon. With another woman. Well, sort of woman*). Molina's totally uninspired boxy navy suit, just the formal side of career dressing for an accountant's office (*so tacky, but then it was probably boxy to hide an arsenal*).

Matt was staring at her hand as if she had just punched him with it.

Molina was staring at Max as if she'd like to tackle him.

Max was staring at them both as if they were Martians.

But he spoke first.

"Is this a . . . date? Are congratulations in order?" Sometimes Max was the reincarnation of Cary Grant in a James Bond movie.

"Work," Molina barked.

"Command performance," Matt said. "What's your excuse?" But he was looking at Temple.

She didn't have to answer. Lieutenant Molina was taking command.

"This isn't my bust, or I'd take you right now," she told Max. "But I'm not supposed to make a scene. So consider yourself lucky."

"I don't know—" Shock had ebbed and he was starting to enjoy himself. Max thrived on other people's tension. "I don't expect much from the show. We could probably have put on a much better one out here."

Molina's strong features hardened, but she resisted a reply.

"We'd better find our seats," Matt the peacemaker suggested. But the look he shot Temple was far from meek.

"What if we're seated near them?" Temple whispered hoarsely to Max as they moved away through the crowd.

"We'll find other seats."

"But they may all be taken."

"We'll find other seats," he reassured her so firmly that she didn't want to know how he'd accomplish it.

But fate was merciful. Temple could see Matt's blond head veering right through the crowd. Max, tickets in hand, steered them left.

"This will be odd," Max noted as if just thinking of it. "To be in the audience for a change."

"Max . . . we keep going forward. We're not in the really close-in seats?"

"Of course, we're in the critic's circle. I definitely intend to criticize the show. If you're lucky, it won't be aloud."

"How did you get such close seats?"

Temple jerked her head around. Matt and Molina were settling into a banquette on the upper tier.

"Seats are sold by computer. I'm learning. Besides, I want to be close enough to see the smoke, mirrors and wires. Also, I want to see this Hyacinth fur-person close up. A Siamese cat is pretty small from the back row."

Temple knew this was not the time and place to object to Max's manipulative seating skills. She would bet that Molina was really steamed that they were so close and she and Matt were so far away.

"Why on earth are *they* here?" Max asked, mirroring her thoughts in the eerie way he had used to be quite good at.

"I don't know! Probably to bug us."

"Don't be paranoid. There's a reason, and I take it unlikely romance is not it."

"Absolutely not," Temple said emphatically.

"Then calm down, quit covering your ring hand and figure out what it is. You're closer to the couple in question than I am."

"Separately, or together?"

"Either way, I assume. The stage is my job; the gate-crashers have now become yours."

"I'm sure they have tickets."

"I'm sure the tickets were obtained by the police about as high-handedly as ours were by me. The key is why Devine is here. What does he know, *who* does he know, that would make him useful as a witness?"

"Effinger."

"But he's dead." Max suddenly settled back in his seat, arms folded across his chest. "Now that might be interesting. A resurrection. I don't believe a stage magician has tried it in forty years."

"If you sit this close up front, you don't get roomy banquette seats around nice tables, but have to put your drink in this dinky hollow attached to the seat arm."

"Aren't we cranky, all of a sudden? Just how many drinks are you planning on having."

"Plenty," Temple threatened.

She hadn't mentioned her real source of irritation: the fact that the pair in the back had a perfect view of *them* all evening but they could hardly return the favor without looking like rubberneckers. Rubbernecks! Not neckers. Oh, shoot.

Max was chuckling. "What a farce. I bet Molina's got a bad case of itchy holster. She can't really arrest me, you know. Not enough evidence for probable cause."

"Maybe she's got evidence you don't know about."

"I doubt it. Now, here's the nice lady with the notepad. What will you have?"

Temple was tempted to ask if they served hemlock, but settled for two scotch and sodas instead. One had to order in bulk, because once the house lights dimmed and the show began, the only interruptions for two hours would be the waiters circulating silently with drink orders.

Max chose white wine, one abstemious glass. Temple wondered what Molina and Devine were knocking back: nothing for Molina if she were working, and who-knows-what for Matt, whose habits of any type were no longer any of her business.

But what was he doing with Molina?

She wasn't aware that she was twisting the ring around her finger until Max took her hand to stop her. "Chill out," he whispered in her ear. "Some questions are better answered later than sooner."

Temple sighed. She remembered them sitting like this at theaters around Minneapolis. How fun it was to settle into their seats, alone together but not alone, whispering back and forth. Max nuzzled her earlobe, his hand moving from her shoulder to her neck.

"Do you suppose this Shangri-La will change the Siamese cat into twins?" he asked. "Why a domestic cat? It's so small for a stage act."

"As big as a rabbit, and bigger than doves."

"I'm glad I never worked with animals." His caressing fingers paused on her neck. "What's this? A souvenir of Effinger?"

Temple froze at his touch, but not from excitement. Confession trembled on the tip of her tongue, but it managed to twist into denial. "No. Louie must have done it."

"A cat gave you a hickey?"

"You know cats." Temple's shrug interrupted his caress. "They'll hook you with a claw here, a fang there and you never even notice it."

"Tooth and nail, huh? Law of the jungle." Max did not sound convinced.

Temple welcomed the nick-of-time arrival of their drinks, and toyed with the evening's program until the waiter left.

"This is clever. Like a Chinese menu."

"With a little Japanese thrown in for good measure. I have a feeling this will be a multicultural evening."

Temple fanned herself with the slick cardboard. It seemed hot in here. She wriggled out of her jacket, Max holding it so she could work her arms out. "Excuse me. Sorry," she murmured as her thrashing impinged on the woman on her right.

"Better?" Max asked as she settled down.

Before she could nod, the Musak that had been barely noticeable swelled into a distinctly Oriental sound, full of crystalline pings and high, yodeling instruments.

"Sounds like the overture to 'Flower Drum Song,' " Max whispered in what was not meant as a compliment.

At once baby-stepping Chinese maidens tripped onto the stage as the opening curtain parted to reveal a set of piled pagodas and distant mountains. A glittering covered rickshaw was being drawn across the stage by a twenty-sandal team of coolies in satin pajamas, pigtails and straw hats.

Temple was about to comment on the politically incorrect clichés when the music grew even higher and shriller. A cloud of shadows crossed the stage, dispersing the coolies and attacking and dissembling the rickshaw with predatory swiftness. Within was a woman in exquisite Chinese robes, which the black-clad attackers rent from her body with flourishes of unraveling fabric.

So many thin, veiled layers flew up into the stage flies that it seemed nothing would be left of the woman, but she suddenly burst upward like the clothes, swinging out of the shadow figures' earthbound grasps on an invisible wire, a tattered kite of a figure, her bare legs and arms flashing through the provocative tatters of her robes.

"Hmm," Max commented, aiming a Clint Eastwood-squint at the stage.

But he was watching the wings, not the central figure of the woman careening above the stage.

The dark cloud was dispersing to the stage's far reaches, separating into a swarm of furies, into black-Spandex-clad ninjas.

"Aren't ninjas Japanese?" Temple whispered to Max.

He nodded, still watching the stage. "This setup blends everything exotic and Eastern into a kind of chow mein. Purist it ain't, but it's perfect for Las Vegas."

By now Shangri-La had come to rest atop a huge elephant figure that had materialized from behind a sheer length of chiffon that the Chinese maidens had lifted from a trembling "river" on the stage floor into a wavering wall of color and softness.

As the show progressed, Shangri-La, while her henchmen the ninja and the maidens disappeared and reappeared, wore less and less and played peekaboo with the almost-living lengths of exotic fabrics that made the stage a fluid space, a kind of cloud kingdom.

Temple was struck by the arch peep-show nature of Las Vegas magic shows. For this later "adult" show, bare breasts were obligatory, though Shangri-La, being the magician star, only revealed glimpses of her acrobatic body.

Her agile movements were even more impressive because of the six-inch platform shoes she wore, which changed in elaboration and grew taller with each of her reappearances in yet another delicately glittering robe. And as the act progressed, Shangri-La's robes intensified in color from the palest pastels to the more lurid and inflamed shades.

"What's the grade?" Temple asked, leaning over to whisper to Max, whose intense surveillance of the onstage and offstage action had turned him into a virtual statue.

"Execution is excellent; originality is pathetic. A very odd combo of strength and weakness. Disturbing. It's almost as if—," but Max's sentence trailed off, lost in the multitude of interior paths his quick mind was following on a journey of its own.

Still, a magic show is a magic show. Impossibly large objects are made to appear or disappear; people come and go in exotic cabinets like Clark Kent dashing into a phone booth and flying out as Superman.

Temple watched, always tricked, like the rest of the audience, despite her best efforts to see the smoke and mirrors, to watch the hand that wasn't waving the red flag of distraction.

And eventually came another patented magic-show moment.

The enchantress, in her tatter-edged robes of black-and-orange chiffon imprinted with silver chrysanthemums, glided across the stage apron on her incredibly high Chinese platform soles. Temple squinted to better see a silver-leafed landscape carved into the six-inch-high platforms. She had never before seen a woman as vertically ambitious.

Shangri-La's mandarin nails pantomimed arcane signs.

"My next illusion requires an assistant from the audience. You, little boy in blue?"

A forefinger nail lunged toward a six-year-old in the front row who was gazing up at her with the utterly round eyes of innocent belief. His wonder was tinged with fear, and she wisely veered away from him.

"Someone older and bolder, but . . . not too large."

Again she strode the breadth of the stage, eerily noiseless despite the clunky-looking platform shoes.

"You!"

A curved nail pointed, and two of the ninja figures leaped into the audience. They stopped before Temple.

"Oh, no . . ."

Somehow Shangri-La threaded her artificially long fingers together, creating dueling fingernails. "This is not difficult. Will not take long. Will be most amusing. And your hair matches the color of my robe."

The audience laughed, having spotted Temple's red hair.

Max was seriously slouching in the seat beside her, giving low profile a new name. He seemed almost in a trance, all observer, rather than actor.

"Will you not be this magician's assistant for a very short time?" the woman coaxed. Her slightly hoarse voice was all the more enthralling, evoking France Nuyen's huskiness in the spate of fifties films that reflected a postwar fascination with the mysterious East.

Like anyone singled out from the crowd to perform as the average idiot, Temple felt bullied, and secretly flattered. She would be cool, refuse to let this professional manipulator throw her. She wasn't utterly unfamiliar with magical hocus-pocus. She would audition as Max's assistant. So she stood, applause encouraging her onward and upward.

The flanking ninjas grabbed an arm each and rushed her to the stage, lifting her up from the pit as if she were weightless, then jumping up onstage beside her and bowing to her, then Shangri-La, then the audience.

More applause.

The dragon lady circled her subject, robes licking like flames at her figure. "Here we have a woman named—?"

"Temple."

"Temple. Are you a tourist, Temple?"

"Oh, no. I live here."

"Imagine. Someone lives here in Las Vegas. Well, then, Temple, you have no doubt seen many magic shows and know what to expect."

Temple smothered a smile. Did she ever!

"That is a lovely ring you are wearing. Show it to the audience, please."

That she didn't like, not with two particular audience members out there, but anyone hauled on stage for shenanigans can't complain when they come too close for comfort.

Temple lifted her left hand, facing her, so the audience could see her ring.

They tittered.

Temple turned her hand around. Her finger was bare. Every finger was bare. She held up her right hand. It too was bare.

Another laugh from the audience. She was performing like an automaton, making all the right, befuddled moves. She didn't like that either.

She glimpsed Matt's blond head at the upper left, amid the overall dark undifferentiated mass of the crowd.

She looked down for Max. His chair was empty. That's when slight unease began to escalate into fear.

"So you had a ring, and it is gone. Surely you felt it leave your finger?"

"No."

"Perhaps you did not have a ring, and will sue the establishment. Can you prove you ever had a ring?"

"Yes."

"Good. Then we will get it back for you. But first you must do as the ring did. You will vanish and reappear."

"The ring hasn't reappeared yet."

"Was it valuable?"

"Yes."

"Of sentimental value as well?"

"Yes."

"Then I take this next task very seriously."

Shangri-La stepped aside, her robes a spotlit flutter. Temple turned to look upstage as the silent lithe ninjas wheeled a gaudy booth to center stage.

She had seen its like a few dozen times. Not in Max's act. He avoided the predictable. But she knew this trumped-up box into which she was supposed to step and from which she would disappear only to be conjured up again.

She didn't really know how it was managed, especially with an untrained subject. A back panel that gave, so she was hustled offstage? A bottom escape hatch that opened onto a stage trapdoor through which she would descend? She supposed a friendly neighborhood ninja would lift her down into the lower depths.

She stepped up into the elaborately painted closet. Shangri-La floated around the prop, her long sleeves and fork-tongued skirt panels making contrails of color and motion.

The door closed on Temple, shutting her in darkness. Then the blackness spun and she felt herself caught in a falling eddy, plunging down into a greater darkness.

Where were the guardian ninja when she needed them?

Chapter 43

Vanishing Act

When Temple's ring disappeared, Max Kinsella's internal illusion warning system went on red alert. The missing ring or watch trick was laughably common, but that wasn't what had alarmed Max.

Maybe it was the primal shock of seeing his ring to Temple vanish, but he didn't think he was that possessive.

It was that the vanishing act happened too soon, like a suspiciously rushed preliminary. Usually the canny magician made a big production of the ring being present before making it vanish. This ring might never have existed. Temple might be a planted shill, for all the audience could tell. Not a wise way to run a magic act.

Max shrugged out of his sport coat. He seized Temple's program from the empty seat beside him, grabbed her half-consumed drink and balanced it atop the horizontal program.

When the onstage action was drawing all eyes, he stood, stooped at the knees so his height wasn't a distraction. Then he darted waiterlike down the row, bending here and there as if delivering a drink. Bewildered show-goers watched phantom drinks hover and disappear as swiftly as departing UFOs.

Sensing a distracting moment on stage, Max darted forward again, heading for the stairs leading up to the dim-lit apron at stage right.

The dialogue between Temple and Shangri-La ricocheted like a racquetball through the house, but despite the mike's booming amplification that distorted the everyday into the unreal, Max sensed Temple's dawning unease before even she felt it.

Beside the stairs he stooped to put down glass and makeshift tray, tearing the elastic from his hair at the same time. He had no ninja mask, but his black turtleneck sweater and pants, and his loose, long dark hair would look sufficiently Oriental, sufficiently sinister, to blend with the ninja assistants for the few moments he needed.

As the trick box was wheeled on stage with every creaking tradition of distracting ritual, Max rolled up onto the dark stage floor, then sprung instantly to his feet alongside the drawn folds of black velvet stage curtain. He risked a glance at the audience. Their faces were tilted as one to the focal point on stage: Temple in her slim hot-pink jumpsuit, her red hair a flame atop a gaudy birthday-cake candle. Temple looking small and wee inside the painted Oriental scrollery decorating the box inside and out, until Shangri-La swept down like a silk *tsunami,* and Temple was gone.

As the ninja contingent spun the now-closed box like a top, Max slipped behind the curtain, hunting the backstage stairs to the lower level.

Hands caught her, held her.

Silk circled her mouth and drew tight as a hangman's noose. Temple started to struggle, but a quick click bound her hands before her in the harsh metal bangles of handcuffs.

She was lifted, and then lowered again into darkness, cushioned darkness, and then she heard the darkness shut above her, and her world was spun away. She was dizzy, disoriented, and a fugitive prick at her inner elbow told her that she was also drugged.

And that was that.

"Why aren't they making her appear again?" Matt wondered.

He wasn't asking Molina so much, as thinking aloud.

"Maybe it's part of the act," she answered him. "Part of the suspense."

"It's more suspense than I like."

"You're . . . oversensitive on the subject of seeing more of Temple Barr."

"Am I? Look down to their first row seats, Lieutenant. I know you marked the spot. Where's Max Kinsella?"

"Damn!" Molina stood, oblivious to hissing audience members behind her.

She pressed a hand to one ear, spoke into her palm. "Any sign of the suspect?"

Matt hadn't realized she was wired. Talk about unobservant. But then his attention had all been on Temple, like the lovesick swain he was. The sick part of the clichéd phrase was growing alarmingly concrete in his gut.

He eyed the elaborate stage scene, a finale of Oriental kites swooping everywhere in silken profusion, like demented paper bats. The eye feasted, but came away empty. Not only was Temple missing, but so was the magician, Shangri-La. Ninjas leaped everywhere, like athletic ants.

Molina abruptly turned to leave. She had forgotten Matt, she heard nothing but the sweet nothings hissing over her hidden receiver. He followed her, their sight-blocking exit drawing more boos and hisses.

For the first time in his life, Matt didn't give a damn about appearing rude.

In the tiny lobby there were also lots of milling men in black, but not Shangri-La's serpentine ninjas. These were heavyset men, or maybe men who just looked heavyset because they were armored in vests reading "Drug Enforcement Administration" that probably covered bulletproof vests underneath.

"They're moving," one said, the moment he spotted Molina. "What's going on in there?"

"The show isn't over," she protested, then shook her head as if to clear it. "We didn't see the suspect. I'll follow up on what's happening here. You guys take it as far as you have to."

They split, the men pouring out the front door like a gang, Molina going to dragoon an usher.

"Get us backstage. Now!" Her ID case was as black as an old stigmata in the palm of her hand.

"Yes, ma'am."

The teenager in the cheesy Chinese pajama outfit—black satin pants, jacket and boxy Philip Morris cigarette-boy hat (except for the phony pigtail snaking down his quaking back)—raced down some narrow, unlit side stairs and then through a maze of hallways.

Molina trailed him like a shadow, Matt a doppelganger behind her.

She stopped the kid as the hallway opened into the stage's shadowed underbelly.

"Got a flashlight?"

"Yeah. I mean, yes, ma'am."

"Out of here."

The kid's footsteps pattered away like a shuffle off to Buffalo as a rope of yellow light whipped through the darkness.

Against it, Matt saw Molina seem to scratch her back.

It took a moment to realize she was now armed and ready.

He supposed she had forgotten him. She faced a maze of stage props, magical mystery machines lined up for tricks done and not yet done. Upright coffins painted up like tarts. Gleaming swords ready for defying the eye and slicing a confined body into mincemeat.

"You too," she said. "Outa here."

But he couldn't leave. He said nothing. Did nothing. He stayed.

Temple sensed movement. Never-ending movement.

Whether it was in her head, or beyond it, she couldn't tell. She was spinning, spinning, spinning. Inside the magic box. Nothing would stop spinning. But the box was moving too, on its ever-ready wheels. Every jolt mashed the metal handcuffs into her tender wrist bones.

Where was that glamorous handcuff of another sort? Her ring. Stolen. She had let it be stolen so easily. Hadn't even felt it sliding away. Surely those long, predatory fingernails would have scratched her flesh. She should have felt something.

Feel? Only movement, and the bizarre upward tingle of some scary snakebite at her elbow. She was like the young Cleopatra in her concealing rug with an iridescent dreamsnake as a hint of the future.

No! Think! They hadn't wanted her to think, why else the prick of fangs at her inner elbow? Her feet were free. She kicked at the edges of her confinement. Soft, upholstered fabric, like the lining of a coffin. Then where were the hyacinths? There should be hyacinths. The symbolism was all wrong if there weren't hyacinths. Where are the clowns? There ought to be hyacinths. Don't worry. Be happy. Kick!

Spinning again, and then bumping up stairs, up a stairway to heaven lined with blue-purple hyacinths, and Effinger there to greet her, wearing wings . . . water wings.

Moses in the bulrushes. Temple's coffin became a boat, and lurched forward into rocking motion. She could almost go to sleep. Sleep of the Deep. Deep, deep sleep.

Where was her ring? That had been the first to go. Why? Petty theft? Or major felony? That sounded like a character from the old board game called "Clue," didn't it? Major Felony. *Look here, Major Felony, Miss Crimson is in the funeral parlor with the handcuffs. Won't you find her, please?*

The gun cocked like a castanet in the understage darkness.

"Put up your hands," Molina ordered.

The flashlight followed a lean dark figure as the arms lifted, and pale, naked palms were crucified with light.

"I don't think you want that, Lieutenant," Max Kinsella said.

The light pinioned his face, making his eyelashes flinch.

"I've got two of your suspects by the pigtails," he added.

A broader sweep of the light revealed paired ninjas, their natural pigtails tied together.

Molina addressed her hand again. "Backup below-stage. Two to go. One to get ready."

"Keep your hands up," she ordered Kinsella.

He obliged, but Matt felt it was more out of form than fear.

"Where's Temple?" Matt asked anyone who would answer.

Max turned his face sideways to avoid the interrogative light of the flashlight. "Not here. Not any more. Maybe the lieutenant has an idea."

"Where's the damn backup?"

She whisked the flashlight behind them. It picked up hunched-over figures heading toward them.

"The pigtails secure?" she asked Kinsella.

"They're not going anywhere."

"Then we are. Come on."

They met the three uniformed cops, guns drawn.

"Two tied up, back there. Approach with caution," she warned them.

"What about the one to get ready?"

"He's with me."

The cops eyed Kinsella and Matt as they followed her and the dancing flashlight beam, not sure which one was the temporarily paroled desperado.

The usher was quaking in his fallen house when they came up the stairs into the lobby. More uniforms had gathered.

"Where'd the DEA go?" Molina asked one.

"Vehicular pursuit."

"Get me wheels."

The man nodded. Molina made for the entrance, pausing only to fix Kinsella with a look half-warning, half-challenge. "Follow if you can."

He sprinted out the door before her and collared a valet in an ersatz Oriental uniform. "The black Taurus. A hundred bucks if you have it here in one minute flat."

With a screech of brakes, a white Crown Victoria careened slantwise across the street.

Kinsella swore like a sailor and then he swore like a French le-
gionnaire.

"I'm going along," Matt squeezed into the backdraft from the
obscenities.

"Watch those taillights as long as they're visible." Kinsella sent
a look after the Crown Vic that Matt hoped never to be on the
other end of this side of Purgatory.

The Taurus screeched up in its turn. Matt barely got around to
the passenger side before it took off in a squeal of tires and the
flutter of a hundred-dollar bill.

"Left onto ninety-five, in the left lane," Matt said, still straining to see the impossible as he jerked on the seatbelt.

The Taurus wove through the late-night traffic like a ninja armored in sheet metal. They must have been doing seventy.

Matt glanced at Kinsella, who grinned. "Had it upgraded.
They're using a Taurus platform at NASCAR, did you know?"

"No." Matt cared little about cars.

"It's what's *not* visible that counts."

Matt nodded, straining to spot the right pair of red taillights
among a host of beady red beams.

"There! Is it them?"

Max nodded. "Look. They're putting the cherry on top.
Thanks, Lieutenant."

"Not for us?"

"Not for us. For speed. But they won't shake us. We'll run in
their wake like Ahab after the white whale."

Matt couldn't suppress his nervous bark of laughter. The big
white Crown Vic was very like the Moby Dick of the automotive
world.

"What's happening?" he asked, hating to ask Kinsella but needing to know more than he needed his pride.

"Drug bust. That was the principal deal. The rest—you and
Molina—were ride-alongs."

"And Temple?"

"Unscripted. Wild card."

"Is she—?"

Kinsella shook his head. He'd probably forgotten his loosened
hair, why ever he'd done it, and didn't realize he resembled a wild

man of Borneo. Matt took in his primitive streak, and wondered about Temple. Wondered about himself. Molina he didn't wonder about. She was doing her job. The rest of them were trying to save their own lives. And maybe each other. He had to give even Kinsella credit for that.

They accelerated like a whip-snake into the on-ramp lane, then were greased lightning on Highway 75, heading north.

Kinsella eased up on the gas. "Don't want to make the cops paranoid."

"She knows we're coming."

"She knows we'll try."

Suddenly they were "we." It gave Matt chills. What if Temple's death were the one thing that could draw them together?

"You're sure she's not back there—?"

"The game is distraction. The aim is a moving target. If Temple were back there, she'd be dead."

"God! Don't say that!"

"It's the truth. As long as someone is running, there's a chance Temple is worth something to them."

Matt grew silent. He couldn't drive like a demon, not without a vehicle; he couldn't pull a gun and flash a badge, not without a license. All he could do was pray. And be there. For whatever would be.

"More taillights at the same speed." Kinsella's chin jerked to-ward the windshield. "It's a caravan. Major bust. Molina and her case is icing."

"And Temple?"

"Temple is . . . an innocent bystander and the point of the game."

"Then you know who?"

"I know who the target is. I don't know why."

Kinsella's hands left the wheel, then pounded back onto it in a death grip.

Matt knew dread, and knew for the first time in his life that prayer was not enough.

Temple rocked and rolled in her padded cell.

Temple despaired. She shouldn't have had that scotch and

water. With all this motion, all this stress, all this hallucinogenic high, she might have to go to the bathroom. And if she died, well . . . it would be embarrassing. If she lived, it would be even more embarrassing.

Amazing what really mattered.

Not being a kid. Not losing it. Not freaking out. Not . . . choking to death on your own fear because you were locked into this human-size jewel case in the dark, bouncing back and forth like heisted emeralds, only emeralds don't have to go to the bathroom, afraid you might die and afraid you might live and never live it down, this awful claustrophobia, this turning of yourself inside out, this delirious buzz that's supposed to be a kick if you pay for it but is sheer hell if someone does it to you.

Oh, Lord. Think how disappointed everyone would be if she died? Poor Max. Guilt would move right in and pay rent. Poor Matt. Another guilty party. They could blame themselves for decades. And her poor aunt Kit, who would blame herself for ever letting Temple leave New York City for the Wild West. And her mother and father, who always knew she should never go off on her own, especially with a man. Especially with That Man. And her brothers, who started all her phobias by holding her under the fruit crate when she was four, and threatening to never let her free, and laughing.

She guessed they didn't really mean it. But it had felt like it at the time, because she was smaller and a girl, both things they didn't seem to like much at their grand ages and sizes of ten, twelve and thirteen . . . she had hated the dark and closed-in places ever since . . . remember how she had grabbed Matt's arm in the haunted house? Not so very long ago. Much more recently than she had encountered her terror in a fruit crate.

Those creepy ninjas, masked men. Weren't going to get her down. Okay, she was down. She was almost out. But she was conscious. Sort of. And her feet were free. Maybe she could pry the lid open. Wriggle her wrists out of the handcuffs. But she'd tried, and it's like they knew her wrists were small. All she did was wear off her skin. And the upholstery was up, down and all around. Muffling.

No one would hear her. She tried chewing the silken gag into a narrow strip and shouting around it. But it was spider's-web strong, the silk and all she managed were a few puny mews, like a sick cat.

Sometimes she thought the dark and the drug haze and the endless nauseous motion would gag her. Or that she'd stop breathing. Just because. And then her heart raced until her ears pounded. And she thought, no, someone wanted this to happen to her, and the last thing she wanted was to give in to someone who wanted her to give in. Did that make sense? No.

They would be so sad that she'd had to leave them. She could hardly stand it. She could face leaving, but she couldn't face leaving them alone, with only sadness to remember her by.

All right. She wasn't dead yet. They could have killed her, but they didn't. She was still alive, and she wasn't quite crazy, although the possibility of that seemed the scariest of all. And her feet were free. And they were wearing very spiffy shoes. If she died, she'd be put in a funeral casket, and then no one would see her spiffy shoes.

Not to be tolerated.

She kicked off one of the shoes, put both hands to her mouth and pulled on the tight rope of silk until it seemed her lips would peel off. But finally she managed to work one side over her chin.

Her handicapped hands tussled the fabric down to her neck, where it hung like a cowboy's kerchief.

Her face and mouth were sore, worn, but it was great to know she could really holler if she had to.

And then she curled her toes, flexed her knee and worked the loose shoe up, up the cushy side of the rolling coffin to her hip. She caught its pointed toe with her fingertips.

She brought it, heel first, to her head.

Temple took a deep breath. It was harder to strangle without a gag in your mouth. And now she could yell. But should she, right now? Better to wait until she sensed that someone beside ninjas might hear her.

The shoe lay on her chest, between her handcuffed wrists.

Now what? It couldn't spring steel. Maybe she could work herself half upright and pry away at the upholstery. There must be wood underneath, and nails or screws. She fought the flutter in her stomach at the word "screws." Screws were hopeless.

No, screws were harder, but not hopeless.

Chapter 44

That Last Time with Temple

The night had settled into a game of follow-the-dotted-line.

The dotted line of the highway center divider.

Max Kinsella drove it, but Matt Devine rode it in his head, on the Hesketh Vampire. A motorcycle was made for following a line, a thin, endless high-wire road through nowhere.

Matt had never realized, until confined as a passenger in this car, how much he had converted to the lone, whining whiplash of a two-wheeler.

He had never understood, until that last time with Temple, how much of himself lay unexpressed, like raw ore in the ground, waiting to be found and valued.

"Why Temple?" he asked. "It began with her ring, but then they took her. Why?"

"Why you?" Kinsella rejoined. "Why were you there at all, with Molina of all people?"

"I was a witness." Matt suddenly saw that role as both horrific and ironic. "I was supposed to identify the woman who cut me.

Why she was supposed to be there, I don't know. Ask Molina. She seemed so very sure."

"She's paid to seem certain."

Kinsella drove like someone who could take it or leave it. Like driving was a means to an end, not an end in itself. It was hard to imagine him caring enough about the Hesketh Vampire to own it.

"What are *we* paid to do?" Matt asked.

Kinsella was silent. Then he hit the door buttons and the windows rolled down, letting in chill desert air.

His unconfined hair blew back like an Art Deco pennant, dramatic, decorative. He looked like the Pontiac Indian: aloof, superior, alien.

"We're paid to care," Kinsella finally said.

Matt tasted the idea. That described his job all right. His hours on the headset, connected to strangers. How did it describe Kinsella's reality? Paid to care? Matt hoped not. He hoped humanity was not a mere commodity.

"Temple cares without being paid," Matt noted after a while, into the wail of the wind.

"Temple is a throwback," Kinsella said shortly.

Matt was silent. The expression made Temple sound expendable, when Matt realized that was the last thing Kinsella had meant to say. Temple was a hark back to old-fashioned values. That was why he was so drawn to her. She looked before she leaped. She weighed right and wrong. She considered other people's feelings. And he had castigated her for trying to spare his.

Matt leaned his head into the wind, felt the fresh, sundown whip of night in motion.

Molina seemed to know what she was doing.

Kinsella always acted as if he did.

Matt would have to count on them being at least half right, because there was nothing else he could do.

A constellation had fallen to earth.

Mars, Venus, the Crab Nebula lay across the long, lone strip of highway, blinking wildly.

Matt took in the convention of red, blue and yellow-white lights.

"Accident?"

"Roadblock."

Coming up fast.

The Taurus's brakes took, but not before the car did a graceful, screeching half-turn on the empty road.

Beyond all the ground-bound official lights blinked an alien vehicle. Twinkling like a rectilinear Christmas tree, big as a double-wide house on wheels.

A semitractor and trailer. West Coast mirrors. Twin trucker CB antennas. Eighteen wheels and chrome Playboy bunny mudflaps. A true UFO brought to earth by a squadron of police vehicles, most of them vans bristling with antennas.

Above them, a helicopter hung like one mighty mad hornet, buzzing.

"Wait," Kinsella cautioned, turning off the ignition.

Wait? When Temple's fate was winking somewhere out there in the chaos.

Matt opened the Taurus door, got out, began walking toward the commotion.

Kinsella they probably would have crucified against the nearest empty van as a suspicious character.

Matt they left oddly alone, as if he were invisible.

Perhaps fifteen men milled around the truck. Matt spotted the white Crown Vic and headed that way. The red light on top still circled endlessly in the night, washing desert and sky and van in sweeping turn.

Molina waited on the road, hanging back as the bulky men in commando gear swarmed over the parked tractor-trailer.

When he came alongside of her, she didn't seem surprised.

"It's their show. We're just a sideshow." She meant the Las Vegas Metropolitan Police.

"And Temple?"

"A featured attraction. I've got to let them do their thing. All we've got is suspicion. They've been working this case for months."

She glanced over Matt's shoulder into the desert darkness. "Hitch a ride with a friend?"

"You know better than that."

"He's still out there." It was a statement.

"Yeah."

Molina nodded, satisfied. "We'll get our turn."

Matt wasn't sure what she meant: that they'd get their turn at Max Kinsella, or at the truck.

Molina leaned against the car fender. "Kinsella's smart. He's got the best seat in the house. We're standing on hot asphalt waiting for a pretty-please chance at the evidence."

Matt shrugged. Only the rotating lights made the site hot. The air was actually chilly.

"Are you saying," he asked, "that their drug bust has priority over a kidnapped person? Temple could be—"

"I frigging know it," Molina said. "These guys have frigging priority. Mess with 'em and you get a slow sentence on their time clock."

But she swaggered forward, finally buttonholing one of the chunky guys in commando gear.

They talked. Hands gestured. Molina returned.

"And?"

"They're not finding anything. I made a deal."

"What deal?"

"You bring Kinsella over for a search."

"Kinsella?"

"This semitrailer is loaded with magic-show gear. The cast of thousands, including the human and feline stars of the show, has vanished elsewhere. This major drug bust has nabbed two drivers whose underdeveloped muscle has displaced their brains. Errand boys. There's apparently nothing in the trailer but elaborate empty boxes. The narcs want to take the truck back to their secured lot and go over it with a fine-tooth flea comb tomorrow morning."

"Tomorrow morning? Temple could suffo—"

"So I told them we have an expert searcher. Better than a drug-sniffing superdog. A human nose when in comes to magical paraphernalia. Think he'll come running if you ask him nicely?"

"I think he'll come running if I tell him that no one cares about looking for Temple until they feel like it."

"I don't care what bait you use. I only care that the fish goes for it."

"Fine." Matt trotted back to the Taurus, angry with both faces of the law.

He leaned over the open driver's side window.

"The drug enforcement unit has priority, but it can't find a thing. The truck will wait in a lot until morning unless you search the magic-show gear for hidden narcotics. If you find Temple, the drug guys won't object."

"Politics."

Max got out and slammed the car door shut. "I suppose my services are Molina's idea?"

"She's along for the ride, just like us."

"She's along for the kill, don't you doubt it."

Kinsella strode forward with seven-league steps, forcing Matt to lengthen his stride. He felt like Chester Goode limping after Mr. Dillon.

Molina greeted Kinsella's arrival with a weary tilt of her head toward the open maw of the trailer. "It's all yours."

Kinsella slicked his hair back from habit, but without an anchor for the ponytail it did no good.

A bulky man in what looked like a flack vest blocked Kinsella's way. "This is what you're looking for." In the light of a flashlight, Matt glimpsed purple-and-white capsules on a palm.

"Pills, or plain powder, like crack. We've done a cursory search, but that truckbed's loaded with mumbo-jumbo stuff. Can't make head or tail of it. The lieutenant said you could."

Kinsella threw a glance over his shoulder. "I guess I'm enough of a politician to be good at mumbo jumbo. Got a light?"

The man handed Kinsella latex gloves and a flashlight as he walked into the squad car spotlight trained on the gaping rear doors. The big rig sat marooned like an island of hollow steel.

Kinsella entered the truck with one superhero leap.

Beside Matt, Molina started, as if afraid he had vanished.

"Always a showman," she commented.

"Maybe he has to con the narcs into letting him have a fair shot at it. Do you think Temple's in there?"

"If she isn't we don't want to speculate where she might be."

"Lieutenant—"

She put a hand on his shoulder. "Do you think I like using Kinsella as a hunt-dog? He's got the best chance. The drug group doesn't believe in magic, that it's possible to hide someone in a hollow box."

"She just . . . disappeared."

"I know. What's worse, she was always meant to."

"Why would drug smugglers care about Temple?"

"Why would Effinger?"

"You like bringing it back to me?"

"No. But that's where it goes back to. So tell me why she was there with *him*."

They both knew they were no longer talking about Effinger. They walked away from the truck doors, away from the Crown Vic into the deep velvet dark of the desert. Where they walked, skitter and chitter and grind halted. They carried their own desert with them, empty and dry and silent.

"They're together again," Matt said. Strange how honest that sounded.

"Not at the moment," Molina noted dryly. "I suspect it's more his fault than yours."

"The kidnapping?"

Molina might have nodded. She sighed. "Right. One thing I like about Las Vegas."

"Yes?" He felt like a straight man.

"No mosquitos."

"No mosquitos," he agreed. But there were sand fleas and chiggers and a thousand other annoying insects of the high desert. "I'm sorry I didn't spot the woman you were looking for."

"I was looking for an untoward event. We got that."

"You weren't looking for Kinsella."

"No. Sometimes I do love this life."

"Not always."

"No. My instincts tell me she's in that truck."

"Then why doesn't anybody see, hear anything?"

"These are instruments of illusion, packed to the gills and probably transporting narcotics. They'd be clever about concealment."

"Powder and pills, maybe, but Temple's a human being."

"Small, though. Give me that. Small. A regular Thumbelina."

"You think that has something to do with why they can't find her?"

"I hope so. I hope so."

They turned without further conversation and made their heavy-footed way back through sand and scrub.

The lights were still trained on the inside of the truck.

When the lieutenant stopped to consult with the drug team commander, Matt moved to the very lip of the stalled semi's storage area.

A forest of strange boxes and pedestals resembled a struck stage set for some Mount Olympus drama from the 1930s. Matt listened, and heard the faint mewling of a seagull.

In the desert?

There was Lake Mead, but how many seagulls were trucked in?

"Do you hear—?" Matt intended to ask Molina, who stood only fifteen feet behind him, but a voice much closer answered.

"Shh! I'm following the sound." Kinsella appeared from around a Gothic grandfather clock with a sword for a pendulum.

"That's the only sound you hear?"

"The way these props are built, sound doesn't much escape the perimeters. Magicians are smooth and silent, like the dead, didn't you know?"

Kinsella grinned into the garish light, then vanished behind a gypsy caravan.

Beyond Matt, impatient combat boots ground sand to silica.

"I heard a mewling sound," Matt said hopefully when Molina came up.

"Please. No more cats. This case was heralded by cats. I don't want to see another one."

"What do you mean?"

"Mister Midnight Louie and Miss Midnight Louise were present when Effinger's soggy body was dredged up from the Oasis barge-pool."

"Louie was there? And that cat from the Crystal Phoenix?"

"Yes. I hope you set as little store by the presence of cats on the scene of the crime as I do."

"I'm not superstitious. Still—"

" 'And everywhere that Temple went, her cat was sure to go?' "

"No, that would be too ridiculous. In fact, lately, Midnight Louie has been showing a marked dislike for his old haunts."

"Has he indeed? Could this be a cat with taste? With deep and eerie instincts? What do you think?"

Before Matt could answer Molina's sarcasm, Max Kinsella appeared from behind a mummy case.

"Might these be what the chaps in the moon-invasion outfits want?"

His palm flowered open to reveal a cluster of capsules, half-clear, half-purple.

The drug team gathered around like hash-sniffing hounds.

"Where'd you find those?"

"Baggies of them. Under the celestial robes of the automated Fortune-telling Mama from Yokohama."

"All right!"

Combat boots beat a tattoo on the trailer's metal floor as the men raided the premises.

Max leaned against the trailer's side. "Now that the smuggled drugs are confiscated, I suppose I'm to be allowed a little peace and quiet to search the rest of the props?"

"Hyacinth!" a muffled masculine voice called from inside the truck. "Bingo."

"That's the name of the narcotic?" Matt asked, incredulous. "Hyacinth? That's what the note in Effinger's pocket referred to?"

Molina smiled and braced a hand on the truck level. In an instant she had pulled herself up to the trailer floor level. Kinsella applauded her feat, not easy in a skirt. Then Matt jumped up.

"Hyasynth," Molina repeated. "S-y-n-t-h. A designer drug fresh from Hong Kong. They needed to get it out before the Communists took over and quashed all sorts of dubious private-enterprise factories. One component is a digitalis replica taken from hyacinths as a base to produce the usual high."

"I don't get it." Matt was honestly confused. "Why Las Vegas?"

"Because it wasn't Hong Kong." Max pushed his long frame

off the trailer opening. "Perfect cover. A magician's props. Are these clodhoppers going to get out of my way soon, Lieutenant? I've got a Very Important Person to find."

"Got your evidence?" Molina shouted into the trailer's long metal cavern. "Get 'em into the van. We've got missing persons to find."

"Missing persons?" Matt asked.

She shrugged. "Kinsella did hear a mewing sound."

The men, carrying garbage bags full of gently clicking capsules bounded off the trailer end in formation, the vehicle shaking as each man leaped to the ground.

The moment the drug-hounds had deserted the trailer, Max began moving his fingers over the nearest cabinet as if searching for Braille.

Matt's alarm grew as he watched the magician's swift and serious search.

Before this, everyone had seemed so laid-back, as if there were no hurry. Now, it was all hurry.

"I've been hearing a faint cry," Kinsella said, finding a hidden spring and clicking open a sword-swallowing taboret.

The cinnabar-red painted interior was empty.

Matt moved among the magical furniture, listening for clues.

A banshee's cry came from far within the trailer.

"*Eeeeeeroooooooow.*"

Kinsella bounded in that direction, still using the flashlight Molina had commandeered.

"That doesn't sound like anything human," Molina pointed out.

"You wouldn't sound very human if you'd been locked in a virtual coffin decorated by mandarin-fingernail painting," Matt said, as Kinsella wrestled another tall case away from the side wall. His long fingers made spider-light tracks across the front surface.

When Matt joined him, he tilted the unit forward just in time for Matt to catch the brunt of its weight, then did the same thorough finger-walking over its lowered top and revealed bottom.

At last a secret lower drawer clicked out and jammed into the trailer floor.

Kinsella rooted through a tangle of rainbow-colored scarves, then rose and pushed the cabinet upright.

Some pieces were covered in tarps. Kinsella began ripping them off. His early handling technique had been cautious, even respectful. Now he was indifferent to the magical cabinet-maker's art.

Matt heard a squeak, or a cry. "There!" He pointed to a low shrouded oblong.

The elasticized ropes binding the piece snapped like suspenders in Kinsella's eager fingers. He knelt before the revealed object.

It reminded Matt of an altar from a Black Mass. Chains and locks crisscrossed its sinister battered leather surface, which was scribed with arcane signs scrawled in the deep burgundy-brown color of old blood.

Kinsella rubbed his hands together, as if stimulating circulation. He tapped on the trunk in various places, tested the chain links, rattled the locks.

"If Temple were confined in something like that," Matt demanded, exasperated, "wouldn't she have run out of air by now?"

Kinsella shook his head. "These props are all made of wood. Wood breathes. It never joins as tightly as it should. These may be built to look as solid as a steel safe, but in magic everything is the opposite of what it appears to be."

"In life, too, I'm beginning to think."

The man grinned up at him in the harsh glare of the flashlight. "Sounds like you're learning."

"If we don't have keys, we need . . . picks, hatchets."

"Violent, aren't we?"

Kinsella's hands roamed the heavy metal keys like a pianist's. He unthreaded a length of chain then jerked. Two loops fell free.

"I suppose," he told Matt in a confidential us-guys tone, "that if I asked Molina for a nail file, and she did have one, she would stab me with it."

Matt dug in his pockets. "I've got a nail clipper, one of those deals with a short pull-out file.

"Good work, Scout Devine! I'll take it."

Kinsella fanned out his bare hand like a surgeon anticipating the slap of a scalpel on his palm.

Matt complied, a little harder than he had to.

"Male nurses can be so violent," Kinsella said, chuckling and handing Matt the flashlight.

Kinsella flipped out the two-inch ribbed-metal file—utterly useless for smoothing off hangnails, Matt had always found—and began probing the keyholes as if they were open wounds in need of cleaning out.

Matt aimed the light at whatever lock Kinsella explored.

Sometimes he gave up and moved on. At other times, a lock conceded with a click that sounded like applause to Matt's blood-pulsing ears. Then Kinsella would draw another long length of chain free and into a puddle on the floor.

Ten minutes became fifteen by the watch Matt's mother had given him, that he wore only on occasions "out."

"You believe she can breathe, if she's here somewhere?" he asked at last.

"These devices aren't made for smothering someone, merely containing them, concealing them, letting them escape. It's too bad I never taught Temple some tricks of the trade. . . . ah!"

Another lock sprung open. More chain pulled through Kinsella's agile hands to coil on the metal floor.

An almost unheard whine hailed the fall of the last length of chain.

Kinsella shook his hands, spread his arms, fanned his fingers over the trunk's front corners, and lifted.

The metal-banded maw cracked, then split, then elevated upward.

Matt felt his blood slow in his veins. The trunk was big enough to hold Temple, especially if her body were curled up. And why would it be curled up? Because someone had forced her into that position to fit into the trunk? Because she had assumed it herself? The ever-comforting fetal position? Or because she had curled up and died. That expression didn't exist for nothing.

The flashlight he held glared like a nova sun into the darkness inside the trunk. Anyone alive in there would have reacted to the bright light, would have stirred or protested.

But all Matt saw were the trunk's dark corners outside the overheated circle of the flashlight beam. No one was inside.

Relief felt like the flu, his arms and legs aching as if all the blood in his body was draining. The next thought was: *if not this casket, what about the next?* And the next. And the next.

This was like playing hide-and-seek in a funeral-parlor coffin-display room and he had very recent reason to be familiar with that grimly hushed arena.

And then the darkness moved, leaped up at him and the flash-light, struck the portable lamp from his hand.

"What the devil—?" Kinsella was caught off guard too.

Matt jumped back to retrieve the light where it lay rocking on the floor.

Something brushed his leg as he did so, and he couldn't restrain a shudder.

He swept the light across the floor, until its beam nailed the perpetrator. Matt saw flattened ears, frown-ruffled forehead blinking eyes with the pupils narrowed to a vertical slit the width of a straight pin. A tail lashed the trunk's outside corner.

"Louie?"

"Oh, no," came Molina's groan from outside the truck. "Keep searching."

Kinsella bent to pick up the cat.

Louie's feet flailed against the magician's chest, and from the expression on his face, a few claws connected.

"Who wants this fireball?"

"Put him down," Matt suggested. "Maybe he knows where Temple is."

"This is a wild goose chase," Molina said from her distance. "We should go back to the theater and conduct a more thorough search there."

Kinsella was quick to answer. "We haven't conducted a thorough search here yet."

Matt heard the mockery as Kinsella repeated her official phrase: conduct a thorough search. He could afford to mock the routine, the methodical means of the law. He was an outlaw.

Before Matt could decide which side to join—stay with Kinsella until every box had been broken down or rush back with Molina to strip-search the theater topside and below—Kinsella spun violently forward and tore the tarp from a concealed shape.

What he revealed made even Matt catch his breath.

"It's the cabinet Temple disappeared from! But how can that be? Did they break down the stage props that fast?"

"Or a duplicate," Kinsella suggested.

He grabbed the pulls centered on the pierced Oriental brass circles. Both doors swept open. Matt glimpsed a figure inside: shadowy, still. Like a statue.

Kinsella mimicked its frozen attitude. Only his lips moved.

"Lieutenant, you better split your skirt seams again and get up here."

He stood as still as a man face-to-face with a striking snake, his tone severe. Matt turned with a swoop of the flashlight beam and ran to the truck apron to help Molina make the giant step up.

Her hand was already reaching up when he got there. Between his alarmed pull and her push she was up beside him as lightly as an acrobat.

Their feat surprised them almost as much as Kinsella's alarm.

They rushed to the rear of the trailer.

Kinsella still stood before the open doors he had forced into re-vealing their contents.

Matt's flashlight beam probed the open space beyond him. The demonic figure inside wore a familiar face indeed: Max Kinsella's.

The box's back wall was a mirror.

"You need to see this, Lieutenant," Kinsella said tightly, like a man afraid to move even his lips, as if something transient and shocking might melt away at too much attention.

Molina stepped past Matt to stand behind Kinsella, so close that she finally saw what he saw.

Matt watched her shoulders stiffen.

He edged next to her place, straining to see the devilishly re-flected light, the mirror-refracted light.

He saw Kinsella's facade, as through a glass darkly. Saw the glass that reflected it. Saw . . . scratches upon the glass. Sand-painting. Scrawls.

The letters were printed in a shade the flashlight illuminated as ox-blood red.

Big letters, lavishly covering on the glass. At a slight angle, up to the right.

R-e-m-e-m-b-e-r m-e

y-o-u b-a-s-t-a-r-d!

Chapter 45

Shoe Time

Matt felt a phantom cut.

This time he knew it for what it was, if not *why* it was.

Like all bad things that happen to supposedly good people it was swift, savage and puzzling.

Kinsella finally spoke. "Someone knew. Someone knew that I would be here to open this device."

Matt stood in the background, faintly reflected beyond the mirrored Max. Matt stood silent, knowing the words had a special, searing meaning for him. And him alone. Didn't they?

Molina's voice was clinical. Calm. "This does seem personal. Anyone here care to confess?"

After the dead silence, Kinsella laughed.

"Confession requires specifics, Lieutenant. This is far too vague. But you're right. It is personal. With me, from now on."

An angry howl from the floor caught their attention.

Louie was pacing back and forth, his tail lashing against the tarps, thumping like a snare drum keeping background rhythm.

His next vocalization was a yowl.

He snaked back and forth against a box shrouded by tarpaulin, rubbed his nose on its corner, first left then right, like a chef honing a knife-edge.

No one wanted to articulate the message they each were getting loud and clear: Midnight Louie wanted them to open this box.

"Must be something fishy," Max said finally.

Kinsella, Matt reminded himself. The man was only a last name and an occupation: magician. He was not a person. He was not Temple's . . . sole savior.

"I don't know about you two, but I'm about ready for ouija boards," Molina said. "Open this thing."

Matt bent to strip off the tarp, anticipating Kinsella.

What they unveiled was another oblong box. Odd how every magic-show container was so coffinlike, Matt thought. How the tricks all involved confinement and escape. Maybe he was missing some subtle erotic content; he wouldn't doubt it. But he was struck by the defiance of death that ran through the art: rising from the dead. No more, no less. Easter Sunday for the unthinking masses. Rolling away the stone.

"Another sword-trick box." Kinsella's voice had lightened for the first time.

They stared at him, shocked by the lilt in his tone.

"Don't you get it? There are already holes slit through, for the blades. Breathing slits."

Molina's glance crossed Matt's, like dueling foils. They were wondering where the swords were, and what they might have already done. Here, among the props of his trade, the magician was an optimist, the master of illusion.

Matt and Molina had no such expectations of defeating the obvious. They pictured the unthinkable. He, from his anxious heart. She, from her professional pessimism.

Max . . . Kinsella . . . bent over the box, checking top and bottom.

"The head and foot slides are shut. Sealed with . . . duct tape!" He laughed. "We've got it! The one. That damn cat must have smelled something, or he saw her put into it." He rapped on the lid. "Temple, we're coming."

Who could demur in the face of such theatrical confidence. Matt found his eyes anchored on Molina's when they weren't darting nervously to Kinsella's delicate maneuvers to crack open the box.

If Temple wasn't here, where was she?

The top of the box lifted off in hinged sections.

They glimpsed a painted interior, something colorful in the bottom. They smelled a potent floral not quite like perfume.

Midnight Louie suddenly leaped atop the closed bottom portion.

The box was like a coffin: top ajar, bottom covered.

Fragile red silk lined the interior. In the open upper portion, next to a satin cat toy in the shape of a gaudy ice-cream cone, lay several blood-red commas, fifteen or sixteen scattered like rose petals.

They were the nail guards one might glue onto a cat's claws.

Kinsella shoved the box hard against the truck side, so the impact rang with a dull, bell-like thrum.

"The dressing room at the Opium Den," Molina said. "All that was left of Shangri-La were a few makeup tins, and the mandarin nail shells."

To Matt was left the logical pronouncement. "The cat Hyacinth was here. That's what Louie smelled."

Louie paced, and rubbed his nose against the corner of the box, like a chef honing a knife.

Max Kinsella began breaking down every cabinet left untouched in the trailer.

Matt and Molina watched as if caught on the sidelines during a sudden-death overtime.

"If she's not here," Matt said, "she must still be *there*. And the issue of air—"

"He's damned if he does, and damned if he doesn't. Either way we go, we risk everything." Molina leaned against the truck side, looking weary. "I could phone in a search, but they wouldn't be able to open most of the remaining cabinets. And the company probably left behind what they did for good reason. Kinsella's got to eliminate the odds somewhere. We're here. It's most economical timewise to stay."

"That's what it comes down to? The least waste of time?"

Molina nodded solemnly. "We've committed. We've got to see it through here before we waste time going somewhere else."

"I'm glad I'm not a cop. Or a magician."

Midnight Louie, as agitated as they were, lurched back and forth from Max Kinsella to the two of them, meowing and pacing, only stopping to sniff at the uncovered cabinets.

"I had no idea," Matt said, "that so much could fit into the back of a semitrailer."

"Great smuggling device." She watched Kinsella shove a rejected cabinet aside.

"We can't help him?" Matt asked.

She shook her head. "Oh, we could shuffle furniture around, try to feel useful. But we'd just obstruct him in an attempt to soothe our own feelings. He's our drug-sniffing dog; let him work."

"Temple isn't 'drugs.' "

"She is if she's hidden in a magician's maze."

"Why can't we hear something, if she's here?"

"She could be gagged. Drugged."

"Or dead."

"Or dead."

Matt found himself looking at Molina as if she were the God of Death itself. But she was only the messenger.

"Is this what I get for tracking down Effinger? Does justice always have a hidden price?"

"Justice is usually damn well out of it."

"But you . . . that's your job."

"No. My job is many things. Justice is something separate. You see it sometime, you let me know."

Matt watched Kinsella, amazed by his stamina. Temple had told him magicians were strong, but he had assumed that meant raw muscular power. It was intelligence, skill and heart, he saw, not brute strength. On those thin threads, on Max Kinsella's magician's instincts, Temple's life now hung.

Another casket lost its tarpaulin. Molina held the flashlight now, quietly led Kinsella's search with its focused beam.

Kinsella bent to pull the latest box from the wall, paused, looked up at them.

"Heavy," he said.

Matt had never suspected the word "hope" was spelled "heavy," but it was here and now.

He and Molina rushed to pull and tug away the ebbing tarp, letting the maestro get to work.

The casket's outside was smooth, unmarked, almost anonymous.

That very smoothness seemed to frustrate Kinsella. His fingers slid over the entire surface, searching for hidden hinges and springs.

He looked up, hopeful. "This is a demonic box. It must be it. And so heavy . . ."

He laid his ear against the polished wood, a guitar player tuning his instrument. His fingers fretted the liquid sienna surface, hunting pressure points like an acupuncturist.

Matt didn't know about Molina, but he held his breath, not wanting to impede Kinsella's sense by so much as an inhalation.

At last Matt heard a tiny click, like a mechanical heartbeat.

Kinsella's breath hushed over the rich veneer. Another click, then the entire top lifted like a grand piano wing. The box was lacquered black inside, with a yellow satin lining. Angled into the lining like a pry tearing it from the wood, was the heel of a magenta suede shoe.

Chapter 46

Panama Purple Haze

Who would guess in their wildest dreams that Midnight Louie would ever wish to be a dog?

Perhaps I should be more specific. I have not actually been wishing complete dogdom upon myself these past tense minutes since my own rescue. I am not that debased, not even in an emergency. Not even in a case of life and death.

No, I merely feel a certain frustrated longing for the nose of the breed in question. They are superior at one act only: smelling. And often, I fear, smelling what is bad as well as what is good. So, in a certain sense, I am glad that any drug-sniffing dogs, such as they are, were pulled off the case in favor of Mr. Max Kinsella, much as I dislike owing my current freedom from the semi to him.

What frustrates me most at the moment is my inability to aid in the discovery and rescue of my lost roommate.

No matter how I sniff up and down and around these magical mystery caskets, I am unable to smell so much as a rat. This is unprecedented.

Why? Why is my sniffer so deficient?

Because all I can smell are three unforgettable scents: that of the demure flower known as hyacinth, that of the far-from-demure hellion from Siam, also known as Hyacinth, and that of the tart, heady aroma of Panama Purple.

So when the Mystifying Max and Mr. Matt Devine pop the lid on a likely-looking casket, there I am, reeling around like Dopey the Dwarf without a hint of what we will find inside. My superior feline sense of smell is of no more use than a smudge pot of sensory confusion.

I cannot sniff life or death or even the likelihood of the contents being human, much less the one particular human we all seek.

I bury my useless nose in my mitts, and swear upon Bastet's right rear paw's left toenail that I will never again knowingly touch the substance called "Panama Purple."

Chapter 47

Found and Lost

The two men stared at the shoe, immobilized as it was.

To Molina, it looked like it was either jauntily hooked there for a fashion shoot. Or like it was impaled there in its owner's extremis.

Molina's job was to know first which case fit the scenario. She stepped forward to aim the flashlight at the casket bottom, automatically using her body to block the others' view.

No use letting the nearest and dearest view the situation first.

The flashlight picked up the steel glint of handcuffs. Molina relaxed slightly. You don't handcuff a dead body. Then again, lack of air, a drug overdose . . . Her flashlight beam on the face produced squeezed-shut eyelids. Molina began to turn.

But as if sensing her verdict, the men jerked into motion again, both reaching for the contents of the casket.

Remarkably, they managed to work in concert. Kinsella pulled up Temple's shoulders; Devine picked up her ankles.

In seconds she was sitting against the box that had confined her, woozy and blinded by the light.

No one asked if she was all right. They simply watched her, trying to gauge her condition.

Midnight Louie had no such inhibitions. He meowed in a forlorn tone and came stalking up to her, rubbing his side against her flexed knees, pushing his face into her arm.

"Louie?"

Temple's voice, always husky, was a dry desert rattle.

"He came along for the ride too," Molina explained. "In his own carrier."

" 'Carrier.' " Temple tried to laugh but it was hard to do with no sound effects. "Pretty good."

Devine knelt beside her. "Water. Is there any way, anywhere—?"

"Gas station," Molina said. "On the way back."

Kinsella also knelt beside her, picked up her handcuffed wrists as if they were Dresden china. He thrust the stubby file from the nail clipper into the mechanism. Presto changeo, the cuffs sprang open like Tiffany bracelets.

Kinsella handed the implement back to Devine.

Temple's wrists separated into a poignant, empty gesture, as if she'd begun it hours before and had been stalled from finishing it. The note of panic in her voice was heartbreaking.

"Max. She took my ring. She never gave it back. It's gone."

He gathered her against him as someone would a hurt child. "It's all right. There are other rings. Dozens and dozens of other rings."

And only one Temple.

The unspoken sentiment was echoed by Matt Devine's silence as he stood, stepped back, ebbed out of the picture.

"Where are we?" Temple finally asked. "It was so dark and the box was jostled around so much . . . and they stuck me. My elbow."

"Left?" Kinsella asked.

"How'd you know?"

"That's usually where right-handed people administer injections, and most people are right-handed." He held her inner elbow up to Molina's flashlight beam.

"Ultrafine needle," she diagnosed. "Probably some of their 'hyasynth' in liquid form. She seems exhausted and disoriented, but not in the throes of an O.D."

Kinsella nodded, a curt agreement.

"Can she stand?" Molina asked.

"Does it matter?" Kinsella's anger was as sudden and clean as a switchblade.

"Yes," Molina said much more gently than she felt like saying. "See if you can get her upright."

Temple rose on the support of his arm, shaky. "My shoe."

"Here." Matt Devine had retrieved it. "But you better not wear it right now. Better give me the other one."

He went down on one knee like Prince Charming while she balanced herself against Kinsella.

The absence of the single shoe restored balance to her body. She leveled her shoulders, looked stronger, leaned less on Kinsella.

"How did you find me?" she asked, looking at them all in turn.

Her unspoken question was: what are you natural enemies all doing here, together?

You, child. You.

"Mr. Kinsella realized something was wrong when you disappeared," Molina began.

"*Before* she disappeared," he corrected.

She ignored him. "Mr. Devine noticed Mr. Kinsella was gone from his seat—"

Temple looked at Matt, with a lucid and questioning gaze that made even Molina look away and hurry on. "Then I decided to explore the understage areas. Devine tailed me, I found Mr. Kinsella shaking up empty prop boxes and a few empty-headed ninjas. We suspected that you were gone, and since the DEA was tailing the show's semitruck, which took off about when you did, they followed, I followed, your swains twain followed. I would say even Midnight Louie followed, except that he was already aboard in his own traveling compartment."

Temple quirked a smile at her. Molina was actually, deeply, momentarily afraid she might have to like her.

"Sounds like Keystone Kops." Temple put more weight on her hose-clad feet. "With accessories before and after the fact." She whispered like The Shadow from the old radio show. "So why do you want me upright, Lieutenant?"

Goddamn, but she could be fast, even after an ordeal like this.

"Let's go outside. Get some fresh desert air."

Devine joined Molina. Kinsella brought up the rear with Temple.

"How did you find me, really?" Temple was rasping like a sick child.

"We followed the yellow brick squad-car light," Kinsella said in the tone of a long-time teller of fairy tales.

Molina sighed. Matt Devine eyed her with some compassion. It should be the other way around, but at the moment she was willing to take what compassion she could find. She certainly couldn't give it. Not now.

He jumped down off the truck bed before her and held up a hand to break her leap.

Poor Matt. No lady fair but a lady lieutenant.

She touched his fingers as a courtesy but landed without his help.

Kinsella loomed over them, preparing to hand Temple down like an Egyptian mummy. Both of them reached up for her, broke the impact.

Matt held out the shoes. "You'll need these on the sand, such as they are."

Temple grabbed Molina's sleeve in one hand, and Devine's sleeve in the other then released each one in turn while she forced her feet into the dainty-toed slippers.

Then she leaned close to Molina and whispered in her ear.

Molina nodded at the men. "We're going around the trailer for a bit. Don't wander anywhere."

Temple put a hand on the truck side and tottered around to the other side.

"Are you sure there's no other choice?" she asked Molina.

"Absolutely sure."

"But I don't think I can."

"You say you can't wait."

"Yeah . . . but—"

"Here's a handkerchief. I always carry one. Leave it when you're done."

"But out here. In the dark. There might be snakes and spiders. I don't know."

"Think of mountain streams," she advised, like any veteran mother.

"Right," Temple croaked, grabbing the handkerchief from Molina's hand.

She tottered into the darkness on her absurd shoes.

Molina sighed again. Someday Mariah would be up to this. Soon.

When they came back around the truck corner together, Kinsella and Devine had the uneasy look of men abandoned by women for reasons not clear.

"What are you up to?" Kinsella, who had stripped off the latex gloves while they were gone, stepped forward to ask.

"I've asked Miss Barr if she'd mind delaying her return to civilization for a few minutes. The DEA has a couple suspects in hand. I asked them to hold them for Miss Barr."

"You had no idea that 'Miss Barr' was even here," Kinsella raged.

"Ah, but I had you to look for her, didn't I? An expert hunter. And she was. And is. So I'd like her to stroll past the suspects and see if she recognizes anybody."

"The men who grabbed me," Temple put in hoarsely, ". . . I think they were the masked ninjas. I didn't see any faces."

"That may not be the question," Molina put in silkily. Her eyes stayed on Kinsella. He was the mastiff. "If Mr. Devine will help me escort you to the front of the truck, this could be over in a few minutes."

"Something you don't want me to see, Lieutenant?" Kinsella jeered, already panicky at losing even temporary custody of Temple.

She could almost sympathize.

"Not something. Someone. Sit tight, magician."

Matt Devine, like a good partner, had materialized on Temple's right.

The two of them steered her over the shifting sand beside the road to the fire-breathing dragon-painted tractor.

Two men stood against the upright bulk of steel, their hands cuffed behind their backs; four men in DEA gear watched them.

Molina walked Temple close enough to see the men's faces in the lurid light of the pursuit-car headlights.

Temple gasped, and sagged between them.

Molina turned and guided her back down the trailer's Christmas-tree-lit length. Kinsella waited in the dark at the end of the overlit tunnel, like a gunfighter.

"Those aren't the men," Temple tried to say.

"Which men?"

"I don't think so. Not the men who grabbed me tonight. But definitely the men from . . ."

She faltered, and it was Devine who held her up. "From the parking garage."

She bent a distressed look on Molina. "Everyone said they were probably dead."

"It's a good cover, isn't it?"

"Max said they were dead."

"Max isn't infallible, is he?"

"He found me, didn't he? He opened my handcuffs."

"But those are the two men who attacked you in the parking garage last summer?"

"Yes. Yes, I recognize them." Temple leaned her head on Devine's shoulder.

"Good. Good work. That gives us something to go on. Now I think we can drive back to Vegas, and then you can go home for some rest."

"Home," Temple said, sounding not only hoarse, but rueful.

Kinsella was waiting for her, but Molina wasn't done yet.

"Wait." She raised a traffic-cop hand.

He almost bulled right past it to reclaim Temple.

"I need to ask you a few questions, Mr. Kinsella. And now, I think you owe me a few answers."

He hesitated, like a trapeze artist on the brink of missing the crucial bar as it swung past.

Then his shoulders relaxed. "Whatever you say, Lieutenant. Where do we talk?"

"Down the trailer a bit."

"I'm all yours." He cocked Temple a smile and turned to follow Molina into the bright dark.

In the distance, the DEA officers loaded the rig's pair of drivers into their sole remaining van. The vehicle spurted into the distance until it was only a pair of red taillights, shrinking like bat's eyes in the night.

Chapter 48

Carmen Miranda Warning

Matt watched Kinsella and Molina amble away like coconspirators.

"What's this about?" He turned to Temple, seeing she was suddenly shivering.

He whipped off his velvet jacket and wrapped her in his borrowed body heat. She still shook like an aspen leaf, and when he was about to say something, she silently threw her arms around him.

He looked up the track. Molina and Kinsella moving away, tall and deliberate, their steps deceptively casual.

Matt clasped Temple to him, covered the only reachable part of her with kisses, the hair on her head.

"It was . . . so awful," she said.

He felt like he was holding a blender set at "grate," her shudders were so sudden and rough.

"Temple. You're all right. Cold and scared, but all right."

"What's she doing?" Temple asked, like a child caught in fretful fever. "What does she want?"

"Answers. You heard her. That's her job."

"I can't believe those men from last summer are here. I guess I'd wanted to believe that they were dead."

"They hurt you. You wanted them to disappear. That's normal."

"But I'm so disappointed that they're still alive. It's like Max promised—"

"Max can't promise anything about other people's lives and deaths."

"Oh, I don't know—"

He crushed her closer. He didn't want to know what Kinsella could and could not do, in any arena—life and death, life and love.

But he also knew these moments for a respite from reality. A few stolen moments. Molina was no accessory drawing Kinsella away, but a cop doing her job.

Matt watched them talk with apprehension, Kinsella leaning against the trailer side. Easy, always easy for him. Molina moving left, then right. Their profiles backlit by the garish bulbs outlining the stalled tractor. Their words a mystery. Their momentary absence a blessing.

Matt became aware of something sanding his trouser legs; looking down, he saw Midnight Louie rubbing back and forth, back and forth.

"Poor Louie," Temple said. "He's had a terrible ordeal too. How did he end up in the same dead-end box I did? Who'd want to hurt a cat? Poor thing. I've upset him with my rotating residences." She was suddenly silent and then she stiffened as she pulled away from him. She let the jacket ebb down her shoulders like a shawl, then handed it back.

She wasn't trembling any more.

The two figures down the road were coming back, slowly, still talking.

"Thanks," Temple said. "I'll pick up Louie and that'll keep me warm the rest of the way."

Matt bent to lift the hefty cat into her arms.

The tomcat actually honored Temple with a lick on the cheek and a burst of purring.

"You'd better get in the car," Molina instructed Temple. "Yes, with the cat."

The trio walked away toward Kinsella's Taurus like a mockery of the Holy Family: man, woman and cat.

Matt watched them go.

Molina still stood facing him, as if she had something to say.

When he finally gave her his attention, she was staring past his shoulder. Her voice was the muted drone of an officer reading the suspect's Miranda rights.

"Infatuation," she said in her best official monotone, "is a predictable chemical process. It floods the brain with feel-good serotonin. Gives a sense of overpowering optimism and shattering insecurity. It lasts about eighteen months at the outside. In primitive times this was long enough to beget a child and let it grow big enough to stay with its mother while both parties repeated the infatuation process elsewhere. Another heat wave, another inheritor of the race. The notion that love has anything to do with it is a medieval artificiality that has been elevated into an obsession in modern times."

She glanced at him once. Eye to eye. "Get over it."

Chapter 49

It's Not Over
Until It's Over

They drove back to Las Vegas in silence.

Matt was beginning to think that being in the passenger seat was his new lot in life. Molina actually driving the Crown Vic felt odd. He supposed her driver hadn't hung around for what was obviously a very private quest.

"Did you learn anything?" Matt finally asked.

"A little. Not where they're going now."

"What do you mean?"

"Kinsella obviously has some place to go to ground besides the Circle Ritz."

"Obviously." Matt tried hard not to imagine where Temple would be tonight. He wasn't much better off than when she had been utterly missing, except he knew she was safe. He needed more than that now.

Molina pushed the window buttons until they lowered four inches. Chill night air played pinball through the car.

Although the pursuit into the desert in Kinsella's car had

seemed endless, the Crown Vic swept into town so soon it made Matt blink. His watch said it was not quite midnight, and he was utterly alert.

Molina drove into the police headquarters' rear garage and parked. Then she led Matt down to another level, where the venerable Toyota station wagon he had seen at the Blue Dahlia was waiting.

"I promised to drop you home, didn't I?" she asked.

He nodded.

"How about dinner first?"

He was too startled to answer quickly.

"Come on! You don't want to go home alone to that empty red couch."

He still hesitated. He may have been used to being up nights, but he was emotionally exhausted. Being a third wheel could do that. He didn't want to stay up and think about it.

"My treat." Molina jingled her car keys like spurs meant to startle a reluctant horse into action.

He was getting curious. "All right. I don't know that I'm hungry."

"You'll be hungry when you get there."

He got into the passenger seat of her Toyota, thinking about buying his own car. Suddenly it seemed important. He had never owned a car. Always it had belonged to the parish. Even the Hesketh Vampire was on loan from Electra.

Molina drove in an edgy, distracted way that made him nervous. He wouldn't have expected it of her . . . such loose, laid-back driving five miles over the speed limit.

Cars still swarmed outside the Mexican restaurant she pulled up to. She regarded it through the dusty windshield like an old friend seen too infrequently.

"*Mi Cocina.*" My kitchen. "Good *fajitas.* Great margaritas."

Matt was getting nervous. She had really rolled the second "r" in "margarrrritas."

Matt stared at her as she entered, and eyes snapped to attention all over the dining room. She was known here. The host led them through two cavernous rooms paved in quarry tiles and past a chittering fountain to a quieter back room. People nodded and smiled all the way.

The back dining room, with its one rock wall, felt like a grotto. A statue of the Virgin of Guadalupe spread her ever-open arms inside a blue-tiled wall niche. Pierced tin mirrors winked from the terra cotta walls like warning lights.

Tables for twelve in the outer rooms were still occupied despite the hour. Here there was only a scattered couple or two, and the murmur of water trickling down the rock wall.

Molina didn't even glance at the menus they were handed. Matt studied the small print, cruising unfamiliar Mexican words, reading past the occasional spatter of salsa.

"Won't they close soon?" he wondered.

"Don't worry. They stay open as long as the guests stay up. No Anglo obsession with when they close, or when they open."

Matt nodded. The waiter came bearing three bowls of salsa of varying heat and a huge hot heap of freshly made nacho chips. Molina had been right; he might become hungry soon.

He ordered the chicken *fajitas*, as she suggested. She ordered a drum roll of Spanish phrases and finished up with a pitcher of "margarrritas" on the rocks.

His objection must have been as plain as one on a defense lawyer's face in court.

"It's cheaper this way," she assured him. "The pitchers aren't that big, the margaritas aren't that strong. Besides, the night is young."

"Not for me."

"That's right. If you were at work, you'd be starting to think about getting off. Off and into the arms of the Razor Lady."

"You didn't find her."

"*We* didn't find her." Molina shrugged, and unbuttoned her boxy jacket. She leaned back in her chair.

Matt wondered if the gun at the small of her back scraped against the chair rails.

"Not a bad night," she said, sipping the first margarita. "You got the girl. Sort of. I got the interrogation. Sort of."

"I trust we are equally satisfied."

"Now that was halfway sardonic, Devine. You're getting better. Not happier, but better."

"Is that what we're celebrating: your getting to buttonhole Max Kinsella against a semitrailer truck?"

"Hmm. You're making it sound a whole lot more interesting than it was."

"Then he didn't reveal anything cataclysmic."

"Cleared up some suspicions of mine."

"Anything you'd care to pass on?"

Molina actually managed to look coy, an odd effect on a woman of her size and authority. "Not at the moment. But humor me. I've been after that guy for, oh, eight months. I'm sorry that Miss Barr had to get roughed up to bring him out of hiding."

She began dipping nacho chips into the hottest of the three salsas. Matt had tried a small broken chip on it and backed off, happy to still have an intestinal track.

Matt suddenly understood why they were there, why he was there. He had wondered if Molina had some misguided purpose in distracting him tonight, but it was far simpler and more straightforward than that: he suddenly realized that he was here to distract *her*.

Molina had realized a very unlikely and difficult goal, and she needed to celebrate. Who else could possibly understand what it meant to her to finally corner Max Kinsella for a few precious seconds. Other than Matt, who knew both the obsession of tracking a man down and the bedeviling presence (and absence) of the once-missing magician?

"How did you meet him?" Molina twirled the short plastic straw in her wide-mouthed glass around and around, until the opaque lime drink spun like a whirlpool.

"He met me. Out by the pool, I think. One second I was alone in the water under the shadows of the palm tree and the passing clouds. The next moment there was a shadow the size of a softball against the moon."

" 'A shadow against the moon.' " Molina savored the phrase with another sip of her margarita. "Very apt. He's a shadow all right."

"Why are you—were you—so . . . rabid to find him? What did you learn tonight that was worth the hunt?"

She laughed and leaned her head on her hand.

Matt began to wonder if he would get home tonight. A woman in her position shouldn't drive with any suspicion of inebriation in her system. Not that it hadn't happened before, but not to her. Not to Carmen Molina. Molina had been high before she got here. He decided that Temple hadn't been the only one locked in a box tonight, not the only who was half-inebriated from getting out.

He knew what he was doing here with Molina now: serving as listening post and bragging wall and keeper. He wondered what roles Kinsella was playing with Temple.

That way lay madness. Molina had been right about that, even before she'd started drinking margaritas. Matt sipped his own. Delicious. Mild. Deceptive.

"A silver-tongued devil." Molina looked up.

In the restaurant's candlelit atmosphere—and every table hosted a dimpled glass bulb filled with a fat wax candle—her vivid blue eyes seemed to pale to match the stormy Caribbean color of the margarita pitcher in front of her.

It was already one-third empty.

"Yes," Matt said.

"Good with those damn locks, though. Good at evading questions. But I nailed him. For what? Seven minutes? I had him pinned to the wall. He was forced to say something. If only because he didn't want to create a scene in front of his wounded dove. Men have such predictable weaknesses."

"You said it. Slaves of chemistry."

Molina's brow furrowed under the fingers she kept running over and over it. "Women too. I'm an equal-opportunity cynic."

"Well, you must have been a chemical slave, sometime."

"What do you mean?"

"It's obvious." Silence. "Your . . . Mariah."

She scooped up a chipful of the tar-and-paint-removing salsa, then thought better of it.

"You didn't care for my advice tonight?"

"I didn't need it. I've read the same lifestyle wire stories in the local paper. Fascinating facts to explain human behavior in a few paragraphs."

"You don't think that, from what we saw tonight, Barr and Kinsella are not together again? The bit about the ring alone . . ."

"I don't need to think it. I know it. So?"

"Well, you didn't seem too thrilled about it."

"I'm not. He's not good for her."

"We agree. He's not good for anybody." Molina lifted the heavy pitcher to top off Matt's glass and refill her own.

"Apparently he's good for opening trick boxes."

"Oh, that. Tricks, sure."

"What did he say? Or should I say, what did you ask?"

Just then their plates arrived. Matt's was empty but hot, and beside it landed a stainless steel platter sizzling with meat and vegetables all slightly seared along the edges.

Molina's was a huge oval ceramic platter filled with the soft tortillas, refried beans and burritos that ran into a sandpainting of red beans, beige tortillas and green chile sauce, like the colors on the Mexican flag.

Matt concentrated on building his first *fajita* without burning his fingertips, while Molina dug into her meal like an excavator.

"He says Effinger was the quintessential errand boy."

"Quintessential? He used that word."

Molina nodded, chewing seriously. When she finished, she drank water from the tall plastic tumbler floating a lime slice.

"Good for nothing and everything at the same time. They could always count on him to do his dirty little job, usually running drugs and money and messages, and then he'd fade away into the gambling joints and bars. Never got into big trouble. Never wanted to move up or know more. He was most valuable for being a nothing."

"That's some epitaph, isn't it?"

Molina put down her margarita glass without sipping it. "I suppose that was an ordeal, the visitation."

"It was bizarre. Memorializing someone you'd wished dead. Wishing you could have thought of some other way to handle him a long time ago. At least I didn't have to . . . officiate."

"What'd you do with the body?"

"Cremated it."

Molina's left eyebrow almost saluted her hairline. "Isn't that—?"

"The church is more liberal on cremation these days."

"And you? What're you gonna do with the ashes?"

"I don't know. I suppose it's quite a test of character," he added wryly.

Molina's face darkened. "Abusers are the worst offenders. Even when you know they've probably been subjected to it themselves. . . ." She shook her head. "The cases I saw in south L.A. gave the phrase 'beaten down' a whole new meaning. It's like abuse is this evil demon that possesses one generation after another. Nobody comes out of it human."

Her vehemence made Matt realize that he'd seen one case of domestic abuse, close up and personal, and had encountered a few dozen more in his work. Molina had probably seen hundreds during her career, especially if she'd started as a neighborhood uniform.

"Effinger," he said quickly. "He was the quintessential penny-ante man. Even in his domestic life. He yelled, he cursed, he stormed. He hit. But there wasn't anything systematically sadistic about it. My mother's pretty 'beaten down,' but I think maybe she could sit up and breathe a little, with the proper encouragement. And . . . I came out of it without a mark."

"A mark that shows." Molina sighed and pushed away her massive plate. "You can't tell me that everything you've ever done, or not done, in your entire life wasn't shaped by that domestic violence."

He couldn't. "How'd we get into this? I thought we were talking about chemical destiny."

"Mariah. You'd asked about Mariah."

"No, I didn't mean to . . . I just meant that you've obviously loved, and lost."

She folded her arms on the tabletop, looked at him as if gauging the depth of his soul.

"You. Know. Nothing. Father."

Matt's head snapped back. There it was. The old accusation of not living enough to know how to forgive others their lives. Priesthood. In his denomination, ostrich-hood. So some parishioners said.

"I was trying to warn you about spells. And demons," she said.

"Sounds . . . superstitious."

"Sounds . . . real. Mariah's mine. All mine. No custody problems simply because I was dumb enough to get pregnant but smart enough not to marry the father."

"Listen, I don't need to know—"

"You mean you don't *want* to know. All right. So I meddled in your emotional life. So you're going to get what you don't want to know in spades.

"You've read it all in your morning Lifestyle section. The classic pattern. The man who's all charm, energy, idealism. He was a cop. I was a cop. Just uniforms. He was Lebanese-American. I was Anglo-Hispanic. I was a big clumsy girl who'd never had much chance of a social life, so I was old enough to know better, but too young to resist.

"We were going to rise together like shooting stars in the department. He . . . encouraged me to sing, to find those funky old gowns, and there were a lot of them in L.A. fourteen years ago. He was flowers and optimism. And then, the thorns. You know how they start out: Mr. Wonderful. You know what they turn out to be, Mr. Control-freak."

"He . . . started abusing you?"

Her eyes said, *What do you think, you think I'd allow anyone to hit me?*

He hadn't thought so.

She turned her margarita glass on its napkin. "He was too smart to use violence. I sometimes think he picked me because he wanted to make sure he wouldn't resort to violence. He liked manipulation. Lived for it. Men. Women. Children. He had a need to lead them astray, into the path most dangerous or self-destructive."

"You're talking about a psychopath."

"I'm talking about Kitty the Cutter."

Matt shut up. Molina was talking. What this had to do with Mariah, he couldn't imagine.

"Simple. He got me pregnant."

Matt tried to digest that, and couldn't. Happened a million times a year.

She leaned inward. "Wasn't supposed to happen. I was using a diaphragm and foam. The foam he couldn't fix, but the diaphragm . . . holes in it the size of a straight pin."

Matt knew she wanted shock, and she got it. She continued talking.

"Usually it's the woman, isn't it? Who's supposed to manipulate in that way? Not this time. He thought my maternal instinct would take over, that I'd never look into the evidence. He thought I was a dumb broad."

"A cardinal sin," Matt put in.

Molina nodded. "I knew the first time I missed my period."

"So. What did you do?"

"I went to an abortion clinic."

The statement was like a slap in the face, and he pulled away from it before he could stop himself.

"Think about it, Mr. Priest. You've never been a woman, but think about being tricked into motherhood like that. By a man like that, who did it just because he could."

Matt didn't have to think long or hard. He thought he carried the burden of Effinger's abuse. But no one had foisted a changeling soul on him, part himself, part the unwanted other, part the demon's.

"Why didn't you have the abortion?"

"Because either way he won." Her shoulders lowered, as they must have once long ago in a clinic office. "He wanted me to be destroyed, or to be a destroyer. I decided to be neither."

"Either way, your life was changed forever."

"So I chose which way."

"And if Mariah asks about her father?"

"She already has, years ago. Kids are ages ahead of us these days."

"And you've told her."

"I've told her that her father was a policeman who was killed in the line of duty."

"Was he?"

Molina shrugged. "Not yet."

"Then he's . . . still out there."

"Out there. And I'm in here, drinking margaritas. There. That wasn't so bad, was it? At least I didn't have an abortion."

"I don't know if I could have resisted, in your position."

"That's just it. You don't know. Thanks for saying so. I am so tired of men thinking they know what women should do. You're pretty sure what Temple Barr should do."

"Not really. But that's why you're determined to run down Kinsella. To you, he's the ultimate manipulator. The ultimate psychopath."

"I don't know if I'd call him a psychopath. Yet." She finished the dregs of the margarita glass. "It was nice to have him pinned down and politely answering my questions, though."

"What about the dead men in the casino ceilings?"

"I can't tell you everything, now, can I?" Coy again, in her hard-edged way. "Part of a scheme to bilk the casinos in question of millions. Someone is always trying to break the bank in Las Vegas."

"And Effinger was a very small cog in a multigeared scheme."

She nodded. "Still, he was connected enough to tip off. Who tipped him off that getting to Temple Barr would get to you, hmmm? That's what the message on the body was about: how to find Temple. Once Electra Lark told me somebody's evil stepfather had assaulted her, I knew my take on the note was right. Too bad none of you three characters panned out as prime suspects."

"Too bad? You want to nail us all to the wall now?"

A smile paired her shrug. "You are my crown of thorns. Anyway, my detective interpreted the note smears as "deadhead" at "Circus Circus," but I immediately thought of "redhead" at the "Circle Ritz," knowing her propensity for trouble and connection to Effinger, through you."

"These big-time crooks would help that weasel out on a personal matter?"

"Your dragging him into headquarters wasn't personal to them, it was messing with their business. Big business. No, Effinger was useful enough to protect; that's why the lookalike was tossed to the authorities. As a distraction. And then Effinger became a liability."

"Yet now, even dead, Effinger still plays a distraction."

"Very good! Yes."

"Can I take it that I'm free to dispose of his ashes as I please? You have no further use of him?"

"Scatter the booger over Lake Mead. I care not, as long as the Environmental Protection Agency doesn't."

"This has been an odd dinner," Matt commented.

"Hint. It's time to go. What time is it?"

"Two A.M."

"Another hour and you can rendezvous with Our Lady of the Can Opener again."

"No thanks."

Matt watched as the waiter returned with a check. Molina signed it, that was all. She had a tab here, but he doubted that she came often. He couldn't see her kicking back like this on a regular basis.

She stood, reached in her jacket pocket and pulled out the car keys.

"I'll have you back at the Circle Ritz by two-thirty."

They passed through the other dining rooms, now cleared and deserted. Matt was impressed. He and Molina were the last to leave, but the staff bowed and nodded, as if they were royalty.

"Influence," Molina said proudly, her face showing the serene placidity of a madonna's. A mellow madonna's.

"Ah," Matt said as their footsteps echoed on the parking lot asphalt.

"Speak up."

"I don't think you should drive me home."

Molina stopped, thrust her hands in her pockets, frowned. "Why not?"

Matt plucked the car keys from her left hand.

"Because I don't think you should drive."

"Agh! Don't be ridiculous. I can drive. It's just a few blocks."

"I don't think so." He'd barely consumed one full margarita.

She'd had three-something. She was a tall woman, but not that tall.

"I can drive! It's an emotional letdown, not a chemical one. My blood alcohol level is barely . . . point oh-oh . . . nothing. Well below the legal limit. Trust me, I know these things."

"I don't think you should drive. It doesn't matter what level you test at; it matters that if you should happen to be stopped, a cop would have to test you. I'll drive."

She folded her arms and glared at him. "You are such a goody two-shoes."

"Hey. You wanted to celebrate your cornering the Mystifying Max. You have. Maybe you should celebrate a little longer and leave the driving up to us."

"Us?"

"The two of me in your view."

"Funny. My focus is perfect. I could hit a target at least in the torso, if not the heart."

"Most encouraging. But I'm driving, or I'm not going anywhere. And if you try to leave alone, I'll call the police."

She suddenly conceded and walked to the passenger side of the Toyota. "If you have to be in control of *something* tonight, I guess it can be me."

The jibe hit home, but he just unlocked the car door and sprung the passenger lock. He knew better than to open the door for her. "I guess everything's chemical," Matt said as she got in. "Get over it."

She took a cue from one of her suspects and refused to answer.

"Past Our Lady of Guadalupe and then north?" Matt asked as they drove deeper into the Hispanic neighborhood. He guessed that she didn't have to live here on her salary, but that she was making a statement.

"Now how will you get home?"

"I'll call a cab."

"Way out here? At night. Get real. This is 'hood, amigo. Anglo drivers don't come."

He didn't answer, realizing she was probably right.

"So I'm stuck with you. What a night! I have to let Max Kinsella go, and I'm stuck with you."

Matt said nothing, but she spoke up at last and began direct-ing him. Her voice was deeper, like when she sang, and he sus-pected she was much drunker than she would ever show.

He recognized the driveway when he turned into it as in-structed.

Molina leaned forward to pull the garage door opener from the console box, and he eased the car into the dark, clutter-crowded garage as gently as if he were cruising the Vampire into a me-chanic's bay.

"Nice landing." She was sounding sleepy.

By the time they had turned on a yellow brick road of lights from the garage into the small squarish kitchen, someone was stirring down the hall past the living room with its lumbering nighttime shapes.

The same Latina woman Matt had seen at the house before came down the passage like an angry locomotive. "So late. You said only midnight."

"Work, Yolanda. A daring chase into the desert, Desperados apprehended on the seething sands. A woman levitated from a coffin."

Molina's woozy theatrics cut no ice with this woman. "Mariah, she been sleeping since ten. Like a good girl." Pointed. A glance at Matt. "I must go home now and leave you alone." Hint. "If you need me tomorrow, do not call until after noon." Bigger hint.

Molina laughed softly when the front door closed behind her.

"You'll have to stay here, I suppose. Don't worry about the evil eye from Yolanda. I've never had a man stay over."

"A cab—"

"Will not come. Not at this hour." Molina looked around with slightly swaying deliberation. "I guess the living room couch it is. There's a half-bath off the garage. Remember there's a preteen girl in the household and undress accordingly. We get up at seven A.M. Need anything?"

"I guess . . . not."

Matt stood and stared at the alien living room after Molina went down the hall on tiptoes. How had he gotten himself into this? By being a good Samaritan, he supposed, and accom-

panying Molina on her girl's night out. Her otherwise solitary
girl's night out.

Matt shook his head and sought out the half-bath. He couldn't
be sorry.

Matt decided that nothing indecent could be read into taking off
his shoes, so he did just that. He piled the sofa pillows on one end
and punched them into the semblance of one wide bedroom pillow. Steps down the hall made him freeze like a cat burglar.

Molina was laboriously tiptoeing back down it, her arms piled
with pillows and blankets.

"Shhh." Her caution now was as elaborate as it had not been
in the parking lot. "What was I thinking of? Bad hostess. Water's
in the kitchen faucet. Good night."

Matt arranged his impromptu bedlinens, smiling. A night in the
convent this was not. And for all the wrong reasons.

At about six in the morning, Alvin and Theodore of singing Chip-
munks fame came squirreling across the waffle-cotton blanket
covering Matt's legs.

"Ow!" he shouted before he could stop himself.

He opened his eyes to the milky pool of dawn leaking around
the edges of the drawn miniblinds and two striped squirrels bar-
rel racing from one end of the living room to the other, using his
epidermis as springboard.

"Ow," he said more softly, sitting up to massage his abraded
legs.

He only saw the girl in the ankle-length Beauty and the Beast
T-shirt when the careening cats returned from a second foray
over his flesh and circled her ankles for recess.

"You're the guy from the church," she said.

For a moment his heart raced in panic. Even out of the mouths
of babes . . .

"You were with the red-haired lady."

"Right. At the blessing of the animals."

"You had the biggest black cat that I ever saw."

"Midnight Louie. And . . . you and your mother adopted these two guys."

Matt attempted to smile benignly on the striped flying demons. They were having none of it and caromed off the top of the Naugahyde recliner all the better to spring at him.

"Girls," Mariah corrected. At her prepubescent age, gender was becoming destiny.

"Girls. Have . . . they been fixed yet? I mean, had their claws removed?"

"They're too young."

He nodded. Everything here was too young, except Molina.

Mariah stepped closer. "You've been here before."

"Once."

"How come?"

"I had something to discuss with your mother."

"My mother's always working."

"She has a tough job."

"I guess." She stepped closer, tilted her head.

Matt didn't see much Molina in her. Mariah's eyes were black-brown, her hair darker than her mother's and her features fuller, rounder. He wondered suddenly what kind of love this was, for a child who might or might not resemble you, or who resembled most her other parent, who might or might not be loved. Or hated. He suddenly recalled his handsome soldier father, his face a mystery in the flickering light of the saint's candles, his staid (now) mother swept away by one night's impulse.

Crazy. It was all crazy, how these children came here, how they were treated when they did arrive. Mariah Molina was unshaped clay in an art department tray. She was, what, eleven, twelve? On the brink of awful girlhood when her ears would have to be pierced and her music would have to be turned up to maximum and when who she was would depend all too much on how other kids saw her, or how she could make them see her.

Matt suddenly viewed the terrible obligations of being a parent and quailed to his soul.

"It's okay." Mariah came closer. "The cats won't hurt you. They're kinda nuts. Like little kids, you know. Antsy."

"I guess." He smiled at her serious, adult attempt at reassurance. And a little child shall lead them. "I'm not used to waking up in strange places, with strange cats."

"Oh, they aren't strange." She sat down on an easy chair and stroked the young cats as they zoomed past. "Tabitha was a witch in a different life, and she runs away all the time because she's afraid someone will catch her and cut off her tail." She related this primal anxiety with the calmness of a school shrink. "Catarina is the sensitive one and wants to be a wire-walker, but she has to go to school first. Do you like them?"

"I think they're wonderful," he said sincerely. Wonderful and terrible in the history she had invented for them.

"They're just alley cats."

"The best kind."

She nodded. "I'd better put the coffee on for Mom."

Matt blinked. Did "Mom" often come in late and a little tiddly?

"She's a sleepyhead in the mornings," Mariah said importantly. "I have to get her going for her job. It's important."

"Yes, I know."

"And I have to go to school." Said with a true martyr's tone. "I get to drink hot cocoa in winter. Instant, though. We don't have much time around here."

"I can see that. Especially with those cats."

Mariah giggled. "Do you always sleep in your clothes?"

"No. But I'm not staying very long. Where's the cocoa? I'll make it."

"Men don't make anything."

"Some can. A little."

"Well, don't spill the hot water on the floor. The cats run through it and dump their food and we end up with such a mess."

Matt was very, very careful with the hot water.

Molina drove him home after Mariah had left for school in her navy plaid uniform.

She wore sunglasses and cleared her throat a lot.

"I'm sorry I left you high and dry," she said after pulling up in front of the Circle Ritz.

"It's fine."

"Those cats are hellions."

"They're kittens."

"Mariah is a handful."

"She's a kid."

Molina pushed up her sunglasses into the headband position.

Her eyes were clear, blue and rueful. "You swim." It was a statement not a question. She had seen him in the Circle Ritz pool.

"Yeah."

Molina looked through the windshield, down the street. "I . . . promised Mariah I'd take her to Wet and Wild this summer. In a couple months. It's closed until then."

"Yeah?"

"I don't swim."

"You don't swim?"

"I didn't exactly grow up in a neighborhood with swimming pools on every block. Not in East L.A."

Matt saw that East L.A. must have been a lot like South Chicago. "I didn't either. But the high schools had swim teams, and the nearby Catholic college had a pool."

"In Chicago they had pools. Guess you Anglos get everything."

Matt shrugged.

"So. Would you go with us? I can't take her on those crazy, zigzag tubes."

"I guess I could."

She sighed. "Then I'll let you know when this adjunct of hell opens for the summer. Got to run."

He got the hint and exited poste haste.

Electra Lark was waiting to greet him at the gate to the Circle Ritz.

Chapter 50

Summit Conference

Temple felt like a neutral country hosting a summit conference.

Poor little Switzerland. So many depending on so little for so much.

Max sprawled on the love seat, his arms and knees spread, claiming every inch of it.

Louie squatted on the coffee table, four paws tucked beneath him, chin pulled into his chest, eyes narrowed to fierce feline slits both horizontal and vertical.

But the territorial dispute in question was not taking place here; Max and Louie were actually getting along for the moment.

It was as if the cat had finally given the magician, if not the man, his due, and conceded Max's vital role in freeing Louie's royal hide from duress vile. Louie's sudden thaw toward Max was about two whiskers this side of severe suspicion.

"You're running around like a snail-darter," Max said to Temple. "Don't worry about our fierce aspects. Louie and I won't bite."

"I know. It's just that Matt's making a big concession. I'd promised him I wouldn't tell anyone."

Temple turned to give Max, and Louie, the full impact of her gaze. Matt was coming down, into their hostile territory, at her behest. He and Max were to be on their best behavior.

Max leaned forward on the sofa, bracing his elbows on his knees. "I appreciate his help. I really do."

"Just make sure Matt knows that. This is . . . very private to him. I know he thinks I've betrayed him."

"And what do you think?"

"I think . . . it's time you two shared what you know, at least. I think it's dangerous to us all to keep secrets from each other."

"Some secrets," Max iterated.

"Some secrets," Temple agreed.

But she wrung her hands while she was waiting, and then realized the gesture would remind Max (and Matt and herself) of her missing ring, and then of that dreadful magic show. . . .

Matt knocked, softly.

Temple started and dashed for the door.

"Hi."

He was already looking beyond her, trying to measure the opposition. *Why* did it have to be like this?

"Come in. Sit down. On the . . . side chair."

He did so, as stiff as the white roll of paper he balanced between his fingertips.

Temple stood before them, between them, like a ringmaster.

You're probably all wondering why I've gathered you together. . . .

"Matt. Max." *Countrymen.* "I thought it was time, given what happened . . . to me . . . at the magic show . . . "—blatant appeal for sympathy . . . *Lend me your ears.*

"Lieutenant Molina—" It was fascinating to read the very different expressions on the two men's faces as she invoked that name. "Lieutenant Molina was looking for someone in the theater that night that she never found, and it wasn't Max."

Max smiled; Matt didn't.

"We agree that no one here wants Molina to be the first to share our secrets. So . . . I think it's important that Max see this woman who attacked Matt. Maybe he can shed some light—"

"Oh, God, Temple," Matt said, interrupting. "If it'll stop this agonizingly roundabout introduction to why and wherefore, I'll show him my high school photograph."

Max laughed like a Marx brother. "Amen. Let me see that thing."

Matt handed over the rolled sketch that was as long and thick as a thigh bone.

Max unfurled it, gingerly. And then his face became very still. "What did she call herself?"

"Kitty O'Connor."

"Any clue to why she was approaching you?"

"I was there?"

"You were there." Max nodded grimly. "So was I."

He stood up, his long arms holding the sketch full width as he stared at the face etched upon it.

"Max?" Temple no longer felt her theatrics had been uncalled for, that they were mere nerves. "What is it?"

He smiled, briefly. His skin looked whiter than milk against the black satin of his hair. He looked like a man from an ancient ballad, pale, filled with dread, and with the name of such a song he answered her.

"*La belle dame sans merci.*"

"The beautiful woman without mercy," Matt translated, perhaps for Louie's sake. "I'll second that. How do you know her?"

Max looked up at Matt, as if their common misfortune earned Matt his respect at last.

"She cut me first, almost twenty years ago."

"Cut you? Max?" Temple wanted to come closer, but couldn't. Something about Max forbade approach.

"Not literally. I wish she had." He glanced at Matt. "I'd wear your scar for a thousand years rather than the one she gave me for seventeen, and counting. My cousin's life."

"Oh, no! Not . . . Sean?" Temple said, remembering the horrible incident Max had related a few weeks before, and again recently.

"Thanks for remembering his name." Max quirked her a smile. "The last thing I gave Sean to remember was watching me go off with Kathleen. That's what she called herself then. It was so simple. Two American boys visiting a charismatic homeland, an ancient land with an ancient wrong riding it. Teenagers. Think they're immortal but they're afraid they won't get a chance to ensure that soon enough. So, a double flirtation, with sex *and* death. A boyish competition. Who'd get laid first. Who'd shoot a gun first. Same, stupid thing, isn't it? Nothing of the rational human in it, just . . . testosterone and territory."

Matt was looking serious, but rather confused.

"You need to tell him what happened," Temple told Max. "Or would you like me to do it?"

"No." Max washed his face with his hands, as if rinsing away the glaze the years had left behind. "He's used to hearing confessions."

Matt stirred uneasily. "Not recently."

Max's smile was ironic. "These are not recent sins I'm confessing."

He sat on the couch then, impinging on Louie's territory, and retold the story Temple had first heard after the death of Gandolph at the Halloween séance.

The two Irish-American boys, cousins from Milwaukee, going to the Auld Sod as a high-school graduation present. Their first solo trip. Of their unplanned foray to northern Ireland to see the "Troubles" for themselves, rash young would-be players of the patriot game.

The game was diverted with their encountering a gorgeous young Irish woman, a bit older and all the more intriguing for that. Gawky gallantries escalated into a grim competition for the first girl who seemed likely to actually sleep with one of them. Good Catholic girls in Milwaukee's parochial schools were too good and too Catholic, but the aura of danger in Northern Ireland, seeing the grinding inequity, made the boys feel passionate and reckless and lucky.

Matt saw Max hesitate before finishing the tale, and cut to the chase, because to him the ending was inevitable, and he didn't want to hear the details of Sean's defeat. "You won," he said. "The girl."

Max shrugged. "She chose me to go with to the cinema that

night. Sean knew better than to come along. She made plain that the trio was now a couple. So I went off to lose my virginity, and Sean went to a pub to brood over his." He began speaking in the fragments of headlines, as if to distance himself from the facts. "IRA bombed it that evening. Sean, a stranger, must not have been thinking too clearly and went to an Orange pub. Car bomb parked outside. Blew off the front of the building. Six killed; three maimed. They had to have a closed coffin at the O'Shaughnessy and Meara funeral home in Milwaukee."

"What did you do when you found out?"

"Went back home with what was left of the body. Went to the funeral. Found out I wasn't the only one who blamed me for it. Sean's family and friends. The Kellys and the Kinsellas ended up at each other's throats. I couldn't stand it so I went back."

"To Kathleen."

"Christ, no. I never wanted to see her again, and I didn't. I did some foolish things to see if I could get myself killed too, and wasn't very good at it." He glanced at Temple who was still standing nervously by, like a referee. "I never told you much about Kathleen."

"Not about the movie and sequel."

"And not this part either: I did hear about her, a couple years later. She was with the IRA, probably had been then too. Her specialty was seducing rich foreigners and cajoling major money out of them for the cause. When I heard this, her turf was South America."

"South America?" Matt sounded startled.

"Lots of Irish emigrated there in the nineteenth century. They intermarried with the Spanish population. Some became quite wealthy. Soldiers of fortune. I think Kathleen was just . . . practicing on Sean and me."

Temple and Matt were silent, each mulling over the final revelation.

"What did you do then?" Matt asked.

"Became an exile. Toured Europe. Studied magic. Became the stunningly successful illusionist you see today."

Matt saw that Temple wanted to say something, but she held

her tongue instead. He hadn't heard all of it. "Then . . . why is she here, calling herself Kitty, after all these years? Why look me up? Why hand me Effinger?"

"My guess," Max said, "is that they planned to eliminate Effinger, and your search for him played into their hands."

"She really thought I was an assassin?"

Max shrugged. "That's the kind of world she's lived in for almost twenty years. So I suspect she was punishing you for not being what she thought you were. She expected a lot from her men, even back then."

"What about 'Remember me, you bastard'?"

Max sighed. "I'm afraid that was meant for me. So was Temple's kidnapping. She didn't like it when I broke off our relationship. She wanted me to stay in thralldom and work for the IRA. I had very different ideas."

"How different?"

Max glanced at Temple. She held herself still, trying not to influence him either way.

Max suddenly leaned forward, his gaze fixing Matt as commandingly as a hypnotist's.

"I suppose you're in this somehow. You've been attacked. You need to know. What I had to do was infiltrate the IRA to find and turn in the ones who had bombed that pub."

"But . . . you were a sympathizer."

"Sure. But that's what domestic terrorism does to a land, to its people, even to passing-through patriots like me. I became as determined to get that particular arm of the IRA as any Orangeman. And, of course, when I did, they became determined to get me. Luckily, by then I'd attracted the attention of some people who wanted to prevent violence by all sides, and they took me under their wing."

"So you've been more than a magician all these years, you're—"

"Basically, we're spoilers. We root out and rat on plans to knock off banks or casinos for money to support terrorist acts; we carry out arms interception raids, we blow the cover on planted bombs."

"We? You're part of a faction, like everybody else?"

"You could say that."

Matt kept silent, absorbing this knowledge. He looked up suddenly. "What was she like then?"

"Kathleen?"

"Yes. Kathleen, not Kitty."

Max glanced at Temple. She understood that current ladyloves weren't supposed to know too much about old flames, about the oldest flame, the very first girl. She eyed the sketch of the woman in question on the coffee table. There was nothing girlish about her now.

"Charming," Max began. "To Sean and me she seemed passionate, endearingly intense about political matters, but we were pretty green. She was . . . flirty, teasing, innocent of the ways of American girls yet always seeming . . . intoxicatingly available. We were bewitched. We jockeyed for position like young colts, falling all over our own big feet and each other's."

"Nothing like the woman who cut me?"

"No. If I hadn't seen that sketch with my own eyes I'd never believe they were one and the same. I'm still not sure," Max added pointedly.

Matt nodded, ignoring the jab at his honesty, or maybe sanity. He too stared at the portrait of Kitty built from his memory and blood. He seemed oddly contemplative for a man considering an enemy.

"Did it ever occur to you," he asked Max very deliberately, like an attorney leading a reluctant witness, "that if Kathleen led you away from Sean that night, she also might have pushed him in the direction of the IRA-targeted pub?"

"Kathleen? But, why? She wanted us both on the IRA side. She must have known that would turn me against them. As a recruiter—"

"Maybe she was always more than she seemed, more than a mere recruiter. The woman I met liked inflicting cruelty. She didn't get that way overnight. What could be crueler than giving you what you wanted at your cousin's expense, not just the cost of losing out at romance, but the cost of his life itself?"

Max was truly confounded. Temple had never seen his guard drop so low. That it would vanish this way in front of Matt Devine was even more astounding. But Max was stunned. The sheltered ex-priest had suggested a dark twist of human motivation that the seasoned counterterrorist had never looked back to see.

"But killing Sean would make her recruitment ploy ineffective," Max reiterated. "It would be counterproductive."

"To the IRA, sure. But maybe Kathleen O'Connor had another objective." Matt stared at the sketch as if hypnotized. "Was she a virgin?"

This was more than Max Kinsella ever wanted to reveal about his first love affair. "How should I know? I was the usual teenage oaf in my own mind, so infatuated with the brave new world before me, with finally crossing the chasm to manhood, so I thought then . . . all I can say is she was willing. Everybody seemed to be happy with how it went, which you may find out some day, unless you already have. Nobody hurt anyone."

"Ah, but they did." Matt ignored Max's gibe at his own state of possible virginity. "That's what I'm trying to get at. You were so hurt by your cousin's death that you broke off the relationship."

"Guilt."

"You turned your political sympathies inside out to pursue a course in reckless revenge that would have easily gotten another boy killed. I suppose your magic training made you more formidable for your age."

"I suppose. Look, the problem is not the past. That's . . . dead and gone. The problem is Kitty now. Why she targeted you and Temple. Where she is. What side she's hiding behind now. It's ridiculous to say she betrayed Sean. I did it, with my horny little hormones. I learned to live with that a long time ago. She was just the means and the opportunity."

Matt shook his head. "I don't think so. The woman I met was lethal. She didn't get that way overnight. Whatever cause she pretends to serve, and may actually believe she does serve, her real motives are more complex than geopolitical agendas. They are deep-down and personal and you're the key. I think she killed your cousin, indirectly, but as surely as if she'd built the bomb."

"But why?"

"Because she needs to wreak the most damage possible. Which is why I was attacked and Temple was taken. She's found you

again. And she is out to make you pay. 'Remember me, you bastard.' That's what she said as she simultaneously kissed me and
cut me. I think she was talking to you."

"She said that to *you?*"

Temple sat wide-eyed, like an audience, as these two men who
competed for a woman—her, omigosh, not Kathleen but her—
also competed for a piece of another woman's enmity.

Matt nodded. "I couldn't figure out why it all seemed so
personal, but it's obvious now that her personal issues are with
you, and that, as before, she'll try to get at you through those
around you."

"But . . . why? Why hate me so much? I . . . Sean and I, we
thought we were in love with her. We were high on Ireland and
noble causes and a beautiful girl who seemed to be part of it all.
Maybe we were selfish in our infatuation, but we were basically innocent, stupid kids. Why hate us?"

"Maybe because you were so innocent." Matt pushed away the
sketch of Kitty, as if disowning it, as if renouncing the fact that it
came from his mind and memory. "All I'm saying is that I don't
think she'll go away, and I don't think any one of us is safe with
her around." He glanced at Midnight Louie still claiming his substantial portion of the coffee table. "Not even Louie."

Temple could be silent no longer. "You mean she'd even hurt
a cat?"

"Especially a cat," Matt said soberly. "The more innocent the
victim—the more helpless—the better."

"You make her sound like a monster," Max objected.

Matt's brown eyes were darkly serious. "You haven't encountered her in, what, fifteen years? I thought I had met a demon."

"Surely you exaggerate."

"No, I don't think I do."

Max buried his face in his hands. "Jesus. I was so close to getting away from that life. And now you're saying that one girl from
sixteen years ago has become a vengeance machine, when she
actually wronged me far more than I could have ever wronged
her? It doesn't make sense."

"It won't until we know why."

"I don't want to know why. I want it to stop."

Matt shrugged. "It won't until we know why. You need to trace her, from then to now. You must have connections."

"I do. If I have anything, it's connections. But she'd dropped out of sight very effectively for well over a decade."

"Tells you something, doesn't it?" Matt stood. "Meanwhile, we'll have to watch ourselves. And each other."

Max's gaze snapped up to his face. "Maybe that's her revenge. Forcing us to depend on each other."

Matt nodded. "*No Exit.* By Jean Paul Sartre. Recommended reading." He picked up the sketch. "I suppose you both should have a copy of this." He glanced ironically at Temple. "This time I'll have the copy place only reduce it to half-size. I don't suppose we want to spread wallet-size copies of this around. Might tip off Molina."

Temple had to jar herself alert to catch up with Matt before he got out the door.

"Thanks for sharing this bombshell with Max. I guess. We need to know. I didn't know what she did and said when she hurt you. That's so sick. . . ."

"You don't want to fall into the hands of her henchmen again." His hands tightened on her elbows. "I mean it, Temple. Be on guard for your life. If he doesn't think of it, it might be best to . . . disassociate."

"I can't. Especially not now. Besides, Max is trained in stuff like this. But thanks for thinking of me." She lifted up to kiss him. "Remember *me*," she said.

The kiss didn't start anything, but it didn't end anything either.

Her life lately, Temple thought as she returned from seeing Matt out, was becoming an eternal ellipsis. Dots, trailing off to uncertainty, like unending sentences . . .

Max was still sitting midsofa, absently patting Midnight Louie's head. The cat was so apparently taken aback by this liberty that he tolerated it.

"Hurt Louie?" Temple sat down beside Max.

"He was taken too. Devine is right. Warnings. And I didn't want to see them. Dammit, I wanted all the past connections to be less of a problem, not more."

"It's not your fault."

"No, on the surface, nothing has been my fault. But it always feels like all of it has been."

"Well, why not? You were brought up in the Church of Mea *Maximus Culpa* too."

" 'My most grievous fault' . . . haven't thought of that old childhood Latin in years. Is Devine turning you away from the Unitarian Church?"

"I was already turned. Too wishy-washy. No searing, impossible moral dilemmas. Obviously, a totally sissy faith."

Max laughed and leaned back in the sofa pillows, sighing. "You certainly got a tawdry glimpse into my sixteenth summer."

"I think you've paid enough penance by now for getting laid, even for a Catholic boy."

"I hate to think he's right."

"But you do."

"I do. And I hate like hell to think he came to harm at her hands because of me. It makes it harder to dislike him."

"Do you have to dislike him?"

Max watched her through the disguising green contact lenses, which only changed surface color, after all, not expression or emotion. "Yeah. He likes you too much, and vice versa. I can't believe I'm back in the past, only now I know enough to worry about something happening to him. If it did, we'd never be the same again, Temple."

"Poor Max. Now you've got three people to look after."

"Four," he added, frowning mockingly at Midnight Louie. "If anything happened to that cat, you'd really never forgive me."

"I did notice that you sprung him first."

"That's because he yells louder than you do."

"Oh, yeah?"

"Yeah."

Max pulled her into an encompassing embrace. "So. We have to fight to survive physically as well as emotionally. So what's new under the empyrean? I wonder if I could use Molina's obsession to tack something prosecutable onto me to help me flush out Kathleen. Or Kitty, as she calls herself now. You realize that Molina had us tailed when we left the truck stop, so to speak."

"Tailed? Molina?"

"I bet she wants to find me almost as bad as Miss Kitty. It's heads or tails which is the more serious stalker. But don't worry, love. I ditched Molina's man, and I can outmaneuver Kitty the Cutter too."

Temple shivered in his arms. "Life is getting too complex, Max."

"So is death, my love. So is death."

Chapter 51

Louie Takes Stock

What a miserable kettle of carp this is!

I hear it all with my own two ears, which have been fanning this way and that to catch every tidbit of meaning that was passed out over the appetizing image of Miss Kitty the Cutter O'Connor. She is certainly an object lesson on the fact that a beautiful visage can hide a shrunken soul. I am also thinking of the svelte but treacherous Hyacinth. No doubt she will be as vengeful as Miss Kitty when she realizes that she has forever lost the sensual services of the only feline sleuth in Las Vegas who is licensed to thrill without any untoward aftereffects, like kitty litters.

And now I learn that I too may be an object of enmity. Well, at least I have had a good long time to study the image of my stalker.

I must admit that I was impressed by Mr. Matt Devine's calm and cogent summary of the facts. Someone must make Mr. Max Kinsella wake up and smell the chloroform. He was so busy trying to escape his immediate past that he overlooked the distant. I would be inclined to look with even more disfavor on his reentry into my darling Miss Temple's life, except that I must admit I owe him for springing me from my fate before I was sent away into a life of enforced fun . . . I mean, sensual servitude.

Of course, everyone present, in fearing for Miss Temple's safety, has overlooked my own humble contributions to this state in the past. Although I myself am now apparently a marked dude, I have often walked hackles to hindquarters with danger, and it will take more than a little doll with a barbering degree from Sweeney Todd to scare the starch out of Midnight Louie.

So I settle down into my haunches to keep an eagle eye on my little doll as she consoles Mr. Max for the sins of his past by encouraging more of the same sort of excess in his future. Perhaps my vigilance will make the lovebirds nervous, but that is just too darn bad.

Wait until Mr. Max discovers my plans for nighttime guard duty over Miss Temple.

Chapter 52

Dust

When Matt came out of the sporting goods superstore, a group of teenagers was clustered around the Hesketh Vampire like pimples around a zit.

He felt a bit possessive, but they looked like ordinary clean-cut kids nowadays: booted, leather-jacketed, hung with Goth jewelry, even the boys wearing chipped nail enamel in Oxidized Oxblood, little rings glinting off enough visible parts to encourage unhealthy speculation about invisible parts.

Three guys and two girls, oddly like a cadre of vampires themselves.

"Cool 'cycle, man," the biggest guy said in a tone half-threat and half-admiration.

"Thanks." Matt had been zipping something into the nylon photo bag he had bought inside and now he slung the strap crossways over his chest.

"What kind is it?" a girl asked. The braces she wore seemed more a high-tech accessory of the wasted look than a cosmetic appliance payed for through the teeth by hopeful middle-class parents.

"A Hesketh Vampire."

"A vamp," the girl breathed in awe. "They really call it that?"

"Well, it's no Harley," a boy said in a down-putting tone. It doesn't pay to impress chicks.

Mr. Big, though, seemed impressed. "I never heard of a Hesketh anything."

"It's British made. Not very many. Probably not as reliable as a Harley."

They nodded seriously. Harley was It.

"What's this silly chicken doing on the front?" the second girl asked, tracing the outline with her chartreuse-enameled fingernail.

Again Matt felt a stab of protective unease. Didn't like strange fingernails scraping the gleaming finish. Having things that other people envied was a pain in the neck.

He moved to the 'cycle and pulled the helmet off his arm where it hung. "That's the Hesketh trademark."

"A funky chicken?"

"What can I say? They're British. Besides, when you've got a product that screams like a banshee when it gets up to speed, you need to have a sense of humor about it."

"Really?" One of the guys looked ready to desert the sacred camp of Harley.

Matt nodded. "Why do you think they call it a vampire?"

By now he was taking back the machine, strapping on his helmet, drawing on gloves and curling them around the handles, straddling it, ready to kick back the stand.

They pulled away, reluctantly.

The key turned. The motor answered the twist of the handles. Matt was cruising away, leaving them surrounding the empty place where the vampire had been.

In his side mirrors, he saw them shrink, still watching.

A couple of the boys had eyed the photo bag, noticing the weight that sagged the black nylon. Sporting goods stores sold firearms.

Matt didn't like to think those kids might mean him harm, but it was lucky they hadn't messed with him. If they'd known what he was really carrying, they'd have thought he was as much a vampire as his motorcycle.

And sometimes it was an advantage to be mistaken for a monster.

The winter had been dry. A fine dust flared up from the highway and flayed the tinted Plexiglas visor. Traffic was light once he left Las Vegas proper.

Midday, heading nowhere. The minute you deserted the extravagant architecture of the Strip and passed the low monotonous rooflines of the suburbs, you were scribing a course across a sandpainting desert, all muted sage greens, sand beige and ferrous reds. Scrub, sand and stone. All of it in the process of being ground away by sun and wind and sudden floods in the washes. All slowly turning to dust.

Farther north, the land grew ruddier near the Valley of Fire. The Vampire droned along the ruler of the road, bored by the level, straight route.

Matt was bored by it too, but he didn't know where he was going and figured the boredom would tell him when, and where, to stop.

He thought about the letter that had arrived that morning from up north, addressed in a loopy, adolescent hand.

Krys. Keeping up with the unattainable older cousin, a traditional outlet for girls on the cusp of womanhood.

A strip of photos from a mall machine had fallen out. Four for . . . how much was it these days? A lot more than it had been when he was young. Younger.

He smiled, though only the desert could see him. Krys's hyperactive prose style, all exclamations and i's dotted with small neat circles. The family was okaying an art major, but she had to go to Loyola, not some California university.

And I took Aunt Mira to the mall the other day. She wanted to see the place where you bought her the blouse for Christmas.

Really was shocked at how expensive everything was, but I explained that was inflation. She is so funny and shy. Never drives to the mall. That's nothing! I told her next time we go, we take her car and she drives. I mean, I sweated blood to get my driver's license, for God's sake, she shouldn't just forget that sort of thing. Anyway, I kept telling her about this place in the mall. Really cool. Great haircuts. She was major not into it, but I got her in for a color rinse and trim at least. So we took pictures afterward. What do you think? I hope you're doing well. Loads of XXXXXXs. Krys.

Matt shook his head. Of the four photos, three were of Krys playing vamp for the camera. The fourth was of his mother, her hair shorter, brighter, bouncier, wearing the earrings he had also given her for Christmas. She looked ten years younger. She almost looked happy.

Sic transit Effinger.

Okay. The memory had set the mood, so Matt turned the motorcycle off the highway and let it jolt a few feet into the desert.

The kickstand sunk hard into the sand before it gripped. Cars whooshed by on the nearby highway, but not many and not often.

Matt unzipped the nylon bag at his hip and lifted out the heavy, smooth bronze weight of the mortuary vase.

Effinger on the gilt half-shell. Boiled down to a few ounces of dust and ash. The eighty percent liquid we all are, burned out from here to eternity.

Desiccated, like the desert. Dry, like old bones. Cold, like dead embers. His to do with as he would.

Keep it? No. Even the ashes of a loved one would make an awkward keepsake. Half shrine, half white elephant.

Matt had wondered what it would be like to hold Effinger in one hand. To feel the outer weight of the container, and the weightlessness of not-being within.

He had often stood over a coffin propped upon its support mechanism over the open grave and intoned the sonorous Biblical line made for ministers, "ashes to ashes, dust to dust." That ancient formula had always made him think, had always seemed new and poignantly specific for each departed soul he had cere-moniously wished godspeed.

And now, Cliff Effinger. A man mourned by no one. A man sur-vived by himself, and his mother. A man ultimately impotent in his anger and the anger he turned on others.

To the end of bitterness, to the lightness of ashes, to the pit-tance of mineral and bone we all are.

Matt pulled the stopper from the bottle, let the genie of death out.

A thin gray veil blew onto the desert air, lifted, swirled, dis-persed in a heartbeat. So many years, eddying away. So much weight and hatred, lofting like butterflies in passage.

Some motes would crash into the swift walls of windshield swimming down the highway. Some would rise hawklike to hunt the upper currents until they snagged on an outcropping. Some fell to earth, for the scorpions and lizards to scuttle through.

Gone. The past. The pain. Gone. Ready for the future. The power and the glory. The pain. Nothing much changed, except how you felt about it.

And that, as the poet said, is all the difference.

Midnight Louie Admits to Nothing

I suppose I am lucky that the officials present at my rescue were more concerned about crimes against humans, such as kidnapping, than crimes against cats.

A close inspection of my condition that night might have revealed that I was still under the influence of an illegal substance, aka Panama Purple.

You can bet that I will not forget the treacherous Hyacinth and her even more sneaky mistress, Shangri-La. And I would be willing to bet that they will not forget me and mine, more's the pity.

Anyway, despite the usual danger and deception, I would think the human dramatis personae would be pretty pleased with themselves after this adventure. Mr. Matt Devine has seen the last of his evil stepfather, and somebody other than himself has done the dirty deed and removed the oaf from the planet. Miss Temple Barr has seen the two thugs who assaulted her a few cases back in custody and under arrest for drug-running as well as suspicion of murdering the late unlamented Cliff Effinger. Lieutenant C. R. Molina has seen the Mystifying Max face-to-face and even has pinned him down (almost literally) for a long-desired, albeit brief, interrogation. And Mr. Max Kinsella has seen fit to play hero of the hour, using his magical skills to uncover a shipment of illegal drugs and a couple of unwilling drug users: myself and Miss Temple Barr.

There is ample cause for celebration at this juncture, and the delicious scent of more mysteries to be solved as recent events resolve even more.

So why is everybody so glum and acting like nobody has what he or she wishes?

Call it the human condition.

You certainly cannot call it the feline condition. My kind is known to be much easier to please.

But I suppose my human companions are suffering from what I would describe as a surfeit of Free-to-be-Feline. The exotic dressing on the top does not seem sufficient to disguise the inadequate sustenance underneath.

What do these humans *want?* Spoon-fed cod-liver oil?

Hmmm. Miss Temple has never tried *that* on my Free-to-be-Feline. I must find a way to drop a few hints. . . .

Very best fishes,

Midnight Louie, Esq.

P.S. You can reach Midnight Louie on the Internet at:
http://www.catwriter.com/cdouglas
To subscribe to *Midnight Louie's Scratching Post-Intelligencer*
newsletter or for information on Louie's T-shirt, write:
PO Box 331555, Fort Worth, TX 76163.

Carole Nelson Douglas
Admits to Confabulation

A reader who has lived in Las Vegas for thirty years wrote to compliment my accurate description of local landmarks.

It's nice to take a bow, but I don't live in Las Vegas; I only visit there (and not as often as I'd like). Also, although I try to describe the environment accurately, I have an easy out around the edges. From the very first, in penning Louie's Las Vegas adventures, I've added fictional structures that are my very own to embroider as much as my heart desires.

Las Vegas, from the founding of Bugsy Siegel's first Flamingo Hotel, has always celebrated making something out of nothing, so it's the perfect setting for fiction.

The Circle Ritz condominium/apartment building, for instance, is an actual building, all right, but imported from Corpus Christi, Texas. I saw it in the mid-eighties and became instantly enamored of its round exterior, which created pie-shaped rooms, and its light-warping arched ceilings. Although built as a coastline pied-à-terre for Corpus Christi's wealthy families, its perfectly preserved fifties decor struck me as perfect for Temple's Las Vegas pad. Another Las-Vegas-dwelling reader recently volunteered that she knows many such buildings in the city.

I invented the Goliath Hotel (Vegas's biggest and most vulgar hotel) and its antithesis, the Crystal Phoenix (Vegas's most tasteful hostelry), over a decade ago for the first series of Midnight Louie novels, now out of print. The idea was to avoid lawsuits by existing hotels on the subjective matter of taste, and also to take Las Vegas to even more extremes than it then seemed capable of.

But since my first visit in 1985, the expanding Strip has overreached even my imagination: the Goliath lobby's "Love Moat" has been echoed several times as new "Goliath Hotels" have sprung up.

Another artifact that brings reader queries is the Hesketh Vampire motorcycle that has belonged to the Mystifying Max, Electra Lark, and now is in the custody of that uneasy rider, Matt Devine.

Bikers have written to ask if it's real. The Harley clubs know nothing about it. Oh yes, Virgil and Virginia, it's real right down to the surly crowned chicken logo on the sleek silver fairing (the front hooding).

This is one case where constructing a character allowed authorial ignorance and the reality of research to fuse. A reference book on V-twin motorcycles covered the field from 1903 to 1985. I browsed through the pinup pictures of these alien machines, looking for one that had Max Kinsella's fingerprints all over it.

Besides gravitating to the sinister model name, trust me to find the only bike in the book that looked like it was speeding while standing still. The Hesketh Vampire was only made from 1980–84, and custom-made for each purchaser. This Rolls-Royce of a gentleman's motorcycle looks like a sterling-silver lightning bolt; its sleek fairing was designed in a wind tunnel. The engine's thick metal walls can take ten reborings; which amounts to a life of millions of miles. And the primary drive does indeed howl. A virtually immortal motorcycle named Vampire: one fact no fiction writer could resist.

Luckily, the real world overflows with just such juicy and obscure facts, along with many much more common permutations on the human (and feline) personality. So the imaginative blend of fact and fiction is an ever-renewable resource.